THE LOST PLEIAD

KELLY BRANYIK

This is a fictional novel. Any information in this novel was created with her imagination or information used in fictious ways.

Write With Light Publications, LLC
Rockvale, Colorado 81244

www.writewithlightpublications.com

Copyright © 2021 by Kelly Branyik

All rights reserved.
Book Cover Design by Nicole Enger Creative

www.nicoleenger.co

Manufactured in the United States
ISBN 978-1-7336265-9-0 (paperback)
ISBN 978-1-7378158-0-8 (hardcover)

Many a night I saw the Pleiads,
rising through the mellow shade,
glitter like a swarm of fire-flies
tangled in a silver braid.

- Lord Tennyson

For Nana.

Who devoured books and

isn't here to read mine.

ple-iad

/ˈplēəd/

noun

1: a group of usually seven illustrious or brilliant persons or things.

2: any of the Pleiades

ONE

Lightning struck the earth, drawing singed black marks into the rocky cliffs. Boulders tumbled down the cliffside, splashing into the dark blue and purple oceans below. The night was black, and the clouds seemed to grow larger overhead, taking up the length of the sky. In the distance, several planets clung to the darkness amongst the stars showing their brilliance. Each planet harbored its own perfect brushstrokes and swirls of colors. A heavy downpour flooded onto the war raging beneath the stars on the terrene, more orchestras of thunderstorms and electric skies quick to follow.

Clans of men and women fought with silver swords against their colossal enemy, consumed with fear and blinded by courage. Each man and woman's skin had a divine glow to it. Each luminous strand of long, golden hair was blood-soaked. Once pristine silver armor was now thick with mud and gore as they sliced their way through hordes of dark green creatures, their skin like snakes.

With each flash from the sky, their scaly skin grew even darker, and yet their bright red eyes pierced into the cosmos. Sounds of flesh tearing, shrill screams, and the deafening yells of defeat echoed into the night as each golden-haired being fell to their knees and perished. Slashes from razor-sharp fingertips ripped through throats and bellies, spilling guts and blood into the soaking wet earth. The sharp teeth sparkled in the bright moonlight, and the hollow snake eyes that sought only blood were gleaming with rage and murder. This wasn't the first or last planet they would destroy, and they would be most thrilled doing it.

Each flash of lightning lit up the dark façade of the Palace not far from the war. Not a single window lit the towers of stone, but few shadows hurried between the spaces where the moon illuminated the structure. The battle raging was distraction enough to help the shadows escape a worse fate.

Atlas rushed into the bedroom where his wife stood frozen, holding their child of a few months old. Looking out the window at the darkness and terror with paralyzed eyes, the cool breeze from the night brushed her skin, and the shrieks of death weren't as soothing. The child let out a cheery coo, her cloudy eyes trying to focus on the human light holding her. She was oblivious to the massacre happening a steep drop from the window. On normal days, this room had high ceilings and oversized windows that let the light pour in. Heavy purple and blue drapes hung on either side of the windows, and when lit, the room expanded. The wind caught the thick drapes, moving them slightly, barely moving her from her place beside the window. Now, that room shrunk into the darkness, making it smaller and more silent than ever.

"We have to go," she said with no hint of calm, yet she stood still as if she was trying to be.

"There isn't enough time," Atlas boomed. "She must descend now." Pleione looked down at her child, who seemed unperturbed by the horror outside the palace walls. Instead, she greedily sucked her thumb and stared up at her mother with her hazy eyes. Pleione, looking into her, felt removed from the sounds of clashing metal and death, the moving winds, the incessantly bright moon and stars, her husband's impatient breaths. Lost in the small child's innocence, she gripped the tiny finger, and for a moment, Pleione forgot her own existence.

Time stopped.

Her baby girl was a bright star in these pitch-black cosmos; a star anyone would rush to at lightspeed. Thoughts of her life flashed before Pleione's eyes. All at once, fierce love and profound dread overcame her. Pleione made a list of all the things she would never see her do and tucked them deep into her mind.

"Pleione!" Atlas shouted, startling her into reality. Without saying a word, she nodded and moved toward him.

"What if we never see her again?"

"We can't worry about that right now," Atlas said, moving to the window. He anxiously looked out at the battle, hearing the screams bellow through the night. Another crash of lighting pierced the earth, followed by another roll of thunder.

"This way," he said. Atlas placed his monstrous hands forcefully on the small of Pleione's back, leading her from the bed chambers into the walkways toward the Great Hall. Pleione's silver hair fell to brush his fingertips. The ceilings towered even higher than the bed chambers, smooth stone pillars holding them up like Gods would hold up the sky. A dim glow from the planets and moons spilled onto the floors illuminating their hurried steps between pillars. She quickened her pace through the narrow walkways with a sort of grace and patience despite the fear consuming her. She wanted to walk slower, savor these last few moments with her daughter, but Atlas pushed her forward. She looked up at him, his silvery beard long and hair even longer against his bright skin. His stoic face carried worry and sadness as he focused on the dark path ahead of them.

They entered the Great Hall and gathered in the middle of the empty space. The massive gathering room recurred into infinite darkness, and their steps echoed into the even darker corners. This was once a place of grand parties, celebrations, and laughter. People vowed their love to each other at the center of these halls. Some honored the life and death of those who had passed. Each new life brought into this world was welcomed here. Now the grand space was empty, lifeless, and dark.

They placed the baby girl on the floor. Above was an open skylight cutting a perfect circle in the sky. Looking out, there were only glittering stars overpowering the thick moonglow. It was the only place where the clouds didn't seem to cover the shimmering stars.

Pleione and Atlas stared into each other, feeling the connection vibrate between them, their slow chanting in Saren growing to a roaring song. The girl wiggled between them, still madly sucking her thumb. With each repeated chant, the room grew brighter as if restoring a million lights all at once; restoring the hall's mass to its original grandness.

Their child's vessel transformed from a dim shimmer to an intense glow. A loud hum filled the hall threatening to burst it open at the seams. A deafening sound that would cause any mortal to spiral into madness. A sound only Gods could bear.

Atlas and Pleione's chants grew in volume; tears showering their cheeks. Pleione felt an emptiness creep into her body, a mass void that would threaten her soul for years to come. A knowingness that this desolation would tear her apart.

The humming grew more deafening as the light grew brighter. With unbelievable force, a beam of light hammered down from the night sky into the baby's tiny center. The ground rumbled beneath them. Pleione looked down on her darling girl fearing the power of the light might shatter her little vessel. After just seconds, the beam disappeared back up into the sky. The small vessel lay lifeless and empty on the cold floor between Pleione and Atlas.

The Great Hall returned to a black silence.

The child's thumb fell limp from her lips and onto the floor beside her. The shouting, the slams of thunder, and the stings of lightning all disappeared around them.

Another crash of lightning.

Another roll of thunder.

Another shake of the earth.

Each passed by them to which they paid no attention.

She was *gone*.

Pleione picked up the delicate little body like she would the broken pieces of a once treasured vase. Atlas stared at his wife, wet with tears and a face already aging with grief. He yearned to reach for Pleione, to comfort her, to love her, to stitch up the void he could already see growing in her. They would never recover from this, and Atlas knew it.

Pleione clutched the child to her chest, desperate to feel her heartbeat or a single last breath.

Nothing.

She wailed up into the stars, penetrating the tumultuous tolls of lightning and thunder, piercing through the songs of death that would inevitably strike down their stone doors. Another roll of thunder woke Atlas from his stares. The Great Hall rumbled above and started crashing down around them.

"MOVE!" Atlas shouted.

Pleione sat still, holding her dead child.

TWO

The mud-caked Subaru splashed through deep puddles in the Colorado wilderness. Above the trees, Anya could barely make out the peak of the mountains she was desperate to get to. She kept her eyes on the road, both hands firmly on the wheel, avoiding any chance to get stuck in deep holes gouged by past adventurers. Anya loved how each adventure on the road would lead her through valleys before grandly revealing the mountains hiding behind them. It was a delightful surprise with every journey. Each time she planned a mountain trip, she was impatient, never reaching them fast enough.

It was the beginning of summer, and Colorado had just suffered one of the worst winters in history. The rivers were high with runoff. On regular days, Anya lived in the mountains outside of Cripple Creek, Colorado. A town of less than two thousand cozied up at the backside of Pikes Peak Mountain. Just four miles out of town was Victor, and not far from there, Goldfield. Thanks to its rich mining history, the area was known to the locals as the Gold Camp District.

Like any other famous Colorado town, Cripple Creek's winters always brought thick layers of snow that coated the area for weeks at a time. A single sliver from Colorado's hottest sun couldn't melt the white powdery blanket. She hated the snow and often wondered why she moved to the mountains in the first place. But her love for the various peaks in Colorado always won over the snowy disasters she had to endure. Even though the winters were brutal, she enjoyed the summer months when it was significantly cooler than any other town thousands of feet lower in elevation. What she loved even more were the forests of green aspens that would change into waves of oranges, yellows, and reds when fall arrived. If she were lucky, she would be able to see the snow-dusted Pikes Peak towering above the autumn tree lines. A display of multiple seasons all competing for attention.

Colorado was her favorite place in the world, and she had been most anywhere. Places like the Great Wall of China, the Eiffel Tower, Rome's Colosseum; marveled at thousands of paintings and sculptures from famous museums across Europe; sailed oceans, bathed in all the seas, slumbered in Alaskan bubble domes with Aurora Borealis looming in the sky.

Anya had seen amazing things, no doubt. But nowhere in the world could compare to Colorado; three-hundred and forty days of sun, clean mountain air, rivers stocked full of monstrous trout, and some of the best stargazing in the country.

If she were honest, Cripple Creek was growing on her each day. She adored taking HWY 67 up the mountain toward the Gold Camp District, coming up the hill that leads down into Cripple Creek where she can see waves of mountains for over a hundred miles until they halted at the Sangre de Cristos.

If she were lucky, she could still see those Sangres topped with snow leftover from the last winter. On other lucky days, the clouds would hang low in town, making the city appear as if resting above the clouds, like someone's photoshopped dreamscape.

The summers in Colorado brought in people from around the country to enjoy its natural wonders. Anya liked being out and about before the tourist crowds burrowed themselves in the mountains and fished the rivers dry.

Colorado was starting to get crowded, and the natives were getting irritated by it. With a simple weed fix being a short drive over the Colorado state border, the appeal of living here seemed to grow on everyone.

Today, she didn't have to worry about the tourists or feel the chill of a fatally cold winter on the way out of Cripple Creek's door. Today, she was off on an adventure further away from the home she had built for herself.

Each summer, Anya went on outdoor adventures with her two closest friends, Bee Wallace and Karmyn Monroe. Like Anya, they loved being outdoors, and that's one of the few places Anya ever really wanted to be anyway. Anya held three places in high regard, the mountains, sea, and night sky. All three of those places were full of secrets and wonders still unexplored. The mountains were the most comforting to journey into. The way she figured it, Earth was an easier place to explore simply because people could breathe in it. Both the sea and space, similarly inexplorable with depths and spaces so vast and suffocating they could crush your lungs in an instant, and yet somehow, people desired to explore them still. Those were places that both intrigued and intimidated her.

Being sisters, they talked to each other about everything; fought about everything too. Yet, no amount of bickering ever kept them apart.

Even with their closeness, one topic of conversation always frustrated Anya. The topic of her romantic relationships.

"How many times have you gone out with him?" Karmyn shouted in Anya's ear. Her voice was loud and unshaken by the rocking of the vehicle climbing the uneven dirt road.

"Who?" Anya said, playing dumb.

"Sam Castleton!" She shrieked loud enough for Anya to cringe.

"Oh," she mumbled. "We've only gone out a couple of times. He seems nice."

"He seems… *nice?*" Karmyn spat. "Anya Allen, you barely give a guy a chance anymore." Anya snickered, glancing at Karmyn to see her scowl. What she knew of Sam was still very little. What she did know was he had a good job, a truck worth envying, and he was an overall nice guy according to the community. Unfortunately, those three characteristics alone were not enough to sway Anya toward jumping into a relationship.

"I just want whoever it is to be the right one," Anya said quietly. "It seems like whoever I date is wishy-washy about commitment."

"Everyone is looking for the right one, but no one wants to be the right one," Bee wisely chirped from the backseat, the moving world outside gleaming in the reflection of her aviators.

"Truth," Karmyn snapped, slumping into the passenger's seat, crossing her arms to look out the window at the aspens, which were finally a crisp, blooming green.

Anya glanced from Karmyn to Bee, whose aviators accompanied a very Indian Jones-looking hat and a forest green handkerchief tied around her neck. She looked too cool to hang out with or ready for a safari. Her hair was a wavy dirty blonde and fell to her lower back. Anya imagined she was a goddess or a mermaid in her past life and always envied her beauty and style. Despite her intimidating fashion and good looks, anyone who met Bee quickly discovered she was the kindest and most understanding person they would ever encounter.

"I don't know why you care so much about who I date or marry, or… whatever," Anya said.

"We are just tired of seeing you alone, that's all," Bee said matter of fact.

"You definitely have a wall up," Karmyn said. She wasn't wrong. After so many relationship failures, it was the only option Anya felt she had left.

"We're here," Anya said, rushing to change the subject. They were about to reach the top of the incline. The steep hill they had been trudging up was now evening out into patches of meadow.

The stinging reminder of her singlehood now hung on her mind, and it was a daily practice to keep those plaguing thoughts at bay. It had been a while since Anya had a real relationship.

And Anya had just turned thirty.

Her past dating life consisted of going on dates, spending a few weeks, or, if she were lucky, a few months with a guy and having a great time.

Eventually, Anya would get invested just enough to see a man lose interest and inevitably end things. Nothing ever really lasted long term for Anya, which left her frustrated and hopeless.

She lacked the patience for men anymore, deciding they were a waste of her time and energy. In her eyes, all men were fantastic con artists that knew clever ways to draw a woman in and get them hooked. Over time, she discovered most of them were terrified of a simple thing called willingness. They didn't appear to be genuine in any way, or they lacked serious depth.

Anya tried dating apps to meet people, desperately attempting to find someone who might see her value and worth. She came to loathe those apps, quickly learning a majority of them were used for hookups or couples asking her to be their special, lusty "Unicorn" in a threesome. When her faith in men met its tired ending, she tried dating women too but didn't seem to find luck there either.

The truth was Anya did *like* Sam. As much as she didn't want to, and as tired as she was with dating, she thought he was kind, humble, soft-spoken, and he seemed content with life. Anyone who knew him only spoke highly of him. For most of the dates they went on, he stared into her, listening more intently than any other had as if he was carving her facial features into his mind.

It was disarming.

But Anya was so far from letting that tear down her wall.

Not *this* time.

Sam was also gorgeous, which made her nervous. Tall with smooth dark hair, a full beard, and eyes like pools of honey. She couldn't make eye contact without feeling flutters in her belly.

What she felt for Sam terrified her and excited her at the same time. Yet, there was so much she still didn't know about him, and she was reluctant to keep learning.

It wasn't the first time she had been both excited and terrified by someone she dated. But, since it happened so often, she never relied on the new and exciting feelings gained from the thrill of a new and possible romance.

Those thrills usually led nowhere good.

What she felt made her not trust any man or herself. It made her back away, hesitant to put in any effort at all. Anya was let down too many times. She didn't want to get to know anyone again. How many times had she told a man her life story?

Too many times to count. So many times, the thought of telling the same story again was exhausting.

"Just go out on another date with him," Karmyn pleaded. "Please! Let us live vicariously through you." She said this as if both Bee and Karmyn weren't already in happy and committed relationships with men who adored them. The last thing they needed was to live 'vicariously' through her crappy dating life.

Anya wondered if both of them missed being single. Maybe that's why they were both so obsessed with her love life to begin with.

Anya parked the car in a grassy area, just overlooking a blue glacier lake. It was a breathtaking sight. Like someone had scooped out the earth to pour a cloudy aqua Jell-O in it. Something out of a calendar or travel magazine.

"I'll think about it," Anya mumbled.

She turned off the car, got out, and slammed the door, sucking in a deep breath of fresh mountain air, which was nothing like the air found in a cramped city. The three of them unloaded camping gear and fishing poles from the back of the Subaru Crosstrek and started setting up camp.

"Look, Sam is great, and you've been single far too long. You have so much to offer." Karmyn spoke. "You got a good job, a good car, a house, and you're stable. I think it's a good time to take a risk here! You owe it to yourself. You're the most gorgeous person I've met."

"Seriously, model material," Bee interrupted.

Karmyn continued to ramble on, her voice fading into thin air. Anya always thought of herself as beautiful but never felt she was an obvious type of beautiful. Instead, she imagined herself as a simple and natural beauty.

"You have goddess blonde hair like Cinderella, an IQ of Stephen Hawking, and you're like the nicest person I've ever met. Seriously, being mean to you is like being mean to Mother Mary. And you have the most beautiful eyes," Karmyn continued.

"And nose," Bee chirped again.

Karmyn turned to question Bee. "Hey, what's that disease called where you have insanely beautiful eyes?"

"Stop it, guys," Anya said, getting irritated.

"And you're an open-minded world citizen who's lived all over the world. Guys totally dig that shit," Karmyn said. Anya huffed, stopped unpacking, and looked at Karmyn, who remarkably resembled Princess Jasmine from Aladdin with her glowing dark skin, thick black hair, and almond-shaped caramel eyes.

"How could you possibly know that guys are into worldly women?" Anya barked. "If anything, being just *that* isolated me from the rest of society and made me super unrelatable," she finished.

"Well, that's because people are fake and can't handle genuine humans. But it's a damn good thing you have us," Bee said. Anya flinched when Karmyn continued speaking.

"Stop being so negative about this! Promise us you'll go on at least one more date with Sam. Please?" Karmyn begged.

Anya looked at Karmyn, who put on her best pouty face and sagging shoulders. She thought for a moment, dropped her head back, and exhaled a frustrated breath.

"Fine. I promise."

Karmyn, pleased with herself, let a bright white smile stretch across her face. Anya and Bee continued to unpack as the sun started to fall behind them.

They were right.

Anya had been single far too long. But was having a good car and a full bank account the only fundamental requirements for mattering to someone? She yearned for deep connection.

How could she know if Sam was that person?

He didn't feel like that person.

Anya stopped moving the camping gear long enough to look into the sky, where the transparent white moon was still clinging to the blue. She wanted a love that consumed her, a passion that never wavered. She wanted nights dancing in the living room. Someone she could be completely herself with. She wanted to be just as sure of him as he was of her. But, in a world filled with billions of people, how on earth could she ever cut through the crowds to find that?

Anya was grateful for her life, and some could call her more stable than most. In Anya's opinion, who she was dating or how secure she was in life were the least of her worries. Bee and Karmyn didn't know about the nights she lay awake thinking about how she truly fit into this big world.

Some days she wanted to take all her belongings, toss them onto the street and disappear down a road that led anywhere else. The real world was consumed by things that never lasted, a hopeless feeling that filled her with rage on days when she let it.

The things that surrounded her mattered less to her than finding the place she belonged. The only time Anya was ever able to escape the material world she couldn't change or control was in books, mountains, sea, and sky.

Anya couldn't be the only one who felt out of place. This world had to be filled with groups of misfits on a journey to belonging.

But where were they?

No matter where she traveled, no matter how much she loved Colorado, Anya still had not found the place she belonged or the place that belonged to her. She still hadn't found that belonging within someone else. Most days, she doubted she ever would.

Anya didn't talk to Bee and Karmyn about her extreme lack of belonging and complex feelings that left her isolated within herself, believing they would never understand or worse, that she wouldn't be able to explain it in a way that made sense.

But when she looked up at the darkness of the sky to see the stars, the chaotic and confusing world around her faded away. Anya felt like, out there, the universe held more possibilities.

Maybe experiences beyond her existence lived there too. That single thought made her doubts about the possibilities of a meaningful life disappear.

But when she realized she might never explore the depths of the cosmos, she fell into a momentary depression.

Her dreams and imagination were too big for this small planet.

She was stuck here within reality's limitations.

That night, they went fishing just feet from where they set up camp. They cooked their catches in tin foil over a fire with roasted vegetables. They drank beer from their favorite Colorado breweries, letting each empty can meet the bottom of their boots, collapsing to metal saucers in the earth.

By nightfall, Karmyn and Bee had curled up in the warmth and shelter of the large Cabela's tent that could easily fit six people. They were quietly snoring while Anya laid out on the wild grass, drinking in the night sky. The fire was burning hot and bright, keeping her warm. The rain fly flapped softly in the breeze playing along with the small symphony of hooting owls within the trees.

Anya snuggled in her sleeping bag. The night was cold during this early part of summer. By dawn, the condensation from morning dew would be rolling off the tent's rainfly to drip onto the earth. Too many times, she woke to water droplets falling on her forehead in the mornings. No matter where she was or what time of year, she always put the rain fly on.

Anya never minded the mountain chill. The air was refreshing, and the only sign of snow was the bit that still clung desperately to the cool rock on the other side of the turquoise lake.

She stared up into the sky, thankful it was warm enough to stargaze again. Winters in the mountains trying to stargaze were brutal. However, on countless occasions, she would power through the bitter winters just to see the stars, but she wasn't too fond of doing it.

She took herself through the different constellations she learned as a child. Cassiopeia, Orion's Belt, the Big Dipper, and the Little Dipper, mapping a trail from one to the other. She stopped at her favorite star cluster in Taurus, unable to recall why it was her favorite, as if anyone could have a close enough relationship with the stars for it to be their favorite. It wasn't like eating your favorite foods, listening to your favorite music, or dining at your favorite restaurant. Maybe it was. Whatever the case, Anya decided it was her favorite constellation a long time ago.

Anya remembered as far back as she could.

Age ten.

Sitting in a giant silver inflatable dome, a projector streamed a small replica of the night sky at the top of the curved inflatable. The teacher was giving the class a lesson on constellations and astronomy. The other students were just as excited to be away from regular classes, but not Anya. She was captured by the fake stars that dotted the roof of the dome.

A whirring fan kept the grey bubble a stiffly round shape, blowing so loudly, it nearly drowned out the teacher's voice. Anya perked up and listened through the noise as the teacher rambled about prominent constellations; ones anyone could easily pluck out of the sky. He finally came to a story that intrigued Anya deeply.

"The Seven Sisters, or Pleiades, is a cluster of one-thousand stars located in the Taurus constellation. It is most obvious to the naked eye, and it is the closest star cluster to Earth. The seven most noticeable stars we see here represent seven women, Alcyone, Asterope, Celaeno, Elektra, Maia, Taygete, and Merope. You'll notice one star seems to be missing or unnoticeable in the cluster. We call that star the Lost Pleiad, and many believe that star to be the sister, Elektra. No one knows where she was lost to or why she is lost." He paused. Anya looked up at the star cluster that could've easily been mistaken for the Little Dipper if people didn't know any better.

"Other lore suggests the seventh sister ate too many onions and smelled terrible, so her sisters cast her away from the family." The class giggled at the story while Anya frowned. It wasn't the first time something outside the norm interested her but not her classmates. What they thought was funny wasn't funny to her. She never adored the same trendy things everyone else did. Anya never fell in step with the cool fads that would cost her parents a fortune. She

was fascinated by unique and odd things, much of which she could always find in books or thrift stores. Over time, Anya was known as the weirdest nerd in school. She didn't care, though. She was never angry at others for how much the material world consumed them.

Ignoring her classmates, Anya raised her hand.

"How do you live on the stars?" The class giggled, the teacher laughing with them. When he saw the seriousness, like a shadow on her face, he shushed the rest of the class before answering.

"It's just a myth, Anya. People don't live on stars," he said plainly.

"But the story makes it sound like they lived on the stars," she argued.

"Yes. I suppose it does. If the story were true, the Seven Sisters would likely live on a planet." He said

"Are there planets in Pleiades?" Anya continued.

"As of today, they have not been able to see any planets in the star cluster," he replied. Anya was glad the darkness of the dome hid her disappointment. "However, future technology may prove differently. There is so much of the sky we haven't seen or learned about yet."

As the teacher opened his mouth to talk about another constellation, Anya continued.

"So, are the people who live there like… aliens or something?" She asked. The teacher sighed, but the indirect light cast on his face showed an amused grin. The class laughed again, and he silenced them once more.

"Some myths say there is a form of aliens known as Pleiadians. Some say they are different than the aliens we usually see in movies."

"Like, different from the Greys?" Anya inquired further. A flash of surprise came over his face as the bell sounded outside the dome.

"Yes. Different from the Greys," he said softly. "Alright, class dismissed. I will see you all in fifth period." The students crawled through the tunnel back into the well-lit gymnasium. Glimmers of light danced inside of the dome as each student passed by the projector. Anya couldn't get enough of the story and waited back to ask the teacher more questions.

"I have another question," Anya said. "How are they different?"

The teacher thought for a moment, as if he was concerned he might say something wrong.

He glanced up at the fake stars.

"Some say that the Pleiadians' greatest power of all was love. The myth says they are the most positive beings of the universe, meant to bring only love and unity to the planet. The myth also says they had incredible healing powers."

Anya looked up at her teacher, stunned and filled with wonder.

It was the only time an adult had ever been so honest with her. Her parents often hid things and put on fake faces—side effects of their religion.

Anya looked up at the stars on the dome one last time before the teacher shut the projector off, the romantic notion of all-loving creatures searing into her. The stars disappeared, and the projector went silent.

Anya crawled out through the tunnel into the gymnasium, where her eyes met the bright orange glow of the large overhead lights.

Anya thought about Pleiades for the rest of that day. How Elektra ate too many onions, how she was isolated from the rest of her sisters. Anya understood that isolation. She often felt like she didn't belong but could never explain why or even summon the courage to tell anyone just how alone she felt.

From then on, Anya dreamed about living on the stars, jumping from one glittering platform to the next as she waved goodbye to the cruel earth beneath her feet. She would transform from Earthling to

Pleiadian, making the Milky Way her celestial road home, skipping along its path to whatever heavens it possessed in the black.

It was a tall fantasy that carried her through some difficult moments in her life. And it was a fantasy she would learn to forget as she entered adulthood and responsibility. Imagination always faded with age.

Anya held the back of her head up with her forearm; her other arm limp across her belly. It had been twenty years since she first learned about Pleiades. Yet, sitting tailor style in that silver dome had never left her memory.

Each time she looked at the stars, she saw a new sky with new balls of burning gas ready to be discovered. Yet, the world was unable to do it fast enough. Unable to see it all in this lifetime.

The Seven Sisters was usually drowning in moon rays or the brightness of surrounding stars. Sometimes if the moon was too bright, Anya would still try to find the constellation using her peripheral vision. Tonight, the moon was dim enough to reveal all stars to her. Beneath the blanket of vast black, she fixated on the Seven Sisters for as long as her eyes would allow.

Anya looked up into the sky, feeling deep loneliness, the child within her suddenly wishing Pleiades was a real place again. She wished she could join the Pleiadians of love and light for once. Maybe she might find a true soul mate there, or she might enjoy her life a little more. Perhaps she wouldn't have to care so much about money, cars, jobs, and whorish dating apps that led her to disappointment. Maybe things wouldn't be so confusing. She could just live in the love and light of the Seven Sisters until she met the maker of her confusing existence.

Anya compared her yearning feeling of living on Pleiades to the same phenomenon people felt after watching James Cameron's Oscar award-winning sci-fi film Avatar. People wanted to live in a alien world like the one depicted in that movie. Where each night, they could run through glowing blue and purple forests and feel the magic of the world around them. The desire to live in that fictitious place was so strong, it sent people into deep depressions, provoking the five stages of grief over an impossible, made-up world. Anya knew her thoughts on leaving this world were that of a child' s fantasy. It was a nice thought, living on Pleiades. But it wasn't real. Anya always had to remind herself of that.

Anya wondered what Pleiades looked like if people truly lived there. She knew there were other beings out there in the universe and anyone who disagreed with her was decidedly ignorant. Earth couldn't host the only species of human beings living within millions of galaxies.

Pleiadians could exist.

All myths come from somewhere.

A crazy thought. A thought like that was never said out loud, even to her closest friends.

She dreamt Pleiades was a piece of earth hovering on the rim of a galaxy, and everywhere there would be passing clouds with stars glittering behind them. Maybe pristine waterfalls cascaded from strong cliffs before they evaporated into the dark void below. Maybe on those pieces of earth, there would be thousands of people living and loving by moonlight. What kind of homes would they live in? Well, that was something she hadn't entirely dreamt up yet, but she imagined it would be lovely, warm, inviting, similar to what people believed to exist beyond the Pearly Gates. She wondered if the stars were even brighter on Pleiades than they were here. She wondered if she could reach out, grab hold of one, and keep it under her pillow.

These thoughts calmed Anya, easing her into a warm slumber next to a crackling fire and the stars telling their stories above her.

THREE

Sam woke to the light of the morning pouring in through his large windows and the smell of coffee already brewing. Without moving, he looked out the windows to let his eyes adjust to the daylight, silently greeted by the large rabbit that hopped around his property and the Stellar Jays fluttering through the aspen trees. A few clouds clinging to the blue sky, and it wouldn't be long before the sun was high and beaming heat onto the mountains.

He climbed down from the loft bed to see the coffee had nearly finished brewing and retrieved a bottle of creamer from the refrigerator.

Salted Caramel.

He poured creamer into his cup as the coffee pot sputtered to a stop. There was far too much coffee. He wouldn't drink the whole pot, and it would go to waste. The coffee gushed into the mug, the dark liquid swirling with the cream to create a smooth tan color. Sam never poured the cream in last. This way, he always saved himself a spoon.

Sam's property was amazing and he knew he was fortunate to have this place in the middle of nowhere, although it needed a lot of work. The outside of his property looked like a junkyard, and the one half of his house looked more like a haunted mansion he dared not walk into.

For now, he had made his home into a little studio while he procrastinated doing any hard work on the rest of the house. From the window, he could see the snow-topped Sangre de Cristo Mountains poking through the hard-rock hills of Goldfield. He knew the high sun wouldn't be strong enough to melt the snow still hanging onto the shadowy corners of the earth.

This really was the perfect place to live.

Across from his house was a small, newer house that obstructed his view of the mountains in the distance. Since living here, he fantasized about buying the property and demolishing that house for a better view. On nights when he enjoyed looking out at the navy-blue night, a single, annoying porch light burned into the evening. It was the only time he wished he owned a gun. When the single blaring light burned like a laser into his home, he could just shoot it out. Buying that property was a nice thought, but that would be a dream for another time. For now, he would have to settle with what he had. Better yet, he would have to work with what he had. And if he was honest with himself, he was lazy and very good at doing the bare minimum.

To the right of the makeshift house, there was an old headframe from the gold mining operation from the early 1900s. Even further to the right was a fully functioning gold mining operation taking place, surface mining to be exact.

If Sam were outside in the evening, the lights from the trucks hauling hundreds of tons of ore would cut through the night. They were so loud some evenings, he swore he could hear them drilling into the earth.

The surface mining operation ran year-round. In the Gold Camp District, they always drill for gold, even on Christmas.

Like anyone else who had moved to the area—or had lived here long enough to see the surface mining operation make its debut—it took a while to get used to the noise. But over time, the persistent drilling in pursuit of glittering flecks of treasure didn't bother him. They extracted over 400,000 ounces of gold from the area each year, so mining wouldn't be going anywhere soon.

But no one seemed to bother Sam here.

It was the perfect place to get away and hide from the ridiculous world. At least that's how he felt most days. It was peaceful, but with long periods alone, things got lonely. It was a daily battle for Sam, being single versus being committed to someone. He wanted companionship but also valued his freedom to check out women. Like his lack of commitment to finishing his house, he usually lacked similar energy toward pursuing a good love. Sam figured it was easier living that way. Yet, there were days he wished someone would share coffee with him in the morning. Maybe they would count the Stellar Jays hopping from one branch to the next. Or they could talk about building a tiny home for the rabbit to live in during the winter.

Carrying his coffee, he carefully moved to sit on his couch in front of the large windows and the sills lined with over a dozen dirty glass bottles. Ones he had dug up on his property—his trash-turned-to-treasure glittering in the morning light. The Stellar Jays were hard at work in his front yard, giving Sam plenty of time to admire their beautiful colors, which were an iridescent blue-black. Their heads were entirely black from the neck up and a stunning blue from the neck down. Sam found their bold presence in his backyard to be most pleasant no matter what season it was. Each day he looked forward to seeing them. He even talked to them.

The last winter soaked into the earth around most places in Colorado, signaling summer had arrived but not in the Gold Camp District. The snow recently started to melt from the cliffs as the warmth of summer seeped through his windows.

No one hated winter more than Sam.

Today, it was warm enough in the house without starting a fire in his woodstove. He preferred it that way. Regardless, mornings were usually always made for sweatpants and hoodies.

He turned on his TV and started watching the news. Reporters talked about the clearing of the winter elements and how summer was here. Updates on politics, community, and crime flooded his screen. After less than thirty minutes, Sam felt he had seen enough, turning off the TV in disappointment. The world outside was usually horrid and depressing. Instead, he chose to play music from his computer, letting the tunes soothe the poor mood he gained from watching the news. The Stellar Jays were now playing in the puddles that once used to be snow.

The tunes boomed through his tiny studio space. Sam downed the last of his coffee, trying to plan out the day in his head while he moved to his coffee pot for another steaming cup. Between sips, he got dressed and brushed his teeth. Toothpaste and salted caramel do not mix. The fishing pole leaned in the corner of his house, whispering bits of enticement at Sam, telling him to drive up to Bison Reservoir and fish for trout that day. Sam wished he wasn't going alone.

Then he thought of her.

Anya Allen.

After a few dates, he knew she was unlike anyone else he had ever met. He was intrigued by her, her thoughts, and her opinions. When he met her, she was nothing short of the most beautiful woman he had ever seen, reminding him of the sandy beaches and ocean people yearn to dive into. Often, he thought about his hands running through her golden hair—swimming in all parts of her just looking at those electric blue eyes. Sam wanted to be near her, but lingering fears that came with giving up his freedom always stopped him.

Anya had lived in the area a while, but somehow Sam had missed her all this time. Sam was fascinated with how she arrived here in the first place since this area was seldom home to new and interesting people. Even more fascinating was her shared enjoyment of things he also enjoyed doing—fishing, camping, hiking, and anything outdoors.

He contemplated texting her and asking her if she would like to join. Opening their text feed, he started typing but then stalled. While he liked her, he hadn't seen her in over a week. She might have lost interest in him already, a thought that frustrated him.

Sam couldn't place why she was different but hoped to learn more about her if she would give him the time. Ignoring the thought, Sam decided not to message her, focusing on his growling stomach instead. Shoving his phone into his pocket, he opened his refrigerator to find nothing of sustenance—just a half-full bag of chocolate chips, a jar of pickles, and a bottle of creamer. In one swoop, he grabbed his fishing gear and left the house, closing the door behind him. Jumping in his Toyota Tacoma, he drove toward Cripple Creek.

Cripple Creek was a short 10-minute drive from his house. The fastest way to get there was to drive through Victor and then snake past the surface mine. On that route, the majestic mountains surrounded the district making for a pleasant scenic drive. For a longer route to Cripple Creek, he took a road that whipped through Goldfield and hugged the backside of the mine. Thousands of people use to populate those lands before they burned in the 1900s. Now, the land was thick with evergreens and aspens. On the way, there are piles of overburden from the mining operation and an old haul truck bed people could climb into. From there, people could view the deepness of the mine from a distance. If they lingered at the overlook long enough, they could see a whole cycle of mining around the 800-foot ledges carved out in search of treasure.

Sometimes Sam took both routes roundtrip just to remind himself of the Gold Camp District's beauty. If he spent enough time being grateful for the area, he wouldn't take advantage of it.

Sam arrived in Cripple Creek, pulling up to the stop sign between Century Casino and the quiet Palace Hotel finding a space in the Bronco Billy's parking lot just across the street.

Home Café in the Bronco Billy's Casino was his favorite place to eat breakfast in the Gold Camp District. They had a $0.49 breakfast menu that outlasted time but remained surprisingly delicious and well portioned for the price. Sam ordered bacon, eggs, hash browns, toast, and a side of French toast. Everything costed less than $4.00. He went there for the food and the friendly bartenders who knew him well. There wasn't any place he could go in town without running into someone he knew.

Sam liked being well-known in the area. The attention made him feel important.

He usually made a stop in at Century Casino for coffee since they had better creamer than the other casinos, but not today.

Underneath blue awnings at Bronco Billy's, he waltzed through the casino doors, hearing the sharp dings sounding from slot machines. The casino was busier than usual now that the weather was nicer and the roads were easier to drive on. Sam worried the bars might be full of people in town for the usually busy weekend, making it difficult to find an open seat.

From one end of the casino, Sam walked to the last room before the table games in search of a spot at the bar. As he sat down, Annie's familiar face welcomed him. She was one of his favorite bartenders at Bronco Billy's. Annie's brown hair was tied back into a bouncy, curled ponytail. A thin black line was drawn across her eyelids, and mascara coated her lashes in many layers. A slender woman, Annie was attractive and Sam never hesitated to admit that to himself.

"Hey, Sam! How's it going?"

"It's going well. How are you doing?"

"Pretty good. Getting my ass handed to me this morning," she said with a smile.

"Well, hopefully, you're getting some good tips out of it," he said.

"I haven't even had a chance to check," she said. "Can I get you a coffee?"

"Hell no. The coffee sucks here. You know that," he smiled.

"I'll be sure to tell the management," she snickered.

Sam ordered a water and then his regular breakfast. He found the TV with the latest hockey highlights from the past season to occupy him while his stomach churned with hunger. Within minutes, Annie arrived at the bar top with his food whipping out three plates in front of him. Devouring everything, Sam felt energy rush back into his body, making him more than lively for his drive up to Bison to go fishing.

Between bites and glances at the TV, Sam shared conversation with Annie, who was incredibly busy but managed to find time to complain about her deadbeat boyfriend and his drinking problem. A touchy subject for Sam since his best friend was a severe alcoholic, so any mention of alcoholism made him sick with worry for his friend.

People in surrounding seats were either with significant others enjoying their short getaways or lone rangers enjoying their breakfast and gambling at the bar top. Every so often, he watched people feed crumpled bills into the virtual card games at the bar, continuing until all bills disappeared from their wallets. Sam wasn't much of a gambler, but he did enjoy it on the very rare occasion.

When he finished with breakfast, he paid, said goodbye to Annie, and left the casino. Walking down the sloping street, he felt the rays of the sun warm on his skin and the chilly winter kissing him goodbye. Up ahead on Bennett Avenue, cars crept by, no doubt to look at the donkey herd roaming loose around town. Ignoring them, Sam hurried to the parking lot, excited to start fishing once again. He drove out of Cripple Creek toward HWY 67 to find his way to Bison Reservoir.

For anyone to visit Bison Reservoir, they had to be a homeowner in Goldfield or Victor. The place was considered sacred to the locals for fear that visitors would be irresponsible with the land, trash the reservoir, and contaminate its precious waters. Since the city only allowed certain people to enjoy the beauties of the reservoir, it became a treasured place in the area.

Being untouched by most everyone, it was an even more serene place than living in the small towns around the Gold Camp District. The crystal waters reflected the sky like a sheet of mirrored glass. The trees were thick, lively, and full of wildlife slinking between them. It was a perfect place to camp and fish without being disturbed by visitors who journeyed to the Gold Camp to pursue outdoor adventures.

Besides the district, and his own home, Sam's third favorite place in the area was Bison. He considered being the Bison Reservoir caretaker for a while, but it meant treating this place as a job rather than a hobby. Something he loved so much shouldn't be work, or else it would lose its value to him. Taking that job would lead to inevitable resentment. He didn't want to look out at the wilderness before him or lose his connection to it because he spent too much time there. Like anyone else, Sam knew he was just as capable of losing interest in something he didn't take in moderation. Instead, he chose to remain a joyful guest so he could forever appreciate it.

He climbed the steep winding hills past Cripple Creek city limits coming past the overlook, which gave a grand view of the town and all the mountains behind it, whipping around each curve he knew by heart as he ascended into the Gillette Flats. Sam tried to imagine what those flats looked like before they were demolished by flames. He imagined thousands of people thriving there, living their lives, driving down unpaved roads in old vehicles, visiting saloons for a drink, and brothels for whores.

Now, the empty flats were just private property or pieces of land shredded up and bought by whoever saw value in the area. Whoever owned those pieces of land never did anything with them, decisions that puzzled Sam. Who in their right mind wouldn't develop a slice of heaven at the base of these mountains?

Over Gillette Flats, Pikes Peak Mountain towered above. In the fall, he could see the kaleidoscopes of green, orange, yellow, and red trees cascade across the mountainside. In the winter, the peak was almost always white with snow. If someone stopped, looked hard enough, and had fairly good eyesight, they could even see the hair-thin line of the road zig-zagging up to Pikes Peak Summit. There, people could eat the fluffiest donuts infamously baked at over 14,000 feet in elevation.

Sam took a right turn off HWY 67, going away from the Gillette Flats but back towards Goldfield. He rode down the long stretch of road which passed by a single empty cabin that had darkened with age and the vacant shooting range he had never been to. He sped toward Cow Mountain, the famous tower of rock and trees that inspired the Root Beer Float, just before coming to a locked gate at the beginning of a winding dirt road. The road led back into a valley and disappeared into the thick of the trees carving a seemingly mysterious destination to outsiders. For all they knew, this was someone's property. Maybe they lived beyond the trees in a cabin, with smoke billowing from a brick chimney. Perhaps they lived off elk, hunted in the winter. Maybe there, no one bothered them.

A road locked with chains and a padlock was mysterious and unquestioned. It was the perfect place for a reservoir to lie undisturbed and unknown to tourists. While always trying to attract visitors, the Gold Camp District kept the many gems of the area hidden away, unable to tolerate sharing them with the average tourist. Like any small town, this place had its secrets. There were three reservoirs in the Gold Camp District, including Skagway and the Cripple Creek Reservoirs owned by a group of men down in Colorado Springs. Of the three, Sam always felt Bison was the most impressive.

Unlocking the gate, Sam felt excitement rush through him, knowing he would soon be fishing after the atrocious winter. It was easy to imagine the fishy smell of Power Bait that would harden like clay on his fingertips. He locked the gate behind him and drove up the road and between the trees, his car rocking back and forth with each passing hole in the dirt road. The aspens were scarred from the herds of elk chewing off the bark for a light winter snack. Big Horned Sheep could be spotted bouncing from one high rock to another, peering down at any strange visitors from the tops of rocky cliffs. The winding road brought him to a long stretch that overlooked a body of water off to the right. Coming around a few more bends, he came to a clearing where two cabins sat lonely and unused. Just a few steps from those cabins was Bison Reservoir begging for company after a silent winter.

Everything around him was serene, untouched. Wisps of smoke didn't billow from the chimneys of the nearby cabins. People weren't recklessly driving through the trees blasting their music. There was just the soft rushing breeze weaving through the trees now thick with green, and Sam soon marching toward a familiar solitude near the water. If he listened more intently against the breeze, he might hear calls from the wild.

He parked near one of the cabins and retrieved his fishing gear from the front seat of his truck. Walking through the brush toward the water, his boots sank into the soft earth, still soaked and muddy from the fading winter.

Nature's aromas invaded his senses, the hearth of the trees, and the sweet smell of leaves, the fresh and wet earth.

Closing his eyes, Sam breathed it all in, giving silent thanks to the warm air surrounding him. He listened for the rustling leaves and snapping twigs signaling wildlife was nearby. While he loved the outdoors, he made sure to proceed with caution around here. Sam was a guest in their home.

With each passing year, the lake aged well, showing a more pristine beauty. He never tired of journeying up here for a short-term adventure. Some nights, he camped here during cool summer, gazing up at the stars he didn't bother to know, clutching a cold, shitty beer in his hand. It was one of his favorite ways to spend the summer. Sometimes he would bring his friends with him, but only if the vibe was right. His best friend often missed those moments. As he inhaled the nature around him, his thoughts trailed off to fixate on an opposite thought.

Anya would like it here.

Today, he decided on fly fishing—his favorite. Sam was a skilled fly fisherman and learned from his father at a young age, although those weren't the fondest of memories. Nevertheless, he considered himself an expert angler in close circles. While others gave up this hobby for the sake of things like school, work, or family, Sam made the time to go fishing, even skipping work to make the day's finest catch. As far as he was concerned, his bond with fishing was the most committed relationship he had ever been in.

For beginners, it took some time to hone the skill and a significant amount of patience. Yet, he was always willing to teach whoever wanted to learn, and there were a surprising many he spent the summer teaching.

Looping the fishing line through the microscopic hole of the fly, he tied a perfect knot, tearing the remaining line off with his teeth, something his dad would smack him for doing. His dad's husky voice lingered in his head, sparking a twinge of sadness and nausea. He didn't think of his dad often, but when he did, it was uncomfortable. Observing the fish swimming in the shallows was the distraction he needed. They were already looking for something to eat, and Sam was already looking for them.

"Don't worry, I'll get to you," he mumbled aloud.

He adjusted the hat on his head, releasing the heat captured in its fabric and hooked two spare flies to the bill.

Working his way up the reservoir, he whipped the line back and forth delicately. Fly fishing was like the same easy breaths he took. Each careful whip rendered him countless small trout. They'd wiggle in his hands, and he'd watch them gasp for air as he admired their iridescent colors before gently placing them back in the water to return home. They wagged their tails as they disappeared into murky depths. If he were camping, he would've kept his catches and grilled them over a fire.

After fishing for a few hours, he sat on the reservoir's shore to admire everything around him. Across the water, a herd of deer took refreshing drinks before leaping off into the trees. Birds flew above, returning home from winter. A few quiet rabbits bounced around him in the wet earth feeding on freshly sprouted grass.

Looking around, Sam felt grateful for his life, where he lived, his low-maintenance job, and being one of the select people in the world who was free of debt. Everyone he befriended seemed to have issues opposite of his. He hated seeing them struggle. On the other hand, seeing their struggles made him feel lucky.

Better to be lucky than good.

That mentality saw him through three car accidents he emerged from unscathed, a pregnancy scare from a one-night stand, upgrades on countless flights around the country, and a job he loved doing.

With essentially no stresses, and nothing keeping him from doing just exactly what he wanted to do with his life, he found he was content nearly every minute of the day. Yet, when it came to finding someone who mattered to him more than himself, he fell depressingly short of lucky.

As a young child, he decided he would only do things he enjoyed. Things that made him feel good. He would do them even if that meant refusing a friend's request to do something he didn't want to do. Being positive every minute of every day was unrealistic, but he decided he would not do anything in his life unless it brought him joy. Why waste time doing things that made him unhappy when he could spend time and energy doing something that does?

Sam didn't care if he refused anyone.

If he tired of something, lost interest, or realized things brought him more stress than contentment, he would let it go without a second thought. It was no use making something out of nothing.

From the sun's position in the sky and the grumbling that returned to his stomach, Sam realized he hadn't eaten since breakfast. It was quickly reaching the early evening. Getting up from the wet beach, he dusted his damp pants off, scraped the fish scale residue from his fingers in the brisk lake waters, and walked back through the brush to his truck, a seemingly longer trek than before as he kept an eye out for any wildlife that could be lurking in the trees. Sam traveled further up the shore than he realized. That was nothing unusual.

When buzzing vibration went off in his pocket, his heart fell into his stomach. When he took it out to see who it was, he stopped in the middle of the dirt road, a smile sweeping across his face.

FOUR

Anya is asleep or awake. She's not quite sure. The air is pungent with the smell of onions, and a small tribe of women surrounds her. All of them with long, silky, and silver hair, beaming smiles, and infectious laughter.

Above was a sky thick with the brightest stars and shining moons. Beneath their celestial rays, the women undressed and ran towards the crystal black waters lapping softly beneath the moonlight, shimmering in the reflection of the night sky. The women dove in headfirst, disappearing beneath the surface.

Anya sat on the black beach, watching the women wade and dive into the waters. Whale-like creatures swam in the distance, breaching beneath the moon rays, seemingly brushing shoulders with the ladies playfully swimming.

An older, more wizened woman sat down beside Anya as she dug her feet deeper into the sand and drew shapes on the coarse canvas. Anya looked out at the water with a heavy frown.

"What's the matter, darling?" The woman beside her asked. "Why won't you join your sisters?"

She paused, continuing to draw strange shapes in the black sand.

"I'm afraid," she said timidly.

The woman stroked the back of Anya's head, a radiant touch vibrating at her scalp. "The waters are so dark, and I'm afraid of what's in them."

"Everyone is afraid of the unknown," the woman said, looking out at the young women splashing in the waters. She turned back to fixate on Anya. "It is the way of life, but we can't let it stop us from experiencing the magnificence of what's in front of us." The woman looked back into Anya's eyes. "Darling, you mustn't be afraid. Great things come to us when we overcome fear and experience cleanse and awakening."

Anya looked back down at her feet and dug deeper into the sand, feeling the coarse grains between her toes. She wiped the shapes away to create a new black canvas. When she looked back up and out at the ocean, she saw the glowing smiles of her sisters in the water and the moon rays dancing on their skin, the spiritual cleanse, and the stars just within arm's reach.

"You must be brave. Give yourself a chance to see how brave you are," the woman pleaded.

Looking out hopefully, she stood up and stripped down to her bare skin beside the woman. Placing her hands in her lap, the woman's gaze followed Anya's path toward the edge of the soft waves lapping at the shore. The water rushed past Anya's toes and feet, grabbing at her ankles, calling her into its black depths. The water was warm, like a pair of open arms ready to embrace her.

The women stopped their play at the sight of her, seeing the hesitance in her posture. They looked into each other's glowing blue eyes, made brighter by the moon and Anya felt shame for being fearful.

Together, all six women approached her at the beach with arms wide and welcoming. Taking her hands, they lead her into the water for cleansing. The warmth of the waves reached past her calves, knees, and thighs until the water met her waist.

She looked back at the woman encouraging her to be brave. The woman was smiling and pleased to see Anya's bravery come through despite what she feared.

"Go on," the woman said. Anya's sisters led her past the first big wave greeting her with mighty force. Those same waves lapped at her waist before another large wave curled into a vortex, tumbling toward Anya, enveloping her from head to toe.

Water splashed into her face waking her from the deep and pleasant dream she was in. She was surprised by how magical the dream was, disappointed she didn't have time to think about it or write it down like usual.

Frustrated with being awoken so abruptly, she rubbed the water out of her eyes and looked up to see Karmyn and Bee already in bathing suits soaked from head to toe. With no makeup and wet stringy hair, they were both the epitome of goddesses—arguably the same goddesses from her very own dreams.

They had already gone for a dip in those glacial mountain waters without her, which annoyed her even more.

"Did someone stay up too late looking at the stars?" Karmyn mocked. Bee was behind her, smiling and eager to rush back in the water.

"Shut up!" Anya said, grinning. She wrestled out of her sleeping bag, which wreaked of campfire smoke. Rushing to her feet, she stripped down to her sports bra and thong, chasing Karmyn and Bee into the waters.

Like tears of Gods, they bathed in the mountain lake, soaking up the sun's already high rays and scaring the fish away. She was eerily delighted at how serendipitous her morning bath with her best friends was, how it resembled the dream she had last night. Remembering it made her ache.

Shaking the thought from her mind, she walked back up onto the dry earth, feeling the grass beneath her feet.

In the pile of her camping gear, she retrieved a towel, taking off her wet underwear and sports bra, drying her body, and getting dressed in fresh clothing before the mountain chill could seep into her bones. While Karmyn and Bee changed, Anya started a fire for breakfast.

Using a fire starter and a wood-burning camp stove she brought with her, she made a spark in a small pile of sticks and tinder she'd made with toilet paper rolls and dryer lint. The fire roared to life while Bee and Karmyn gathered around, snuggled up in dry clothes. They boiled hot water to make cups of pour-over coffee, and fried up enough eggs, bacon, and potatoes made for an army.

They had enough time for a quick hike to the top of the peak just on the opposite side of the lake. Once reaching the top, they screamed at the top of their lungs, hearing the echoes of their voices against the tall mountains. Sometimes they could hear the sound of wildlife calling back.

There was no other feeling like climbing to the top of a mountain after cursing your way to the top. Being there and seeing the world for hundreds of miles in the distance made Anya feel alive. Like she could do anything. Like she was invincible and fearless. If she could build her house at the very top of a mountain, she would.

After coming down from the hike, the three of them went fishing in the lake, catching cutthroat trout they would eat for dinner that night.

By nightfall, Sam was on her mind, as was the promise she made to her friends. Eventually, she would have to deal with scheduling a new date but knew her trip in the mountains could reduce her chances of a message getting through. Regardless, she sent him one anyway, asking to see him tomorrow night. Anya wondered if maybe she liked him a little bit more than she let on.

"Who are you texting out here in the middle of goddamn nowhere?" Bee said over her shoulder, startling her.

"Sam," Karmyn and Bee exchanged excited looks. "No need to make a huge deal out of it, okay? I'm just keeping my promise to you guys."

"Sure you are," Karmyn said with a wink. "I think you like him more than you think you do."

"What did you say to him?" Bee asked.

"I asked him if he wanted to meet up for dinner tomorrow night after I got back from our camping trip."

"He probably only read 'camping trip,'" Karmyn laughed.

"Probably," Anya snickered. "We'll see what he says. Maybe he's moved on by now."

"Dude, I doubt that. He's Prince Charming, you're Sleeping Beauty, and from what you've told us, he wants to kiss your face," said Karmyn.

"Girl, I still have major problems with a random guy kissing a girl he barely knows while she sleeps. Just sayin'," Anya said. Sam still hadn't kissed Anya.

As the sun set, the campfire became their light. Karmyn brought six clean and gutted fish to grill while Bee took charge of cleaning and cutting fresh veggies. Anya manned the fire, making sure the flame was high and hot for grilling. Flecks of burning wood jumped into the sky, letting the wind carry them off and turn them into harmless wisps of ash.

As she watched Bee and Karmyn work together to grill fish and veggies, she admired them for how beautiful they were in their genuine ways. When Bee and Karmyn shared parts of their hearts with her, she found them to be the most stunning. The raw act of sharing part of yourself and being vulnerable was so rare to Anya. When people felt comfortable sharing sensitive things with her, she appreciated and loved them that much more. Over the many years the three of them had spent together, they had gone through so much. So many times, they had relied on each other when their strength had wavered. When one of the three was going through their difficulties, the other two were beacons of hope, bright lights in the shadowy distance, and a real good kick in the ass if they sat in misery for too long.

The smell of fish singed at the tips of the flames roaring from the fire, and the skewered veggies had imperfect char marks on them. Soon, the tails of the fish would be dry and crispy, and the veggies would be salty and smoky. The three of them shared more of their favorite beers, raising them to the oncoming summer.

Tonight was their last night in the mountains, but it was also the celebratory welcoming of a summer full of adventure. Tomorrow they would go home and continue with their regular workdays, just trying to make it through the week so they could leave for their next adventure together. This night was the perfect way to start the summer. It was hard knowing it would end by morning.

At dinner, Anya found herself staring up at the stars again, thinking about her dream, the mentions of awakenings and bravery, the women bathing in the waters, what that all meant. Anya felt Bee's eyes on her as she stared up.

"When you look at the stars, what exactly do you look at?" She asked. Anya paused for a moment, wondering if this was a test, if they were planning to make fun of her or if they were genuinely interested in her answer.

"You really want to know?" Bee and Karmyn nodded seriously.

"Usually, it's the same constellations in the sky, but they change positions depending on what time of year it is. Usually, I am looking up and going through the ones I already know. But I mostly look at my favorite constellation."

"You have a favorite? What is it?" Asked Karmyn. Anya hesitated, looking up into the sky.

"It's called Pleiades, or the Seven Sisters."

"What do you like so much about it? Seems like a weird thing to be your favorite," Anya didn't disagree with that.

"I first learned about the constellation when I was in elementary school. The myth of the story was most interesting to me because it was a bizarre folk tale."

"What's the tale?" Bee asked further, more interested than usual. Thinking on it now, the memory was the first instance of spiritual awakening she could recall. The first time she felt woke to the universe and not just the observable world around her.

"The best way I can describe the story is from that Jodi Picoult book, *Picture Perfect*."

A long time ago, when the world had just begun, six young women lived in a village set beside a huge boulder. As was their custom, one day while their husbands were out hunting, they went out to dig for herbs. Some time passed, each of the women rooting with their digging stick, and then one of the wives found something new to eat.

"Come and try this," She told her friends. "This plant tastes delicious!" Within minutes, the six women were all eating sweet onions. They were so tasty that they ate until the sun set. One of the wives looked at the dark sky.

"We'd better get home to cook dinner for our husbands," she pointed out, and they all left.

When the husbands came home that night they were all exhausted but happy, since they had each killed a cougar. "What smells so awful?" one man asked as he stood in the doorway of his lodge.

"Maybe it is some food that has spoiled," another husband suggested. But when they leaned over to kiss their wives hello, they realized where the odor was coming from.

"We found something new to eat," the wives said, bubbling with excitement. They held out the onions. "Here, try them."

"They smell terrible," the husbands said. "We won't eat them. And you're not going to stay in the same lodge as us, not smelling like that. You'll have to sleep outside tonight." So the wives gathered their things and slept beneath the stars.

When the husbands left to go hunting the next day, the wives returned to the spot where they had dug up the wild onions. They knew their husbands didn't like the smell, but the onions were so delicious that the wives could not help but eat them. They filled their bellies and stretched out on the soft red earth.

The husbands came home that night, gruff and irritable. They had not caught any cougars. "We smelled like your onions," they accused, "so the animals ran away. It is all your fault."

The wives didn't believe them. They slept outside a second night, and a third, until a week had passed. The wives kept eating the onions that were so delicious, and the men could not catch any cougars. Frustrated, the men yelled at their wives, "Get away from us! We can't stand your onion smell."

"Well, we can't get any sleep outside," the wives countered.

The seventh day, the wives took their woven ropes with them when they went to dig the onions. One wife carried along her baby daughter. They scaled the large rock behind their village and turned their faces to the sinking crimson sun.

"Let's leave our husbands," one wife suggested. "I don't want to live with mine anymore."

The wives all agreed.

The oldest wife stood on the boulder and chanted a magical word. She tossed her rope into the sky, and it hooked over a cloud so that the ends hung down. The other wives tied their own ropes to the one that was swinging and then they stood on the frayed edges of the ropes. Slowly they began to rise, swaying around like starlings. They moved in circles, passing each other, reaching higher and higher.

The other villagers saw the wives ascending in the sky. "Come back!" the People called as the women floated over the camp. But the wives and the little girl kept going.

When the husbands returned that night, they were very hungry and lonely. They wished they had not driven their wives away. One of them had the idea to go after the women, using the same kind of magic they had. They ran to their lodges and brought their own ropes, and soon they too were rising in the nights.

The wives glanced down and saw the husbands coming after them. "Should we wait for them?" one woman asked calmly.

The others shouted and shook their heads. "No! They told us to leave. We won't let them catch us." They danced and swung on their ropes. "We will be happier in the sky."

When the husbands were close enough to hear, the wives shouted for them to stop, and the men stayed right where they were, a little behind their wives.

So the women who loved onions stayed in the Sky Country. They are still there, seven stars that we call Pleiades. The faintest of all is the little girl. And the husbands, who will not go home until their wives do, remain a short distance away, six stars in the constellation Taurus. You can find them shining up at their wives, wishing maybe that things had turned out a different way. –Monache Indian Legend.

Bee and Karmyn stared at Anya in gaping awe.

"That *is* a bizarre myth. But it's kind of great," Bee said.

"Did you seriously memorize that whole story?" Karmyn said, still in admiration. Anya nodded. "That's impressive."

"Guerilla recitation for an English class in college. You kind of don't forget after repeating a piece of literature over and over for the sake of passing a test," Anya said. "I don't know why exactly I enjoy the constellation. But the myth that went along with it just made it so memorable that it became my favorite."

"Makes sense," Bee said.

"Ever since I learned about it in school, I kind of became obsessed with stargazing. I liked imagining all the possibilities that exist in the universe."

Bee and Karmyn sat quietly as if they were also contemplating what actually *could* exist out in the universe. Maybe the idea that more possibilities existed in space frightened them. Anya understood how that could be intimidating to anyone, realizing they are such a small part compared to the magnitude of all existence. Still, she suspected they might be just a little curious.

To Anya, Bee and Karmyn resembled the little girl in her dream the night before. Like the little girl, they were scared to dive into the dark ocean, or outer space, for fear of not knowing what was truly out there, unlike Anya, who felt so small and confined to such a grand universe.

Maybe they were scared of a true spiritual awakening, but in this world, who wasn't?

Perhaps knowing the possibilities or what the universe is capable of is just too much for people to comprehend. Maybe the ignorant bliss in believing humans are the universe's superior race is easier. Or perhaps people are severely in the wrong by casting out extraterrestrial possibilities. Anya had to quit thinking about it, or Bee and Karmyn would think she was having a seizure.

"So, what other adventures should we go on this summer?" Anya asked to change the subject. The conversation was uncharted territory, making her shift uncomfortably in her camping chair. The girls perked up at the chance to discuss that topic.

"You know, it might be nice to visit California or something. It has been a long while since I've seen the ocean, kayaked, and just enjoyed the beach," Bee said.

"I like that idea," Karmyn said. "We can do a road trip together and rent a nice house close to the beach. We could probably try and fish from the shore, maybe go whale watching too!"

"Sweet," Anya giggled. "California it is."

They finished their meals, cleaning up their campsite to avoid attracting any bears or other predatory creatures. Anya opted to slumber in the tent with her best friends that night instead of gazing at the stars. She would have a lifetime to stare at the stars. As she climbed into her sleeping bag to go to sleep, her phone went off. She picked it up to see her message to Sam had gone through and that he responded.

"Dinner with you sounds great. See you at 6:00 p.m. tomorrow."

FIVE

Anya dropped Karmyn and Bee off in Colorado Springs, then drove back home toward Cripple Creek. The drive was a pleasant one, full of winding curves and the greatness of Pikes Peak towering above her. On occasion, deer chomped grass on the side of the road reminding Anya to drive more carefully.

When she took long drives by herself, Anya played her soothing music from Spotify and thought about Sam.

She met him several months after moving to Victor and after her most recent relationship. Her last breakup made her want to swear off all men for a while. Thoughts of him still tortured her. Anya couldn't figure out how she was unable to find someone suitable to date or someone that chose her every day.

People often told Anya that she was too nice and that men preferred dating bitches. Anya thought women tended to date assholes, which she didn't find exciting or enjoyable. It took too much energy for her to play games. But Anya was guilty of giving people too many chances, and she knew it. She wanted to see people happy. She saw the good in everyone. But when it came to dating, she figured out whoever she dated was hurt by someone or something and just hadn't let go yet.

Just like Anya.

Most everyone she dated would leave her using the iconic reasons, "I've been hurt, and I'm afraid of getting involved" or "I don't know what love is" or "I'm not ready." Whether or not those statements were true or false, she wasn't sure. As much as she hated those excuses, they became her own drumbeats for never getting involved with anyone.

Humans are weird in that way. Someone hurts them, and instead of taking time to heal, they carry the hurt around with them, indulging it and even cherishing it. When they move on to a new relationship, maybe something with potential, they invest their time and energy into them, discovering that person still hadn't released their pain either. It's just one big, miserable cycle of hurt that no one bothers to break.

Anya never understood that behavior, why people couldn't let go of their pain to welcome new possibilities into their lives. Yet, here she was, adopting the same behavior after years of dating disasters. Even so, Anya still tried to be compassionate and understanding, realizing people were complex and often stubborn to change. At the same time, she kept her distance until it was safe to let someone in.

It was for this reason Anya gave people too many chances. She wanted to prove to everyone she ever encountered that not everyone is out to break their heart. That there are people out there who will love them for who they are.

People hurt her, and she knew she carried those hurts around, although she tried not to. For that, she understood how easy it was to be a victim of heartbreak, sit in those feelings of being unwanted, and suffer in her confusion after doing everything she could to make things work, only to feel like love was hopeless.

Perhaps that's why Karmyn and Bee were so frustrated—because they could see Anya's hope and faith in love slowly fading away. Anya didn't want them to worry about her anymore. So she decided to make it her mission to heal her hurts and break the hurt cycle. Maybe Sam was a good start.

Maybe not.

Anya had no intention of meeting anyone after her last relationship. She liked Cripple Creek because it was isolated, and the dating pool was scarce. It was the perfect place to escape dating, be left alone, and focus on things she wanted to do without the complications of tempting and fleeting romances.

And then she met Sam, who was comfortable in social situations but wasn't keen on talking about himself, which bothered her. What she did know was he wanted to know her and was upfront about being interested and impressed by her.

"How did you end up here?" He asked her. She wondered the same thing. But in his many attempts at asking her out for coffee, she didn't feel compelled to say yes too often, which made him chase even more.

Anya tried not to be attracted to him but let herself shamelessly admire his backside more than once.

Sam was funny and social, the life of the party in many settings, and Anya didn't know much of anyone in town outside of work. Just having known him, he had introduced her to a mass of people in the area that she could be friends with. Slowly but surely, she was starting to feel a little more welcome to the area.

After nearly an hour of driving winding mountain roads, Anya pulled into the paved driveway at her house. She couldn't believe how far her thoughts had carried her on the way home. Some days, she arrived home so quickly she was convinced she went through a wormhole.

She loved her house, and although she lived outside of Cripple Creek and there wasn't much to offer in the area as far as entertainment and necessity, she carved her little place on a hilltop that gave a grand view of the many mountains she couldn't get enough of.

Anya's home bordered on a tiny home concept but was slightly wider than a typical tiny house. Anya needed enough room for her books. After moving to Cripple Creek and finding she enjoyed the area's beauty, it seemed like a good choice to build her own home. Renting was horrible, especially in this area. Most of the houses were old and never upgraded or outrageously high in rental cost.

From her front door was a large nook, which looked at out the thick trees but gave a clear view of the sky above her. Her spacious kitchen was to the right of her, and in the corner was a small dining area. Next to the nook was an open space with a cozy couch, a small TV, and bookcases overflowing with books. To her left was a bathroom big enough to fit a tub, and to the back was a small but still relatively spacious bedroom. She had decorated the whole house with navy blues and whites, giving it an almost nautical feel. The floor was a beautiful hardwood, and windows were abundant, looking out into the trees.

After getting inside, she glanced at her watch to see it was already 3:00 p.m. She had a few hours before she was meeting Sam for dinner. Walking into the house, her black Manx cat, Sugar, welcomed her with soft meows that rose to meet Anya's ears.

Anya felt terrible about leaving her alone when she went on adventures, imagining how miserable Sugar was when Anya was gone. She picked Sugar up and snuggled her face, kissing her nose.

"Did you miss me, Sugar baby?" Anya spoke in a high-pitched voice. Sugar licked her face.

"I'm going to take that as a 'yes,'" she said, kissing her nose one last time. Anya filled Sugar's food and water bowl, serving a small plate of wet food, which she devoured within minutes.

Anya took her dirty camping gear down the short hallway to her stacked washer and dryer wedged between her room and the bathroom. She tossed her clothing directly into the washer, stripping down and tossing today's clothes in with them. Pulling the hair tie from her long golden hair, she felt it fall down her back, tickling her skin soothingly. It was greasy and unkempt from the camping trip, and the smell of campfire was clinging to each strand.

Sugar jumped onto a window ledge to observe the birds fluttering about the property. The soft patter of her paws and quiet chirps communicating with the birds put a smile on Anya's face.

Why couldn't people love each other like they love their pets and vice versa?

After a quick shower, she turned on the TV for background noise and ran a towel through the length of her golden hair, searching her closet for something to wear to dinner. She might even put on mascara tonight. She settled on a pair of dark skinny jeans and a navy blue crew cut t-shirt. Black canvas shoes would be her shoe of choice.

It took Anya about 45 minutes to get ready, shower, blow-dry her hair, and put mascara on. She didn't like to take too much time getting ready. Since a few hours were left before going to dinner, she decided to read a book, opting for *Eleven Minutes* by Paulo Coelho. It was a story of a Brazilian prostitute who finds herself living in Geneva, where she sexually pleasures high-paying clients. But the twist is—she finds love.

Anya had done lust and hated it. So, she loved this story.

Maybe the person she was destined to love would be coming soon. Perhaps he was already here. Or maybe she had met him. It could even be Sam. She shook that thought from her mind, knowing her past held far too much optimism for people who were interested in her, only for them to decide she wasn't 'the one.' The less pressure she put on this, the less likely she was to be disappointed.

The time passed too quickly, and having to leave for dinner was fast approaching. It wasn't easy putting the book down, and she considered canceling on him so she could live in the fantasy for a bit longer. Feeling ridiculous for wanting to ditch her date, she ended the chapter and placed the book on her dining room table beside her nook.

She lifted her sleeping cat from her lap and placed her on the floor. Sugar stretched and strutted over to her food bowl. The clock on her stove read, 5:45 p.m. After admiring the simplicity of her outfit, she took her purse and keys and left her house to drive into town.

SIX

Sam arrived at the restaurant early to get a table. He ordered a drink—whiskey, neat. The dining area was small and filled with people smiling, enjoying their meals, going on dates. There was a TV above the bar playing all types of sporting events, but he wasn't paying attention to any of them. Instead, he glanced anxiously at the opening, waiting for Anya to walk through the door. He read the clock on the wall above the host stand—5:56 p.m.

Anya arrived right at 6:00 p.m. She swept through the doorways, waving her silky golden hair. Her eyes seemed a brighter blue than normal, which could have been a trick of the light. When she saw him, he could feel a smile curl along his face. She responded with the same, drifting toward him with a sort of grace.

Sam got up and embraced her. Their bodies connected, chest to chest, pelvis to pelvis. The good hugs were the ones you could fall into, or so he thought. The lavender aroma of her hair was thick in his nose, and he could feel himself relax. The hug didn't seem to last long enough, but it made surrounding tables dance with silence. Feeling the awkward looks of others, they broke the hug and sat down in their seats.

Sam subtly looked up and down at Anya, admiring her slim form. The outfit she was wearing was simple; a shirt and jeans, reminding him how low-maintenance she was and how much he liked that about her. Sam knew being a simple woman helped her fit into this area more than the bedazzled ones who came through town.

Not knowing what to say to start the conversation, he started with something plain.

"So, how are you? What have you been up to?" He asked, opening a menu.

"I'm good. I just got back from a short camping trip with my girlfriends," she said. He perked up when he heard, 'camping trip.' Running quickly through his mind, he listed all the places he would love to take her camping.

"Really? How was that? Where did you end up going?"

"We had a great time. We went up to Clear Lake. It's so beautiful up there. Have you ever been?"

No. But I'd go with you.

"No. I've never even heard of it before."

"It's amazing," she said. "It's just this little tiny lake in the mountains, and you can climb up to the peak if you want. We did some fishing and grilled our catch over the fire. It was a long-awaited trip. Winter sucked."

"Yeah, it did. I hate winter," he said.

"God, me too," they smiled in unison.

They looked over the menu in silence for a few moments and then ordered. Anya didn't get a drink but instead sipped a glass of water while Sam sipped on his whiskey.

"So, what do you do in the summertime?" She asked him.

"I like camping and fishing too. I like to go up to Bison Reservoir in Victor," he said. "In the summer, I'm usually out wandering in the mountains somewhere." He finished his sentence and noticed she was watching him intently. Palms sweaty, he took a shaky sip of his whiskey, feeling her blue eyes pierce into him. Their dinner arrived, and they ate together, carrying on a conversation about Anya's cat, the Colorado outdoors, the music they liked.

It was so easy to talk to her about anything, and he liked that. What he liked most about her was her desire to help others. She talked at length about her pursuits with volunteering at places that needed it most, mostly animal shelters and soup kitchens. Anya believed greatly in self-care and mental health. Her passion for connecting to others was made blatantly apparent by how she yearned for travel. Not only did she visit places, but she also immersed herself in them as if she were a local herself, visiting less-traveled roads.

She talked about all the languages she wanted to learn so she could connect with more people around the world. Sam had known for a while that she was compassionate and an empath. The way she talked, he could tell she felt things deeply and was a little bit sensitive. She spoke of her love for whales and dolphins and how she wanted to be a whale trainer before she saw the killer whale, Tilikum, kill a trainer at SeaWorld in Florida. He could see her discontent for the way whales were treated in captivity as she talked about movies like The Cove and Blackfish.

The things she loved and the way she talked about loving others were topics she didn't fear discussing. Sam sat there, taking everything about her in, wholly captured by how interesting and honest she was about the things she loved. He inhaled every single thing she released with each breath, admiring how refreshing she was, especially in this area. The conversation, like any other, led to movies, and she had seen a lot of them, to his surprise.

"Do you like the Marvel movies?" She asked excitedly. She had nearly cleared her plate at this point. Sam liked a woman with an appetite.

"Oh yeah! I love the Marvel movies," he exclaimed. "You know. I feel like all these very celestial, science fiction movies are easing us into what's really out there in the universe."

At that comment, she straightened in her chair.

"That's an interesting theory," she said. "Continue."

"Do you believe in all that stuff? Aliens and whatever?" He said.

"I definitely do," she said. "I think for us to believe we're the only living species in the universe is ignorant and naïve."

"Me too!" He said. "I just think, there are so many movies about people living in the universe and life outside of our Earth, it just feels like they're gateways or messages to help us realize there are other worlds out there. So if we're watching it in movies, it won't be as shocking when it appears in our current reality."

"I like this perspective, and you could be right," she smiled. "So you know about all the alien races and stuff? Reptilians, Greys, Pleiadians?"

"Yeah. I watch a lot of YouTube videos on that stuff. I prefer videos over reading books." He said. She was silent for a minute, looking down at the now-empty table, making him feel slightly uncomfortable with her silence.

"You okay?" He asked her.

"What? Oh, yeah! I was just thinking," she said, looking up at him.

"Can I ask about what?" He said. "Is it because I don't like reading?"

"Ha! God, no. I'm a total book nerd, but not everyone is. I was just thinking about the Marvel movies and your perspective on them," she said. But then she fell silent again.

"Oh. Okay," Unsure of how to carry the conversation, he tried something else. "Do you want any dessert?"

"Sure. I love the flan here."

"Flan it is," he grabbed the nearest waiter and ordered two plates with two coffees. They ate their dessert, finding the rhythm in their conversation again. With each passing minute, he felt himself relax a little more, divulging some of his thoughts on the world, how depressing it was, how he wished people could just be happy and live in harmony. Each time he said something honest, she would perk up at him.

After paying for dinner, Sam walked Anya of the loud casino building to her car to say goodnight.

"Dinner was nice," she said as they approached her car.

"Yeah. I had a great time," he said. Before their evening together started, he thought about kissing her goodnight. She groped her purse for her keys and then looked up at the sky with faint disappointment.

"Don't you hate how city lights drown out so much of the night sky?" She asked. Sam looked up with her hoping to find the same place in the sky where her eyes were fixated. He saw the faint twinkles of stars, but she was right. City lights obstructed the view.

"Honestly, I never really thought about it, but I guess they do," he said.

She continued to stare up at the dark sky. "Do you like stargazing?" He asked. She tore her gaze from above and looked at him.

"I *love* it," she said.

"Well, how about we go stargazing this next weekend. I hear there is a meteor shower happening." A huge smile extended across her face, and in the darkness, Sam saw her blush. He found the single thing in this whole evening that made her glow brighter than the golden hair falling past her shoulders.

"That sounds wonderful," she said. "I know a great place I always go to. So, maybe we can go there? Unless you have another place in mind."

"Sounds great," he smiled. "I'll pick you up at like 6:00 p.m. on Saturday? And I'll bring blankets."

"It's a date. I'll bring some sort of hot beverage," she said, staring at him as if waiting for something else. He could've gone in for the kiss but decided against it.

"I'll see you then, Anya," he moved away from her, and she smiled. Jingling her keys between her fingertips, she unlocked her car with the touch of a button. The chirps echoed in the corners of the parking lot.

"Goodnight, Sam," he walked back to his car, hearing her car door slam behind him.

It was a mistake not kissing her.

But another date meant another chance, and that thrilled him.

SEVEN

Getting in the car, Anya realized she was more connected to this person than she expected to be. She didn't realize Sam would be near as interested in the things that she only thought about. Yet, the thought of going more into the conversation with him terrified her. She could handle her friends making fun of her love for the stars and her secret fascination with aliens, and the massive universe hanging above her at all times. But, facing any judgments from Sam would be a shot to the heart she would never recover from.

She drove home with thoughts of Pleiadians and Reptilians on her mind. Surely if he believed in them and she believed in them, there were others out there who believed in them too. In Anya's mind, she thought there is at least one person out there in the world who believes in something or can do something others can't. Those are the odds as she wishes to believe them.

When Anya got home, she greeted Sugar with open arms and kitten kisses. The house was pitch black, and the stars were intensely bright outside her windows above the tree line. She looked out to see which constellations were revealing themselves and searched the sky for the Pleiades constellation, finding it hanging within the Taurus cluster. She stared at Pleiades, her small furry creature brushing against her leg.

"For as much as I love stargazing, I don't know much about our galaxy," she admitted to herself out loud. Sugar looked up, letting out a soft meow. Anya placed her hands on her hips and glanced at her computer.

"What do you think, Sugar? Should I go down that rabbit hole?" Sugar brushed her body alongside Anya's leg again. She could feel her soft purrs against her skinny jeans. After changing into a pair of leggings, Anya grabbed her computer and situated herself in her cozy nook to be closer to the night sky. Sugar hopped up to be near her and found a comfortable place between Anya's calves, where she curled up and fell asleep.

Opening her computer, she started searching the internet for information about the Milky Way.

She settled on a long and detailed documentary about her galaxy, courtesy of National Geographic. She learned that what people could see in observed space was one-half of one percent of what existed out there. At this rate, Anya would never see every corner of the universe, and that depressed her.

She learned that the Milky Way is one galaxy in a sea of millions of other galaxies, but the Milky Way is one of the oldest galaxies in the universe, competing for space in the black, next to younger, more persistent galaxies in their orbit. Astronomers theorized the Milky Way has existed since the birth of the universe some twelve billion years ago.

The Milky Way is a spiral galaxy, and at the heart of our galaxy, 26 thousand light-years from Earth, there is a tremendous density of stars shining and moving at superspeed. In the center of stunning stars is a small black hole four times the sun's mass, disguised as a star. Black holes grow with time as gas, dust, and other things fall on top of it.

The Milky Way's spiral holds two-hundred billion stars whipped around in various spiral arms. But, people can't see the galaxy from an aerial view. The model presented in the video was all just speculation drawn from observing similar spiral galaxies outside the one she lived in. This galaxy is just a swirl of gold, white, and black existing as a giant disc.

Anya learned the spiral arms are littered with nebulas too. Many of them with unique puffs of color. That nebulas are clouds of gas and dust left behind after the death of a star. She learned the creation of a new star happens from that same dust and gas left behind after a star's death.

A beautiful cycle of life, Anya thought.

Dying so you can be reborn.

Repeating that cycle for trillions of years.

For a star to beam back into existence, gas and dust must be pulled in by gravity to make a disc. The denser the disc becomes, the hotter it burns. When it reaches 18 million degrees, the hydrogen atoms come together to create helium.

Thus, a star is born.

Fascinating.

The Milky Way is a galaxy stretching over 600,000 trillion miles in diameter. Astronomers theorized it would take 100,000 years to cross. The documentary answered millions of questions she had never asked, like how the galaxy was held together.

Anything with mass has a gravitational pull.

Large mass means a bigger pull.

The mass consists of dark matter, something people can't see, hence the limited visibility when staring into space. A galaxy held together by dark matter and gravity amused Anya, proving that even powerful things like galaxies couldn't exist without darkness. Like them, Anya couldn't exist without her darkness.

As Anya finished the documentary, she learned Astronomers had theorized the model of the universe, calling it a Bolshoy, which meant 'big' in Russian. The model of this structure insists galaxies aren't randomly placed throughout the universe.

The Bolshoy looked miraculously like the blue sphere of electric light she used to see at toy stores. When she touched it, the electricity followed her fingers, reminding her of what neurons might look like firing in the brain.

It was a good documentary, but all it did was spark other questions.

Most of which revolved around Pleiades.

Her fingers ticked away at the keyboard, looking for information about the star cluster. There was far less about it than the treasured Milky Way, but she was able to settle on a much shorter video.

Pleiades was also known as M45 and suggested to be one-hundred million years old. When looking at the star cluster from a telescope, astronomers saw them as blue, meaning they were burning brighter and faster than other stars. When people on Earth look at Pleiades, they're viewing it as it was four hundred light-years ago.

"Well, that will screw with your brain," Anya said out loud.

After watching the video, she searched using the term "Pleiadians."

To her surprise, there were Facebook groups, Instagram accounts, books, YouTube videos, spiritual gurus and Pleiadian channelers, and websites full of knowledge and myth of the Pleiadians. She started consuming everything she could find, reading more on the tale, getting lost in videos of beautiful women speaking to their Pleiadian family.

Anya chose one video of a woman speaking to her Pleiadian family using a language that resembled nothing like anything Anya had heard, and she spoke three languages. The woman rambled on in very long-winded sentences, smiling during some parts. Anya couldn't help but wonder if the woman was making all this up. Thousands of people had already upvoted this video, so it was clear there were many out there who believed it. On some level, Anya thought it was too ridiculous to believe. On another level, she believed it all.

This is crazy. I can't believe people believe in this. If my parents found out I was looking at this stuff, they would lose their minds.

Anya was the daughter of Christian parents, and they were very judgmental of any other religion or belief system that didn't match their own. However, they never showed their indifference to anyone's beliefs. They would just talk about it in the safety of their home. Anya never liked that. She always felt it was more helpful to let people just believe what they believe.

Anya spent years wondering why she needed a church to pray to God each day. God was there for her whenever she needed support, and she never needed a church to practice her faith. The boundaries of the church always made her feel like she was trying to be controlled rather than inspired. When she left the house, she stopped going to church and silently promised herself she would practice her faith when and where she wanted. Although baptized Christian, she never identified as one as she grew up. As a woman who had semi-abandoned the Christian institution, Anya didn't quite know how to identify her religion anymore, but she knew it was more than the strict confines of Christianity.

Anya kept searching the internet, learning Pleiadians were often called Starseeds, or those sent down to this planet to help others and instill love and connection. She learned they reincarnate on other planes across many other galaxies and are multidimensional, coming from other star systems and galaxies. To her surprise, many people in this world identified with the Starseed persona and felt they were a part of the cosmos. Many of them linked their connections to spirituality, a realm Anya was aware of but never explored.

The more she searched the internet, the more she stumbled onto strange videos that twisted her ideas of herself, begging questions she would never fathom on her own. Ones like "Signs You Are Pleiadian" sticking out to her in large bold letters.

She hovered her mouse over the video for a moment.

Do I really want to go here?

Curiosity getting the best of her, Anya clicked the video.

"More and more, people are realizing they are Starseeds..." the video began. Each slide showed different things. "You may be a Starseed if you're: empathic, love whales and dolphins, love jewel tones, feel you don't belong, have a deep love for the cosmos..."

Anya listened to every word, watching beautiful images of all the things she loved flash by, instantly making her weep.

"...desire an unrooted lifestyle... have vivid dreams or spiritual experiences, feel drained by reality... struggle to fit into economic and societal norms... reject religion and accept spirituality, are creative."

With each slide, Anya recalled moments in her past where she resonated with all of these. How she had seen countless places on Earth and still yearned to see more, her vivid dreams like ones she had the other night, her struggles to fit in, her disdain for religion.

It was all there.

By the end of the video, Anya was sobbing uncontrollably.

She had never felt so seen until this moment. How had it taken her this long to see this video? How could this four-minute video understand her more than any human close to her ever had?

Anya watched the video a second time, checking each thing off her list.

She loves whales and dolphins.

She isn't a huge fan of religion.

She loves blues, greens, and purples. Especially together.

She loves nature.

She's sensitive and empathic towards others.

She has golden hair and blue eyes.

She's a traveler and often thinks about escaping reality.

She loves books, movies, and other ways to escape reality.

She's a creative person.

She felt like an outsider, even to her friends.

She's obsessed with the universe.

She hates how people define a successful life by material things.

Anya was crying powerfully, and Sugar was at her chest, licking the salty tears from her cheeks. The small and abrasive tongue started to leave red marks on her skin, and she could feel it. She cradled the black furball, who found great comfort in being held like a baby.

"I'm alright, Sugar," Anya giggled through her tears.

She kissed Sugar on the nose and stroked her soft fur until she stopped crying.

Anya looked out the window again, admiring Pleiades. This was still very new, very uncertain, very *insane*. Most likely not true. Childish. Yet, she wanted more than anything to call her mom and dad, to call Karmyn and Bee, so she could tell them everything. But at the moment, she was met with a deep fear of being judged, that she might feel shame for these crazy thoughts on her connection to Pleiades. Plus, she hadn't spoken to her parents in weeks.

How could she possibly talk to anyone about this? How would anyone believe that this resonated with her? Surely they would think she was crazy. She decided then that she would keep this to herself for a while, if not forever. Anya knew this was a cruel world, and people were quick to judge. Knew there were a lot of people out there who were afraid of anything unknown. Karmyn and Bee had made so much fun of her already, she clammed up without a second thought. She considered telling Sam, the only person she had met who believed half as many things as she did. He was nearly a stranger anyways, and talking to strangers can be easier. But in the Gold Camp District, no one was a stranger. Everyone knew everyone and knew everything about everyone. If he thought for a moment she was batshit crazy for identifying with *this*, it would tarnish her reputation in town.

There was still so much she didn't know and so much she wanted to learn about Pleiadians. Part of her was still resisting the idea and terrified of what else she might learn, but the possibility this was her origin made her feel relaxed, complete, and understood.

She glanced at her clock. It was 3:00 a.m., and she had to work at 7:00 a.m.

"I think that was enough for this evening, don't you?" She asked Sugar, who chirped in her arms. Anya picked Sugar up and carried her into her bedroom. Anya took one last look at the stars from her bedroom window and found a comfortable space under the covers. Sugar curled at her feet and fell asleep.

While Anya's mind was racing, her eyes were tired enough to entice her to drift off to sleep. She thought about Sam's theories on the Marvel movies and how they were helping awaken us to the possibilities of other lifeforms in the universe. Maybe he was onto something. Would Anya have been this shocked about her realization if that were true? Would she not feel as connected to that theory if so many movies about beings from other universes hadn't already been made? She said a quick prayer out loud, looking to her ceiling.

"If this is true about me, please show me," Anya said. Within minutes, she was asleep.

Anya was putting her legs into a harness.

The sun was bright out, and in the background, she could hear planes taking off from an airstrip in the distance. People chattered behind her as she looked up toward the sun, shielding her eyes from the circular glare in the sky. She could see tiny figures floating down from the clouds with parachutes easing their fall. She felt fear. She began to imagine the sensation of jumping out of the plane. The thought both excited her and terrified her.

At first, it would be scary falling like that and having no control. But she thought, after a while, the fear would disappear. After the fear disappeared, the only thing she would feel around her was the cool air blowing her cheeks up to make ridiculous faces. Then she could see the world from above through the tight goggles clasped to her face. After just a short while of free-falling, the parachute would open, and from there, it was smooth sailing. This scenario soothed her and her decision to go sky diving.

But as soon as she felt soothed, the 'what ifs' and the fears of everything that might go wrong during this short rush of adrenaline attacked her optimism. What if the parachute doesn't open? What if I'm so afraid I pee or shit myself? What if I pass out? What if something happens to the guy tandem diving with me?

The diving instructor was talking to the two other people joining Anya on the excursion. They were gleeful, excited, and suiting up in their harnesses with enthusiasm. Meanwhile, Anya was frozen in place, having a panic attack. He was in the middle of explaining the process of the sky diving adventure when Anya interrupted.

"What if the parachute doesn't open?" She asked the guide anxiously. He stopped mid-sentence, sensing her fear and anxiety, and then chuckled aloud.

"Everything will be just fine! You just have to trust," he said with a smile. This did not ease Anya at all. She was paralyzed in place with her harness tight around her body, squeezing her legs so tightly her pants became highwaters. The guide continued giving his spiel and then ushered the two people toward the plane to bring them to their sky-high destination.

"Are you alright, miss?" The guide asked. Anya jerked out of paralysis.

"I don't think I can do this," she said." I don't think I'm ready."

"Really?" He asked. "I think you are. Otherwise, you wouldn't be here." He had made a good point, but it didn't make her feel any less fearful.

There were so many uncertainties and no guarantees that she would walk away with her life if she decided to take the dive. On the other hand, she was afraid of how much she would enjoy it. Sky diving could be the gateway to other crazy adrenaline rushes. What if she became addicted and couldn't stop doing things that made her feel something of such incredible magnitude. She wasn't sure if she could handle it.

"Come on. The plane is about to take off," he said.

"I'm not ready," she replied.

"Suit yourself," he said.

Anya woke to the sound of her blaring alarm clock sounding off in the corner of her bedroom.

"Alexa, turn off the alarm," she said tiredly. She rubbed her forehead and laid in bed, going through the dream she just had. Sometimes she hated how real and how vivid her dreams were. In some cases, she experienced incredible fantasies, ones where she would wake up sad because she couldn't stay asleep in that world. Other times, she couldn't wait to wake up and escape the dread and horror of her nightly imaginations.

Anya never had recurring dreams, but she did consistently dream of Zombies. In some zombie dreams, she imagined herself a total badass cutting through fear to slay dozens of the undead. Other times she hid in dim corners of her mind trying to escape death. Anya was always two kinds of people—fearless and fearful. A balance of both, and one never really overpowered the other.

She laid in her bed and curled beneath her sheets. Going through the dream again, she recalled each feeling within her gut—the thrill, the excitement, the fear, the anxiety, the panic, the paralysis.

What had she asked last night?

"If this is true about me, please show me," she remembered.

"Interesting," she said out loud to herself, unable to make sense of it.

Sugar chirped at her from the doorway and jumped up onto the bed to pad the comforter with her paws. The cat's yellow-blue eyes stared at her. Anya felt the soft shift from paw to paw ripple beside her as she tried to decipher the meaning of this dream.

"Obviously, I'm afraid of something. Afraid of taking the dive," she said. "But afraid of diving into what?" She thought of her newfound knowledge of Pleiadians and her sudden unexplainable connection to it all. She thought about Sam and how much fear she felt around the potential of falling back in love with someone again.

Knowing there might be some other existence out there that could explain why she felt so disconnected from everything. However, all of it being so incredibly unknown to her and seemingly made up, she was afraid to even go down that road. Did she understand it to the fullest extent even? Was she prepared to learn everything about it? Was she prepared to turn away from everything she already knew to explore something one-thousand percent foreign to everything else? Was she willing to look insane to everyone?

"Obviously, not," she said out loud to herself. "If I truly was ready," she said, Sugar creeping up beside her. "I would have jumped. Right, Sugar?" Sugar looked up at her and tilted her head as if she understood.

"Yeah. I most certainly would've jumped."

Instead of thinking about childish fantasies, she thought of a different idea taking up space in her mind. Sam and their stargazing date was something far more familiar and easier to confront.

Even with her excitement to stargaze with Sam, Anya wouldn't be able to stop thinking about the times someone hurt her. She had gone through heartbreak and liked to believe she had recovered from it. Either way, she would still get back out into the dating pool. Eventually.

With each breakup, she grudgingly found some sort of courage to date again. But with each breakup, she also felt herself harden to the world around her. Anya felt her innocence and her spirit for tackling the unknown start to fade. She felt the need to protect herself with tall walls that could keep anyone out. But even the optimistic parts of her still secretly hoped for a glorious love. Truth be told, she had too many trust issues to count. She held onto each failed relationship like sad trophies, taking them out to examine them from time to time to see where exactly she went wrong.

But also, she was tired. The effort it took to teach someone about her again and then learn about them too just overwhelmed her. How many times was she going to share her same story, build trust, and instill a routine with a guy all before it came crashing down around her? The thought depressed her.

Even the thought of sex with someone again was an unfathomable idea. Too many of her partners had been boring lovers, selfish lovers, or she couldn't get it up for them, no matter how hard she tried. After so many, her sex drive had its own carefully crafted wall.

All aspects of dating were too daunting, but she loved stargazing and couldn't think of a good reason not to go, and stargazing was a far more comforting thought than accepting she was Pleiadian. She decided to throw out the possibility of the Pleiadians.

For now.

All of it was too much to think about. She wanted to focus on something simpler, less risky. According to her dream, it was clear she wasn't ready to handle it anyway.

"I promise not to entertain myself with silly thoughts of me being an alien," when she said the last sentence out loud, she cringed, feeling even more ridiculous than the previous night she had considered far-out possibilities. Saying the words out loud was her way of signing some secret contract with herself. If she said it out loud, then God would hear it. Then, somehow, he would hold her to her word.

But saying the words wasn't enough. She laid in bed thinking of what it meant to be Pleiadian, how this might fit into her life now that she knew it. Her curiosity wouldn't leave her that easily.

She sat up in bed, writing down her dream and the thoughts that came with it, so she didn't forget them. After getting out of bed, she went straight to her computer, where she did some quick research before going to work. She hoped to find more answers or something that would ease such a shocking truth.

The first search of her day brought her a wealth of overwhelming information, flashing through page after page, image after image, reading through information similar to what she discovered last night, thinking it would put her at ease, but it didn't. If only someone could help her understand this identity or realization better. A spiritual guru or a Pleiadian master, maybe. Yet when she searched for such people, she found those who claimed to channel Pleiadians speaking the same gibberish language she heard last night, which suddenly annoyed her. Some claimed to have seen Pleiades through astral travel, but when people asked on Facebook groups what it looked like, they had incredibly vague answers. Instantly, she was turned off, thinking all of it was phony, a ploy, or an opportunity to capitalize on new age spirituality. Maybe this was all just a fake world people dreamed up and followed just because it sounded good.

It reminded her of Christianity.

Astral travel seemed to be the only somewhat tangible thing she could run with to find any possible answer, but even then, she didn't know where to start or how to learn such a skill.

She glanced at the clock and panicked. If she didn't get ready now, she'd be late for work. Anya rushed off into the bathroom to take a shower. The hot water rained down her skin as she lathered up her favorite almond soap. She loved that smell and how it calmed her. Now and then, Sugar would take her black paw and move the curtain aside, peeking into the shower with wide eyes.

"I'm okay, Sugar baby," Anya said. She always thought Sugar's reaction to her being in the shower was comical. Sugar hated showers and baths, so when her human was joyously bathing herself, she checked in on her to make sure she was okay.

After showering, Anya got out and wrapped her hair neatly in a pink hair towel. She let her naked body dry off in the coolness of her apartment and walked to her closet to find something to wear to work. She stood there for a while before settling on a pair of dark jeans, a stylish plaid button-up, and a pair of hiking boots. After getting dressed, she blow-dried her hair and added a faint under curl to it.

Anya loved mornings. She especially loved them on weekends when she could really slow down and take the day in. Even on workday mornings, she loved making her hot cup of honey, vanilla, and chamomile tea. She loved her bowl of hot oatmeal with maple syrup and brown sugar. She loved sitting at her table and seeing the light from the morning pour in around her. The magnificent tree line sat so idly outside each day, and while nothing ever changed, she felt it was more beautiful each day.

Getting to work, Anya started making a list of everything she needed to do that day. While not the most glorious of jobs in Colorado, Anya had gotten a job working for the City of Cripple Creek as their marketing director.

Although a small town of just a few thousand people, Cripple Creek was a well-visited tourist destination thanks to its extensive gold mining history and reputation for gambling. Before introducing gaming to the area, the streets crumbled as people walked on them, the roads were paved with dirt, and people could still find pieces of Turquoise on the side of the road. Finding gold was forbidden and difficult if you were looking specifically for nuggets. Most of the high-grade gold was mined decades ago when underground mining was in heavy production. Sure, the high-grade gold was long gone, although the occasional gold kiss or nugget was found. But there was enough low-grade gold in the thick rock to keep the mining operation busy for more than fifty years.

So much land in the Gold Camp District fell into the ownership of Newmont Mine's operation. If anyone were caught on the side of the road picking up ore thick with flecks of gold, they could get in mighty big trouble and face some hefty fines. That's not to say people hadn't done it.

Newmont Mine also seemed to be battling with the underground mining operation just on the other side of the hill. They were known as Mollie Kathleen and were even more known for their thrilling excursion, which led tourists one-thousand feet underground for an old-school mining tour. The story running around was that Newmont had some of its employees break into Mollie Kathleen to steal their secrets. What secrets, no one knew exactly. Everyone knew Newmont was hard-pressed to take over Mollie Kathleen's operation since they were still finding veins of high-grade gold and who didn't love gold?

One of the strangest and most wonderful things about Cripple Creek was the herd of donkeys that would roam in the summertime.

After a long winter in their pen just past the Public Works facilities, the donkeys were released and allowed to wander the City of Cripple Creek. Surprisingly enough, the herd never left Cripple Creek, nor did they wander over to Victor. In the summer, tourists would visit Cripple Creek, sometimes just to see the donkeys. They would feed them carrots, donkey treats, and other things they weren't supposed to, fattening them up for the next winter.

Part of Anya's job was to promote the city's tourism and history, among other things, but she was also in charge of organizing the city's annual events, and there were many of them. It was stressful, and she only had two other people on her team with her to help get the job done. The job was even more intimidating and difficult since she was an outsider. The position as the city's marketing director was cursed, and anyone who had ever filled the job role had never stayed longer than two years. Anya came into the job with a good attitude, hoping she could be a person of influence. But after a few months, she saw the town, its shop owners, and its locals constantly at each other's throats. Essential leads of the community couldn't stand each other so bringing a functioning Chamber of Commerce together was impossible. Anya knew she had her work cut out for her, but she was determined to do her best at the role.

She arrived at the office at 7:00 a.m., switching the light on to reveal a large whiteboard that stretched the length of her office. It was filled with tasks, all color-coded based on the priority or category in which they belonged. Each week, she had her marketing coordinator, Sami, join her in the office to update the board. Since Anya had taken the job, the long list of tasks she needed to complete never seemed to get shorter. Something was always hot and needed immediate attention, whether it was a poster for an event, a meeting with the casinos about an event, registering an old firetruck for the parades, or organizing tours for the Colorado Welcome Centers.

Looking at the board didn't overwhelm her. She looked forward to the challenge of crossing everything off the list and showing the City Administrator she could make significant impacts on the community. But each time a space cleared, another task occupied it. Some days she wasn't sure she would ever make a dent in it.

She sat down in her chair and turned to the desk behind her to find her Keurig. She brewed herself a cup of coffee, using less water to make it stronger. Being up all night exploring the internet for information on Pleiadians was a poor life decision she regretted this morning.

Like the list on her wall, Anya was determined not to let the topic of Pleiadians be the looming presence trying to steal her attention, but she was losing that battle.

The Keurig gurgled behind her while she scanned through her emails. Some days she would get hundreds, but today, she had very few. Most emails were from companies trying to sell their outsourcing services. Other were alerts from event sites where they had posted their annual events. No matter what, everyone tended to shove their newsletters into inboxes, and that was Anya's least favorite aspect of marketing.

The coffee sputtered to a halt, and she swung around to snatch it as the last black drop fell into the mug. She took one small sip, testing the heat to her lips and the tip of her tongue. She was ready to feel energized this morning and anxiously blew on the scalding liquid. Soothing hickory and caramel scents invaded her nose.

She loved coffee. She sometimes drank it more than water which she knew was bad for her. But it reminded her of her first trip to Paris in college. On those summer mornings when Paris was already soaked from rain the night before, she would get up early and mix Folger's instant coffee for herself. Not her choice of coffee, of course, but that memory and the scent stuck together. Other times, coffee reminded her of her Nana and Papa's house on Christmas morning. That day, she could always find Papa at the dining room table with a cup in his hand. He had thick shaded glasses, a full grey beard, and curly salt and pepper hair. When he would get up to hug her, he always smelled of coffee and pipe tobacco.

Coffee reminded her of impromptu breakfasts with her father when he felt adventurous enough to take short road trips somewhere on weekends. Anya loved coffee's ability to waft through each room no matter what building she was in.

When the coffee cooled down a bit, she took a larger sip, feeling herself perk up. She set the cup down periodically to answer a few emails. She had at least forty-five more minutes to make progress with tasks before Sami arrived, and they stepped into their weekly meeting. Time passed quickly, and she wasn't even through half of her emails when she spotted one that had gone unnoticed. There was a tour group coming up today, and they weren't ready for anything.

And there were twelve of them.

"Shit," Anya spat, feeling a wave of panic cross over her.

She needed a few days in advance to organize a day with the tour group, and she barely had that. But, lucky for her, this was just a day trip instead of a weekend, so not having to book hotels was already a huge relief. She took another drink of coffee, hoping it would soothe her nerves, and started making notes, hoping she could pull a few strings.

Bakery.

Mollie.

Newmont.

Maggie's

Donkeys.

Shops.

Casinos.

Crippled Cow.

Just as Anya finished her list and was about to pick up the phone, Anya felt Sami's presence enter the building.

She marched in through the large green door, a whirlwind of air forcing its way through the doors with her. She rushed past the ancient slot machines sitting next to towering boxes of travel guides reminding Anya that she needed to organize that front room so badly. She looked up at her whiteboard, wondering where on there she could cram that task in.

Sami was a force and a force Anya was particularly fond of. Sami was on staff before Anya took the position. If she didn't have Sami, she would've been walking into a world of marketing chaos and feeling her way around completely blind.

Anya loved Sami for many reasons. She knew that if she needed a straight answer, Sami was not afraid to give her that, no matter how harsh or cruel it was. At the same time, Sami was a kind person and didn't like hurting people's feelings. Before she told you the harsh truth, she would preface by saying, *"Okay. So do you want my advice? You may not like it."* The consideration alone earned Sami Anya's respect. On days when things were particularly hard, Sami and Anya had no problem closing the door and bitching for an hour to get their frustrations out. Anya loved that too and felt it was healthier than holding in everything that made this job stressful.

Sami hurried in through the doors carrying one too many bags. Just as Anya thought she had made it to her office, Sami poked her head in.

"Blech, coffee," she squeaked. Sami was a short Chinese woman, a tiny thing with dark brown eyes hiding behind a pair of glasses, milky white skin, and nightshade hair. Her clothes were free-flowing and earthy. Like most Chinese women Anya knew, Sami was very blunt, very honest, worked hard, loved naps, and always brought Anya snacks—a way of showing they care about someone. Sami's personality wasn't everyone's cup of tea, but it put Anya at ease.

"Yeah, you want a cup?" Anya said jokingly.

"Absolutely not," Sami said. "You know I like tea."

"Are you sure? You might need it," Anya said in barely a whisper.

"What's that now?" She said with an alarmed look, almost letting one of her bags slip from her hand.

"We have a tour coming today that must have slipped through our fingers."

"Son of a bitch," Sami said wide-eyed. Sami only cursed when she was frustrated. "Well, let me put this down, and I'll be right back."

Her silky black head disappeared from the doorway to the office behind Anya. There was a single small window between their offices and above both their desks.

Anya felt the light switch on behind her. She swiveled around to start brewing a big cup of hot water for Sami. Anya chose a cup with the words 'Sprinkles Bitch' on it, feeling like it was the perfect cup for this morning. Anya looked down at hers, not remembering which one she picked; hers said, 'It's Motherfucking Coffee Time.'

Anya got up from her chair and stood on the seat to look through the window separating the two of them. She lightly tapped on the glass, and Sami looked up, pushing her glasses closer to her face. Anya mouthed, "Tea?" Sami mouthed back, "Yes, please!" Anya stepped down from her chair and glided around her desk toward the clerk's office just on the other side of the building. She opened the wooden door with a large creek and found Marcy squinting at her computer screen in a creepily quiet office. She was an older lady who had worked in City Hall longer than anyone else had. Anya never dared to ask her age, nor was she able to guess. Her aptitude for the computer and her ancient appearance was a confusing combination.

"Morning, Marcy," Anya said, moving through the swinging door and past Marcy's desk toward the next room.

"Morning, Anya. How was your weekend?" She asked. Anya made it to the break room, where there were extra green tea bags.

"It was good. Went camping at Clear Lake. How about yours?" She asked, already moving past Marcy's desk, where she hadn't stopped squinting. Anya picked up her mail from the box just on the other side of Marcy's desk.

"It was alright. Didn't do much of anything. Just sat around with my cat," she said.

"Oh, cool. Well, tell Zola I said 'hi,'" Anya said.

"She doesn't like people, but I'll tell her," Marcy said back.

The entire conversation, Marcy hadn't stopped squinting. Anya disappeared back into the darkness of the marketing department and found Sami already sitting in the chair staring at the whiteboard. She appeared to be sweating a little while she waited impatiently for her tea.

"Ugh, tea bags are an abomination," Sami said. "Remind me to get loose leaf at Yellow Mountain Tea House next time I'm down in Colorado Springs."

Anya handed her the steaming cup of tea. "I will."

Sami looked up at the board. "I'm freaking out."

"Don't freak out," Anya said, sitting down.

Sami took a long swig of tea, ignoring the tongue-burning heat. Anya touched her hand to her coffee; the warmth had already faded. She took another sip anyway.

"What are we going to do?" She shrieked. "We need a few days to make reservations!"

"We're going to tag-team it, alright? I've got a list of the places here that we need to call. Luckily, they are only coming down for the day, so we don't need to reserve hotel rooms." Anya said.

"Thank God," Sami said, gulping down another large sip of tea. She let her eyelids fall for a second of peace before returning to panic.

"So, they're going to be here around 9:30 a.m. That gives us a little over an hour to make this work. I'm going to call the Gold Camp Bakery and the mines. I need you to call Maggie's to make a lunch reservation for fourteen at 2:00 p.m. After that, call the Crippled Cow. See if they have the conference room available around 5:00 p.m. We'll probably need three to four large pizzas in a variety. Then, take the truck up to Venture Foods and get a couple of two-liters of soda and a case of water. Cancel anything else you have to do today, and let's just have some fun with this."

Sami exhaled.

At the clear demand to forget all else and have fun, Sami seemed to relax, slumping further into the chair for just a moment before hopping to her feet.

"You got it, boss," she said. Sami left the room, and Anya started making her phone calls. First to the Mollie Kathleen to reserve a party of fourteen for the trip downstairs to the mine. Anya could feel her heart beating faster and noticed she was tapping her pen fiercely on her desk. Summer tourism was picking up pace more quickly than the year before. She would hate to do anything that might make this little town have eyes on her. She feared the locals and their opinions more than she feared her boss. Word tended to spread quickly here. She learned that after the Public Works director got off for driving drunk in a city vehicle. The news of that went around town within the hour.

Lucky for Anya, Mollie Kathleen had a reservation cancel at 10:00 a.m. Leaving a giant open space for her tour group. Anya thanked them multiple times before hanging up.

The second call was to Gertrude at Gold Camp Bakery. This was Anya's favorite place to get breakfast, and if she hadn't been so tired this morning, she would've stopped in for a cresson roll. She loved their ham and pepper jack cheese-filled pastries. If she was lucky, she might get one with cheese that had oozed onto the pan and became crispy. Combined with Gertrude's fluffy homemade dough, it was a divine savory concoction she had never tasted anywhere else. And it was simple. Anya loved simple things.

To her surprise, Gertrude had made an extra batch of cresson rolls by accident that morning, giving them plenty for the tour group already on its way. It would be a nice little breakfast snack for the older men and women working so hard to promote Colorado tourism.

Her next call was to Newmont Mine, and she knew their schedule might not be as flexible. She closed her eyes and whispered a quick, 'help me' before picking up the receiver. In the other room, Sami was already onto making reservations with the Crippled Cow. Soon she'd be off to the store to get beverages. They were moving fast, thankfully.

"Hey, Steve! Sorry to drop this call on you like this, but I was wondering if you could fit me in for a tour around 11:00 a.m. this morning. I have a tour group coming in today, and we need to schedule one. I'm so sorry it's last minute," Anya was tapping her pencil again, now adding the rhythm of her bouncing knee to the anxiety orchestra.

"Ahhh. I don't know Anya," he said with a bit of Southern twang. "We're already so busy with tours today. The only other person who could do it is me, and my lunch break ain't 'til around then. I've been working eighty hours straight this past week. I don't know if I can handle a tour. I'm beggin' for a break."

He groaned on the other end. "Man, I totally get it," she paused quickly to think. Not having this tour wouldn't give them much of an exciting day. She needed this to make it the full package. "How about this, though. What if I buy you lunch today and then as another 'thank you,' I bring you a case of your favorite beer."

He was silent on the other end of the phone and then exhaled the breath he had been holding in.

"Make it lunch for the rest of the week, and I'll do it," he said.

"Deal. You saved my ass, Steve. Thank you so much. We will be there around 10:50 a.m."

"You're welcome, darlin'," she slapped the phone on the receiver triumphantly and leaned back in her chair. Sami ran into the office to collect the truck keys and the company card and then sprinted out the door. When Anya glanced down at her watch, it was 8:45 a.m. She still had forty-five minutes left to add a few more treats to this tour. She called the casinos to see if they were willing to cough up any vouchers for the group, and to her surprise, they did.

How was it that everything was falling into place today?

Anya downed the rest of her now cold coffee. She threw on a Visit Cripple Creek ball cap. With her dark jeans and hiking boots, she looked the part of a country mountain girl.

Within twenty minutes, Sami had returned. After unloading, Anya took the keys from Sami, and they mounted their seats in the truck to make a quick trip out to the bakery in Victor.

On the way, Sami talked about her boyfriend and how they were looking to buy a house out in the Cripple Creek Mountain Estates. Most of the homes out there were newer homes and cabins carefully constructed and mostly by people with a lot of money. To get there, people had to drive past Venture Foods toward Florissant. Looking up from the road, she saw the homes tucked in a cozy thick of trees. No single place in that area had a terrible view, and it was quiet. Sami rambled about the cost of the house they were considering. She complained about the HOA fees being so astronomically high she was close to abandoning the idea of moving out there altogether.

"I'd be fine living in a tiny home at this point. But home buying is so much more stressful than I thought it would be," Anya wished she could give her some advice to comfort her, but she was right in a lot of ways. Home buying wasn't the easiest. It took Anya an exceptional level of patience to carve out her little piece of heaven on this rock.

Within ten minutes, Sami and Anya were driving through the more adorable of the two towns, Victor. The streets were nicely paved and the town bustling. To the left was a beautiful mural painted on the wall next to the Fire Department, and homes were clinging to cliff edges everywhere. Anya took a right turn down 3rd street, arriving at the bakery. They parked on the street in front of windows blanketed in the shade. They had a painted logo on the front that had seen many years making its colors fade. Inside the farthest window to the right were tables and chairs occupied by locals. To the left of the building was an open patch of grass between buildings. In that unkempt patio area were metal garden tables with more chairs, some of which had fallen over into the grass to show how unused they were. There was also a single bicycle with a broken wheel. The door jingled when it opened, and there was a pink box sitting on the bakery case stocked with cakes, pies, and other sweet and savory pastries. To the left was a window lined with various rocks, some smooth, others with sharp edges.

"Hey, Anya," Gertrude said in her thick German accent. "Here are your cresson rolls. You lucked out today."

"I appreciated you having my back there, Gertrude."

"Well, if I didn't give them to you, they would've gone to waste, so you're the one helping me." She said, her German accent getting thicker with each word. Anya paid the bill with the company card, glancing at her watch as she signed the receipt. It was 9:10 a.m. Just twenty minutes left before they arrived. They had enough time to speed back to Cripple Creek and up the hill to Mollie Kathleen.

"Hey Sami, once we get back in range, I need you to take my phone and call Marty. Tell her to meet us at Mollie Kathleen Mine instead of City Hall," Sami nodded, taking Anya's phone from the center console. Anya focused on the road back to Cripple Creek, snaking past the towering ledges of overburden on the side of the road to make new mountains. All that rock was piled behind the fences, and trying to swipe a piece was still considered stealing, even if there wasn't a speck of gold in it. As she drove around each curve, she noticed a white truck speeding toward her in the oncoming lane. It was Sam. She knew it too. As he passed by, he waved, and she could see his giant smile. She waved and smiled back.

"Was that Sam?" Sami asked Anya.

"Yeah, it was," she answered.

"He's well known around here. How did you meet him?" She inquired again. For some reason, Anya felt nervous about her answer.

"We met at Ralf's. He asked me out for coffee a couple of times," Anya was surprised she was being so honest. She had hoped Sami could sense the neutrality of her feelings for his person from her tone, but she wasn't sure.

"Have you gone out with him?" She asked. Anya was growing more nervous with each question.

"Why do you ask?" Anya said defensively.

"Just watch out for him. He's sort of a player in this area," Sami said, and Anya's heart sank. She could feel her skin heating up.

Not another fucking one.

If he was a player, she didn't want a single part of it, and she was angry someone had tricked her *again*. She had taken a deep vow to avoid anyone else who might break her heart again. Any slight hint toward a huge risk of heartbreak was enough to make her abandon someone entirely.

"We went out on a few dates, but nothing has really happened," Anya said again as they approached the first stop sign entering Cripple Creek.

"Good. Just don't go there."

EIGHT

Sam woke with a smile. Feeling energized, he readied for the day ahead of him. He danced through his morning routine of coffee, shower, and getting dressed, filling idle moments with silent conversations between the Stellar Jays. The day was sunny and bright, too gorgeous to be spent inside or at work. Momentarily disappointed with his commitments on a beautiful day, he grabbed his wallet and set off for breakfast at Bronco Billy's.

On most days, the ringing of slot machines irritated him. Anyone who wanted breakfast in town had to brave an ear ringing trek through the casino to get a meal and most of the restaurants lived in the middle of the gambling action. There was no escaping the songs of gambling, even if he was just trying to wake up with a cup of coffee and dry toast. But this morning, the jingles didn't bother him. He simply smiled, ordered his breakfast, and recalled his date with Anya the night before, swooning at the very thought of her.

He thought about the strands of golden hair that fell down her back, how her skin looked soft to the touch, how her eyes glittered in the light. She was a thoughtful woman who stood firm in her opinions, and more than that, she was interesting. Anya was full of life and adventure. Sam had never met a more worldly woman. In the moments she talked, and he listened, she had not seen the way he examined her closely. How she hesitated when it came to talking about herself but gleamed when she spoke of the people she loved. How she would get lost in her big thoughts and never say them out loud.

Sam deemed her a humble woman who just wanted the best for all people but wondered if she had always been that way. Had she always been this kind of person, or did she go through journeys of self-discovery and pain to be the person sitting beautifully in front of him? Sam intended to find out. He was determined to learn anything and everything about her if she let him.

He was desperate to.

Her avoidant posture was evident and could pose a problem in his efforts to know her. She avoided letting people get close to her at all costs, a characteristic that made him want to try that much harder. Whatever made her close people off, he wanted to know it, understand it, fix it, if she would let him. Sam had seen this behavior before. He had been there. Been famous for keeping people at a distance because the past had hurt him too much. Sam had done this with many women, but all of them were far less interesting than Anya.

Recalling times when he cruelly told women he didn't feel a connection was always miserable, and each woman would inevitably cry. In his guilt, he would shower them with compliments that would make them stay so he could fuck them one more time. Sam was fucking all these women without the promise of commitment, and they let him do it. It was good for a while, getting sex without being responsible for anyone's feelings. It made him feel carefree. If there was one thing he was good at, it was making them feel close to him while at the same time keeping them at a distance.

A man could only do that so many times. Could only watch women cry so many tears. After so many women and no connection, life became hollow. Not waking up to a person he wanted to see every day, instead of seeing a bunch of random women that never lasted, it was getting old. No amount of just getting laid could ever occupy what he, or anybody, actually needed. That was an inevitable truth that took years for him to overcome.

He regrets it now, treating those women that way, holding them close, making them feel like they mattered when he knew that they wouldn't last long. Then, he would dump them in abrupt ways, offering little to no explanation other than the "I need to work on myself" excuse. Women didn't typically argue with him when he spat that bullshit. Some did. He knew who he was, what he wanted, and was very aware of what he was doing to pull these women in. Who knows what kind of heartbreak they had to overcome because of his selfishness. Sam was a coward and insensitive.

He openly tells himself this or discusses it with the Stellar Jays in the mornings.

Knowing how he had treated women and that countless men had done the same, Sam wondered what heartbreak happened with Anya. If she trusted a man with her heart and he didn't care for it. It was likely and common with most everyone these days. But the thought angered him.

Thinking of Anya, she was someone he could see himself waking up next to, but he still couldn't pinpoint why. Maybe it was her energy. The thought of her cozying up next to him during cold mountain winters made him surge with excitement. Making coffee and breakfast for her in the morning was a fantasy he considered writing her into.

After breakfast, he drove back to Victor to start work. It was always difficult to focus on the road when this area was so goddamn beautiful. Some days he imagined himself as one of the Stellar Jays living on his property. Wishing he could swoop down into the valleys and brush his blue feathers at the tips of the trees. He wished he could skyrocket through wisps of clouds and feel that wind glide freely over him. Then, life would be perfect. Today, he wasn't a Stellar Jay. He was Sam, on the road to work at the museum. Mutating into birds would have to be saved for the afterlife. He cruised down HWY 67 toward Victor, seeing the same leaning cabins and abandoned cars on properties near the road. Coming up on Newmont Mine, he saw a familiar truck.

Anya.

A whirlwind of bats circled in his belly. He couldn't help but grin. There she was.

In small towns like Cripple Creek and Victor, it would be impossible to never see her. And he would see her. It was like a new car coming out on the market, and suddenly he saw it everywhere. It was likely he would just run into her at any given time, meaning he could probably see her as much as he wanted or as much as the universe would allow. The only place he might never see her unless she asked was her own home. No one knew where she lived in town, and usually, everyone knew where everyone lived, which only added to all her mysteries worth solving.

As she drove by, he could feel the tension in his cheeks burn as he came upon her truck.

Don't screw this up. Give her a good wave.

She waved back at him, smiling. What was she doing in Victor this morning? What was her day like? He wanted to know everything.

"Get some goddamn restraint, man," he said out loud. "You don't have to know everything so fast." That morning, he decided to make a better effort with controlling his sudden excitement and potential impulses to be near her. Fixating on work for the day would be a better choice.

Most of the jobs in Victor didn't pay very well since the area was so remote. Sam didn't need much. Everything of his was either paid off or paid in cash. A simple job for him would do. His love for the area and its history always fascinated him. That's why he took the position handling the desk at the Lowell Thomas Museum in Victor. The museum was an organized clutter of historic mining tools, photos, and information about this area when the gold rush was bustling. It was also home to the history of the American writer and traveler Lowell Thomas.

People who knew of Lowell Thomas rarely knew he was from Victor, Colorado. They didn't even know where Victor was. Even with the tourism Victor gained from its sister town, Cripple Creek, a shocking amount of the nation still knew very little about the Gold Camp District. As someone who loved the area dearly, he enjoyed educating travelers passing through or visiting the area. Watching their eyes switch from curiosity to wonderment was something that always pleased Sam.

The Lowell Thomas Museum was two floors of history housed in a building constructed in 1899. The Newmont Mining Operation also ran tours out of the museum, so people usually came through during the summer. On those days when the tourist traffic was booming, visitors would join Newmont to tour around the surface mining operation, coming back filled with astonishment. When they finished, they could pan for precious gems and gold in the trough just outside the museum. Children especially loved pulling multi-colored gems from the dirty water. They held up their precious treasures with soaking sleeves and t-shirts. Watching them beam over something so simple was the kind of life Sam wanted to live. He wanted to be someone with a life full of simple things that he treasured. He wanted a life without complications or drama, similar to the world children usually live in before life slaps them in the face with the harsh truth.

Most days, his time at Lowell Thomas Museum was easygoing. In the summer, he got to talk to people from all walks of life. Hearing their stories, however brief, helped him understand the world and people better. Sam had met every type of person possible. What enamored him most was how all of the people he met would share their life stories and ideas without hesitation. He had the pleasure of talking to those old and wise with decades of experience under their belt. Even the youngsters full of life and naivety were just as interesting as the wizened elders.

Many of them were on journeys to discover the world outside their home, something Sam always felt was brave. People all over the world never leave their home state, let alone their town. It happened in the Gold Camp District all the time. People ended up working for the local schools, opening up a bar, or were attached to a toxic situation or relationship. The people who did get out of their homes to discover the world were people he admired deeply. Stepping out of their comfort zone, out of everything they know, is terrifying. It's easier to be cozy in the known than shocked by the unknown. But that was a mindset Sam always felt would consume people from the inside out. If people never left their homes to learn about the outside world, how could people in the world ever really understand each other?

Seeing so many people walk through the doors of Lowell Thomas Museum, he had learned how to be more empathic, to listen to a stranger's story with intensity and the utmost attention. He figured someone sharing their story could be the difference between shattering to pieces or being set free from what ailed them. People he interacted with were all different; some vibrant with life, others deep in despair. With either one, Sam wasn't able to dictate how close someone was to falling off a cliff. Those who sat in their sadness and shared it with Sam in brief moments between tours were the people he considered the bravest. Sometimes he would hug them; other times, he would just listen. On occasion, he would offer advice.

Truthfully, working at Lowell Thomas was something he could see himself doing long-term. It was a way for him to preserve a history he adored so much, but it was also a place where he could learn the stories and adventures of others. He loved people. There was no denying that. After meeting him for just a few minutes, anyone would be able to tell he was an extrovert utterly thankful for making so many friends, whether temporary or permanent.

Today, Sam wandered through the museum, looking at aged and somewhat rusty tools from the Gold Rush, marveling at the headlamps that used to be lit by a single flame. Checking to make sure everything was in order was a daily task of his.

While most people were honest and curious, there were a few tricksters who pranked the museum. He'll never forget coming into the museum one morning to find two large pieces of ore sitting at the base of a drill bit. The worst phallic representation he had seen yet, but okay. Or the time someone graffitied over the sign outside. What originally read Lowell Thomas was now read Lowell Homos, the 'T' crossed out and an 'O' painted over the 'A.' Zero points for originality, in his opinion, but he laughed anyway. No use getting upset over them, and it's not like Victor, Colorado would make news for a bunch of kids being insensitive jackasses. Sam climbed to the second floor, where a great homage was paid to the American writer and traveler.

"Thanks for journeying, sir," Sam said out loud. He looked around to make sure no one else was there, observing how quiet and dark everything seemed when people hadn't arrived. When he was comfortable with the silence, he walked back down the hall decorated with various well-aged artifacts to find his perch in the gift shop.

After doing a once-through, he returned to the front desk, making sure everything was stocked well; candy, vials of fool's gold, booklets and guides on the history of the area, Gold Camp District swag. The museum had it all. They usually did pretty well with selling it all in the summer, but when winter came around, business slowed to a dreadful crawl. Sam hated the wintertime. He hated how many days the snow landed heavily on the area and how it kept people from venturing out. During that time, Sam felt the most lonely. Without people coming through the museum and most of his friends not daring to brave the winter streets and mountain cold, Sam faced brutal loneliness and isolation. In the winter, he was thankful for Sunday mornings and his ability to play hockey all night.

Maybe this winter would be different because of a certain someone.

Sam's morning routine and thoughts of the museum could only distract him from the real thing on his mind this morning. Seeing Anya.

He wondered how her day was going, and if she was enjoying her job in Cripple Creek. Sam had lived in the area his whole life making him very privy to the shortcomings of the City of Cripple Creek and how they run their town. He was well aware of how difficult working for the city could be. They had gone through at least ten marketing directors in five years.

Beyond that, Cripple Creek and Victor were at odds for decades thanks to old feuds held onto by the old-timers. The way Sam figured it, these towns resembled two kinds of sisters. Victor was the kinder and more free-spirited sister. Cripple Creek, on the other hand, was the materialistic and condescending sister that pissed everyone off at Thanksgiving. Despite it all, Sam decided the two towns were not so different. He believed they should be working more closely together, being four miles apart and all. It was harder to get people on board. Old-timers were so tense and stubborn in their ways; change was never an occurrence here. It drove out the young minds that were once eager to live in this area. After a year passed, newcomers couldn't pack up their homes and leave fast enough.

At thirty-three years old, Sam rallied with some of the other locals who had a vision for the area. With any young and nubile person who came to the area, Sam and his friends made it a mission to welcome them warmly. They wanted those young minds to stay and tough out the stubborn mindsets. Eventually, the old minds would deteriorate, leaving a fresh path for new ideas, new ways of running these communities, and new ways of bringing people together. Each time one of their prospective new friends came and went, the young welcome committee was furious and disheartened. And yet, they all stayed because this was home.

Victor was not like Cripple Creek. It was full of people who enjoyed the area and regarded it as a precious gem of the area. When people moved to the area and came to Victor, they said, "Goddamn, this place is wonderful!" The locals replying, "Right?! Isn't it just? Now, shut the hell up and don't tell anyone." Smile and winky face.

Victor was intent on kindness and unity over division, unlike the sister town. Yet, Sam was determined to hold firm to the idea that things may change someday. Maybe the combination of people was just not right. Not yet. But he was more optimistic than most.

Like so many others who had come and gone, Anya was a breath of fresh air. People knew it too. Some people didn't like it either. Especially the shop owners in Cripple Creek. They wanted a Marketing Director to come into town, sit in their office, shut the fuck up, and do as they were told. While many of the old-timers were good friends of his, Sam felt that kind of attitude was helping no one. People talked about Anya in circles, voicing both excitement and upset over the changes and attitude she brought to the role.

"This is how we've always done it," that was the town motto.

Anya did not strike Sam as the type of person to follow that motto. It would be interesting to see how she would impact the community. If the old-timers didn't back her up, he was sure the few youngsters in the crowd would or at least attempt to.

Sam went to the break room and brewed himself a cup of coffee. It was his third cup today, but he didn't care. It was just past 10:00 a.m., and the museum was already open. Here and there, tourists started to filter in. They poked around the gift shop before purchasing self-guided tickets to the museum. Each walk-through took about an hour, give or take. But people were quiet today, not as talkative. Sam was okay with this since he had other things on his mind anyway. He stood behind the counter, staring out the big windows to look at main street running through town. The sky was an ultra-blue above, and cars crept slowly by. Some people walked through the empty streets, and he could see people walking in and out of the General Store. He took another sip of his coffee and blinked to adjust to the light.

The phone rang, startling him enough to spill his coffee onto his shoes.

"Shit," he put his coffee down, quick to find a paper towel to mop up the mess and the brown liquid already making a perfect ring on the counter.

"Lowell Thomas Museum, this is Sam."

"Hey, Sam. It's Steve."

"Oh, hey, Steve!"

"Hey, man. I just wanted to give you a heads up. We're adding an extra tour today at around 11:00 a.m. It's for the City of Cripple Creek," Sam's heart leapt. Perhaps he would get to see Anya today. The thought excited him greatly.

"Oh, cool," he said, his voice shaking slightly.

"Hey, you going to karaoke this weekend?" Steve asked.

"Yeah, of course, man," Sam said enthused.

"Awesome. Do you plan on *actually* singing this time?" Steve laughed.

"Psh. Dude. You know I don't sing. I'm just there for the beer," Sam scoffed.

"Well, one day, I hope to see that. I don't care how many beers it takes," said Steve.

"Wouldn't do it for all the gold in the world, my friend," Sam said.

"Yeah, yeah. We'll see. Alright, buddy. See you in a bit," Steve said.

"Sounds good," he hung up the receiver and stared back out into the streets again, this time with a smile.

Sam didn't care as much about karaoke this weekend, and looked more forward to his stargazing date with Anya. He wasn't sure if he could even wait that long to see her. Outside of stargazing, Sam thought of all the dates he could take her on. He could pay the owners of the ISIS Theater to let him have a whole screen to themselves for the evening. They could watch MARVEL's Avengers for hours, laugh, and talk shit about Thanos. Maybe they could go to all the museums in Denver or get dressed up and go to dinner in Colorado Springs at the Rabbit Hole underground restaurant. Lord would he love to see her dress up. Sam could teach her to skate on the hockey rink he flooded every winter. He wanted to cuddle up with her in the mornings and introduce her to the Stellar Jays. He wanted to take long drives to Pagosa Springs to soak in a hot spring. The things he could imagine doing with her were endless.

He stared at the clock. 10:24 a.m.

These next thirty-six minutes would drag along as he waited for her arrival. Busying himself with *something* would help him pass that time. He jumped on the computer to read the news, read anything that might occupy him. After one article that he didn't read nor understand, he glanced back up at the clock.

10:26 a.m.

Reading would not do anything at all. Plus, he hated reading. What was he even doing? YouTube was a better choice. He chose one of the first videos on his screen, something about the Federal Reserve being full of shit, and started watching. Before he knew it, the infinite rabbit hole of YouTube sucked him in. By the time 10:58 a.m. rolled around, the ding of the front door's bells chimed. In walked Sami, along with a cohort of about a dozen people much older than her.

She was alone. Anya wasn't with her.

"Hey, Sami!" He said.

"Hey, Samuel," she joked. No one ever called him that. "Is Steve not here yet?"

"Nah, not yet," he said, anxiously looking for the familiar golden head of hair to enter the front door. "Where's your fearless leader?" He asked.

"She had to make a call. She asked me to take care of everything," she said.

"Right," he grunted with a hint of disappointment. "How many people in the party?" He asked.

"14," he started ringing up the cost of 14 tickets in the system. He handed her a receipt. The group wandered around the gift shop, a quiet chatter lingering among them.

"Alright, everyone," Sami piped up. "Have a look around. We're just waiting on our tour guide. He'll be here soon! Remember, after the tour is over, your ticket is valid for entry to the museum, so we'll be spending some time here." The group nodded and wandered around the gift shop.

Sam waited impatiently behind the register looking at the window, expecting to see Anya walking along the street, phone pressed to her ear, but he didn't see her. He couldn't leave the museum with the people here.

So we waited.

Within minutes, Steve frantically barged in through the front door.

"Hey, folks! I'm Steve. I'll be your tour guide for today. First, I want to lay down a few ground rules and then give you a summary of what you'll likely see today on your tour. The tour is about two hours long, so…" Steve's voice trailed off. It was a spiel Sam had heard hundreds of times before.

Where was she?

Steve's voice played like a recording in the background. Sam wanted to tell him to shut up so he could concentrate on manifesting her presence in front of him. But, with each of Steve's words, time passed, and she never appeared. Before he knew it, his spiel was over and they were walking out the door. As the group left, Sami stopped in front of Sam.

"Hey, you alright?" He jumped at her voice. "You're like creepy staring," she said, pushing up her glasses.

"Oh, yeah! I'm good. Was just thinking," he muttered. "You guys have a good time. See you in a few hours."

NINE

Anya and Sami sat in the truck at Mollie Kathleen Mine, waiting for the tour group to arrive. The pastries from Gold Camp Bakery were steaming from the seams of the pink cardboard box. She could smell the meatiness of the ham and the buttery aromas of the dough. She couldn't wait for the group to arrive so she could sink her teeth into that ham and cheesy goodness.

Sami scrolled through her phone in the passenger's seat while Anya admired the metal pully system operating the elevator. When it was time to pull the elevator up, there were rhythmic rings from a bell in an operating room nearby. Soon, a mechanical clunking of cogs pulled the thick metal wire up from the ground below. The slim red elevators emerged from the earth, holding a chattering tour group. Behind the elevator and the staging area where people readied for the trip below, there was an old train car topped with a giant-sized hard hat. It was empty. In the past, it was a dining car, but that part of their business hadn't panned out like the underground mining tours had. Around the dirt property, Mollie Kathleen had very subtle decorative elements that one might overlook unless pointed out. Shoved in flower pots were old flat water spigot knobs painted pink and orange to look like flowers. Looking even closer, the establishment had also used old drills and drill bits to construct patio awnings. They had very thoughtfully made sure every aspect of their business shouted mining.

As the elevator came up, Anya noticed a white van pull into the dirt parking lot to find an open space that pointed toward the sea of mountains before her. Anya and Sami hopped out of the truck. Sami walked around to the bed, dropping the tailgate. She returned to the passenger's seat to retrieve the now less steamy pastries, making a very casual spread at the edge of the truck bed.

Anya met the group leader from the Colorado Welcome Center in the middle of the parking lot.

"Hey, Marty! How've you been?" Said Anya.

"Hey! Nice to see you again! Everything is going great. How about you?"

"Can't complain," she said, shielding her eyes from the bright sun.

"Damn, it's so cool up here," Marty said.

"Sure is! A benefit of living at 9,494 feet. That cool mountain air never stops," Anya said.

"You're not wrong there," she replied. She turned to her group of elders. "Hey, guys! This is Anya and this Sami. They're going to be taking us on our tour of Cripple Creek and Victor today," Sami gave a quick wave and a cute smile.

"Nice to meet you all! Sami and I brought you some fresh pastries from Victor's very own Gold Camp Bakery to get this day started. You guys dig in, and I'll go inside to get your tickets," Anya walked toward the front door, hearing the shuffles of feet travel across the dirt parking lot.

"I'll save you one," Sami whispered as Anya passed her.

"You're the best," Anya said. She marched inside, taking off her sunglasses to let her eyes adjust to the dimmer lights. Anya paid and collected fourteen green tickets like a kid at an arcade.

"When you hear them call your ticket color, that's when your tour starts," said the man behind the counter. Anya went back outside to see people almost done with their pastries. She was so thankful Sami saved her one. Anya picked up the less than warm pastry and took a huge bite. She let the savory meat and the spicy pepper jack move across her tongue. Quite literally, heaven. Food would always be her weakness. She was surprised that she wasn't three hundred pounds with how much she loved food.

Anya couldn't believe this day was working out as well as it was. She wouldn't dare say it out loud, fearing she might jinx the rest of the day. The City of Cripple Creek invested in the welcome center visits since all Colorado Welcome Centers were hubs for information about destinations around Colorado. She figured that if they were excited about the place they had visited, they would pass on that same excitement to travelers visiting Colorado. Most of the time tours came up here, they left full of energy and enthusiasm. And Anya had never met more splendid groups of people.

"Group green," someone announced over the intercom. Anya looked down at the green tickets in her hand.

"Alright, guys! That's us," she handed out a single green raffle ticket to each member. "You guys go on over, and we'll get this all cleaned up really quick," Sami and Anya grabbed everything from the truck bed and tossed it on the passenger seat. The two of them followed the group over to the gated area, where they would get a summary of what would happen today.

"Alright, folks! Welcome to Mollie Kathleen Mine. My name is Zeb, and I'll be your tour guide for today. We will be traveling one thousand feet underground to take a look at what unground mining was like during the gold rush in the late 1800s. This whole tour will take about an hour, so I hope you all went to the bathroom. Before we take a trip down, all of you will need to select a hard hat and a jacket. It is quite chilly down there. Once you get your hard hat on, turn the knob at the back of your helmet to tighten it." The group put on their helmets and jackets. Anya felt her jacket heavy on her like a weighted blanket. The jacket was so oversized she looked like a toddler putting on her dad's clothing.

"Now that we've got you all dressed up, we're going to pile into the elevator. Now, back in the 1800s, we were able to fit twelve people in this little elevator," whispers fell over the group. In today's world, unless you were an athlete or a model, there was just no way twelve people were getting in there. "Now, there are two elevators. Today we're going to put as many of you in each elevator as we can, sort of like putting together a puzzle. It will be a tight fit, so I hope you know each other well. Now, I need the first group to pile into the top one. Once we get you guys all situated, we'll raise the elevator and let the next group enter the bottom elevator. After that, we'll make our way down."

The guide piled the first half of the group in. This was Anya's favorite part. As each person went in, the space between grew tighter. Butt to butt. Hip to hip. Gut to gut. Everyone inevitably giggled at the process, which was always Anya's favorite way to start this tour. Anya joined the last group and the tour guide, who gave a final thumbs up to the elevator operator in a separate building across from them.

There was a jolt from the wire where the elevators hung, and suddenly gravity did its thing. The elevator traveled down at five hundred feet per minute. On the way, they could see open tunnels lit by a single light, illuminating the dark spaces where some old planks of wood rested. Once they passed the red light, that's when they knew they were halfway down. With each passing foot, the temperature dropped. In the summer, it was almost refreshing. Within another minute, they reached the bottom. All group members were let off the elevator, stepping onto solid and damp ground. The air around was chillingly damp. The mixture of hard rock and condensation was quick to enter your nose. Just ahead of the elevator was a carved-out tunnel lit with LEDs. Running through that tunnel was a track for the ore carts.

Anya loved this part of her job. She had never loved mining or its history until she took this job. Being part of these tours made her feel so blessed to work for the city. Anya and Sami situated themselves in the back of the group, having done it many times before.

Zeb started his tour, telling everyone about the history of mining. He led everyone through the evolution of mining, first showing them just how dark it was in the tunnels. Headlamps back then were lit by a single flame. Zeb demonstrated what that might look like, turning off the lights in the tunnel. It was so dark, she could barely make out the flicker of the single flame that powered through the darkness. Over time, headlamps evolved, getting brighter as history moved on. After showing them the evolution of the light in the dark tunnels at the start of the gold rush, Zeb demonstrated the process of mining through the hard rock to find gold.

"At the dawn of gold mining, miners were using a single hammer and chisel to mine through the rock," he picked up a hammer and a large chisel. He jabbed the chisel into an existing hole and then rotated the chisel. "Each time you hit your chisel, you had to turn it." Whispers hung between the members.

Mining wasn't as easy as people thought.

Zeb led them to the next tunnel to show the evolution of drill bits. Some of them were longer than a human was tall. The end of each drill bit looked like the inverse of a screwdriver. Alongside this drill bit display were two poorly constructed mannequins dressed as miners, a thick layer of dirt and damp covering them, one of which was striking the drill bit into the rock while the other miner held it. Like the flame headlamp evolved into more practical ways of lighting their mining efforts, the drill bit would soon evolve into a mechanically powered one. He picked up the heavy drill, holding either side up and pressing the back of the drill into his hip.

"Y'all might want to cover your ears for this one," he said. As soon as everyone's ears were covered, Zeb powered on the drill, and it let out a rumbling roar through the tunnels. Anya felt the vibration in her body. The rock around them shuddered as Zeb plugged an existing hole in the rock to demonstrate how it worked.

"After a while, miners started working with dynamite, cutting down the time it took to get to those gold veins," he said. In this tunnel, fuses connected to multiple sticks of fake dynamite, which plunged into holes in the solid rock. "These blasts were very controlled to make sure the miners were safe while mining. Since we obviously can't set off any dynamite in these tunnels while you're here, we've made a recording so you can hear what the explosions sounded like," Zeb clicked on a recording from a CD player hiding behind an information board.

The soundtrack of exploding dynamite boomed through the tunnels sounding remarkably like a true controlled mining explosion. The soundtrack even sent a vibration around the tunnel. Another gasp of wonderment fell across the group. Zeb led them through the next tunnel showing them how hauling ore had improved throughout history.

"Miners used donkeys when they first started mining here," the group looked around at each other, confused by how donkeys moved up and down through the narrow elevator shaft each day to complete their work. "The donkeys didn't just work down here. In fact, they lived down here. Inevitably, donkeys were even born down here. Many of them lived out their entire lives in the mining tunnels. Donkeys were used to haul ore between tunnels because they can hold five times their body weight," he continued.

"When Teddy Roosevelt came to visit the area in 1900, he believed the way donkeys were kept in the mines was inhumane. So he mandated that the donkeys spend at least one hour above ground each day. The miners harnessed the donkeys to the bottom of the elevator, which carried them up to the surface. However, the donkeys, who had spent years in these pitch-black tunnels, kicked out of their harness at the first touch of daylight, ultimately falling to their deaths below," the group gasped again. This was not Anya's favorite part of this history.

"Because of the way donkeys lived in these tunnels over one-hundred years ago, Cripple Creek felt the best way to honor their memories was to let a herd of donkeys roam the City of Cripple Creek in the summers. Today, we have a small herd of donkeys that wander around town. Some donkeys in the herd are direct descendants of the donkeys serving in the mines during the gold rush."

As the tour ran on, Zeb showed them the mechanically powered ore carts and small front loaders that helped load the heavy rock without using donkeys. They transported rock through different parts of the tunnel to the designated drop-off areas. As they neared the end of the tour, Zeb showed them one of the larger tunnels of the tour, which extended into the rock above them and seemed to go on forever.

"One of the ways you will always be able to find gold is when you find fluorite," Zeb slid his hands over the rock wet with condensation. He found places where purplish rock swirled in with the brown rock. "If you found fluorite in the rock, you were sure likely to find a vein of gold nearby." Looking up, the tunnel was over seven feet wide and once filled with gold. Anya couldn't begin to fathom what that looked like. Just masses of smooth gold, some pieces bigger than her. How incredible it must have been to see something like that in person. There were seven-foot-long logs wedged between the tunnel walls where miners would sit and chisel away at the rock towards their golden victory. Some of those same poorly made mannequins sat on the logs to demonstrate just how large the void in the rock was.

Their last stop before leaving the tunnels was an air-powered ore cart train fitted to sit fifteen people and carry them through the rest of the dark tunnels toward the end of the tour. For several hundred feet, the group was led through dark tunnels once again, a short journey on the track with a single headlamp lighting the way.

After everyone disembarked the makeshift train, Zeb flipped a switch that sent it hurtling back through the dark tunnel to its resting place. Zeb went through a list of minerals living in these tunnels, fluorite, and copper, being the two most common. The very last stop in the tour was the small area where many historic mining tools were kept, many of which had seen better days. Time had turned them a bright orange-brown shade showing signs of rust formed over the years.

"Mollie Kathleen Mine is still mining gold today," Zeb said, nearing the end of the tour. At the end of the tour, Zeb led them to the mining communication system, a short rope with knots and a strange morse code system. He taught the group about the bells and their specific signals, which alerted the team above. Some of the signals alerted everyone above of mining collapses or told them when it was time to go back up to ground level. Some group members tried out the rhythmic bells, using the metal chart hammered into the rock as their guide.

The group piled back into the elevators, trying to remember their same Tetris-style positions. Zeb thanked them for joining him on the tour, and they ascended through the dark tunnel to the surface. The groups left the red elevators with an enthused chatter, similar to the group that disembarked before them.

The next tour would be at Newmont Mine. She knew some of them would not be able to fathom a more fascinating tour of mining history. Anya thought the same thing after her first Mollie Kathleen Mine Tour. How could any other mining tour ever possibly live up to that one? By the time she finished her Newmont Mine Tour, she was amazingly proven wrong. Seeing the surface mining operation and the magnitude of its endeavors was a sight to behold.

Anya loved these tours.

Today especially, they took the thoughts of a specific someone off her mind. It wasn't until the tour was over that she realized she had been able to ignore his presence in her thoughts. An hour of keeping busy wouldn't be enough.

The sick feeling of Sam being a player in this town returned to her stomach. For an instant, she felt awful, but thankfully her attention would soon focus on the group long enough for her to forget about him again. As the cheerful group behind her put their helmets and jackets away, they remarked on how amazing the tour was. Anya was sure today would be a disaster, and yet here she was, listening to the group gush over the tour. The rest of the journey hadn't even been completed yet.

"Alrighty, guys. Our next stop is going to be Newmont Mine. This will be a two-hour tour. After that, we'll grab some lunch and then give you some time to wander around Cripple Creek. From there, you can hit the casinos and shops," she said.

"I don't know how a surface mining operation could be any more amazing than this one," said one of the group members.

"I promise you the next tour will be just as amazing as this one was. Now, Sami and I are going to hop into the truck; you can follow us down the hill and out to Victor," Sami and Anya jumped in the truck as the older group members shuffled back to the white van. Anya turned the key and let it idle while the group took their time getting in.

"Are there any more pastries in there, Sami?" Anya asked. Sami looked in the pink box.

"Looks like there are two left," Sami said.

"One for me, one for you," Anya said.

Sami didn't complain.

They pulled out the last two to munch on. Even cold, the flavors and texture were perfect and delicious.

"I love how excited people get after they do this tour," said Anya smiling.

"Oh, me too. Old people are so sweet," Sami laughed. The white van pulled out of the parking space, and Anya did the same, holding the remaining chunk of her cresson between her teeth. She drove up to the edge of the parking lot and took a right, moving away from Cripple Creek. She drove toward the Gillette Flats, where she would take a right toward Bison Reservoir. She would pass Goldfield and then enter Victor shortly after.

As she drove, Sam returned to her mind. She recalled the moments she had spent with him, looking for the red flags that would signal he was a player. Most of what she did know, which wasn't much, demonstrated he was a gentleman. He never placed his hands on her unless she let him. He was smart, he was funny, and even after their last date, he didn't kiss her.

Nothing in her memory indicated he was a bad person.

What she did know is he believed some of the same things Anya only ever really thought about when she was by herself.

Admitting she was actually into Sam was something she was too stubborn to do. Instead, she held onto anything that would keep him at a distance. Since she couldn't find a single red flag burning through her memory, she remembered the advice Sami had given her earlier that morning, "Just don't go there."

Anya wanted to ask Sami what he had done, who he had played. But she didn't. Anya was suspicious of herself—that maybe she was looking for a reason to back out, even if it was gossip.

Since getting in the truck, Sami had returned to scrolling through her phone. Anya glanced at her, watching her glasses slide to the edge of her nose. She pushed them back up to the space between her eyes and kept scrolling.

Anya thought it was crazy how people could drive through this area and still just scroll through their phones. So much magic and beauty existed outside, especially in Colorado. It bugged her how the digital era helped people miss so much of that beauty. As much as it angered her, Anya wasn't the one to openly criticize. She wasn't a person to point out this behavior to others, nor was she the person to give people grief about how they spent their time. Trying to make people care about the environment around them or make them see the beauty of things wasn't her job. Eventually, people would see those beauties when they were ready. Plus, people's definition of beauty was different.

As she drove, it dawned on her that Sam was likely working at the museum. She silently cursed to herself, not letting Sami know how plagued she was by a guy she had warned her to steer clear of. Anya checked the rearview mirror to make sure she wasn't driving too fast for the group and then returned to trying to devise a plan that would get her out of seeing Sam.

They rounded the curves that snaked between the aspen trees, which were now thick with leaves. The wind flowing through the branches caught them just right, so they shivered underneath the sun. The shiny topside of the leaves caught the sun rays, making them glitter in the daylight. The aspen bark stood out, a blaring white with the dark notches speckling up and down the trunks and limbs. Today would have been a perfect day for a long drive in another mountain landscape. Anya loved those kinds of drives, but she didn't enjoy that as much when she was alone. Maybe Bee and Karmyn would go with her sometime this weekend if they weren't busy.

Shit.

Anya forgot she agreed to go stargazing with Sam this weekend. How in the hell was she going to get out of that one? Making a plan to get herself out of that date needed to be her first priority, the second being her trying to avoid him in the next five minutes. Anya whipped through Goldfield, a place that once thrived with thousands of people before the whole area burned to the ground. She knew Sam lived in Goldfield, but she didn't know where. Looking amongst the houses, she tried to guess which one might be his. On the right side of the road were numerous headframes still standing tall and black in the cliffsides. At one time in history, around two hundred headframes existed in the area. That's how thick with gold this area was. It didn't take long to pass through Goldfield since much of the town was just homes, some of which would crumble if you put so much as a finger on them. She passed over one of the highest points in the area, Victor Pass, which stood at 10,201 feet and honestly wasn't much of a pass compared to others around Colorado like Wolf Creek and Independence Pass. After coming down from the pass, she slowed her speed to a fifteen-mile-per-hour crawl, passing by Phantom Canyon Road and a sign that said, *Welcome to Victor.*

She drove a block and a half before turning left onto 3rd street. There at the corner of Victor Avenue and 3rd street, was the Lowell Thomas Museum. Parked just up the road was Sam's truck. He *was* working today.

Goddamn it.

Sami drove past the intersection and parked on 3rd street, just past the big windows that looked into the museum. The white van pulled up behind her. Everyone started getting out of the vehicles while Sami jumped down from her passenger's seat.

"Hey, Sami. How about you get the tickets paid for? I'm going to make a quick call," she handed Sami the company card.

"Sure thing," Sami closed the car door and walked off, taking the cohort with her. Anya held the phone up to her ear, pretending to be on the phone until they disappeared around the corner. She sat in the truck doing nothing but breathing as a twinge of guilt rose in her. She knew it would be cruel to avoid him like this and wondered if he would even notice or care that she hadn't come in with the group. Avoiding it all entirely made her feel somewhat better. While she waited for the group to come out, she let herself stare off into the distance, thinking nothing in particular. Within several minutes, Steve pulled up behind the tour van in a commercial bus with an orange flag towering high and flapping in the wind. Anya took this time to get out of the truck to greet Steve.

He opened the power doors and hopped down the steps onto the sidewalk.

"Hey, darlin'!" He exclaimed. Anya was surprised by his mood, given he was doing this tour on his lunch break.

"Hey! Thanks so much again for doing this," she said. "You're doing me a solid."

"I'm glad I could help," he smiled. He wore a grey Newmont Mine polo, a yellow hardhat, and an orange reflector vest along with a pair of black-rimmed sunglasses and his very grey beard fluffy on his chin.

"Well, after this tour, I got lunch set up for you over at the Side Door. Just head on over and order whatever. I told them to invoice me for all your orders this week," she said

"Much obliged, Miss Anya," he said with his Southern accent. Around the corner, the volume of an excited group rose as they emerged from the front doors of the museum. It was time to go on the next ride. She noticed Sam had not emerged with them, which both relieved her and disappointed her. Although she had made up her mind about not seeing him again, she wanted to see him again. A frown crossed her face just long enough for Sami to catch it.

"What's wrong?" She asked. Anya didn't realize her face was thinking so much out loud.

"Oh, nothing. I was just thinking about all the stuff we will have to catch up on tomorrow," she lied.

"Don't even get me started," Sami growled.

TEN

Since this tour wouldn't be done for another two hours, he decided to close the store for lunch. The heavy door sank into the doorframe behind him, and he locked it shut, hearing the muffled rings of the bell sound into the shop.

He walked to the corner of Victor Avenue and 3rd street. Looking down the hill, he stared at the City of Cripple Creek truck, which was empty. He stared much too longingly at it as if Anya would evince herself into the front seat, hop out of the truck, and run to him with a smile. He shoved his hands in his pockets and turned to look up 3rd street, thinking how odd she didn't come inside to see him.

Sam walked across the street, taking a left to walk a block up towards 5th street. The Side Door would be open about now.

He wasn't hungry at all on account of eating less than a few hours ago but he needed to eat something to calm the bats. It was a short block to trudge up, and he did so without much enthusiasm.

Just this morning, the Stellar Jays were singing with him, and the rabbit was hopping around just as joyously as he was. All of his excitement seemed to fade away within a matter of minutes. His gut told him something might be off.

He rounded the corner to the Victor Hotel, finding himself at the front of two wooden double doors with oval windows cut out in the center of each one. From the windows, he could see the Side Door restaurant lifeless just in the corner. He grasped the gold handle, smashing the smooth button-down with his thumb and pushing hard.

A musty wave of air rushed him. Music played faintly in the background, something modern which didn't match the feel and aesthetics of the outdated interior design thrown on the floors. Parts of Victor Hotel hadn't been updated in quite some time.

The floors were a deep and blinding maroon floral print. A large and dusty wooden piano sat in the center of the lobby with a few mismatched couches resting behind it. The ceilings were high and white. And the windows barely caught the edge of the ceiling, giving people a good view of the sky. The windows extending tall and wide, allowing light to brighten the horrific carpeted floors.

Up the steps from the lobby and tucked in the corner was The Side Door, where not a single person was clanking their forks and knives on plates. Between the lobby and the restaurant, the only sign of life was Bruce, who muttered to himself behind the bar top.

"Hey there, Bruce," Sam said, startling the old black man behind the counter. He turned to look at Sam, who was already pulling out a bar chair to sit down. His borderline pornstache quivering.

"Goddamn son of a bitch, Sam. You scared the mighty hell out of me," his voice was gritty. He wore an old grease splattered trucker cap with a yellow 'The Side Door' logo printed on it. Thin strands of grey hair poked out the sides above his big ears and stood out against his black skin. His tattered shirt dripped from his slim body. And his kind face had seen many years.

The gold band on his left ring finger looked weary.

"Sorry. Where the hell is everyone?" Sam asked, throwing his hands up.

"Who knows," Bruce shrugged. "You're a might early for lunch today. What can I get you, son?" Sam looked down at the bar, smearing invisible infinity signs on the clean bar with his pointer finger.

"How about just a beer," Bruce froze, his hands locked onto the corner of the bar.

"A beer?" He tilted his head to look at him, his thick lips frowning. "You alright, Sam? Not like you to have a beer at 11:00 a.m.," Bruce had known Sam long enough to know his chipper and extrovert character.

Bruce's observation of him annoyed him for an instant, and he considered getting defensive but then remembered how much he loved Bruce. He had gone to him often for advice, finding he had many wise perspectives on thoughts that troubled Sam. Bruce was the closest thing he had to a father.

"Sort of," Sam said, not looking at Bruce.

"You want to talk about it?" Bruce asked. Sam was still drawing infinity symbols on the bar top, delaying an answer that might make him look like a weak young boy.

"I met a girl," he stopped. "Not a girl. A woman," he finished. Bruce moved toward the tap to pour him a beer.

"Well, if I remember correctly, you've never really had trouble meeting women," Sam glared up at Bruce, who threw his one empty hand up in surrender, while the other held a beer. "I'm sorry. Continue," he said, sliding the beer over and wiping his hands on a towel.

"We've been on a few dates. She's not from around here," he started. "But she's most definitely different from the women who live around here. She's interesting, beautiful, smart..." he trailed off, getting lost in the thought of her hourglass body and golden hair. Sam felt Bruce's black-brown eyes focus on him.

"So, if she's great, what's the problem?" Bruce probed.

"Well, she came by with a tour group today, planning to go up to Newmont with Steve. But when they all got here, she never came inside. I never saw her, and I don't know... it just worries me," Sam exhaled with force like he had been holding in a heavy breath all morning.

"That's it? That's not much to go on, you know," said Bruce. "You don't know what's actually happening, son. She could just be having a bad day, or she could be busy. It may have nothing to do with you at all," he said.

"I guess," Sam said, taking a large swig of his beer. It was cold. Little bubbles darted to the corners of his mouth, and a bitter taste sunk to the back of his throat. His intuition was telling him differently.

"Here's the thing," Bruce said, shifting his weight from one foot to the other. "Everything happening under that head of hair you carry around, it may not even be a real story. Right now, you don't know if she is avoiding you or not. That's a story you're making up to justify your anxiety," he paused. Sam took another large swig, listening without looking at him. "The only way you will ever know if she is feeling indifferent toward you is to ask her yourself," he said.

Sam stared into the beer, trying to count the bubbles in the transparent yellow liquid, which was now half gone. He thought for a moment, letting Bruce's words run through his mind once more.

He was right.

Sam didn't have the full story, nor did he know what kind of day she was even having. Slowly, Bruce's words started to soothe him, or maybe it was the half beer he had already drank. Bruce continued to study him as Sam flipped through his thoughts.

"She'll be back after her tour," Bruce knew the routines of everything around here, and he knew them well. "See if you can talk to her. You might be able to get a better gauge of what's going on if you just talk to her in person," he said.

"Yeah, you're right," Sam conceded.

However, he wouldn't feel any better until he saw her and heard for himself what might be going on with her.

Sam stayed at the bar with Bruce for the remainder of his lunch break, chatting with him about other things, which inevitably and always lead to conversations about Bruce's wife. Bruce carried on about her, beaming with love and gratitude for her very existence in the world, recalling how difficult it was for Cripple Creek to see an interracial couple all those years ago.

Each time he told the story, he told Sam how much he didn't give a shit. She was the love of his life, and that love of his passed away fifteen years ago. Sam didn't know her well around then.

Sam was amazed by how a man could love a woman long after she'd gone, no matter what way she left him. From her grave, she still had a stubborn hold on his heart, so much so, Bruce never considered scenarios of moving on.

As he spoke of her, his dark eyes glistened with tears, and Sam wondered what their vows were like on their wedding day. He imagined Bruce with his smooth ebony hands interlaced with her ivory ones, vowing to love her and no one else for this life and all other lifetimes that followed. How every word he said to her as he stared into her eyes was true. He imagined those vows to be the most sacred promise he had ever made to the universe. More precious to him than any material thing that would fill his home.

Things faded, but the obvious love Bruce felt for his wife was a thing that filled up a home more than things ever would. He imagined how much emptier his life felt as memories of her loomed on the shelves, in the kitchen, and in the empty side of their bed. Without a doubt, Sam knew Bruce would never trade in the current loneliness he felt from her passing. To him, it meant he had loved greatly, wholly, and perfectly until her very end. That was the greatest gift this world could have ever given him. He'd rather sit in that loneliness, sadness, and her fading memory than trade in the many years he spent with her.

A love that incredible was something Sam only ever dreamt up.

In a digital world where those kinds of connections seemed to be fading, Sam yearned for it more than ever. Listening to Bruce, Sam realized he wanted their kind of love more than anything else in this confusing world.

ELEVEN

Sami and Anya joined the tour group on the bus, squeezing into the grey fabric seats. As Steve talked, he drove. The moment Anya got him on the phone this morning, the frustration in his voice was clear and tired. His voice carried a heaviness and exhaustion that almost made her feel bad for asking. Yet, listening to him talk about the mining operation, she could tell he very much loved his job. She could hear the smile and happiness in his voice even though she couldn't see his face.

Newmont was an exhausting operation that required attention 24/7. The operation never stopped, not even for Thanksgiving or Christmas, and employees working twelve hours a day. She pictured Steve going home at the end of the day, falling face-first into his pillows, and slumbering for as long as humanly possible. Kicking up his feet with a cold one wouldn't be enough for this job, or so she believed. Even Anya's ten-hour days did a number on her, and she only worked four days a week.

Steve drove back toward Goldfield, taking the same road they came in on. He gave brief histories of the mining headframes dotting the hillsides, noting the efforts of the many local citizens who have worked to preserve the ones still able to stand. They looked similar to oil rigs, pointing up into the sky like a crooked arrow. Ghosts of the 1890s Gold Rush. What it must have been like, to see them in action. See their big wheel at the base turning fiercely beneath the wooden tower as miners worked hundreds of feet below the surface of the earth.

Steve listed off a few of the most notable headframes, the Gold King, The Independence, and the American Eagles. They continued down the road until not a single house was in sight, just the rocky landscapes and the tree-dotted rolls of the mountains. Pikes Peak hovered above them in the background as they drove; a once white-dusted peak was now a pale brown. Before she knew it, the white van pulled into a gated enclosure where the van would enter Newmont Mine.

"Be forewarned, folks. We will be driving on the left side of the road for the rest of the tour," said Steve, a statement that sparked whispers. After he passed the small house situated between the draw gates, the truck immediately switched to the left side of the dirt roads. "The reason we drive on the left side of the road is that our haul truck drivers operate from the right side of the vehicle, much like you would in Europe. We do this because these haul trucks are so large and unable to make turns as easily without potentially driving into someone." As he forewarned them, he drove up the heavy dirt roads, passing a fueling station, and a vehicle smashed to the ground.

"That, folks, is what happens when you get in the way of our haul trucks," Steve said, referring to the smashed car. A silence fell over the group. They drove up the left side of the road, an odd sensation Anya could never get used to even though she had taken these tours a dozen times already. She consistently reminded herself that this was perfectly normal. The more they pressed forward, the more they climbed up the dirt road. They went to make a right turn and immediately came upon one of the hauls trucks, which were three times taller than the small van that enclosed the cohort.

A single man sat at the right side, the dirtied yellow of the truck almost blending in with the rock piles. The truck bed had an awning that extended over the helm and created a bit of shade over the small area where the driver could stand to come down. Anya imagined the inside of that truck stayed pretty cool. What always astounded her was how a worker would spend a full twelve hours in these trucks, not counting necessary bathroom breaks. How could monster trucks be cool when gold mining haul trucks existed? The wheel alone towered just above the height of the van.

"This is one of the haul trucks we use to carry ore to our crusher," necks craned through the windows, looking up at the oncoming truck. "You'll notice the three-digit number on the windshield. That's not the truck number, my friends. That is the amount of ore carried in tons," the bright red numbers blared the number, two hundred and fifty.

"These babies can carry a maximum of two hundred and fifty tons of ore. For every one ton of ore, we'll be able to extract one ounce of gold," Steve said.

He continued to explain how most of the high-grade gold had been extracted from the earth back during the gold rush, but that didn't mean gold wasn't still here in Cripple Creek. They discovered this place was still rich with low-grade gold and little flecks sparkling in a chips of rock. So there was still a lot of it.

They continued up the dirt road to their first stop, which overlooked a massive pit with over a dozen tiers of rock swooping around all sides like an inverted tiered cake. Each tier looked small in the distance like someone could climb each step easily.

When the group left the vehicle, the rush of air was refreshing against her face but smelled heavily of dust. Steve showed them the bottom of the pit thousands of feet below. Some trucks drove around down below like little Hot Wheels.

"If you look at all these edges where we carved our way down into the rock, they look short to you, I bet. But, I assure you, they aren't short at all. Each ledge you're seeing right in front of you stands at about eight hundred feet," the hard rock was a fleshy pink, and from where they stood, it seemed to be carved out with precision, although Anya knew if she were up closer, she would notice all the uneven and imperfect areas. "Now, if you look down at the bottom of the pit here, you'll see we are fixing to blow up some dirt," he continued. The group shuffled their feet in the rock, making their way toward the edge. A handmade wooden fence stood between them and a steep plunge looking down to see the trucks and people organizing a controlled blast. "Once we blow all that rock up, we dig it out, and we take it over to our crusher," he finished. After he finished explaining other specifics of mining in the pit, they piled back into the van to make their way to the next stop in the tour.

The group continued up the dirt road, this time viewing the world happening on the left side of the road.

This was one of the best views of Cripple Creek Anya had ever seen. From the seat of the van, she could see even more of the earth and how far it stretched across the horizon. The blue sky seemed to add even more blue to the mountains and trees below. Clouds crawled above, and it was on days like this that she understood why people call this a 'city above the clouds.' As the mountains and sky hypnotized her, she was jolted alert by Steve's voice.

"Because of all this rock and dirt we've kicked up here with the mining operation, I'm sure you're wondering how whirlwinds of dust don't just cover the towns of Cripple Creek and Victor below. Be on the lookout for the water tanks driving on these dirt roads. We use water throughout the day to spray down the dirt roads. This keeps us from kicking up more dust and causing a big ol' dirt storm in town. We do our best to care about our area and consider ourselves an eco-friendly operation. All old tires from our haul trucks are chopped up and given to playgrounds. We make sure that when we cut down trees, the wood is offered to the locals first, and in our contract with the area, any rock we move from these pits will be replaced once we've extracted as much gold as we can out of this area. We predict that we will be mining here well into 2050," he said. "All the rock we dig out that doesn't contain any gold is placed into piles we call overburden," as he finished his sentence, the bus pulled into a large, flat dirt parking lot where a haul truck even bigger than the ones driving on the roads was resting. The truck was a dirty white and appeared to be twice as tall as their regular haul trucks.

"Now, this is Big Bertha," he said, pulling up to the pile of rock and putting the vehicle in park. "Back in her hay day, the beauty could haul up to three hundred and fifty tons of ore. She was retired because of her size, and now we just resort to using our two hundred and fifty ton haul trucks. Feel free to climb up into Bertha and take yer pictures. Just make sure when you come down from the truck, you climb down like you would stairs and not a ladder," he finished. The group dispersed. Although many of them were older, Anya was delighted to see how adventurous they were. She admired their vigor as they climbed up the steep steps to take a seat in the haul truck and take pictures on digital cameras. She looked over at the massive tires, which also seemed to double in size compared to the regular haul trucks. When she stood beside them, she only reached about a third of the height of one wheel. She wondered what it would be like to assemble something of this size. How in the world did they even transport things like this anywhere? Better yet, how the hell did this even get up this mountain? Anya loved that there was so much she didn't know about the world. Realizing just how little she knew about anything humbled her. It was a fantastic adventure for her to learn something new each day, even if the information was small and insignificant.

From this area, with nothing obstructing her view, Anya could see the entire length of the sky; how it curved out of sight. She noticed the wispy white trails left behind by airplanes crossing the great blue and the few other wisps of nearly transparent clouds. The crescent moon was a white shadow hanging on the sky, stubborn to leave in the daytime, reminding her that there would always be a night.

Anya suddenly missed the stars.

Each night, she looked forward to seeing them. It's why she chose to live so far from town—less light pollution, more darkness, brighter stars. The drive to work in the winter was a pain in the ass when she still lived in Colorado Springs, but if her being far off the grid meant darker, more star-speckled skies, it was worth it to her. It was midday, and she was already looking forward to the darkness that would fall across this part of the world. Transitioning from dark orange to a fading pink to a navy blue and then a deep purple and black, it was beautiful. Like hearing a really good song. She looked forward to going home and sitting in her favorite nook next to an open window where she could feel a cool summer breeze. It was there she could finish reading *Eleven Minutes* and nuzzle with her favorite furry companion. From there, she could steal longing glances at the sky and pretend it was possible to live somewhere else in the universe.

The tour group, tired from climbing steps and exploring all nooks and crannies of Big Bertha, retreated to their small mob, where they loaded back onto the bus. En route to the next stop, the ore crusher, which sounded like a lousy metal rock band, she examined the sky for as long as she would allow, ignoring all conversation around her since she had heard the words of a mine tour many times already. Most days, she was fascinated by the new words and how each tour guide put a different spin on their information. Today, she could care less about what she already knew on the topic.

Her mind drifted to the things she discovered about Pleiades the night before, revoking her promise to forget. Thinking about it brought about a fear she couldn't explain away. She could feel her stomach rumble with uncertainty. Believing something as far out there as potentially being an alien was something her body was forcefully resisting. Her heart could be more forgiving of that truth. But everything she had grown to know and understand about her world, getting rid of that kind of indoctrination was difficult, and she knew it.

Over the many years she had spent traveling the world, she met the people who refused to believe something new simply because they didn't know anything about it. Anya knew what that kind of fear could do to a person. She knew that believing a new concept would toss out the ego entirely. Seeing the ego cling to the body was a nightmare to watch. It was something she vowed never to put her own body through.

Yet, here she sat, in her ego and fear, rejecting the very thing that could explain her entire existence.

Being a Pleiadian? It was absolutely too much.

It was absolutely *not* real.

As the fear and the curiosity rose within her, she felt as if she could burst at the seams.

Her chest and throat felt tight.

Air.

That's what she needed.

Just when the van pulled up to the site of the ore crusher, she felt a wave of relief creeping up on her mild panic attack. The bus unloaded slowly, and Anya did her best to cover her panic with a calm face. Following Sami out, she stepped down into the soft rock and dirt, taking a deep breath, the ore crusher in the distance drowning out her desperation for air. She pulled at her collar to release the choking sensation. She turned away and moved toward the group to listen to Steve talk about the ore crusher. She knew this part.

The ore was brought over by one of the haul trucks and dumped into the ore crusher. The crusher would then crush the ore into smaller sediment, allowing workers to sift through and find remnants of gold. This was just one of their methods for finding low-grade gold.

The other method was displayed plainly on HWY 67 between Victor and Cripple Creek. Mountains of ore built on the hillside where black hoses ran down to almost meet the road. The hoses dispersed a mixture of water and cyanide. The combination would dissolve the ore, letting the gold fall to the bottom of the hill like rocks to the bottom of a river. The gold would then be extracted. The different kinds of methods concocted to extract gold from the earth were pretty amazing.

They watched the ore crusher go through a few rotations of crushing ore and then piled back into the bus for one last stop outside the mining operation. They drove down the dirt roads, past several haul trucks, past the street graders, past the spraying water tanks, past white work trucks with the same waving orange flag. The high sun was starting to swoop to the west and out of view. She couldn't believe it was almost 1:00 p.m. already. In some places, there were a few aspen trees still standing strong amid a dirt clearing. Like they were desperately trying to hold on to the earth.

Leaving Newmont, Steve took them onto solid pavement once again, driving the back roads on the way toward Cripple Creek. There wasn't a structure in sight, except for a lonely headframe standing next to a red barn and a haul truck bed painted bright Tonka truck yellow. To the left was a massive hill of overburden, which appeared unmoved for ages.

The group pulled into the large empty parking lot, disembarking one last time. Climbing to the top of the empty truck bed, there was a different view of the first stop they'd made during the tour. The pink fleshy color of rock was even brighter from this view while the sun was still somewhat high.

From this angle, they couldn't see the bottom of the pit or the demolitions happening below, but it was still a beautiful view of the area.

Anya looked to a member of the group who was standing in the farthest corner toward the pit. Her silver hair blew behind her ears in the high wind. Tears sparkled at the corners of her eyes as she clung to her coat. If Anya could reach that age and see the beauty still left in the world, she would consider her life an innocent and a full one.

Even with the hot sun above, the high winds brought in that chilly mountain air. Once the group had enough, they were back on the bus and back on the road toward Victor.

This whole time, the tour was helping Anya forget the inevitable. Eventually, she would have to face Sam. She pulled at her collar again, feeling the panic return to steal her breath.

It will be okay. Just tell him something came up.

Anya decided she would settle on the bullshit excuse that something had come up that weekend and she wouldn't be able to go on their date. She would not offer to reschedule, but he might suggest it. Drawing nearer to the museum, she felt more anxious. If he came out and talked to her, she decided to make their interaction as short as possible.

The bus pulled into the space behind the group tour van. The group slowly got out of the bus, and Anya worried they would be too tired to continue today's journey. The older men in the group helped off the less capable. Anya wondered where that same chivalry was in her generation.

The worry she felt for her elders left her when she remembered the tickets to the mine tour were also good for an hour-long wander around the museum.

Fuck.

She would probably have to survive an hour talking with Sam.

Well, fuck it.

Anya was the last to get off the bus, following Sami.

"Alright, guys. Remember, our tickets to the mine tour today also give us a free one-hour tour of the Lowell Thomas Museum," she shouted at the corner of Victor Avenue and 3rd street. "We can do this tour and then head off to lunch, or we can just head off to lunch," she finished hoping they would choose the latter.

"I'd like to check out the museum," said an older woman with glasses slipping from her nose.

"Me too," said another man in a pale blue collared shirt.

The rest of their heads nodded in agreement, and soon the group was off into the museum.

Anya closed her eyes and took a deep breath, following them in.

TWELVE

Sam left The Side Door feeling lighter. Time with Bruce tended to do that. After his one beer and talking to Bruce, he felt hungry again, so Bruce served him a thick cheeseburger, which he wolfed down in a few minutes. As Sam left, his chest held a little higher as he walked back down the street to the museum.

 Sam decided he would take Bruce's advice and just ask Anya what might be up. He didn't know the true answer, so why should he assume anything different? He crossed the street to the museum, unlocking the door to let the heavy door swing open. The air drifting in was pleasant, so he left it ajar. It would be another hour before the tour group came back, and he could talk to Anya. Obsessing over her imminent return wouldn't do him any good. It was clear she was already driving him mad. He paced back and forth in the gift shop, organizing a few items out of place. When the shop looked tidy enough, he returned to his spot behind the counter and sat on the stool to look out the window. If the museum was ever too slow, he would sit on that stool and watch the few people going by who were curious about this small town full of very few things to explore.

People watching was an adored pastime for Sam. The world was full of odd and curious types of people he found most interesting to observe. Some of them were so rightly oblivious to their own wild existence, which he loved to watch. His world held so many walking anomalies. He guessed their life stories by observing how they carried themselves, the clothes and shoes they wore, if they wore makeup or not, if they smiled or frowned, if they listened to music. He dreamt up wonderful stories for them, journeys of love or despair. If he had a chance to meet everyone who came through this town, he would make it a point to learn about them, no matter how briefly they stayed. As he watched the people outside, he barely noticed a lone woman who had come in. She was so quiet, she could have slipped past him into the museum without a word.

"Hey there!" He exclaimed. He loved having customers—an entire day without any bored him.

"Hello," she said somberly.

"Welcome to the Lowell Thomas Museum," he looked at her. She had a short cut of platinum blonde hair, electric blue eyes, a slim waist, and tight curves. Gorgeous, in his opinion. "Have you ever been here before?"

"I have not," looking at Sam coyly. This happened a lot. Sam was never one to boast about his looks, but he knew he had them and that it was easy to attract women.

"Are you interested in wandering through for a bit?" He asked. She looked around the shop, which gave little indication of what she might see in the museum.

"I don't know. I was just kind of browsing," she said, averting her eyes to continue wandering the room. The classic, 'I don't want to commit to paying for anything' response. He had heard it hundreds of times.

"Well, if you're nervous about it, I can go through it with you. It will take about an hour, maybe less if I take you myself," he said. The look on her face told him she might not be having the greatest day. An hour with him, and he was sure to make her smile at least one time. She pondered the offer for a moment. When the silence was starting to grow uncomfortable, she opened her mouth to speak.

"Okay, sure," she agreed.

"Great!" He said. He took out a small bell and a sign that said 'ding for assistance.' "This one will be on the house today," he said.

"Are you sure? The tickets can't be that expensive," she said. Sam didn't know if that was a good or bad thing but insisted the offer stood. He took her on the winding journey through the museum, going upstairs to observe the room dedicated to Lowell Thomas' memory, letting her admire the artifacts organized around each room in particular manners of chaos.

At certain moments, he would interject and feed her information about a picture, a type of mining tool, or an old chair someone sat in over one hundred years ago. Sometimes she would ask him questions for clarity. Other times he would attempt to make jokes. With each of his quips, he could see a smile threaten to stretch across her face. Her stubborn efforts to prevent herself from enjoyment were truly admirable. Sam would wear her down by the end of the tour. He was sure of it.

They came to a very old picture of a couple standing side by side. The picture was fading away, cracking in the corners. It was a heavy sepia tone making it difficult to see the outlines of the male and female bodies standing side by side. The woman stood in front of that picture, staring at it for several minutes. She crossed her arms, placing her fingertips on her lips. She was choking back tears. For a split second, Sam thought she might know this person, so he started constructing the woman's story.

He decided she was an adopted child who spent her entire life in foster homes, never feeling like she would ever have a sense of home. She was looking for her family, her past, the parents that gave her up. That family started here. Maybe this picture was one from her past. Perhaps she saw herself in those two characters fading away in that frame. When he couldn't take the secrets anymore, he delicately asked about her sadness.

"Are you alright?" He asked, leaning over to look at her.

"Yes," she squeaked. "It's just… this has been a supremely awful week."

Sam thought for a minute. It was only Monday.

"I'm so sorry to hear that," he frowned. He let the silence rest there for a while, watching her struggle between the choice to cry it out or keep it in.

"Would you like to talk about it?" He asked. She didn't answer. She just stared at the picture, removing her fingertips from her lips to touch the faces on the picture. He was desperate to see if the story he made up in his head would pan out. Sam also wanted to make her feel better. Sad people made him uncomfortable.

"I just…" she started. "I was supposed to come here with my fiancé this weekend," she said.

Damn.

Not a long-lost family story, after all.

Sam returned his attention to her.

"Just before I came here, I found out he had been cheating on me with my best friend," she continued. "Not only that... she is pregnant with his child." Sam remained silent, unsure if she had finished the story or not.

"I caught him fucking her on our bed," she muttered.

Men really are pigs.

Sam liked his story better.

His story had a happy ending. This one certainly did not.

"Because he couldn't keep his dick in his pants, I'm here alone feeling like absolutely nothing," she finished. Sam saw tears roll down her plump cheeks. She closed her eyes to squeeze out the rest, wiping them away quickly. "The funny thing is, I paid for this entire trip. He had always talked about coming here because he loved Colorado. His family spent a lot of vacations up here, so he wanted to show me this place," she said. "I figured I would try to surprise him with a visit."

Sam felt awful, his insides twisted in knots that he knew couldn't compare to what she was feeling. No one had ever cheated on Sam before, and he was grateful for that. But, if he had been cheated on, he would beat the hell out of the man screwing his girl, and Sam considered himself a calm man. Sam looked at her, swearing he could see relief in her small confession. He stayed quiet, waiting for her to add more. Rushing in with advice or opinions of situations like this tended to shut people down.

If people were hurting, Sam felt that grieving until you couldn't anymore was the best way to heal. Only they could move on and heal, so he let her cry. She didn't reach for him, just stared at the old photograph, as if it was a portrait of her and her now past love.

"I decided to come on this trip anyway. I fucking paid for it. I got a nice hotel, organized tours, everything. Fuck him. Fuck her," with that, she burst into tears, sobbing into her hands. Sam stood there, shoving his hands in his pockets. He felt useless, standing next to this stranger who needed comfort. Hugging her would be out of the question, inappropriate in many situations, but this woman just had her heart torn out and stomped on. Sam quickly recalled the various times he saw a stranger and felt compelled to hug but never did because it would be too weird. Against his better judgment, he asked anyways.

"Would you like a hug?" He asked. Inhaling a breath, she removed her hands from her face to look at him blankly. "Consent is important," he said. "I know I'm a complete stranger, but I think a hug could help," he finished. She sniffed, looking at him long enough to stop crying as if no one had asked to comfort her.

"Okay," she said.

Sam embraced her, hugging tightly, but not too tightly. She curled into his chest. More sobs followed, giving her the massive release she had been holding, likely for days or weeks.

"I'm so sorry that happened to you," Sam said. "I don't know you, but I know no one in the world deserves that. Not at all." With those words, she cried harder, drenching his shirt in tears. His beard tickled her platinum head, and she smelled of coconut. After a short time, she gently pushed away from him, wiping the tears from her face. Her posture straightened, and she let out a deep breath.

"Thank you," she said. "I don't think I realized how much I needed that. I've barely talked to anyone about what happened. I just sort of took off and came here," she finished, looking at him. Her blue eyes were now swollen and pink, along with her button nose.

"Well, in my opinion," Sam said, stepping back and returning his hands to his pockets, "you don't owe anyone a goddamned thing right now. You should be doing what you can to get past this first stage of grief."

"How many stages of grief are there?" She asked.

"Five, I think?" Sam guessed.

"Ugh, motherfucker," she sighed. Sam started laughing, and she did too. When she did, the smile she had been avoiding appeared. It was a brilliant one, possibly one of the best he had seen. He knew he would get that smile out of her somehow.

"It'll get easier," Sam said. He put his hand out to lead her through the remaining parts of the museum. They were nearing the large windows looking out to Victor Avenue. This room was full of mining artifacts and scenarios built to demonstrate what living situations looked like during the gold rush.

"I'm sure you're right," she said. "But it's not easy right now. We were together for a long time," she said. Sam stayed silent. Asking her more about their relationship would likely send her back into sadness. A trip down memory lane reliving moments with that asshole was not worth any more of her time. She looked up at him, the redness disappearing from her face.

"What's your name?" She asked. Sam looked back at her.

"Sam. What's your name?"

"Mandi," she said.

"Nice to meet you," Sam said. "I hope you take some time to enjoy your weekend here. After it's all over, you can go back to your life and pick up the pieces. This place is too cool to be wasted on guys like him," he finished.

"Yeah," she agreed. "You're probably right. So far, I have done everything I've planned to do instead of sitting alone in my room and ordering room service."

"That's a really good start," Sam said.

"Thank you for the great tour," she said. "I know I was sad, but I still learned a lot."

"Well, good. I'm glad to hear it," Sam said as the bell rang from the gift shop. "Sounds like someone is here. You're welcome to poke around some more," he said.

"Nah, that's okay. I'll come out with you," she said. The two of them emerged from the final room of memorabilia. Sam unhooked a rope separating the rooms and lead Mandi back to the gift shop. As he went to move the rope, he saw Anya standing right next to the door. His heart jumped at the sight of her. Before he knew it, he was smiling. Anya, however, was not.

Anya's eyes darted back and forth between Sam and the stranger he had just met. Sam looked at the stranger and then back at Anya. The two pieces hooked together like a puzzle. She had suspicions of him seeing someone apparently, but how? The time between their last date and now was short. Anya glared at him for a moment before looking away. Then she opened her mouth to speak to the tour group.

"Alright, you guys, don't forget, you have about an hour to walk around. Meet back here at 1:45 p.m., and then we'll grab some lunch," she said. Sam could see the anger hiding behind her fake smile. Sam tried to put the rest of the puzzle together and couldn't fathom crafting a bullshit story around this woman. The look on her face told him she did not want to talk, and he didn't want to ask unless he had some kind of idea what he was up against. She pushed the group through the same route Sam had just taken Mandi through. Mandi lingered in the gift shop while the group moved on.

"Thanks a lot, Sam," she said. "I hope you have a good day."

"You're welcome, Mandi," he pulled his eyes from Anya to focus on her. "Thanks for giving the museum a chance. Have a great weekend here in the Gold Camp District." At the last sentence, Sam elevated his voice, hoping Anya would hear him, but she was already out of earshot. Mandi left the store as silently as she came in. Sam stared into the empty gift shop, listening to the chattering group recede as he sulked back to his place behind the counter.

It was possible she might have encountered someone who knew him and his history with women. It was the only explanation for her reaction to this complete, albeit stunning, stranger standing beside him in the museum. Sam had a strong desire to explain himself, and he intended to. But who on earth could she have run into that might divulge this information to her? He was friends with virtually everybody on this mountain. Who would throw him under the bus like that? Whoever it was, he promised he would kick their ass or give them a good talking to at least.

It had already been a torturous three hours that passed with him feeling this unexplainable tension between him and Anya. He would have to wait almost another full hour to talk to her. If he let her in on his intentions, how she was already making him feel, she would understand and give him a chance. She had to.

THIRTEEN

Anya stared at Sam, standing there next to the blonde lady. Jesus. Sami had warned her just in time.

Hot with rage, she took the group through the museum, trying to go through as quickly as possible. She didn't want to be in the same building with him any longer than she had to. Anya couldn't wait for this day to be over. Getting home, sitting down with her book, and forgetting her foolishness was her plan for the evening. She planned to turn off her phone and talk only to her black cat.

That hour felt like a year. This day felt like an eternity now. Once the tour group finished their lap of the museum, they spent a few more minutes in the shop buying their last few souvenirs. Anya hovered near the door, watching them all, trying to be polite while also distancing herself from Sam. From the corner of her eye, she could see him stealing glances at her, a face dripping with sadness and confusion. As the group filtered out, she was left alone with Sam while he stared at her. Anya yelled out the door to Sami.

"Hey, Sami? Can you take the van over to Maggie's with the group? I'll follow you in the truck. I need to talk to Sam for a second," she said.

Sami stepped back to look at Anya with a quizzical look but didn't argue.

"Okay, I'll see you there," she replied, disappearing out of sight. There was another brief stint of silence between them as they waited for everyone to leave. Anya crossed her arms and looked down at the floor. It was old, polished to look new.

"So, I'm guessing we don't have a date this weekend?" He asked.

"Yup," she replied, eyes still fixated on the floor.

"Can I ask why?" He inquired calmly. Anya kept looking at the floor. "Will you please look at me? I'm not even sure what exactly I did wrong here. This morning, I woke up hearing birds singing, feeling great about last night together," he spilled. She looked up at him, saying nothing, opening her mouth to speak.

"I've heard some things about you," she said as Sam shifted uncomfortably in the stool behind the counter.

"What things?" He asked. She dodged his looks, glancing out the window. She wanted to feel justified, rooted in her anger, stubbornly holding on to anything that would protect her from potentially loving someone again. Anya was terrified. Grasping for the slightest thing to use as an excuse to keep him away, she didn't even stop to think she had no proof he was a player, just the words from a friend.

"I was told you're quite the player here in town. That I should stay away from you if I don't want to get my heart broken," she blurted. Sam sighed, slipping off the stool to close the space between them.

"All of that is true," he said. She scoffed, turning away from him to fiddle with the keychains on the rack behind her. "That was me once. It was a fun life," she laughed, turning to stare hard at him, hoping it would make him uncomfortable, but he advanced on her. "It was also a lonely life, Anya. One I have since left behind in pursuit of greater things," he scanned her face, holding his stare.

Sam was cyanide and water solution, and Anya was gold flecks swarmed with hard rock. She felt her stubbornness melt away like the stone attached to those gold flecks.

The words were what she wanted to hear, but this wasn't the first time someone tried to convince her to let him in using sheer words. How did she know he was telling her the truth?

"I've heard words like that before. So I'm not quick to believe them anymore," she said plainly. "I don't cling to words. Just gestures and actions."

"I'm sure you have heard them," he said. "I can't imagine what men have done to that pretty heart of yours." She folded her arms tighter, holding up the wall between them, closing the space around her heart.

Not today, Sammy boy.

She let the silence stand once again. Anya didn't want to give him another inch, not another piece of herself.

Asshole. Being naturally charming.

She tried not to look at him, tried not to let her heart dance when his amber eyes caught hers. She tried not to see his gorgeous and worried face or feel his desire to keep her close. All of that, she wanted none of it to sway her.

"I can see you're stubborn in believing me," he said, but it didn't stop him from closing the space until he was right next to her. Anya could feel his soft breaths near her. Now, his hands were shoved in his pockets.

"Give me a chance to show you instead of tell you," he said.

Anya turned back to the keychains, searching for the one that might have her name on it. Her name was not a common one, so she could never find keychains at gas stations or museums where names like Tom and Sally were abundant. She glanced sideways at him to see he was still looking at her, waiting for an answer. She didn't want to say yes. Remaining stubborn and alone, free from getting hurt by anyone ever again, it was something she held tightly to. But he was patient. He didn't rush her answer with the sighs of a frustrated man who wasn't getting his way. Sam was trying to understand her, intent on protecting her. She turned back to face him, stepping a little closer until there was barely any space left. Sam's shoulders relaxed, and Anya saw a smirk form on his face.

"Okay," she said. Sam lifted his eyebrows, removing his hands from his pockets.

"Okay?" He smiled. "You're going to give me a chance?" He asked excitedly.

"I guess so," she rolled her eyes, trying not to smile at his joy. She had no idea one mediocre, and stale word could bring such happiness to a man.

"I promise, Anya, I will prove it to you," he said.

Anya didn't want to believe him, but as he looked at her, she couldn't help herself. "I know you have to go. We can always talk about this stuff later. You can ask me anything you want about any of this, and I will tell you the truth," Anya perked up at this.

"Anything?" She said. He laughed nervously.

"Yes," he said. "I'll do anything to show you how serious I am about pursuing this," he finished.

"I'm holding you to that," Anya said.

She jingled her keys between her fingers. "I have to go."

"I know," he said. "We can talk later. But, please don't change your mind about me." This was the third person convincing her to give Sam a genuine shot. Unrelentingly, she fought against all of them, maybe not as hard as she thought she had, but she fought nonetheless.

"See you later, Sam," she said, moving away from him, expanding the space between them again. Sam didn't reach out to touch her or embrace her. Admitting that she wanted him to was stuffed deep down. Her guard was up, and she would keep it that way. They hadn't touched much, except for the hug that stopped the restaurant last night. The closeness they shared at that moment, Anya wanted it more than she could say.

"See you soon," he was smiling.

Anya left through the open door. The air had been coming into the open space but not enough for her to feel like she could breathe. The building was now hiding in shadow as she disappeared around the corner toward the truck. She inhaled the cool air lingering in the shade and opened the truck door to get in. When she sat down, she smiled. Against all her judgment, she was letting a man give her possible hope or happiness.

I better not regret this.

Shifting into drive, Anya took off down the road back toward Cripple Creek. She wasn't far behind the group and found she was looking forward to lunch and the rest of her day.

A huge weight had lifted from her chest, letting full breaths enter and leave her lungs.

She opened all windows in the truck and let the summer air flood in. Her hair whipped in the wind, strands catching on the curves of her face. The sun was falling over the dome shape of the earth, and she was thrilled she was that much closer to night.

Despite feeling shallowly better about Sam, she still had every intention of keeping him at bay. Anya decided she wouldn't text him or chase him. She would let him do what he said he wanted to do, and prove himself.

Tonight, she would go home, cut off all communications to the world outside her own, and finish reading her book. The plan for the night was to remain unbothered by anything, including her thoughts and desires. Escaping into that story, finding out how Maria was faring in her sexually tense life was more interesting to her than her own sexual tension. It was something she could experience without taking ownership of its presence in her own life.

Minutes passed, and she was pulling into the parking lot behind the Brass Ass Casino. She crossed the street to the heavy double doors leading into the Maggie's and wandered to the restaurant's back room, where most large parties usually sat. Maggie's was always dark, carpeted with an awful floral print laid beneath darks walls and heavy drapes hiding the windows. The tables wobbled, which annoyed her greatly. However, Maggie's had debatably the best burger in the area. She always ordered her burger with pepper jack cheese, extra pickles, and fries.

The meal was pleasant, and so were the people. Anya loved lunchtime with the tour groups. It was her chance to learn more about each person, hear their thoughts and opinions, how years of life and living in this world shaped their wisdom.

Anya sat at the corner of the table, deep in conversation with one of the women. Janice was her name. She had an entire head of silver-white hair. Spectacles rested at the edge of her nose, a string of beads holding them in place if they ever fell off her face. Anya was rare to reveal lots of herself to people her age unless she knew them well. With people who had seen more life, she could say other things, deeper things better comprehended by people who had been around. After their 60s and 70s, they were more forgiving, freer, less caring of everything. Years of putting up with shit would do that to them. What it did was make them more carefree. Today, Anya and Janice talked about perfection, how people always strived for it.

"For as long as I can remember, I have been striving towards some type of perfection. It even happens in my work. If it's not one-hundred percent perfect or something doesn't go my way, I beat myself up horribly for it," Anya said. Janice looked at her, wisdom brewing beneath the brim of those witchy glasses. Her elbows were on the tables, fingers crossed. The gold ring with the big diamond sparkled in the dim restaurant.

"If you were dealing with someone who was going through that, would you allow them to feel that horribly about themselves?" Janice asked.

"Absolutely not. I wouldn't. I honestly wouldn't be able to bear seeing them that upset," Anya replied.

"Mmhmm, then why would you do that to yourself?" She lifted her eyebrows and smiled. Anya smiled back, nodding. "Perfection is an illusion and usually cultivated in us by the those who raise us and surround us. We have been made to believe we can't disappoint others. So we strive to please them, yet we end up disappointing ourselves in the end. Got to let all that stuff go, honey. Just go with the flow." She took a sip of her low-calorie sweetened tea. Anya saw her pour two pink packets into the glass earlier, watching the sugary morsel dissolve before reaching the bottom.

"You're right. I think this happens in my relationships too. My generation sucks when it comes to being perfect. I always feel pressure to be perfect and without any kind of issue. For men and women my age, if one single thing about a potential partner isn't perfect, they toss them out and look for something else, like you would change out a phone case. It could be over the smallest thing too. People tell me to heal my crap, to love myself before I can love anyone else. I think it's bullshit, and it makes me feel like there is something wrong with me. Loving myself, that's an ongoing journey. I've seen people more miserable than me in perfectly healthy relationships," Anya confessed. Janice nodded along as Anya spoke. She stopped to think for a second, removing her elbows from the table to take a deep breath.

"Everyone has baggage. It's impossible to find someone without it. If they say they don't have any, they're probably lying. Everyone is usually carrying around some type of pain or belief system that's creating their limitations. Don't let this be a matter of finding someone who is perfect or you being perfect for someone else. You are perfect as you are, even if you're at your worst. Make a habit of searching for someone you can be raw with. It may not always be pretty, but it will be real. It will be love. But only if you're both willing to accept each other as you are, shortcomings and all," Janice said.

Anya looked down the length of the table to see if everyone was listening to this glorious speech about being loved as you are. No one was listening.

"Thanks for that, Janice," Anya said, taking a sip of water from her glass.

"Thank you for coming to my TED Talk," she replied.

Anya laughed at Janice, choking on the water in her throat, knowing this was a phrase coined by younger generations when trying to make a point. Anya's surprise and laughter pleased Janice, which made her laugh too. She must have grandchildren younger than Anya.

When lunch was over, Anya paid the bill, keeping the receipt for work. Before leaving the restaurant, she quickly called Bob at Cripple Creek Transportation.

The fleet of transit vehicles was a bright red and always easy to spot in town. She could give them a call, and they would be at a location within minutes. The town was so small, it was easy to remember every place in town. The fact that Cripple Creek had its very own transit fleet in a district of just thousands was impressive to Anya. It was even more convenient in the winter when people didn't feel like driving anywhere. It was not convenient for Anya because of where she lived, but she was grateful she had her Subaru.

"Hey, Bob. Can you give me an idea of where the donkeys might be lingering right now?" The drivers for the fleet always knew where the donkeys were during their drives to and from locations. They could usually spot them on whatever random route they were on.

"Depends. Where are you right now?" Bob asked.

"Hanging out in Maggie's," she said.

"Well, you're in luck, missy. The donkeys have been making their way toward Poverty Gulch for a snack. They're right behind you."

"That's excellent news. Thanks, Bob!" She hung up the phone.

"Alright, y'all, the donkeys are nearby. Less than a block away, actually," Anya said. They chattered excitedly, getting up to leave the restaurant.

The Lost Pleiad

On her way out the door, Anya bought some donkey treats from the host stand, handing a clear bag full of brown cubes to each person. From what Anya understood, the treats were a combination of hay and dried apples, so the donkeys loved them. The group walked down toward Poverty Gulch, where the herd of twelve donkeys stood. At the sight of people, their ears perked up, and they stared, curious to know of just one thing; did they have treats.

The rustling of bags had their hooves clacking on the pavement as they slumped toward the group. They moved excitedly closer with their treats, feeding them to the incoming herd of donkeys, all of which were close enough to be petted. Anya felt the roughness of the dirty donkey hairs brush her palms, finding her way to Wendi, the Alpha female, who was named after Steve's wife.

"Hey, Wendi girl," Anya came up and petted her, feeling the pocket of fat on the top of her neck. With other donkeys, this pocket would become so heavy, it flopped to the side. "Gaining that weight already, huh? Good for you, girl." Wendi was the prettiest of them all. She was swirls of white and brown, had a small furry growth on her left hind leg. It was the only reason Anya was able to tell her apart from the rest. However, Wendi did have a sort of poise different from the others.

As soon as the treats disappeared, the donkeys left empty hands to search for more grass to munch on. Wendi led them up the road moving farther away from the Brass Ass Casino.

The group spent the rest of the day shopping in the tiny stores up Bennett Avenue. Some ducked into casinos, disappearing until it was time for dinner. After eating their various pizzas at the Crippled Cow, Marty loaded the group in the van as everyone hugged goodbye. Sami and Anya stood on the corner of Bennett Avenue and 2nd street, both letting out a heavy breath.

"Goddamn," Sami said. "I cannot believe we pulled this off today."

"Me either, honestly," Anya agreed. "I think we deserve a beer. You know, since we worked so hard having all this fun," Anya said.

"At least one. But wine for me," Sami said back.

They walked Bennett Avenue toward City Hall, which swooped up and down as a wooden roller coaster would.

Steve, the tour guide from Newmont, always joked about Bennett Avenue. When people were out of breath just walking around town, he would say the road was 'uphill both ways.' Anya, amused by this, adopted it for herself. For any newcomer visiting the town, Anya found the phrase amused many others too.

Anya and Sami shared their drinks for about an hour at Ralf's after leaving work an hour early, but Anya didn't care after the day they had.

For all the city manager knew, Anya and Sami were out doing some kind of promotion. This job was part desk job, part boots to the ground. The bar was nearly empty at 4:30 p.m. on a Monday, and she was glad. Having been surrounded by people all day, she needed space to breathe.

After just one drink, the two of them left Ralf's. Anya couldn't wait to get home, take off her bra, put on her stretchy leggings, throw her hair up in an ugly bun, and snuggle with her cat and book. Sami and Anya walked back to the office together, where they collected their belongings. After parting ways, Anya took off in a fast walk around the corner to her Crosstrek, speeding off but careful not to alert Cripple Creek PD of her excitement to get home. The sooner she got home, the more time she had to read. Anya was intent on finishing her book this very evening. She wanted to see how Maria's relationship with the painter panned out.

The winding roads between trees and rocks led her to the paved driveway and her little slice of heaven. A big window faced her driver's side. Sugar was already in the window, the single pane silencing her loud meows.

"Hi, baby girl!" Anya moved toward the door as Sugar disappeared from the window. Sugar was now loud enough, she could hear her over the jingles of her keys in the door handle. When the door swung open, Anya found the nearest place to drop her things and picked up the small black puff. She snuggled her nose and kissed her on the head. Sugar returned the love with a few abrasive licks to her cheek. Anya placed her gently on the table nearby and left the living area to change into a loose shirt and her leggings. Getting her day clothes off could not happen fast enough. She whipped the hat off her head and threw her hair up.

A blanket lay unfolded on her bed which she grabbed on the way to her nook. Grabbing the book off of the table near the nook, she powered her phone off and slumped into her favorite reading spot. Anya opened to her current page, the beginning of a brand new chapter.

Sugar jumped into her lap, finding her resting place. Everything fell away within reading a few sentences. Sam was cute, but she didn't care about him right now. She cared about the love story that wasn't hers. One last look out her window, she looked forward to the night that would fall across the trees and cover them in black. Stars would sparkle above while she immersed herself in the story. Sugar would purr in her lap. No buzzes would vibrate in her pocket.

This was her haven.

FOURTEEN

Sam remembered watching Anya leave, not looking back at him. He had no intention of tearing his eyes away from her. What he was feeling was beyond just better. He had hope.

He couldn't mess this up. If he did, he could lose her forever. She was teetering on the edge of losing all hope of love. With the way he cared about people, he wanted to make sure he never hurt another woman, including this piece of magic in front of him. Sam wasn't even upset that she was having doubts about him. He honestly didn't care either, as long as he made the most of his second chance and was able to show her exactly how she deserves to be treated.

Sam was eager to prove to Anya just how serious he was about her. Serious about learning who she was, proving to her he wasn't like the others, proving to her he was ready and willing, that he was ready to turn himself over to her completely, even though she had her trepidations. He was ready. Sam was not keen on appearing desperate, and he would do his best to keep cool, trying to wait until their date on Saturday without bothering her too much between now then. For the rest of the week, Sam spent time learning about constellations, knowing how much they intrigued her. Having rich knowledge of something she loved so much, he thought that would be a good way to her heart.

Sam could think of several topics he could talk about with her. Camping, fishing, her worldly travels, stars, otherworldly possibilities, music, movies, cats and dogs, the people they meet, science, anything. He would talk to her about anything, even if it didn't interest him at all.

The week painfully crawled by.

As each day passed, Saturday felt like it was getting farther away. Not communicating with her every day worried him. But today's digital world did that to people; caused a wealth of anxiety.

Each day, people could get served up with a nice dose of instant gratification. One text could spiral you into a lovely and poisonous dopamine hit that only leaves a desire for more. Communication and dating weren't like it was with older generations. People didn't wait days for a phone call anymore. Sam couldn't believe people waited days just to get in touch with someone they were into. If someone doesn't respond to a text within minutes, something must be wrong, and that was the digital culture. Somedays it sickened Sam. Responding to every text instantly so people felt seen or remembered was exhausting. He didn't know how others weren't just as exhausted.

In a way, Sam liked waiting days for phone calls. Anticipation would build, the absence would increase fondness until two people were so obsessed with each other, they would fall madly in love. They weren't constantly smothering one another with attention. He wished that this kind of dating routine still existed. Now, any silence between messages could cause skepticism and insecurity. People checked their phones, seeing if red notification bubbles appeared in large quantities, watched Facebook messenger like a hawk to see how long it had been since someone was on, and *why didn't they read my message?* It was disgusting and draining.

By the time Friday came around, Sam's excitement made him feel as if he would burst from the seams. He found himself staring at the clock, obsessing over considerations on whether to text Anya or not. She had been silent all week, and it was killing him. Some days, he wondered if she had forgotten him or if she had lied to him in the museum about their date. Against all of his doubts, he still held out for hope.

Friday nights were reserved for karaoke. It was one of Sam's favorite nights, not because he particularly liked karaoke, but because he loved watching the bar pack with people laughing, smiling, and dancing.

Sam dressed in a backward cap, a flannel shirt with the sleeves rolled up, a pair of jeans, and a pair of Pumas. He fluffed up his beard and left the door without locking it. He agreed to meet Steve at Ralf's tonight.

When Sam arrived, the bar was packed, but Steve was in the corner near the quiet wood-burning stove saving them a table. Ralf's had a cabin feel to it, the inside dim from the dark wood accents that were consistent throughout. Two pool tables and a couple of dartboards sat in the room to the back, and beside them was a slightly elevated stage already set up with a soundboard and microphones.

No one was singing yet, and the tall white man and his Vietnamese wife who ran it were nowhere in view. They usually started the night with a song. On the walls were metal signs, some of which said, *Be careful. Don't drink the Cyanide.* Some pick axes hung from the walls, and a line of different liquors was stacked behind a bar that curved into an L shape.

In the front room was a single shuffleboard table near the front windows and crane games for kids to play. Sam walked over to the table, cutting through the crowd already on its way to a drunken stupor. In his path, he greeted many of the other people he had grown up knowing—a familiar ritual each time he made a public appearance.

"Hey, Steve," Sam said when he finally reached the table.

"What's up, buddy?" He said, taking a sip of his icy beer. Sam could see Kim rounding the bar with a tray full of drinks.

"Not much, man. It was a hell of a week," Sam said. "Dragged ass, actually."

"Your usual, Sam?" Kim shouted, passing him, handing out drinks to a nearby table. Her blue eyes were wide and cheeks red. Her blonde hair rested on her right shoulder, tied into a braid.

"Yeah, Kim. That would be great. Thank you!" Kim sped off, delivering more drinks to other tables before returning to the bar.

"You didn't bring Wendi with you tonight?" Sam asked.

"Nah. She was too tired. It was a long week for everyone, I guess. It's good, though. I could use a bit of guy time myself," Sam nodded, nearly ignoring him as he thought about seeing Anya Saturday. Kim came around to drop off his beer. The green bottle told Steve it was a shitty pale ale.

"Dude, when are you going to stop drinking shitty beer?" Steve joked. Sam took a swig in with his laughter.

"When they start serving good beer up here," Sam replied.

"It would be amazing to see a brewery up here," Steve said.

"Yeah, man. We should open our own," Sam said. "The only problem is getting the materials up here to build anything. Most of these buildings wouldn't work. They're not fitted for an entire brewing system."

"Shipping materials up this mountain would probably cost more than building the damn place," Steve agreed, taking another swig of his beer.

Sam thought about it. It wasn't a bad idea, opening a brewery in Cripple Creek. Ralf's was a great place, and during the winter, it would keep the locals occupied. It was unlikely they would follow through.

"I think if I were to open up a brewery, I would craft my own root beer. Then we could make root beer floats for the kids too, honor that heritage," said Sam.

"That's not a bad fucking idea, man. I bet most people don't know the root beer float was born here. Man, somedays I wish these two communities had the money to really do this place justice," Steve said.

"Right? This area is badass, but it's hard to glean from just driving through. I feel like people miss the true gold of this place," Sam said.

"Maybe that's because the casinos are so prominent here," Steve said.

"Yeah, but without them, these streets would have crumbled to dust. That's just the truth, and I don't care what the old-timers say," Sam took another large swig, leaving the clear green bottle half empty.

He raised two fingers to Kim, who caught his eye. She nodded. Somewhere in the corner, someone dropped a glass, and the sound of pool cues cracking against pool balls sounded in the back. The music still hadn't started yet; still just symphonies of a busy bar.

"I'm with ya," Steve said.

The Lost Pleiad

At that moment, someone came in the door, sucking the air from the bar like a vacuum—no one in particular. Just a visitor to the area. Sam knew everyone and could usually tell who wasn't from here based on the clothing they wore. He looked down at his nearly empty bottle of beer as Steve studied him.

"Expecting someone, Sam?" Steve said, sipping his dark beer from a tall glass. Sam looked up at him and shook his head, saying nothing. He had sort of wished Anya would walk through that door. He wanted any reason to run into her.

The Vietnamese woman appeared from the storage room. Soon music was blaring throughout the bar as she sang a shrill rendition of Fleetwood Mac's *Dreams*. Watching people get on that little stage was something to be admired. Having the courage to get on stage and sing in front of strangers, or worse, people you know, whether you were really good or really bad, was something Sam commended. He would never do it himself.

The night cycled through some very impressive singers and some less than impressive ones. After several songs, Sam and Steve were down three beers and laughing hard at the table, telling ridiculous stories of the dangerous things they'd done as young men, counting the many times they had escaped potential jail time. They made vulgar jokes and laughed until they were in tears.

Now and then, the front door would suck the air out of the building. After a while, Sam stopped checking to see who was at the door. He would see Anya tomorrow.

After one more beer, all the singers started to sound good, even the bad ones. Some people found their places on the small dance floor to sway their hips.

Air was sucked from the bar again. Steve looked up and gave a friendly wave. Sam figured it was Steve's wife changing her mind about a night out. He didn't bother to look and instead worked on finishing his fourth beer. When the person who entered came around the back of his chair, he could barely move.

It was Anya.

Jen, one of the youngest members of the Cripple Creek City Council, was with her. She had pale blue eyes with a streak of black across her eyelids and her hair was dimmer compared to Anya's blazing gold mane. Her nose was pierced, and she was already bouncing to the room's rhythm, pumping her fist in the air. Jen was always the life of the party. Her presence alone was a surefire way to ensure a crazier night.

Sam straightened his posture, looking at Anya, who was dressed in a sleek pair of faux leather pants and high-heeled boots to match. Her blouse was a dark navy with a sparkling string of jewelry dripping down to her navel. She hadn't straightened her hair today. Instead, it was curled. Anya placed her hand on the back of his chair and smiled down at him.

"Hi, Sam," she grinned coyly. Sam could feel himself melting in the seat of his chair. He squeaked out a 'hi,' and Steve looked over at him, realizing he was indeed waiting for a specific somebody.

"Would you guys like to join us?" Steve asked before Sam could get to the question.

"Hell yeah, we would!" Jen shouted. "Gotta get me a whiskey first, though." She bounced off to the bar. Sam got up from his chair and moved a new chair for Anya.

"It's about to be a rough night," Steve said. Sam just stared at Anya, who was still smiling, wondering where this new, striking version of her suddenly appeared from and how everything about her in this moment turned him on. Steve knocked the bottom of the beer glass on the table, drawing an alarmed gaze from Sam. He mouthed the words, 'don't be creepy,' to Sam, who nodded agreeably. Sweat was forming on his brow and in his palms.

"Would you like a drink, Anya?" Sam asked.

"Sure, I'll take something dark," Steve raised his eyebrows.

"The lady likes beer," Steve said. "Unless you meant a Starry Night?"

Intrigued, Anya clapped her hands together. "Well, that sounds magical. What's in it?

"Goldschläger and Jäger," he laughed.

"Ew!" She exclaimed, which sparked a chuckle in Sam. "What a terrible drink for such a lovely name. I think I'll pass—just a dark beer for me. I'm going to run to the bathroom really quick, though. Speaking of which, I owe you a case, Steve," she was nearly shouting over this next singer who was screaming into the microphone.

"I didn't forget, my dear," his southern accent sounded even thicker after a few pints. Anya strutted off to the bathroom. Sam watched her hips sway back and forth as she walked away.

Goddamn.

He headed to the bar to get her a dark beer, returning to the table with a glass nearly full to the brim and another green bottle for himself.

"Anya, huh?" He said, tipping his beer glass to clink with Sam's. All he could do was smile at Steve. The liquor was settling into his bloodstream, bringing out a more talkative side of his extrovert personality. If he didn't stop drinking now, he would surely do something foolish in front of Anya, and he still desperately wanted to prove himself to her.

"What about Anya?" Said Jen, who had returned with two neat double whiskies.

"I was just telling Sam how amazing she was, but I think he already knew that," Steve smirked. Sam rolled his eyes, a wave of red flushing his cheeks.

"Anya is my girl. She is incredible. It's nice having a woman my age in that stuffy city hall," Jen said. She was usually this blunt about things, yet, at the same time, she was very respectful toward her work on the city council. When she threw house parties, Sam always saw her dining room table covered in the laws and rules of the city. She understood how everything worked in the town government better than everyone else *supposedly* more seasoned in small-town politics.

Being a woman in a clan of old white men, they had trouble with some of her more progressive ideas. Although a massive and intimidating challenge to most, it was not something that would stop her. Sam heard she was relentless during City Council meetings, but was always honest and clear-headed when presenting information and offering new ideas.

Anya returned to the table, glowing with each step. She was like a perfect painting, looking just as stunning and capturing up close as she did from a distance.

Anya sat down at the table, quickly letting herself fall into conversation with them about the town. She took large swigs of beer, and Sam swore he was falling for her. He did his best not to stare but couldn't help himself. Somewhere amidst the conversation, Kim brought him a soda. He could feel the liquor's numbing sensation subside with each sip, quickly sobering up to a clearer state that wouldn't make him out as a fool in front of Anya. They talked about the various odd instances that seemed to gravitate to this town. Sam settled on telling one of his favorite stories of all time.

"So, this one day, and this isn't my story, I just heard it from Jacob at CCPD, the Cripple Creek Fire Department got a call about a fire over on Carr Avenue between 1st and A street," he began. "It was raging hot that day. Easily over a hundred degrees. The whole area was on a fire ban, so any type of fire anywhere scared everyone," he said, leaning back in his chair.

"I love this story," Jen said.

Anya was halfway through her beer, one hand propping up her perfect chin. Jen was sitting in front of four empty shot glasses, now dry from the whiskey shot that momentarily lived there. Her eyes were now half open and soft pink.

"CCFD got in their gear, called in the EMTs and PD, drove over to Carr to find a single pile of donkey shit on fire in the middle of the street." A round of exuberant laughter circled the table between Jen, Anya, and Steve, tears burning the corner of their eyes.

"Apparently, the summer heat lit the damn thing on fire! So, the whole fucking team went out to Carr to put out that fire. They circled around it, pulled out this little hose, and put out the pile of shit," he looked at Anya, who was laughing so hard she could barely catch her breath. Sam wanted more than anything to make her laugh like that as often as possible.

"Jacob said it was the most ridiculous thing he'd ever seen. When he was coming up in his squad car, he saw the whole gang just circled around a pile of flaming donkey shit like a bunch of idiots. Only in

Cripple Creek, man," Sam chuckled. He swirled the ice cubes at the bottom of the glass, noticing Anya's beer glass was now empty.

"You want another one?" He asked her.

"Sure, I'll come with you. We can do a shot or something," she said. They got up together and walked toward the bar. Jen and Steve were leaning into one another, whispering behind them. When they reached an open space at the top of the bar, they were silent for a moment. Kim was busy but nodded to let Sam know she was on her way.

"So, you don't come out on Fridays very often, do you?" he asked Anya.

"Not usually. I'm not a very big partier, honestly. I'd rather be at home reading a book," she said. "Jen convinced me to come out and begged me to dress up, which I also don't do very often."

Sam tried not to look her up and down as she remarked on her outfit. "I think you look great."

Anya smiled at him.

"What are you reading right now?" He asked.

"I just finished reading *Eleven Minutes* by Paulo Coelho. God, it was good," she said. Kim made her way down to the end of the bar.

"Another beer for you, girl?" Kim asked.

"Yes, please. And two shots of Butter Crown."

"Coming up."

"Butter Crown?" Sam tilted his head.

"Half butterscotch schnapps and half Crown Royal. Much better than whatever that damn Starry Night shit is," she said, cocking her head to the side, letting her Disney princess eyes glimmer at him. Smiling idiotically any time she did anything seemed to be his normal reflex when he looked at her. Mesmerized by her smile, he shook his head, gripping the edge of the bar, forcing himself back into reality.

"What was the book about?" He asked, leaning into the wooden bar top, his forearm muscles bulging. Her eyes lingered on them for a sweet minute before darting to the floor.

"It's about a Brazilian prostitute," she said sharply, looking for his reaction. Sam's eyes widened as Kim came to the end of the bar with the two shots and her dark beer. If he had a mouth full of beer, he would have spit it out then.

"Well, that's interesting," he laughed. "You'll have to tell me more about it when we're in a place that's not so loud." Karaoke was still raging in the background, booming music at a deafening volume. Anyone on Bennett would no doubt hear them over the sound of slot machines.

"I'd love to," Anya said, raising her glass of clear caramel liquid in his direction before shooting it back. The shot was a fusion of sweet, creamy, rich, and spicy. Fucking delicious.

"Damn, that's good. Tastes like Christmas," Sam said. She smiled, lifting her beer from the bar top. The pair of them were just about to sit down when the karaoke host called Anya's name.

"Oh! That's me!" She said. "Be right back."

She waltzed over to the stage and snatched the microphone. The bar was still a rowdy chatter before piano sounds rippled over the speakers signaling a familiar song everyone knew, *I Want You Back* by The Jackson 5. Everyone in the bar shouted and wolf-whistled at Anya. No doubt, this song was a crowd favorite in any bar amongst any age group.

Anya belted out the song on key, hitting every note perfectly and shockingly resembling Michael Jackson's high pitch. The bar was loving it. It was clear she had won crowds over with the song before. People left their chairs to find a place on the dance floor. Sam tapped his foot and lifted his hands to the clap with the rhythm. The rest of the bar joining him. People stopped playing pool and shooting darts just to listen to her sing.

Sam couldn't believe he found such a captivating woman in a strange place like Cripple Creek. He wanted more than anything to kiss her, to feel her soft lips on his. With every note she sang, he could tell he was a goner.

When she finished the song, applause erupted all over the bar. She stepped off the stage, wading through the applause with an impossibly large grin on her face and a shade of pink invading her cheeks. She sat down in her chair, out of breath, trying to adjust her smile to a normal expression, but she just couldn't.

"That was fucking amazing!" Sam shouted.

"No kidding!" Steve yelled.

"How come you never told us you could sing like that? We've known you for how long?" Asked Jen, who now had six empty glasses in front of her.

Anya was glowing, but she was embarrassed too. Sam could glean the reason why she never told anyone. She didn't want the attention, but he could tell she loved it just a little bit.

"You are a woman of secrets," Sam piped up.

"You guys flatter me," she said, taking a sip of her beer. "When I was in college, me and a buddy of mine, who was also my landlord, used to bar hop all week long, going to every single place there was karaoke so we could just sing all night. We would order pitchers of shitty beer, play darts, and sing. Sometimes he and I would sing duets too. I miss those times," she finished.

Sam briefly wondered if she missed the moments or the man. Feeling a twinge of jealously for all the times before this that he never knew her.

The four of them talked into the evening as the bar slowly cleared out and the clock hand ticked its way to the early hours of the morning. The four of them closed down the bar. Sam was not ready to leave. Not ready for this night to be over. Not ready to let Anya slip from his view.

His desire to kiss her grew as each minute passed. Kim wiped down the bar in the background, the jukebox was now playing, and Jen was still surprisingly upright in her seat. They all got up from the table sticky with beer and whiskey rings. They wished Kim a good night as she followed them out to lock the front door. It clanged shut behind them.

The night was warm and cool at the same time. Like pockets of crisp mountain air were just hanging there, ready to pop like soap bubbles kids blew at parks. Anya and Sam waited with Jen and Steve until the transit bus came to get them. After several minutes, the bus arrived. Jen and Steve said their goodbyes and climbed into the red bus. It sped off, leaving Anya and Sam standing together on Bennett Avenue in front of the Double Eagle Casino.

Alone.

Bennett Avenue was always quiet at 2:00 a.m. Sam shoved his hands in his pockets and looked at Anya.

"Are you okay to drive home?" He asked.

"Oh, yeah," she said. "I live so far away from here I try not to have more than two beers at a time, and if I do, it's with food." She looked down nervously, admiring her black boots. "How about you? Are you okay to drive home?"

"Yeah. I stopped drinking a while ago," he said. They let the silence rest between them again, and Anya laughed nervously.

"Well, can I walk you to your car?" Sam asked.

"Of course," she said. Anya's car was parked on the block up the street from Ralf's in front of City Hall. He put his hand out to lead the way. They strolled, side by side, the soft skin of her forearms brushing his own. Sam's skin was burning, his entire body racing to an uncontrollable tremble. The wanting and yearning for her touch surged through his veins, reaching the very center of his bones.

Touching her, even in the most innocent ways, would lead him to eternal infatuation. How men didn't lose their minds just being around her was something he would never understand. Anya's golden hair sparkled under the few street lights dimmed by the black night.

They were crossing the street now. Sam tried to slow his footsteps, hoping doing so wouldn't spark suspicion. Sam's time walking with her was running out. Soon, she would get in her car, drive away from him, and he would wait even more unbearable hours until he could see her again.

When they arrived at her car, he was so hot, he was sure she might see how ablaze he was. The town was quiet. It was just the two of them. He wanted to take her in his arms and dance with her beneath these dim lights and bright stars.

And when she looked up at him with her ice-blue eyes, he was struck down from his high, grounding him to the very pavement beneath his feet. She was a force of gravity pulling him into her orbit, something she had been doing for a while now. But tonight, he had seen another side of her, a stunning and daring one, and just another subtle piece of her intricate puzzle. This would be the moment where he would kiss her. Those blue eyes flickered with that same idea. The noticeably rapid breaths between them told him so.

Sam removed his hands from his pockets, moving closer to her. His heart was a relentless pounding beneath his ribs, a drumming he was confident she could hear. The world was dissolving around them.

Sam let one hand reach up to touch her cheek, feeling the softness of her skin in his palm and the golden strands of hair brush the back of his hand. Those ocean eyes were wreaking havoc already, tearing his guts out. Any minute, Sam might crumble at her feet, letting her command him in any way she pleased. Sam relinquished his control, respecting the power she had over him. Those blue eyes disappeared behind her eyelids as she savored his soft touch. Her hand met his wrist, feeling the heat of his burning skin. Sam couldn't move. Now was the time to kiss her. It was the perfect time. Not a single soul was in sight. The silent night was the only one watching.

Sam leaned in, a serious expression falling across his face as she waited for his lips to meet hers. He let them brush against her cheek, smelling her lavender hair, breathing softly into her ear. Anya shuddered at his touch, the swell of her chest rising quickly toward his own as she sucked in each rhythmic breath. Sam was still intent on showing her just how happy she would be with him. This was just the beginning. He wanted to build this anticipation and tension, not just for her but for himself. Sam wanted to take pleasure in every single touch and moment with her, including this one.

He planted a soft kiss on her cheek, feeling Anya's body shake as if she would fall into his arms at any second. When he pulled away, she released her loose grip from his wrist. She opened her eyes to look at him, her chest rising and falling even more rapidly now. Grinning, as if she appreciated him even more for being a perfect gentleman, her eyes twinkled with want, knowing just exactly what he might be up to.

"I *really* look forward to our date tomorrow," Sam said, smiling even wider than ever. Returning a smile, amused by this game they were playing, Anya turned to the car door opening it to slide into the driver's seat.

"Goodnight, Sam," she flashed one last sinful grin.

She sped off, leaving Sam alone in the street, grinning ridiculously beneath the dim streetlights.

He watched her taillights disappear into the black cliffs. Shooting his fists into the air victoriously, he whispered 'thank you' to the sky.

FIFTEEN

Anya drove down Bennett Avenue, feeling her cheek hot with the remaining brush of Sam's lips. To stop when he did, to stop from kissing her, it restored a sense of her innocence. It reminded her of her days as a teenager when she only ever went as far as kissing, how those kisses were so intense and passionate, how those fifth-grade make-out sessions never led anywhere beyond a lip lock. The rush she felt then was now rippling through her veins, burning hot on her cheek where his lips met her skin.

She dared not touch it, fearing the sensation would wear off if she did. She wanted to keep it for as long as possible. The moment made her feel excited for the possibility that she might experience the same impassioned anticipation she felt in her younger years.

She glanced in her rearview where Sam had become smaller, disappearing beneath the dim street lights. He was watching her down the road while her stomach did backflips, feeling jolts of eagerness for tomorrow's date. From what she knew, they would be going to stargaze, but she didn't know where they would be going yet. Anya remembered one place she loved to see the stars, but it was a bit of a drive.

As she drove, she realized she wasn't just eager for the date and seeing Sam, she was nervous about what her body might do. How two people attracted to each other would react under darkness, as they do behind bleachers, in dark closets, in bedrooms, in places they're not supposed to be. How those places make people animals for each other.

Anya could entertain all the ways he would make love to her beneath the stars. How that would be the most romantic way any man had ever entered her. But she tried not to think about it. After a majority of her relationships formed on lust, she learned fantasizing about sex or creating any expectations at all usually ruined intimacy by the time it happened. The times she had been disappointed dreaming up mind-blowing sex, she could remember them all, how they would implode because of these expectations. Some men talked so highly of their ability to please a woman it created false stories of their passionate sex lives in her head. They were heavenly, but they were dreams.

By the time she had gotten in bed with a man, the sex she dreamed up was usually always better than the sex he promised her. But Sam leaving her with a single kiss on the cheek and nothing more, it inflamed her, left her wondering, left her anticipating. There might be some mystery in this romance after all. Overthinking it would ruin it, and with this flaming kiss still blazing on her cheek, she would fight every urge to imagine his skin on hers until the time came.

When she arrived at her house, there was a familiar black shadow sitting in the window waiting for her. The stars peeked out over the tree lines, quick to remind her of that newly discovered part of herself she was trying to forget. Anya had other things on her mind. Things that would set her ablaze in ways balls of flaming gas lightyears away would never be able to promise her.

She thought about what she had experienced already. The hug that stopped a restaurant and that single innocent kiss. How he closed the space between them. How his brown eyes turned to a shade that wanted and needed with a sort of primal hunger. Anya didn't know what color to call that. She remembered his soft hand sweeping the side of her cheek. The shivers that raced up her spine as his gentle breaths tickled her ear. How his very touch made her so dizzy she thought she might collapse. Anya could relive that fleeting moment over and over until the next encounter became her new favorite.

Anya unsnapped the lace bra, letting her breasts fall. She let out a sigh, accompanied by a smile. How would Sam react when he saw her naked? She put on a pair of leggings and a loose shirt and climbed into bed. That night she would go to bed, replaying his touches, how he had stolen her breath. How every rational part of her would fall away each time he touched her. How that simple kiss had transformed her hesitations into fantasies.

Tonight, her fingertips wouldn't find the warmth between her thighs at the very thought of Sam. She would not give in to her temptations. The more they raged on, the more intense their first time together would be. Anya wanted their relationship to be like Maria and Ralf's in *Eleven Minutes*. Their intimacy happened far before sex did. And when the time was right, sex intensified their bond in ways lost within minutes of passion and lust. Lust was so often disguised as love, which ultimately led to heartbreak. But if they could be like Maria and Ralf, that would be a dream well fulfilled.

Tonight, Anya wouldn't bother to sit with the stars or tell them goodnight. She would try to sleep and stop herself from counting the hours until she saw Sam again.

SIXTEEN

The sunshine burned through Anya's cozy nook early in the morning. She had slept far past sunrise on account of coming home so late. There was no hangover or headache this morning, which delighted her. She laid in bed, a bit of light filtering in through the curtains and her black poof ball resting at her feet. As Anya shifted in bed, Sugar perked up, her yellow eyes bright and alert. Anya looked out from her small bedroom, the white walls on the inside expanding in the residual light.

When Anya got out of bed, Sugar trailed behind her, yawning to show her tiny sharp teeth. She walked through the doorway, feeling the dark sun-warmed hardwood beneath her feet. She moved to the bathroom to brush her teeth, throwing her hair into a bun. Saturdays for Anya were usually days of recovering from the week, listening to music, reading books, or spending time outside in the wilderness. Since she had her date this evening, she decided she would read through half of her next book. The trouble now would be choosing which one to read next. Leaving the bathroom, she glanced at the stack of books in the nook. She took one, *The Invisible Life of Addie LaRue*, strapped Sugar to a harness, and walked outside barefoot with her in tow.

Anya walked down the step and onto the bare earth, feeling its coolness beneath her feet. The one thing she wished her property had was a proper grass yard—a difficult thing to achieve on a sliver of hard rock mountain terrain. Maybe one day, she would be able to carve it out. Grass was always a pleasant sensation between her toes. Even in parks or grassy areas uninterrupted, she found herself taking her shoes off and feeling the cool grass blades swarm her feet. What she loved even more was wading into icy rivers and feeling the stones massage the bottoms of her feet. Without the grassy yard, she was still grateful for what she had since there were plenty who wished for even her worst day.

Anya sucked in the mountain air and sat down in the chair closest to the house. The shade of the trees had cooled the dirt under her feet. Like the music playing in her home, it soothed her, gave her energy.

When she was a child, she enjoyed being barefoot, although her parents scolded her for it, saying it was dirty and she should act more like a lady. It was common for them to look down on anything carefree, natural, or liked by Anya. They expected her to be proper, a certain way, like them, but that wasn't Anya. She was far from the lady who sat up straight, said polite words, and wore pretty and proper dresses. Anya was rugged, she loved nature, she didn't spend hours getting ready in the morning, and as an adult, she spent as much time possible doing the things her parents told her not to, especially putting her feet in the dirt.

Anya tried to remember the last time she had seen or talked to her parents. She was often scolded for not going to church on Sundays. She hadn't been going for months, mentioning that fact without thinking, which usually sent her mother into a raging lecture about how she's damned for not appreciating God more. In reality, neither of them knew the extent of her relationship with God or the talks she had with him on her best and worst days. Anya didn't understand why reading a bible or going to church were the only ways she could pray to God, honor his memory, or call upon him for guidance.

Beyond that, there were occasions when Anya tried to show her deepest thoughts or truest self to her parents only to be fiercely judged. Judgment seemed to be a common thing among them and religion in general. When it came to her church, it was clear a myriad of things were unacceptable, like the LGBTQ community. How could anyone speak of an all-loving, forgiving God who hated gay people? Anya felt like she could empathize with them somewhat and the judgment they faced in their pursuits of being unapologetically themselves.

Anya's parents were indoctrinated, unwilling to change, and she knew it. Rather than waste her energy trying to show them anything different, she just quit talking to them. Anya was stubborn that way.

She had rarely seen text messages from her mother, but in reality, Anya spent more time engaging with her father anyway. Overall, Anya didn't see the point of staying around for anyone who didn't appreciate her, or others, for that matter, and that included family.

If she wanted to shout 'Jesus Fucking Christ' because someone almost ran her off the road, she would, and she would not feel bad about it.

She knew where she stood with God. She counted her blessings and was kind and loving to people even when they lived in their darkness. Anya was her own type of religion, and that religion was kindness and love. There were some days where she wasn't her best at it.

Still, she would spend her moments outside barefoot on her property in a sort of rebellion, proud of the life she had built here. It was simple, everything she had ever wanted. She didn't need much more than the mountains, the stars, and her books. Summer was her favorite season, and looking through the trees and their glittering canopy of green leaves, she knew it would come and go as fast as a single breath. There was never enough time in a day, let alone a summer or even a year.

Sugar had moved on to climbing a broken tree nearby, sinking her tiny claws into the bark. The little black poof where her tail should've been gave her a remarkable resemblance to a mini black bobcat. Anya giggled at her, trying to reel in the wild spirit she wished she could mirror more often. Anya wasn't the free spirit she used to be. She hardened over time after learning how harsh the world could be.

When she let herself think about the segregation of the people in the world, how the earth beneath her very feet was dying, how people harbored greed and possession of things, she felt deeply depressed. Most of the time, she wouldn't let herself think about any of it. It made her feel helpless. The more she lived, the more she learned life wasn't always the perfect gift wrapped up with a pretty bow. It was complex. It required adaptation, patience, understanding, nurturing, and above all else, love.

Anya tugged lightly on the leash, feeling the sharp bits of rock plunge into the arches of her feet. Sugar, reluctant to come inside during her exploration, eventually conceded to follow mother back inside. Anya looked at the clock. It was just four o'clock. If she got ready now, she would have enough time to read another few chapters before leaving for her date. She showered quickly, got dressed, blow-dried her hair, threw some pillows and blankets by the door, and sat down with her book to get lost in a new story.

Life rang like an alarm when she got a text from Sam. "Hey, I'm on my way."

Looking at the clock, it was a 5:45 p.m. and she was now running late, all for the sake of a good book. She brewed a fresh pot of coffee in a hurry, adding a few shots of cream and spoonfuls of sugar to the thermos. Once the coffee finished brewing, she filled the thermos, watching the steam rise into the less lustrous bits of sunshine that found their way through the window. Anya gave her furry companion a quick kiss, grabbed all the items near the doorway, and rushed out to her car. Cruising down the road, she would be just a minute or two later than she had hoped. Being fashionably late tended to build more anticipation.

She slowed her speed in Cripple Creek, minding all the stop signs before reaching 2nd street. There in the Bronco Billy's overflow parking lot, Sam was leaning up against his truck, staring down at his phone. He looked up at the sound of her car passing by, pocketed his phone, and watched her pull into the parking lot. Anya smiled, almost running a stop sign at the sight of him. She pulled into the same parking lot, trying to find a place close to him. Once she got out, she took the blankets and thermos, carrying them over to him. Sam ran over to her, taking a few items off her hands.

"Hi," he smiled without touching her.

"Hello," heat rushed to her cheeks.

"Do you have everything?"

"Yeah, I think I have everything. Any idea where we might be going tonight?"

"Well, unless you have a place, I know just the perfect spot," he said. Anya was curious about what he had conjured up and decided to just go with it.

"Let's go with your plan," she said. They made their way to his truck, where he stuffed the blankets into the back, situating the heavy thermos in the center drink holder. Stuffed in the back seat were even more blankets, pillows, and what looked like sleeping pads.

"It's a long way. You up for an adventure?" He questioned.

"I'm always up for an adventure."

SEVENTEEN

Sam arrived almost twenty minutes early, feeling glad Anya hadn't arrived sooner for fear he might seem too eager. Sam watched each minute pass by like the cars driving slowly through town.

Now, sitting in the car next to her, Sam could barely tame himself. At any moment, he would spontaneously combust in this summer heat, even with the cool AC blowing directly on him. He held a burning desire to spend every second in Anya's presence. Last night, he could barely sleep thinking about her reaction to his kiss.

Anya was in the passenger's seat as they drove out of town toward the Cripple Creek Mountain Estates past the silent and tall Mount Pisgah. He was desperate to tell her where they were going but wanted to keep it a surprise. Even more curious, she hadn't asked where they were going yet. Maybe she already knew. Maybe she was content with wherever they were going, no matter the destination. Sam glanced at her to see she had relaxed into the passenger's seat, now comfortable in the silence of the cabin staring out the window as the world blurred by, her eyes glimmering with fast-moving images from the outdoors. The desire to reach out and touch that cheek again, brush that golden hair from her ear, was nearly unbearable. How easy it would be for his fingertips to touch that beautiful skin. But there would be time. That was something he would have to remind himself. There is time.

After several minutes of driving, her silence started to make him anxious. A thousand questions stopped at his throat. Learning every single part of her in a day was impossible. Instead, he started with a simple question.

"Don't you want to know where we are going?" He asked. She finally turned to look at him, the electric storms in her eyes even more brilliant in the daylight filling in the inside of the truck. They stopped him dead. If it wasn't for his peripheral vision kept keenly on the swerving roads, they were sure to crash.

"No," she smiled brightly. "I'm sure wherever we're going will be great." She said calmly. Anya held her stare to really looking at him. By now, his peripheral vision had stopped working.

Removing his gaze from hers was a task he couldn't achieve. He had no desire to crash this truck, intending very much to live, to gaze into those eyes millions of times until he could no longer count the shades of blue in them.

After getting out of the paved curves of the road, there would be long stretches to speed down. Sam planned to steal glances of her on that entire stretch of road if pronghorns didn't leap into his path.

"I'm sure you'll like it. It's one of the best places to stargaze in Colorado," he said, grip firm on the steering wheel.

"I think I may have an idea of where we're going, but I'll pretend like it's a complete mystery," she said. Sam laughed. From the corner of his eye, he saw Anya slip a single shoe off and prop her foot up on the seat. A sign of comfort in his eyes.

"I'm sure that by the time we reach a certain point, you'll realize where we're going. We should be there just in time for nightfall," he replied.

Not only had he planned an entire evening under the stars to observe their static existence, he had even curated a stargazing playlist. Most of the songs had names of constellations or referred to astronomy in some way.

It had been a long time since he had made a playlist for anyone. Doing that in his younger years was about putting genuine thought into each song's placement. It told someone the story of how you feel about them and linked memory to the song forever.

People didn't curate playlists for each other anymore, and if they did, they were seldom really listening. All the feeling and thought once placed in a perfectly good playlist became lost. Sam wanted to bring back that tradition with Anya.

"If I'm right, and I think I know where we're going, it's one of my favorite drives in all of Colorado," she said.

Sam was curious about whether or not she was right and if she was envisioning that drive. He would take Teller County Rd 1 hanging a left on County Rd 11, following it until he hit 9. From there, he would drive until he hit HWY 50 and take a right toward Poncha Springs. They would take a left on HWY 285 and drive until the road veered off onto County Road 17.

After that, it would be a straight shot to the sandy dunes, past Moffat, past Joyful Journey Hot Springs, following the Sangre de Cristo Mountains like a car speeding beside a moving train. That was the long stretch of road that would allow him to focus less on the road and more on the stunning woman sitting beside him.

"Well, let's see how right you are," he said. "Curious though, what are some of your favorite drives in Colorado?" She thought for a moment.

"Well, the drive past Twin Lakes and up Independence Pass is a top one. Going through Wolf Creek Pass too. That's probably one of my favorite ones, especially in autumn when the leaves are changing. For me, that sight is just unmatched to any other landscape in the world," she finished.

"I love that pass. It's one of my favorites too. Where are you usually going when you travel that way?"

"In the past, it has been a much-traveled road on my way to Pagosa Springs, Mesa Verde, or passing through on my way to Page, Arizona."

"You ever stop at the hot springs in Pagosa?"

"Hell yes. It's one of my favorite hot springs," she said. "The way it sits on the river and looks up at the stars. It's complete magic." He smiled and nodded.

Her and her stars.

"Have you ever been to Strawberry Hot Springs?" He asked.

"No, but I've seen pictures! I have always wanted to go but felt like that was more of a romantic hiking trip," she said, looking hard at him. Sam focused on hugging the curves of the road, feeling her stare burn into him. Taking her up there, just him and her, he would add that to their bucket list if she chose to have him.

"You're definitely right," he said, implying he was documenting this subtle request.

"What's in Page, Arizona?"

"Antelope Canyon. Turns out it's one of my other favorite places in the whole world," she said.

"Sounds like you have a lot of those."

"I really do."

"What do you do when you visit Antelope Canyon?"

"I go down there to get out of range, clear my head, take a few days to camp, and kayak into the canyon. It's such a beautiful and peaceful adventure. Remind me to show you pictures from my last trip."

"Oh, I will," he said.

"How about you? What are your favorite paths to adventure in Colorado?"

"Definitely Wolf Creek Pass. The drive to Breckenridge is a good one too. I love any drive that will lead me to the Sangre de Cristos. I just love those mountains so much," he said.

"Me too!" Anya interrupted. He smiled at her shrill excitement.

"I also love driving through Rocky Mountain National Park," he said. "Especially during the fall season when Estes Park, Colorado has elk roaming everywhere."

"We like a lot of the same places," Anya said.

"It sounds like we do."

"I still haven't seen every place in Colorado," she said.

"What places haven't you seen?" Sam wanted to add more to their travel bucket list and was silently taking notes.

"I'm not sure. I just know there is plenty I haven't seen," she said. "What's so great about this world is there is so much to discover, and new things are always being created. The adventure is truly endless."

Anya was right. Sam particularly liked that there was so much he hadn't seen in the world. There were many hidden places he could still journey to but knew it was impossible to accomplish all adventures in his lifetime. However, he would still try his damndest to visit those hidden places. There were some locations he had been to various times, ones he would love to take her to. As he thought, she continued speaking. "I would really, really love to go to Dunton Hot Springs one day," she finished.

"Tell me about it," he said.

"It's nestled in the San Juan Mountains near Mt. Sneffels. It's a renovated ghost town. Real luxurious. It's also really expensive to stay there even for two days. But it has an amazing hot spring and incredible scenery. It would be a perfect trip to go on one of these days when I can get around to it."

"It sounds really nice," he said. If she said it was expensive, he would take her word for it.

The drive to the Sand Dunes would take around three hours. He already loved how easy it was to talk to each other, how comfortable it was in the silence

By the time they had come to HWY 50, they had made it through their lists of family members. Anya had a short list since it was just her and her parents. Sam learned her parents were only children. He also learned her parents were incredibly religious. While he didn't care who believed in what religion, he could sense she wasn't thrilled about being the daughter of extremely religious parents. When he asked, and she answered, it was the first time he had seen her tense up since getting in his truck. Arms crossed, closing her heart—confusion on her brow with a hint of frustration. Sam wanted to ask more, but they were still getting to know each other. After just a sentence describing them, he figured the topic was extra sensitive.

Sam told her his parents died but didn't dare tell her how. She didn't pressure him with more questions, which put him at ease. Sam told her about how Bruce and how the town raised him into a man. As he spoke, he admitted to himself that he was a bit of a friend hoarder. Like people who had lost so much and then hoarded every single object they came across, Sam hoarded friends until he had so many he would never be lonely. He would simply not allow anyone else in his life who mattered to be gone from him again. So he held onto everyone.

Sam wanted to tell her to make things right with her parents if she could—what he wouldn't give to have two parents who were around. Anya probably never considered the grief and guilt she would feel if her parents left this planet too soon. The thought of her feeling that kind of pain worried him.

Eventually, he would want to hear everything about her parents and the frustration she felt there. Eventually, he would have to tell Anya about his parents. It would be a difficult story to tell.

Today's adventure was about getting to know each other, enjoying the meteor shower and stars, certainly not opening up family wounds. They would get to all that eventually.

Now, they were driving along the Arkansas river toward Cotopaxi. The glow that had left Anya during the conversation about her parents returned as she watched the slow river collapse into stints of white water. The river was high from all the winter runoff. Surely, a river rat had already died trying to run those rapids. Every year someone did. She went on about her love for the Arkansas and all rivers, pointing out some of her favorite fishing holes, talking about some of her rafting adventures in detail.

Delighted by her love for the outdoors, he pointed out his favorite fishing holes too. Together, they tried to spot the Big Horn Sheep that blended in with the cliffsides.

"One of my favorites things about this stretch of road," she said. "Is coming out of the valley to see the mountains. And when you take that turn at Texas Creek toward Westcliffe, seeing the Sangre de Cristos, it's a nice little surprise. I love bringing people up these roads and watching their expressions when they come in view of the mountains," Sam wondered if those people were friends since her family was small. He even wondered if she had brought men up here. If so, how many? How many people had she brought to the places that captured her? How many of them took advantage of that? Anya rolled down her window, letting her delicate hand surf in the wind.

"Would you ever live anywhere else in the world?" He asked.

"Where else could there ever be?"

"I don't know. Page, Arizona?" He laughed.

"Yeah, right! It's hot as fuck in Arizona," she exclaimed.

"How about somewhere colder?" He asked.

"I hate the cold," she laughed. "Snow is pretty as long as I don't have to go out in it."

"Wait, what?" Sam laughed at her, adjusting his position in the seat to look at her. He was smiling. "Why in the hell do you live in the Gold Camp District then? You know it's a couple thousand feet short of a 14er, meaning winter is most certainly happening, right?" He asked.

"I know, I know. I don't make any sense at all. I love it up there in the summers and fell in love with the mountains. At least I can snuggle inside during the cold rather than sweating my ass off in the desert heat," she said.

"That's very true. So, do you not like snowboarding or skiing either?" He asked, playing with the fluff of his beard, anticipating her answer. Anya bit her lip and laughed.

"I've never been snowboarding before, and I've only been skiing once. I just don't think I would like it very much," she whispered. Sam clutched his chest with his free hand.

"You've broken my heart, Anya!" He said dramatically. He dropped his hand to his lap, looked at her, and winked. He swore he could see her blushing.

"I'm sorry! I always meant to at least try snowboarding but never met up with any of my friends who do like it. Plus, it's cold," she said. "I also know my ass print would be all over the mountain after the first day. How about you? Do you snowboard or ski?"

"Every single year," he said. "I actually hate the snow but love snowboarding as long as I am properly suited up. Plus, I run the ice rink in Victor," he said.

"Do you really?" She turned in her seat, forgetting about the cliffs in the valley and the rushing river waters. Her leg was still propped up on the seat, and she had both arms wrapped around it.

"Yeah, I help flood it every winter when it starts getting cold enough. Every Sunday until Spring comes around, we have a drop-in, and then we sit around in the warming hut and drink beer afterward. It's one of my favorite times of the year," he said.

"I'm awful at ice skating," she said. Sam looked at her again. Her posture turned directly toward him now. He reciprocated by turning his body to her as best as he could.

"Don't worry. I'll teach you."

"Okay," she smiled.

He looked at her, desperate to grab for a hand or twist a lock of her hair around his finger the way he was getting wrapped around hers.

"So, I still don't know where we are going," she said.

Sam looked at the clock. It was nearly 8:00 p.m. The sun still had not fallen over the horizon, and they still had an hour or so to go before they arrived.

"Really? You haven't figured it out yet?" He asked.

"No. I have a guess. But without knowing how many hours until we get there, it's hard to say," Sam smirked. But he knew she would figure it out by the time they arrived at Poncha Springs to drive down HWY 285. He wanted to see the look on her face when she figured it out.

"You'll know soon enough, but I'm not going to tell you how much time until we get there."

"Well, alright then."

When they neared the end of the valley, the towering Collegiate Mountains came into view, blending so well with the Sangres, it was almost impossible to tell they were two separate mountain ranges. Not a single speck of snow clung to the peaks. They were completely bare. A hot summer melting away the snowcaps until the rivers and lakes were full of cool glacier waters. It would be weeks before the dirt and rocks carried with it would clear out and make for perfect fishing. They talked about the CFS level of the rivers, recalling the highest CFS they had ever rafted and where. As they drew closer to the Collegiate Mountains, Anya thought she might know where they were going.

"Are you going to Mt. Princeton?" She asked, looking at the sign that suggested Salida was just a few miles away. What lies near that area was one of his favorite hot springs. "If we are, I'm totally screwed because I don't have a swimsuit," she said.

"Good guess!" He chirped. "But no."

"Damn. Where the hell are we going?"

"You'll see."

They followed HWY 50 toward Poncha Springs, rounding Poncha Mountain. When Sam drove into town, past the Walmart, turning to 285, a light flicked on in Anya.

"We're going to the Sand Dunes!" She yelled. A smile stretched across her face.

"Yahtzee!"

"Oh my gosh! I have never been stargazing in the Sand Dunes," she said.

"Well, that makes two of us," he replied. It would be several more minutes until they hit 17, and from there, it was about an hour and a half.

"So, it's both our first time. How simply lovely," she said.

Lovely couldn't begin to explain it.

Their first adventure together was an adventure neither of them had embarked on. An adventure Sam hoped would be the catalyst for something grander between them.

They came to Mears Junction, where they would follow the long stretch of road beside the backside of the Sangres. The sun was lowering on the horizon, setting the sky on fire. The clouds left on the wind streaked the sky in fuchsia, trying to cover the incoming darkness. Soon the stars would flicker into existence, but not before the night started its descent on the mountains to the left of them. A battle of who was greater—the earth that had shifted into tough peaks or the vast space that echoed into infinity.

As the day faded, the view of Anya in his passenger seat fell into a shade. The sky was a darkened rainbow that would inevitably end in a deep navy blue. They drove down the straight road, passing Moffat, watching each star sparkle into view. After an hour, they could see the tan mounds of sand crash into the mountains like ocean waves. The tan shade was changing to deep violet, reflecting the sky above. From a distance, the dunes appeared massive, but with each mile they drew near, the dunes became larger, reminding them of their greatness. By the time they neared, the dunes were their own mountains but made of softness, like bread or cookie dough. Yet, if the wind was high and fast, the smallest grains would pierce your skin like thousands of mini knives.

Tonight was quiet.

The wind wasn't blowing, and the clouds were clearing. If this weren't a sign that this is where Sam needed to be, he wouldn't believe in higher powers anymore. They passed by the Gator Park just minutes away from the turn to Lane 6 N leading toward Sand Dunes, taking a nice drive around the mounds until they hit CO-150. The sun continued to set, and Sam flipped on his headlights, clearing the dusk with a path of light. After reaching CO-150, they took a left. The desert wasteland slowly dissolved into the mounds like beaches do into the sea, yet unmoving. They came to a near-empty parking lot, seeing the dances of small fires where the nearest campground resided. By now, Anya was on the edge of her seat, staring anxiously at the mounds, rambling in excitement.

After parking, they got out of the truck, feeling the heat wearing off to make space for the cool air to settle. If it got chilly, the two of them had plenty of blankets to get them through the evening and a thermos of coffee if that wasn't enough. Anya took the coffee and a lump of blankets and sleeping pads.

"I can't believe you drove us all the way out here," she said.

"Well, go all in or just go home," he said. "Stargazing should be done properly."

"And you know how to stargaze?"

"Well, no, but I can certainly dream up the proper ways," he said. "Come on. Let's go."

They walked to a line of trees blocking the parking lot. There was a faint sound of rushing water. Medano Creek was flowing well this early on in the summer. He hadn't accounted for that and knew the water would be glacier cold. They passed through a doorway in the trees and came to a panoramic view of the dunes and the creek rushing over the sand. The water was mid-calf deep.

"Okay. We have to wade through the water," Sam said. He took off his shoes and socks, rolling up his pant legs. Anya stood in the sand, looking down at her jeans.

"I don't think my jeans are going to roll up," she said. He looked at her legs. Her jeans were so tight, they were practically painted on her body. "Unless…" Sam looked at her.

"Unless what?" He asked.

"Unless I take my pants off," she said. Sam stared at her, eyeing her figure in the approaching darkness. He toyed with the idea of agreeing to this. The coy look on her face made him smile as she waited for his response. She was serious. Sam walked over to her, his pant legs rolled up nearly past his knees. Her posture shifted from shy and apprehensive to bold and sexy.

God. He wanted her. He stalked over, putting his hand out to take hers. "While that would be a lovely sight, how about I carry you over on my back?"

She smiled. "You're serious?"

"Dead serious. You can piggyback and I'll come get everything else," he said.

"Okay," she snickered, taking his hand. That laugh made him smile every single time he heard it. Sam led her to the rushing water and let her jump on his back. He felt her legs around his sides, her breasts hugging against his back, and her arms feeling the hardness of his chest. Her hair fell to the side of his face as he trudged through the surprisingly strong currents of water that washed over the sands. The water was freezing, fresh off once snow-packed slopes. Anya held tight, pressing all parts of her body into his. Every encounter, every touch, no matter how innocent, made the heat rise in his chest. He wouldn't need a blanket tonight if he stayed near her.

"Excuse me," she said. "Can you please hurry up? You're wasting the night. I just saw twenty meteors fly by," Sam could hear the smile in her voice and smell the lavender in her hair.

Giggling, he gripped her tightly. "If you want, I could just drop you in this cold ass water instead." She tightened around him.

"Absolutely not," she giggled.

"We're almost there."

Sam made it to the other side of the wide creek and waded back across to get the blankets. While she waited, Anya took off her shoes, dipping her bare feet into the chilly waters. Sam could see her, hands on her hips, watching him in the distance. Her golden hair nearly reflected the light from the stars, which continued to brighten.

After a few trips, Sam came back to dry land to find Anya with her shoes in her hand and her feet snug in the fading heat from the sand. She helped Sam carry the blankets, pillows, and sleeping pads further away from the creek. They found a place to set up a nice area to lay down. No other person was in sight. Sam smoothed the blankets out over the sands and invited her to sit down.

While they waited for total black, they faced each other, sharing the thermos of coffee Anya brought, which was still steaming when she unscrewed the lid. Anya glanced anxiously at the sky. It was well after 9:00 p.m. now. Closer to 10:00 p.m.

"I think there's a meteor shower tonight, but we probably won't see any until after midnight," he said, looking up.

"Once the cities go to sleep," she said, taking a sip of her coffee. "And you did your research."

"I did," he grinned.

"Well, we have time. I'm not worried," she said.

When the evening crept in with a desert chill, they snuggled underneath blankets, laying their heads on the pillows to stare up at the night sky.

"What's your favorite constellation?" He asked.

"Pleiades." In the Taurus constellation. He was glad he covered that one.

"Where is it right now?" Answering quickly, she aimed a pointer finger to the sky.

"It's the little one that is hard to see and sort of looks like a microscopic little dipper. I can't exactly point it out to you," she laughed.

He searched the sky for it, ultimately finding it in the darkness.

"What do you love about it?" This question she did not answer quickly.

"I really don't know," she said. "It's not my favorite so much as I'm just heavily drawn to it," she finished.

"Interesting," Sam said, devouring her words. "How so?" Anya remained silent.

"It's ridiculous. You'll probably think I'm crazy," she said. As if that wasn't more intriguing. Now, he had to know why it was ridiculous being drawn to a constellation. They had already talked about life on other worlds and Marvel movies preparing humans for the imminent introduction of extra-terrestrials. How much weirder could it get?

"Try me. Let me in on those big thoughts," he said. She stayed silent longer, but he could see her searching her thoughts, trying to find the right words.

"Well..." she began. "I've loved it since I was a kid. Some say there is a race of aliens who come from that constellation. And... I don't know. I watched this YouTube video about what they are like. Basically, they are incredibly loving and kind people. Some of these videos say Pleiadians actually walk among us. I guess I just identified with that," Sam stayed silent. He had not researched all the alien races.

Damn it.

"So, you identify with a race of people who are meant to be loving and kind to others?" He asked to clarify. She nodded.

"Yes," She said softly.

"That doesn't sound crazy at all."

"I guess that crazy part is me thinking I could actually be one."

"A Pleiadian?"

"Yeah. But that's impossible and absolutely absurd. That I would be this great super being shot down from the stars to spread love and encourage connection."

"Why?" He asked. Anya shrugged.

"Why is it possible to believe in God without question, who we've never seen, but then not believe in the presence of otherworldly humans, which there is growing evidence and theory of?" He asked.

"That's a good question," she said.

"I don't think there is anything wrong with wanting to be that, let alone think you are, especially if the point is to love people and bring them together," he said frankly. "You could be an alien or an angel. Who's to say you can't?"

"Society as they're sending me to the looney bin," she said.

Sam scoffed. "If you want to be a cosmic angel, spread love, and encourage connection, that's your choice. You don't always have to let people in on that."

Anya laughed. "Cosmic angel. I like it."

He heard her smiling again. "Have you told anyone else this?"

"No."

"Why did you tell me?"

"You asked."

"That's true," he said. "Thank you for sharing that with me."

Sam could feel her fingertips dancing beneath the blanket, the movements rippling in the fabric. A nervous tick. The stars twinkled above. It was still not dark enough for the meteors to show themselves. The Milky Way started to reveal its starry path above, drawing a line from each end of the horizon across the middle of the sky. He moved his hand to Anya's, lacing his cold fingertips into hers, and she let him. It was only then that he felt her shaking.

"Are you cold?" He asked, alarmed.

"No."

"Are you sure? Your hands are ice, and you're shaking."

"I'm just nervous."

Sam's touch left hers and turned onto his side to look at her, ignoring the second most important reason they had made the trip here.

"About what?"

"You."

Sam's heart jumped. This talk was happening, and suddenly he was shaking too. She turned onto her side, wedging her hand behind the ear closest to her pillow to look at him. His eyes softened, but he didn't close the distance between them.

"You make me nervous too," he said.

"Why do I make you nervous?" She asked.

"I feel like, when I look at you, I'm running full speed into the light, and I can't stop. There is this magnetic force pulling me to you, and I can't stop it, even if I wanted to, which I don't. You just amaze me." Sam saw tears glistening at the corner of her eyes, the stars above reflecting in them like flecks of glitter.

She was not going to come to him.

Sam had to go to her.

He inched closer to her, and her eyes flicked up to meet his.

"What did I say?" He asked.

"Nothing bad. It's just probably the sweetest thing I've heard," Sam paused. "The problem is, I don't know how to believe it."

Sam ached. "You've been hurt."

"Yes," she said. "A lot."

"I understand," he placed a hand on her shoulder, moving to her shining hair to brush it from her neck. With his thumb, he smeared a tear trail from her cheek where it found a resting place on the plump curves of her face. Sam could go to war with those men. "How could you possibly ever believe that truth when every single man has used it for any other intent other than something genuine?"

"Yeah. I'm sorry that I don't believe you," she said.

"You don't have to be sorry," he said. "It's not your fault for how they treated you." His hand was still resting on her cheek.

"Being vulnerable like this, it's embarrassing. Terrifying," she said. Sam traced the line of her cheek down to her chin, lifting it to meet his gaze.

"I'm going to do everything I can to prove that I'm one hundred percent invested. I know you may not believe those words right now, but I hope you will be able to trust my actions," Sam said.

Anya looked into his eyes. Those pools of blue were still bright in this vast blackness, stars sparkling in them and dotting each iris in random wavy patterns like unpredictable ocean waves. Anya reached up to his wrist, massaging his skin with her small hand, choosing not to say anything.

Sam drew her close to his chest, and she fell into him as if she had fit there all along. The night grew blacker as they lay beneath the stars. Meteors swept across the sky, leaving trails of light in their wake. Sam spent the evening making wishes. His cosmic angel, his lavender goddess, his delicate lady resting at his chest, marveling at the unearthly miracles streaking into orbit. Like her unexplainable and strange connection to the stars, he couldn't explain his draw to her, the wonder settled in his arms.

When they had little to say, Sam remembered the playlist he had made for her. He rolled over, the one arm holding her, a gesture reminding her he would not be going anywhere.

"What are you doing?" She asked.

"I made you something," the hue of his phone screen flashed into view, blinding him into an eye squint.

He searched his phone for the playlist—one of the many actions he would use to show his devotion to her. When the music started playing, she smiled, falling deeper into the crevice of his chest.

"You made me a playlist?" She asked.

"I did. It's a playlist of songs all singing about stars," he said.

The pace of his heart quickened at the shared anxiety of being vulnerable. It was a terrifying thrill, one that he hoped to learn well with her. The first song that played from the small speaker was *Under the Stars* by John Legend. As if the moment could be more perfect.

"No one has made me a playlist since I was in middle school," she said. "I love it."

Sam planted a single delicate kiss on her forehead, feeling her softness at his lips. That night, he thanked the stars over and over until they fell asleep beneath them.

EIGHTEEN

Anya laid in Sam's arms, listening to his heart pounding fiercely in his chest. She laid with many men, rested this same ear on chiseled chests rising in calm breaths, listening for any beats that might skip within her presence. Seldom did she hear a heart pump behind a ribcage like Sam's was.

Anya wanted to believe every word he said to her. Felt foolish and embarrassed by her display of sadness and incredulity. For telling him the outrageous notion that she was a product of the stars. Not realizing, in those words, that all people are. It was the first time she had uttered that possibility out loud and still didn't believe it herself. Either she was resisting greatly, or it was inane.

It took great convincing for Anya to enjoy this transient moment in time, him holding her like she mattered. By tomorrow evening, he would be gone. That's what being genuine and vulnerable usually left her with.

Nothing.

He would tell the town she was crazy. They would believe him over the stranger. Inevitably, she would be forced to move from her slice of heaven to avoid all people and their judgments. She would start her life from scratch again, adding an extra layer of protection to herself, along with a vow that she will never show these parts to anyone again.

Anya was preparing herself for another rejection, coating herself in a thick layer of shame and embarrassment. No sane person would be with someone who identified with a bullshit extra-terrestrial story made up by people on YouTube.

No one.

She could barely convince herself of this outlandish idea. Why on Earth would Sam believe it before her?

As if he could hear the destructive thoughts stampeding through her mind, Sam gripped her tightly, enveloping every inch of her in his own warm and inviting energy. It pulsated between them. The bulge of his chest was soft like a pillow. The set of arms holding her were strong, ready to protect, an embrace that felt like home.

If she invested too quickly, too enthusiastically, he would leave her. It was the routine that she had become accustomed to. There was no denying one thing. Sam was not pushing her to go too fast. He wasn't pushing to fuck her and still hadn't kissed her. Instead, he just held her and listened.

It would take a lot more than this for her to relax, to let him in, and feel safe about that decision. The very thought made her panic. To find a sense of calm, she listened to each of Sam's breaths entering and leaving his lungs. Felt the rough curves of sand beneath the place they rested. Let the distant chirps of crickets and crackles of campfires rock her to a near slumber as music played beside them. Watching the sparkling stars glitter in place and the silent meteors dash through the universe, a calm finally settled, and she felt safe again.

They didn't do what they came here to do.

They didn't watch the meteors.

They didn't play connect the dots with the stars.

They didn't recite the stories for each constellation.

They didn't pretend to be people they weren't.

They were just two fleeting souls in one of four billion galaxies passing time before dissolving back into the very dust that drifted from the stars they slept beneath. Two infinitesimal blips on a boundless black map just feeling their way through the most bewildering and necessary journeys of all.

Love, connection, and belonging.

She is walking through a field of bright green, towers of smooth rock hundreds of feet high above her. The rock is a faded red against the cerulean sky. She followed a narrow dirt trail around the rock towers leading her into a clearing that opened wide to show the infinite horizon.

Beneath the sky was more red rock, but the green grass blowing in the wind was now turning a sad tan. From her spot on the grass, Anya looked into the distance to see a giant, majestic piece of slanted rock sliding down from another mountain of rock lined just to the right of it. From a distance, Anya saw a perfect square gouged out the side of the sloping rock was cut out as if someone had done it with a large hammer and chisel.

She squinted, trying to make out the definition completely. Perhaps her mind was playing tricks on her. Anya tried to move her feet, but they wouldn't budge.

When she looked down, she saw rock had solidified around her feet, keeping her from any movement. Anya wiggled in place, desperate to leave the place she was now rooted to. Desperate to make it to the rock and soothe her curiosity. The rock wrapped around her ankles, knees, thighs, hips, stomach, chest, neck. Anya started to panic, hyperventilating, clinging to breaths as the rock circled around her chin, threatening to choke her breath and words.

"Please, no! Let me go!" The rock covered her mouth, and her eyes widened. As the rock swallowed her, the view of slanted rock disappeared from her view.

Anya woke up, trying to push herself out of Sam's embrace. Dawn was breaking, and the sky was a marbled orange, pink, and blue.

"Whoa!" Said Sam, who was startled awake. He released his hold on Anya, throwing his hands up in the air in surrender. "I'm sorry, Anya. What did I do?"

Anya looked around, remembering that she was at the Sand Dunes with Sam. They had slept through the night on the beach not far from Medano Creek. They hadn't moved all night. When she looked up at him, he was staring back at her, eyes wide with fear.

"It's okay," Anya whispered. "It's okay. I just had a bad dream," she finished, putting her forehead to his. Sam put his hands down and relaxed his shoulders, letting his panicked breathing slow. "I'm so sorry. I didn't mean to startle you," Anya said.

"It's alright. I didn't want you to feel like I was doing something I wasn't supposed to," he said. Anya looked up, smiling at that comment.

"Well, I appreciate that," she laughed. Sam still kept his distance. With the incoming sunlight, he looked beautiful in the morning. His thick beard was now awry, and his eyes were dark shades of amber.

"Let's lay back down and watch the sunrise," Anya said. Sam smiled at this, intertwining into a comfortable embrace, finding the sun as it rose to kiss the mountain tops. After the sun started its intense shine on them, they packed up their things, waded through the creek, and found their way back to the truck.

Anya's stomach grumbled so loud it nearly embarrassed her.

"Oh, man," Sam said. "We need to get you some breakfast! Can you last until we get to Poncha Springs? I know a great restaurant we can go to," he said.

Anya's stomach felt like it would eat itself, but she could wait that long.

"Oh, yeah. That should be fine," Anya said, putting on her seatbelt. "You know, there might be some coffee left in that thermos," she said. Unscrewing the cap, she could see wisps of steam rise from the mouth of the bottle. Sure enough, there was coffee in there. As Sam got the truck started, she poured herself a small cup.

"Would you like some?" She asked.

"If there is some left," he replied.

"There's a little bit. I'll give you some of mine. I don't mind sharing," Sam smiled, taking a right turn out toward the main road. Anya found the other cup and carefully poured the rest of the coffee and a little bit of hers in the cup. Careful not to spill it, she handed it to Sam.

"Thank you, kindly."

"You're super welcome," she took a sip of the hot coffee. They drove back the way they came, moving alongside the familiar speeding mountains toward Poncha Springs.

Within an hour, because Sam was speeding, they arrived in town. Sam found the little restaurant he had talked about, Robin's. Her stomach grumbled again knowing what was coming. She hadn't eaten since yesterday—the newest book and time with Sam consuming her life.

"God, I'm starving," she said.

"Me too," Sam said, leading her in. The hostess led them to a table outside on their patio. Each one was black metal patio furniture with matching chairs. The awning was built with 4x4s and canvases stretching over tables and chairs and surrounded by green trees. After ordering more coffee, they ordered their breakfast. Sam ordered bacon, eggs, hash browns, and French toast without looking at the menu as if it were routine. Anya had huevos rancheros with a side sausage links, salivating at the thought of each salty bite of eggs, beans, and hash browns. This was one of her favorite breakfast plates.

"So, what did you dream about?" Sam asked, sipping coffee and looking above his cup at her.

"Oh, it was sort of weird. I'm not quite sure what I was dreaming," she said.

"Well, I'd love to hear it," he said, taking another sip, eyeing the waitress who walked by with three plates of food stacked up the length of her arm.

"Okay. Well, I'm walking through a meadow, and these huge rocks were towering above me. I'm following this path that eventually leads me to a huge clearing. From a distance, I see this big rock, but it looked like a square was cut out in it. When I moved to take a closer look, I couldn't. Rocks were creeping up my legs. Within seconds, the rocks had covered my whole body. That's when I woke up," she finished. Sam was studying her as she spoke.

"Hmm," he said. "Very interesting."

"It is?"

"Of course. I think dreams can tell us something about ourselves. Although, I'm not sure what they are trying to tell you," he said. Anya thought back to some of her most recent dreams.

Bathing in celestial oceans.

Potentially jumping out of airplanes.

One thing she couldn't do. Another she wouldn't do.

She wasn't sure what messages she could get out of any of those.

"Do you dream?" She asked.

"Not really. If I do, I usually forget," he said.

"Well, that's a bummer. I love dreaming," she said. Anya thought about some of the dreams she had in the past. How each one was a miniature adventure that seemed eternal when she was experiencing it, and she loved any kind of adventure.

"You must dream a lot then," he said, looking intently at her.

"I do," she said. His gaze on the waiters passing by had stopped. Sam was now focusing on her completely. Anya always forgot how intense his stare could be when he looked at her. For a moment, she panicked, realizing she hadn't checked her hair or her make-up since she woke up. She must have been a mess,

"I'm going to go wash my hands really quick. Get all the sand out of them." He didn't argue. She found her way to the bathroom. When she got to the mirror, her appearance was better than she expected. Some flecks from her mascara had fallen to her cheek, so she took a single paper towel, drenched a small portion with water and then wiped the blackness from her eyes. After fluffing her hair, she looked somewhat normal again. Leaving the bathroom, she returned to the table to see that their breakfast had arrived. Sam was waiting for her to come back before eating. A polite gesture she instantly adored.

"Thank God," she sat down. "It felt like this would take an eternity to get here."

Anya and Sam devoured their breakfast in near silence, but Anya could still feel his eyes on her. She was sure he was laughing at her as she wolfed down her breakfast like a wild animal. When she looked up, he affirmed her feelings and chuckled nervously with a mouthful of food puffing up her cheeks. She swallowed her bite and spoke.

"Sorry, I'm such an animal. This is just so good," she said.

"Oh, I love a girl that can eat," he said.

"Well, get ready then. I eat everything I can. I love food."

"I do too."

"Do you cook?"

"Oh, yeah. I love cooking," he said. Anya took another bite of her toast. "We should do it for our next date. Cook something together," he said. Anya looked at him but kept chewing her food. She must have misheard him.

Did he just say next date?

"You want to go on another date with me?" She asked.

Sam giggled. "Why wouldn't I?"

Anya replayed last night's confession in her head. How she had divulged information to him about being a creature of the stars. She was sure he would not want to date her after that. Perhaps he was just saying that to make her feel better. To let her down easy before he stopped seeing her. But Sam looked at her with serious eyes and a sly smirk.

"No reason," she said. "I would like that, though." Sam finished the last few morsels on his plate, washing it down with his last bit of coffee.

"How about later this week? Maybe Wednesday or Thursday night?" He said. Anya couldn't believe it. Sam wanted to see her again. He was making plans with her right now.

"How about Wednesday?" She asked. Anya wanted to choose the closest day from today, hoping he wouldn't change his mind. "I get off at five," she said.

"How about we meet at 5:30 p.m. Where do you want to cook?" He asked. Anya thought for a moment. She hadn't invited anyone to her home since building it. Sam would be the first one to visit. Anya regarded her home as her safe place. A haven. She needed to be careful with who she let enter it. Making it a place of memories, happiness, love, and acceptance was her priority. Inviting someone over, especially someone she still didn't know the true intentions of, made her nervous. Anya didn't like the idea recalling memories of someone in her home after they had long left her life. Having Sam overexcited her and scared her. After that innocent kiss, the one that threatened thousands more kisses, she wasn't sure what she would do with him in a private space.

Oh, that kiss.

However, Sam had been a gentleman. Perhaps it would be alright if he came over to cook with her.

"How about we do it at my house?" She said. Sam perked up at the suggestion. His entire posture smiling at her.

"It's a date," he said.

NINETEEN

Sam couldn't wait to see Anya again. It had only been a few weeks since he'd met her. If Sam looked at himself in the mirror, he might not know the man who was staring at him. The one so overtaken by this woman. How had she captured him in such a short time?

If this was love at first sight or the kind of love spun from films in a theater, he could finally understand what everyone was fussing about. Whatever he was feeling, the profound need to be near someone, to care for their heart, or ensure their protection, that was what he felt for Anya. If it came down to saving her life, give him dozens of horrid ways to die, and he would carry out each painful one.

Sam was sure he had never felt *this* before.

Each morning since the Sand Dunes, when the heat had risen to the loft, he woke up with an intense yearning for her to be next to him. One that made him writhe beneath his blankets, looking for comfort. An aching restlessness in his body that wouldn't afford him solace in a place that was once cozy and inviting.

These mornings started with a vow that he would keep it together, exercise patience. There was no need to rush this extraordinary thing happening between them. Men around the globe would try to convince him this was animal instincts, his need to procreate, that this wasn't love, just a vigorous lust consuming him. Nothing more than the lizard brain unable to think rationally. Sam convinced himself this was more than the poor excuse for the animal need. That was a sensation he knew well. He had acted on that sensation countless times before. This was a longing. A desire for the missing piece that made him whole, the single instance in his eternity that would define him, the entire reason he was living this human life. To return to the split essence hurtling across the universe in search of its match.

Sam laid in bed, no longer caring to get up for the Stellar Jays or the lone rabbit that had already made its rounds. He stared up at the ceiling tiled with old planks of wood much too close to his own face. He wondered if Anya was feeling this same way about him. If he had driven her near a pleasant madness like she had done him. Had she seen him as the other half of her split soul?

At the Sand Dunes, she allowed him to inch a smidge closer. Anya was mysterious and odd but in a captivating way. She was plagued with monumentally complex thoughts that she wouldn't burden anyone with. But those burdens ate her up, threatening to swallow her very existence. He could tell she was anxious to release them.

With no place to air these thoughts, she would inevitably implode. She needed a place to feel safe, and it was clear she hadn't found it yet. She had burdened him with one single shocking thought that wouldn't sit right with others and felt honored for knowing it.

With her in his arms on a bed of sand, the flickering stars faded away. Who needed billions of galaxies, stars, and handfuls of planets when Sam had captured his very own star?

Sam replayed that night. Wading through the creek, lying in the sand, her in his arms, falling asleep beneath the stars, waking to her pushing him away, the misunderstanding, breakfast together.

All of it.

Even Sam couldn't dream up such a perfect and genuine instance in time.

TWENTY

Anya was running out of reasons to avoid Sam or push him away. If she tried to make up a reason, none of them were good.

Sam taking her to see the stars was something no one had bothered to do for her before, even if she told someone she dated about her love for the stars. Anya remembered the black. After her eyes adjusted, she could see swirls of purple and navy in the sky just along the bright trail of stars known as the Milky Way. She dreamed of walking that trail with her own feet. The need to follow those stars to a different world was always a consistent and lofty desire. If anything, it was the single most familiar feeling she had ever known, even if it was unfathomable.

Anya was standing at her kitchen window, drinking her coffee, letting her mind wander amongst the stars hiding behind the day. This morning she was up early, unable to sleep. Her thoughts were not affording her that luxury, legs kicking through her blankets to find some sort of space to feel comfortable. Sugar was not brushing up against her leg like normal. Anya laid in bed for what seemed like hours thinking about her confession to Sam, thinking of the Pleiadians and how much she identified with them.

It wasn't unusual to exaggerate narratives in her head instead of seeing them as they truly are. Humans tended to do that. Maybe that's what was happening here. Maybe this truth just kept growing out of proportion to threaten her sanity.

She moved from the kitchen to her dining room table, grabbing her laptop on the way to sit down. There must be someone out there who could help her find more answers. Anya opened her browser to do a search. Her fingers hovered over the keyboard. She wanted to look for something that would explain this better, or someone. She searched her thoughts until a single term popped into her mind. Although weird, she decided to go with it.

She typed in 'Pleiadian Master.'

"Not my best search, but okay," she said aloud. When she hit 'Enter,' pages of results came up. Some talked about a council and ascended masters. Many websites still lived in the 90s or hadn't been updated since then. She deemed them not relevant or remnants of people who had tried to talk about Pleiadians decades before her. She searched through each page, glancing at the clock to make sure she left for work on time. There, she could continue her search between daily tasks. Disappointingly enough, none of the pages were helping her find the answers she needed. Although a common trend in her search was the mention of the spiritual self. Sugar stalked into the living area, giving Anya a chirp on her way to her food bowl.

"Come on," she said out loud. "You're in marketing. Expand your search." Anya stationed her fingertips at the keyboard again.

This time she typed in 'Spiritual Counselors.'

To her surprise, even more results came up, prompting her to narrow her focus to something more local. She added 'near me' at the end of her search term and hit 'Enter.' The first result was a website about Awakenings and finding your spiritual path—a topic more real to her than Pleiadians or religion. A potential route to understanding.

Clicking on the website, she started reading everything about the services offered by a couple out of Coal Creek, Colorado. Surprisingly close to her. They did energy work and helped guide people toward understanding their spiritual selves. There was no picture of the couple or description of who they were—just a description of what they do and glamorous shots of the Wet Mountains. Energy work was their specialty. They promised a combination of readings and clearing the blocks from your spirit body. It was a concept Anya was undoubtedly unfamiliar with but open to nonetheless. They also boasted their ability to help people connect to their true selves, something that intrigued Anya.

A single session with them wouldn't cost that much, and she was allowed to book an appointment online. Anya chose the intro session for this coming Saturday, setting a calendar reminder on her phone so she wouldn't forget. She would have to get through the week before getting any closer to her answers. Lucky for her, she had something else to keep her mind occupied until then, concentrating on her date with Sam later that evening.

He was going to come over so they could cook together. He would be the first person in her house since it was built, which was a big step for her. Since their last date beneath the stars, they discussed what they would cook together in flirty text messages, agreeing on a simple Indian dish, Butter Chicken. Sam was bringing all the ingredients, including the key ingredient for this recipe, masala, which couldn't be found in town. Sam had to go to the Asian Pacific Market in Colorado Springs to get it.

Anya looked at the clock again. It was almost time to leave for work, and she wasted too much time filling her morning with ideas of living in her fantasy world. It was time for reality. Anya sometimes felt like the real world was just as much of an illusion as those she usually dreamt about.

Giving Sugar a pat on the head, she took her bag and left for work.

There would be absolutely no time to learn about her star fantasies at work. Not today. Sami and Anya were busy finishing up tasks that would organize Cripple Creek's biggest event of the year, Donkey Derby Days. It was an event put in place to raise money for the herd of donkeys roaming the town. Any funds raised usually covered food, medicine, and other supplies for all twelve of them when winter came around. But the very name, Donkey Derby Days; Anya still couldn't believe this was the kind of thing she promoted in her job role, but she liked it anyway.

Anya and Sami danced through the routine of ordering generators, contacting vendors, placing those vendors in the appropriate spaces on the street, getting food trucks to come down, reserving stages for the bands, and confirming the bands that would be playing. By noon, the both of them had gone through three cups of coffee and tea each. This work was a lot for just two people.

They had one person who helped with the heavy lifting, an older gentleman named Paul, who was in his 70s but had more energy and strength than the average thirty-year-old. The work overwhelmed Anya some days, but she was always proud of how things turned out once the event was over. She even enjoyed cleaning everything up at the end.

Cripple Creek was a mini Las Vegas. It didn't usually sleep. The bright neons and the outside lights beaming on the sidewalks were a pleasant illumination on those nights. Depending on how tired she was, Anya would even stumble into one of the casinos to have herself a 'good job' drink before going home. Sometimes Sami came with. Other times she just went home.

Anya and Sami had a little over a week until Donkey Derby Days would start. Most of the intense work would take place the day of the event. Once everyone set up on the street, she and Sami made rounds up and down the booths to ensure all the vendors were happy.

Sami and Anya spent most of their day finalizing aspects of this event while also trying to organize for the Fourth of July event. Most of the events felt like they existed right on top of each other. Somehow, they were able to stop for an hour to have lunch at Rudy's Diner in the Christmas Casino, an extension of Bronco Billy's. It was the only place they could get a veggie burger since Sami was mostly vegetarian. Rudy's also served the best pumpkin pie milkshakes, which used a whole slice of pumpkin pie.

The busy day flew by even faster than she realized. Soon, 7:00 a.m. turned to 5:00 p.m. By the time she was walking to her car, she realized Sam would be at her house in just thirty minutes.

When she arrived, she rushed into the house, making a direct line to her bedroom, where she changed her outfit from country girl to comfy-at-home girl. Sugar followed her, placing her little paws in each of Anya's footsteps.

Sam would be here soon, but she hoped he wouldn't be here any sooner than 5:30 p.m. Anya straightened the books on her windowsill. Cleaned out the coffee cup she left on the dining room table that morning and closed the laptop. The last thing she needed was Sam to look at her recent searches on Pleiadians.

It was 5:25 p.m.

As she frantically fluffed up pillows at her nook, she heard the crunch of tires on gravel, and his white Toyota pulled up behind her Subaru. He waltzed in the door in seconds, holding all the groceries in his hands.

"Hey!" He said.

"Hi!" Anya said back, debating on whether or not to hug him. Sugar chirped at the stranger before dashing away into a corner for safety.

"Wow. This is some house," he said. "It's literally incredible."

"Come on. I'll give you the tour," Anya led him through each part of the house, feet bare on the floor.

Sam reveled in the masterpiece that was her home, admiring all the details as she let him wander. Anya followed his eyes as he looked in every corner, unable to believe there were that many details for a person to marvel at.

To her, the house was very simple. Yet, Sam seemed like a 'find joy in everything' kind of guy.

"How was your day?" Sam asked.

"Really busy. Sami and I are getting ready for Donkey Derby Days."

"Oh, yeah. The biggest event of the year."

"It is definitely the most time-consuming. But I really love organizing it. How was your day?"

"Pretty good. We were busy too—a lot of tours and a lot of customers. But I'm starving. Are you ready to cook?

"Absolutely."

Anya and Sam started preparing the ingredients, cutting the chicken into cubes, getting the rice cooker going. The recipe for Butter Chicken was quite simple.

They let the chicken soak in a marinade of yogurt, garlic, ginger, masala, turmeric, cumin, chili powder, and salt for thirty minutes. The rice cooked in the corner, sounding through the small vented hole, and resembling a train tooting its horn. Anya welcomed Sam to one of her favorite beers. After the thirty minutes were up, they dropped a few tablespoons of oil in a pan, letting it heat to a pleasant sizzle.

By that time, the rice had sputtered to a stop and sat warming in the rice cooker. Sam added the small portions of chicken to the pan, letting them cook until they were brown.

Once all pieces cooked through, they removed them from the pan to add a healthy portion of ghee and chopped onions, letting them sweat. Sam scraped remnants of chicken stuck to the bottom until they disappeared in the onions. After the onions reached a caramel and translucent appearance, Anya added the garlic, ginger, coriander, cumin, and masala, letting it cook for another twenty minutes. As they waited, the two of them cracked open their second beer. Next, they added crushed tomatoes, chili powder, and salt, followed by another fifteen minutes of chatting as they finished their second beer. With each sip, Anya could feel herself ease into the comfort of the evening, realizing this may truly be a safe place; he may be a safe place.

Sam and Anya removed the tomato mixture from the pan and added it to the food processor, blending until it became a smooth reddish color. The pureed mixture returned to the big pan, where they combined heavy cream, a dash of sugar, and fenugreek leaves. Mixing that up, they added the final ingredient, the cooked chicken. They let it simmer for another ten minutes while they set the dining room table, letting the savory aromas invade their senses.

The creamy orange mixture and the large chunks of chicken bubbled in the pan. Sam helped Anya scrape small portions into clean white bowls filled with steaming rice. The kitchen was a mess of dishes, which wasn't usually Anya's style. She was a clean-as-you-go type of person. Instead, she constructed the small fantasy of washing dishes with Sam after enjoying the first meal they made together.

"We're really good," Sam said. "We should do this professionally."

"There isn't an Indian restaurant in the Gold Camp District. Maybe we can open one up!" The steam from their hot meals rose in the daylight, still shining through the windows, dancing in midair like a coy ghost. That was always a sight Anya wished she could photograph.

"They've tried so many restaurants in this town, even corporate ones, and they all went belly up."

"Why, though? They seem to get a lot of tourist traffic here."

"They just don't last through the winter. No one comes up here because of the roads."

"I've seen those roads in the winter. They're almost always clear. I heard Newmont had something to do with that. Being a 24/7/365 operation and all. Really, it's not that bad driving up here in the winter."

"You'd be very right. It doesn't change people's fears, though. Fear is a compelling motivator," that was something Anya could agree with.

Once they had cleaned their plates, leaving much of the butter chicken and rice leftover, they grabbed another beer and sat at the table, falling into that same easy conversation that started to feel so normal.

The more they talked, the more Anya felt at ease. It was effortless talking to Sam. As easy as breathing, as habitual as brushing your teeth or combing your hair. There was always something to talk about, and when there wasn't, the silence was easy to exist in. Anya didn't mind silences as long as it was in the comfort of someone she trusted. The painful silences that left two people searching for something to say, those silences were clear indicators that things just weren't clicking. Anya felt that sensation with many friends and lovers. But not Sam.

After their third beer, they cleared the table. Anya portioned the rice and butter chicken into separate containers, leaving enough for Sam to take home with him and enough to keep for herself. Next were the dishes, another innocent interaction she looked forward to sharing with him.

To Anya, this felt like an act of teamwork. How they work and problem solve together would be a great testament to how they could work in their relationship.

She believed in teamwork and equality. She believed in splitting checks at diners and both partners pulling the same weight. No single burden should fall on either sex just because of social constructs.

Anya scrubbed the plates, bowls, and pans while Sam rinsed and dried them off. After so many dates, Anya still wondered why Sam hadn't kissed her. It seemed odd to her since most men couldn't be patient enough to wait. Anya felt respected, but the growing sexual tension was on the brink of sexual frustration. Without thinking more rationally, she decided to ask.

"Can I ask you a question?" She asked while washing dishes. Sam glanced at her while she trembled beside him.

"Of course."

"Why haven't you kissed me yet?" Sam was in the middle of drying a plate but paused to look at her. Putting the plate on the counter, he turned to Anya, retrieving the soapy plate from her grasp, stealing away the nearest towel to take her free hand to wipe off the soap.

Turning her around, he faced her, closing the space between them until she was pressed against the counter and the edges dug into her. His closeness was a reminder of the night her cheek burned with his kiss and her whole body tensed.

Anya prepared for him to kiss her, thinking he might do it now that she asked. She hadn't dreamed up what it might be like to finally kiss him for fear of ruining the real thing when it came. Sam's golden eyes blazed into her, catching the bit of light still draining from the day. Depending on how he looked at her, his eyes turned a different shade of brown. Sometimes it was a shimmering amber. Sometimes it was a dark, almost black brown. Other days his eyes were like golden sun catchers. But today, his eyes resembled those of a hungry wolf's bright against a pale winter.

"Close your eyes," he commanded. Anya looked at his sun catcher eyes, realizing his serious but delicate tone. Closing her eyes, Sam took his fingertips and grazed them across her forearms. She trembled at his touch before settling into the tickling sensation. Anya felt her heart pound beneath her ribcage as he leaned into her ear and whispered.

Dropping his voice and octave, he spoke. "When I touch you, what do you feel?" Sam moved his hands along her skin which rippled with goosebumps. They moved to her hips and waist, where they danced around her belly button. Anya gulped, inhaling a sharp breath.

"I feel... skin tingling, my heart racing and... shivers up my spine," Anya felt her eyes soften and her body tense. Sam grazed the sides of her legs with his fingertips so slightly, Anya almost didn't feel them. Sam took it a step further, letting his lips hover at her neck. Anya ached for them to connect with her skin. Feeling the tremble of his breath flutter in her easiest spot for arousal.

"Anya," he whispered, sending a hot stream of shivers coursing through her. "You deserve to have every inch of your body worshipped to a blinding ecstasy," Anya tensed at his words, holding back a groan. Awaiting his next silky batch of words that would swallow her entirely.

"My every touch should light you on fire. And when the time comes, every inch of you I take in my mouth will be devoured, wholly and delightfully." Her knees nearly gave out. Anya was on the verge of begging for him, all parts of him.

"The waiting… The wanting… it builds that anticipation," he whispered, taking in the scent of her skin and hair.

"I'm waiting until you're on the brink of exploding. From there, you will be sick with desire. As will I. I want your lips and your body. That's certain. But what I desire more is your mind; for it to surrender at my touch, so you're lost in the very cosmos you dream so fondly of." Anya was already sick with desire. She was just good at hiding it. The words slipped off his tongue, and she wished he would continue.

"That's why I haven't kissed you yet," he finished returning his sultry tone to the regular cadence of speech. Anya had barely let out a sound, barely breathed. Whatever place she was lost to right then was made glaringly apparent on her face. Anya lost in the deep cosmos all because of a man's sensual, poetic words.

"You can open your eyes now," he said. Anya struggled to open them, feeling dizzy. She stared back into his eyes, still a blazing amber.

Anya's mouth was dry and her throat choked like ocean waves drumming at the backs of empty seashells. Wetting her lips, she watched Sam's coy smirk curl beneath his nose. Clearing her throat,

Anya and Sam returned to the dishes. Anya couldn't help but smile, silently replaying the last thirty seconds of Sam's sensual words, wishing they had turned into something more.

Sam left her with more than a plain wanting but desperation for him. One day, she would burst. If this was a game he wanted to play, she would work up the courage to play it too. Making him want her as much as she wanted him. She was intent on seeing who would cave first.

TWENTY-ONE

That Saturday, Anya woke up early and got ready for her trip to Coal Creek. She had never heard of Coal Creek before. She didn't even quite know what was in store for her in this session. What she did know is she needed to find answers. Solve the mysteries of herself. If only they could help solve the mystery of when Sam would kiss her.

Like any human, meeting the needs of your curiosity would always be a hot pursuit. It was strange how people in the world always seem to be on a quest for categorizing themselves. Finding that little box they fit in, so they felt they belonged. The hope they might find another person or two in that box who fits in their same category. Over time, Anya had gotten good at pretending as if she had never questioned her place in the world. By all definitions, Anya was normal.

Coal Creek wasn't too far away, about ninety minutes there, somewhere around Florence and Cañon City. Her nerves churned with anxiety and excitement. Anya had barely researched the ritual of self-discovery she was about to go on and wasn't sure what to expect. She figured she would just be ready for whatever might happen to her rather than try to prepare herself for it.

Driving along the hillsides dotted with trees, past a lake she didn't know the name of, she wondered how she might feel after she learned the truth about herself. If it would be the real truth and not the truth of some crazy alien cult. It was hard to know what was true in this world anymore. Everything concrete provides facts or evidence. Yet, Gods are well-believed stories that lack proof at all. People use books to tell their God's story. Some use it as a tool of manipulation. Claiming to carry out their acts in the name of God, whether lovely or cruel. God is so real, yet the concept of other worlds and beings is entirely out of the question. Concepts of people being products of another world, that's out of the question too. The world had already set its boundaries and limits on what was real and what wasn't.

If anyone didn't follow along, they were outcasts, misfits.

Somehow, people had grown in the mindfulness category over the years. People she knew in high school were suddenly finding themselves, improving their spirit, practicing mindfulness and kindness, now that they were old enough to make their own decisions. Anya wondered if her former classmates had told their parents about these lifestyle and belief changes. If they did, were they accepted?

Would her parents accept her if she believed something far different from their religion? It was a thought that plagued her.

Eventually, Anya would have to see her parents again. But she knew every piece of news she fed them would be an alteration of the absolute truth. Anya would tell them that she goes to church every Sunday and that she doesn't drink alcohol. She'll pretend she is still a pure and untouched virgin, even though she had been touched and by many; many of whom had never met her parents. She won't bring up any topics that stray from their belief systems. Anya had tried that before, and it only ever resulted in battles in the living room. It was why she hadn't talked to them in a while. If they knew where she was going and the answers she was looking for, they might disown her.

Anya came onto HWY 50 just outside of Cañon City, about thirty minutes away from Coal Creek. The anxiety was growing in her with each passing mile. Maybe she wasn't quite ready for the answer. Perhaps she wouldn't get any answers at all. Worst case, she would still be left wondering about herself. Either way, no matter how nervous she was, she was determined to start finding the answers, even if the first place she looked was odd.

She took a right turn off HWY 50 onto MacKenzie. The road was a slow crawl toward HWY 115, another curvy journey that would veer up a hill and off into countryside. Anya drove past dirt roads, towering bluffs dotted with trees. She drove through a place called Williamsburg, which looked like nothing more than a town of junkyards. People's homes were boarded up with old sheets of wood and metal panels while brand new trucks sat out front. One yard had a giant neon "m" sitting in their front yard, pointed up at the sky as if projecting a sort of weird bat signal.

Anya passed through Rockvale, realizing she had missed her turn to go to Coal Creek.

She drove past the oldest cabin still standing in the area, an empty park, and a post office—much more civilized than Williamsburg. Soon finding her way out of Rockvale, driving past an adobe house, she veered off the main road toward Coal Creek. The road took a swerving dip, and she was passing more houses. It was surprising how many people lived out here. Even more surprising was how nice some of the houses were.

She followed her GPS to a home tucked along a dirt road far off all other main roads. The house was sitting behind a lush green lawn fenced in with chain links, unlike so many other homes in the area. It was covered in white stucco and had a red metal roof. Four trees had grown tall enough to brush the clouds. One of them was a drooping juniper, and the pale violet berries littered the ground beneath it. The big windows had all the blinds and curtains drawn. Anya could only see dark outlines of the objects inside but noticed a light gray striped cat perched in one of the windows. Out back was a smaller house with the same red metal roof. Two older 300SD Mercedes sat in the dirt driveway along with two white trucks.

As she approached, a man and woman sitting at a table on their front lawn drew nearer in view. Both of them were barefoot, wiggling their toes in the soft grass. The man wore a light teal polo over his broad shoulders and khaki shorts. He had silver hair and Colorado sun-kissed skin. The woman was a rainbow of color in a flowing skirt that appeared to be made by hand and a tank top that hugged her slim waist. Her dark curly hair could easily be spotted from space. Anya finally pulled into the driveway next to one of the trucks. When she got out, the man and woman stayed seated but waved happily from their lawn chairs.

Anya shut her car door and made her way through the front gate. The cat in their window was wild-eyed with curiosity around this stranger entering the yard. As she neared the couple, they stood up to greet her.

"Hi, there! You must be Anya," said the man walking forward, the woman close by. "My name is Gwynn Roundtree. This is my wife, Sage Augustine. And that is Silas," he said, pointing to the cat in the window who struggled to meow through the glass barrier. Sage cracked a bright smile at Anya while she shook both of their hands.

"Nice to meet both of you," Anya said.

"Nice to meet you too, honey," said Sage. "Have a seat," she said.

"Would you like a cup of coffee?" Gwynn asked.

"Absolutely," Anya said.

"Cream and sugar?"

"Yes, please," she sat next to Sage while Gwynn retreated into their home.

In the sunlight, Sage's skin sparkled with flecks of glitter amongst the brown freckles that seemed to cover every inch of her. Up close, her curly hair was even more out of control but in a beautifully wild way. On her shoulder was a tattoo of the half-moon and star. On her ankle, a tattoo of Egyptian Goddess, Iris. Both pieces of body art had seen many years. Bangles upon bangles hung from her wrist, and she wore rings on nearly every finger. Her nose was pierced too. For a woman aging and aging well, her young spirit was obvious by her posture. Anya felt a motherly comfort vibrating off her.

"So, where did you come from?" Sage asked to break the silence. That was the single question she was looking to answer, but Anya knew that's not what she meant to ask.

"I drove down from Cripple Creek."

"It's beautiful up there."

"Yeah. I really love it. I built a house on a mountain there."

"You and Gwynn will have a lot to talk about then. He is a mountain man himself," Anya noticed a beehive off in the corner of their property, which was alive and buzzing.

"Do you keep bees? " Anya asked.

"Oh, yeah. I've been keeping bees ever since I was a child. My mother was a beekeeper," she said, looking over at them. "They're busy today." Just then, Gwynn emerged from the front door with a cup of coffee clutched in his hand.

"Sage doesn't bother to wear her suit when she keeps her bees," he said, placing the cup in front of Anya. He sat down to take a sip of his coffee. The strange motherly feeling she felt around Sage had now increased to a profound warmth Anya wasn't able to identify. She tried to focus.

"Aren't you afraid they'll sting you?" Anya asked. Sage looked back at the hive.

"No. I've been stung before, but if you don't swat at them, they'll leave you alone," she said.

"So, I heard you're from Cripple Creek?" Gwynn asked.

"I am."

"There are some awesome lakes up there to go fishing in," he said. "Do you fish?" Anya could feel her anxiety fade a little more with each minute of conversation. Up close, Gwynn was built like an athlete, carrying himself with that kind of confidence. But he had delicate features and kind eyes. Around his wrist was a bracelet of agate beads swirling in green and deep reddish-brown.

"Whenever I can. River fishing is my favorite, though. I usually catch more fish," Anya said.

"You know, I've been all over the state of Colorado, grew up in Pueblo. I have to say, river fishing is one of my favorite types of fishing too. Do you fly fish?" He asked. Anya noticed how the teal polo brought out the blues and greens in his eyes as they darted around the yard to follow a single robin.

"I do. I love fly fishing," Anya said.

"I like you already," Gwynn said. Anya smiled, taking a sip of her coffee. It was delicious, different from her blend. She couldn't identify what about the coffee was so tasty. It was just normal freshly ground coffee. Yet, there seemed to be something else in there, something she couldn't taste on her tongue. It was more of how it coated her core, soothing her from the inside out.

"So, what brought you here today, Anya?" Gwynn inquired. Anya hesitated, shocked with how quickly they were getting to the point. She wasn't sure if she was ready. The original reason she came here was disappearing in her fear and shame. She wasn't sure if she could handle telling these strangers her secret and revealing herself for possible rejection.

Shifting uneasily in her chair, she picked at her cuticles. The wind blew through the few wind chimes that hung just below the edge of the roof—suncatchers from the inside of their home projected specks of rainbow onto the green grass outside. Silas was now resting on the ledge near the window, giving up his desperate attempt to close the gap between him and his owners.

Anya searched the yard for something to ease her anxiety. She could feel Gwynn and Sage's eyes on her as patience radiated from them.

"I think…" she started. "I discovered something about myself," she said. The two of them waited for her to continue. "It seems so crazy to say out loud."

"Try us," Sage smiled. Anya slumped in her chair, crossing her arms in defense in preparation for rejection. She looked down at the ground.

"I recently discovered a video that made me think I may not be part of this earth," she glanced up at them, searching for any kind of shock on their face.

"Go on," Gwynn said.

"I've always felt like I just don't belong here. Like I'm... different," she continued.

"What makes you feel that way?" Gwynn asked, placing his elbow on the table to prop his chin in the palm of his hand. His blue eyes sparkled with wonder. Sage shifted one crossed leg to the other, and her bangles jingled with each movement.

"I've always had this strange connection to the stars, a single constellation in particular," she said, looking up at the blue sky as if she could see the constellations poking through the day. "Not a night goes by that I don't look up at the sky to marvel at those stars," she finished.

"Which constellation?" Sage probed further. This would be the honest truth, a sentence she wouldn't be able to take back. Saying it to another person would make it more real than its existence in her mind.

"Pleiades," she squeaked. Sage and Gwynn looked at her with a bright smile and then looked at each other, holding back giggles. As if they were speaking jokes telepathically. Anya felt rage rise in her. She knew it was wrong to tell more people such absurd beliefs. She felt the urge to get up and storm out the gate to her car, spin out and whip gravel into the sky and leave a path of dust behind her. Yet, she was rooted in place by the gravitational force these two people seemed to be. What kind of sorcery had she walked into?

"What's the problem?" she said, irritated.

"Nothing. You're Pleiadian. This is great!" Gwynn said, smiling more. Anya's arms dropped from their defensive posture.

"It is?" Anya was shocked.

"It is," Sage agreed.

"What made you realize you were?" Gwynn asked.

Anya straightened in her chair, ignoring her almost full cup of coffee. "How much I love the ocean—my connection to whales and dolphins. My favorite colors are jewel tones. I believe in compassion. I feel like I can't fully be myself emotionally. I'm deeply empathic and intuitive. Like, I can feel the pain in others sometimes to the point where I almost weep for them. My deep-seated detachment from everyone. To name a few," Anya said, waiting for their next question.

"Pleiadians," Gwynn started. "We've learned a lot about them over the years," he said.

"You believe in that stuff?" Anya asked.

"Of course, we do! We'd be ignorant not to," He replied. "The reason it's not more widely discussed is that people fear what they don't know."

"That's a painful truth," Anya said. "So, what can you tell me about them?"

"Well, Pleiadian Starseeds are known as a force of angelic nature brought to the planet to heal and bring teachings of love and compassion. Generally, they tend to be very attractive as human beings. They're typically recognizable by their physical looks and tend to have more feminine features. They also possess an intense magnetic draw. It's impossible for people not to feel a gravitational pull toward Pleiadians," he said. Anya was hanging onto every word, remembering this very explanation from her childhood as she searched his words for the sentence that would solidify her place in this identity. "From what I've learned, Pleiadian Starseeds are sent down in groups, spawned in human vessels and masquerading as these angels to be that positive and loving influence. If you strongly feel you are Pleiadian, it's likely you are here for that purpose. Do you feel like you identify with this truth?" Gwynn asked.

"I honestly don't know. I feel crazy for believing it. My family is really religious, and part of me feels like I throw out everything I grew up knowing if I believe this. I throw out everything they taught me and exchange it for their disappointment. I feel so much guilt and shame around it," Anya said. "I came here to find some answers, and I was hoping you could help me," she finished.

"What questions were you hoping to answer?" Sage questioned.

"I want to know if I am Pleiadian and what that means if I am. What do I even do with that information? How does it help me find where I belong? I thought about trying astral projection but don't know how real that even is." Anya huffed out all the words, feeling out of breath but lighter for saying it out loud to someone.

Gwynn looked out into the bluffs which cut across the blue sky and fluffs of scattered clouds. He closed his eyes to feel the air and listen to the wind chimes ring out into a silent echo. Sage opened her palms up to the sky. Normally, Anya's judgments would tell her to view this as odd, but she still felt a strange sense of comfort and ease in their presence.

"Your judgments and fears are blocking you, Anya," Gwynn said. "It will take several sessions to open you up to new paths. Awakenings can bring profound enlightenment. Don't expect to get your answer overnight. They will come, but don't judge them as they do. Together, we can work on opening your spirit up, offering you a place to search for these answers safely. Sage and I cannot give you the answers, but we can assist you in finding them for yourself. We can also guide you with astral projection but may need to clear some blocks first. Is that something you're interested in?" Gwynn asked. After hearing what he had to say about Pleiadians, Anya was more convinced about this being a possibility.

A large part of her was still holding back, protecting herself. Another part of her wanted to satisfy the curious thoughts that weighed heavy in her mind.

"Yes. I'm interested," Anya said.

"Before we begin, we are going to have you draw a picture," Sage said. "From that picture, we'll do a reading on you and ask you some questions. We'll take you out to the awakening room where you can draw your picture. Everything is ready," she said. Anya nodded. The two of them got up from their chairs. Anya followed them as they glided down the stone path to the front door of the awakening room that lived behind their home.

Just outside the door, there were two large rocks on either side of the path. One appeared to be a rather large piece of meteor, and the other was a large cluster of smoky quartz. Next to the quartz was a cast-iron cauldron looking rather witchy and filled with nothing but ash. On the outside wall next to the door hung a large white angel.

Gwynn and Sage welcomed her into the small room painted a pale yellow, bringing even more light to the room, a single slim window helping the light filter in. The aromas that invaded her senses were a calming clary sage and the looming smoke from a recently burned smudge stick. To the right of the door was a long shelf stretching from one side of the room to the other. It held dozens of stones and precious gems, all in different colors, shapes, and sizes. A line of pendulums laid evenly next to one another. In the middle of the room was a massage table covered with a plain sheet. Underneath the table were large pieces of rose quartz towers pointing north. There was a single electric fireplace in the farthest corner just before the small bathroom.

In the northeast corner was a small desk and chair where a blank sheet of paper was set up with a box of crayons opened wide. A single candle was lit next to the blank sheet of paper. Soft meditative sounds played in the corners of the room, soothing and relaxing her.

"We're going to give you as much time as you need to draw your picture. Once you're done, the two of us will do your reading. The reading could take some time depending on how willing you are," Gwynn said. He motioned to the chair, and Anya sat down.

"I just draw anything?" Anya asked.

"Yes. If you have trouble drawing, close your eyes, try to quiet your mind, and draw the first thing you see," Sage said.

With that, Gwynn and Sage disappeared from the Awakening room, leaving Anya alone with the music. She stared down at the blank piece of paper, and the candle flame danced alongside her while she closed her eyes. Meditation was not something she practiced often, and she struggled with quieting her mind at times. Most of her thoughts carried worry, anxiety, doubt, angst for her belonging, and, on occasion, deep sadness. When she closed her eyes this time, the first thought that entered her mind was the judgment of her situation. Although she felt safe and heard, she questioned the truth of it all. Anya reminded herself to let it go, working hard to quiet her mind's uncertainties.

"Focus, Anya," she said aloud. She relaxed her jaw, her shoulders, her breath, settling deeper into her seat. With each deep breath, she felt her body in the chair, the weight of her feet on the floor, and her arms firmly resting on the table. Slowly moving toward a more relaxed state, her mind cleared enough to see an image.

Anya took her first crayon from the box, connecting it to the paper, drawing hard and soft lines in color to eventually form a picture. She decided to use all colors of the rainbow and then some, blending them into an abstract portrait. When she had finished filling the page with color, she got up from the chair and wandered around the room, admiring the different crystal towers, stones, and tools used for healing.

Some of the stones were shaped into hearts, some of the tools were pieces of wood polished smooth with one feather at the end and seashells dangling from leather strings on the other end. A set of singing bowls dominated the corner of the shelf just beneath the sound system. A picture of Jesus laughing hung on the wall just next to the window above the shelf.

Within a few minutes of finishing her picture, Gwynn and Sage returned, ready for the reading. They instructed Anya to take off her shoes and socks and sit on the massage table. She did as she was told, feeling the cold floor tile beneath her feet. Gwynn took her freshly drawn crayon picture and folded it in quarters. He stared down at the drawing for minutes and then handed it to Sage, who did the same. Several minutes of silence passed.

"You done, babe?" He asked.

"Yes," Sage gave the picture back to Gwynn. Anya's feet hung from the table. She observed the two of them, wondering what was about to happen next.

"You've used a lot of great colors in the image. A lot of brown, some great greens," Gwynn looked at the picture. "This tells me you're grounded, but maybe a little too much. But it also tells me you are very prosperous, very endowed with good things. Do you feel grateful for those things?" he asked.

"I do," Anya said. "Not often enough sometimes."

"Why do you think that is?" Anya knew the answer right away. Her parents.

"My parents always taught me to be modest. To never gloat about what I have. I guess I always thought if I were too outspoken about how grateful I was, it would make me seem arrogant or entitled," Anya said. Gwynn continued to examine the picture. All Anya wondered was if she is passing the test. Then, Sage posed her first question.

"You seem very grounded like Gwynn said. It's marvelous how connected you are to the earthly life, but how connected do you feel to spirit?" One of her biggest upsets was her connection to her faith, but that felt different from her spirit.

"I don't feel connected to my faith. I feel as if the things the bible and church taught me were fake, like a form of brainwash. So, I avoided religion altogether," Anya said.

"Do you meditate?" Sage asked.

"No. Never. People always tell me to," Anya replied.

"Do you have visions or dreams?" Sage asked her.

"All the time. I have very vivid dreams."

"Dreams are an excellent way of receiving messages from the universe. We can help you interpret your dreams at another time," Sage said. "In your picture, there is a thick and heavy line drawn through the middle of your picture at the center," Sage showed Anya the picture she had drawn, seeing a kaleidoscope of color and the giant line through the middle from left to right. The light caught the dark colors existing at the top of the page versus the bright and joyous colors living at the bottom.

"The half of the picture below the crease represents connection to the physical body or Earth. There is a lot of brown and green there, which is good. It shows us you are very grounded and rich in your physical self. The half of the picture above the crease represents your connection to spirit or the universe. Your use of red and orange amongst gray and black tells me you're holding onto a lot of anger and a lot of judgment around your spiritual self or your faith," Anya felt her heart sink.

It was a truth she swore to never bother dealing with. If it were out of sight, if she buried it deep, she would never have to face how her parents and faith anger her. She would never have to feel the hurt they had caused her.

Anya had never told anyone how she felt betrayed by the faith that indoctrinated her, how it brainwashed her parents, and how it made them believe only certain people were capable of God's love. It was an utterly conditional love. And when Anya searched for other ways to express herself to her parents, they judged her in the name of God, telling her she was a sinner if she didn't follow the same path they had.

Some days, she hated her parents for having their conditions and judgments, not realizing she encompassed them at times, that she was far from the kind and loving Pleiadian teachings Gwynn and Sage just shared with her. Her capacity for love, compassion, and understanding were diminished because of her parents. Her blood boiled thinking of it. But it couldn't be their fault forever. She sobbed. Sage and Gwynn's few questions hit her precisely—hit her trigger with extreme accuracy. Her life was spectacular in all other areas except this.

"I hold a lot of judgments and anger. I've approached my parents to express who I am to them. They've judged me a lot for it. Each time I try and explain to them how that makes me feel, they never take accountability. Ever." Anya started to cry hard. "I can never understand why they can't just accept me and love me for who I am." As Anya wept, Sage was crumpling up the picture into a ball. The colors disappearing into the center until it was nothing but a white, imperfect sphere.

"Anya, listen to us. We know this is a difficult thing to accept after so much conditioning," Gwynn said. She looked up from her hands, sniffing hard while the tears still ran. "You are perfect. It is perfectly normal to seek acceptance from your parents, but it's not a defining factor of who you are. You must learn to love and accept yourself. Easier said than done. We know."

Anya continued to cry. She hadn't cried like this for a while. Hadn't confided in her closest friends about the trouble she faced with her parents. She never did anything but hold it all in.

"Why am I crying so hard like this? I barely know either of you. I don't even talk to my friends about this," Anya just couldn't explain to herself how it was this easy for her to release it all in front of two strangers.

"This place is filled with love. Most people feel it once they walk through the gate. We've blessed the place as a haven for those in search of healing. Plus, you came here willingly. You came here looking for answers and healing. That's half the battle," Gwynn said. Anya's crying was beginning to subside. She glanced at Sage's hand, which still held onto the crumpled paper.

"Once there is a break, we don't continue with the reading," Sage said, squeezing the paper ball. "From here, we'll burn the picture, releasing it from yours and our grasp. After that, we'll begin clearing the blocks and filling the void you just emptied with something more spectacular," Anya looked at Sage, who was still sparkling in her flecks of glitter, the curly dark hair springing wildly upward.

Sage lifted herself from the chair, taking a box of matches with her. She left the room, letting the door drift open behind her, and squatted down to meet the cauldron. Her flowing skirt caught the wind as she lit the paper ball on fire. It blazed with orange flames as she dropped it into the cauldron. Anya imagined it evaporating into blackness and then sad gray ashes. While she burned her picture, Gwynn was in the small bathroom filling a silver pitcher with hot water. He tapped a few drops of clary sage essential oils in and carried it over to Anya along with a matching silver basin. Her feet dangled from the side of the table, and Gwynn sat down in the chair just in front of her.

"The next step is to wash your hands and feet. This will open your energy fields and allow energy to run through you when we eliminate any negative blocks you have," Gwynn said. He took her feet in his hands, the scent of clary sage thick in her nose, relaxing her again. Anya felt even lighter than before. It was amazing how confession always made a person feel better. Having not gone to church for some time now, not making confession, she forgot how relieving it was. Gwynn washed both her feet and hands, urging her to release tension from her body until her limbs were limp. Gwynn rubbed the palms of her hands and the arches of her feet, kneading out blocks, cracking her knuckles. Sage was drifting around the room, lighting candles placed in every corner and nook, while Gwynn dried her hands and feet.

"This next part," Gwynn said. "We will brush the blocks from your energy field. We won't touch you unless we place stones or objects on your body. We typically do this in certain areas where intense blocks reside," Anya nodded. "Go ahead and lay down on the table with your feet facing north." She laid down, letting her head rest on the softness of the table. Gwynn and Sage helped her align her body on the table. The music in the room played on, and candles lit up every corner. Sage stood at the foot of the table and Gwynn at the head of the table.

"Now, Anya, just close your eyes and try to relax. We're going to say a prayer, and we'll begin the energy work," Gwynn said.

"Okay," Anya said. She realized she hadn't muttered a peep since she had finished crying, feeling content and relieved. Closing her eyes, she held her palms face up. Gwynn took a deep breath. Anya opened her eyes to see Sage at her feet with her eyes closed and palms raised to the ceiling.

"Mother, Father, God, spirits of love, light, and compassion. Join us here for our sister, Anya, as she embarks on the journey to find herself. Release her from anger and judgment around her spirit and faith. Allow her to let go of the resentment she feels toward her parents. Allow her to start her journey toward self-acceptance. So be it," he said.

"So be it," Sage repeated in a whisper. There was a brief second of nothing before the music escalated in volume. Anya relaxed, admitting to herself she was more relaxed than she had been in a while. Anya felt the weight of her body sink into the softness of the table, felt the wisps of breeze from the two bodies moving in circles around her. Air from their hands pushing in downward motions around parts of her body.

Anya could *feel* it all.

She knew she should be relaxing, attempting to meditate, but her mind was busy, trying to see if she could feel what they were doing with their healing hands. Curious what sensation she would feel when it was over. A tingling vibration quivered on her skin, encapsulating her entire body. Anya felt strange relief and acceptance the moment she stepped on their property, although it took her time to let go and admit it. Savoring the vibration she felt, she let go, not thinking anything, but just drifting into the space between sleep and wake, feeling heat balling up in her palms and at the bottom of her feet.

Random images flashed, one after another, behind her eyelids until she stopped on the image of a flat and calm ocean. Anya felt her body lighten, lifting from the table to enter this image in front of her. Drifting over the waves, her feet grazed the still waters, but she couldn't feel the wetness.

Anya spun around in circles, looking for any other presence. A ship, a seagull, a fish, or a spurt of water from a whale or dolphin. But nothing, just complete calm and silence, the water beneath her feet and the sky enormous above her. This wasn't just an image she viewed like a portrait in her living room. Anya was in the picture, living it, but still unable to touch the cool waters, smell the salty air, or feel the humidity.

Anya was snapped from her relaxing picture when the music lowered and she heard the door creak open and close, sensing light from behind her eyelids. The heaviness of her body sank into the table, making her feel more aware. It was quiet around her, even with the music in the background. Any quieter and Anya would have laid on that table for hours. Although relaxed, she felt eager to speak more with Gwynn and Sage. Remaining there, she didn't move, knowing doing so would interrupt the comfortable sensation vibrating every cell of her being. She never had an aptitude for science, but if it taught her one thing in her youth, it was that everything is energy, and she was certainly feeling everything she was made up of right then.

Anya lifted herself from the table, realizing all tensions had left her body, much like a massage would do for a person. When she looked down at the table, she saw a single smoky quartz pendulum attached to a silver chain and stones placed around her body and in between her calves. The music was still a soothing beat in the room, pleading with her to stay. Anya swung her feet over the side of the table and slid off, feeling the cold tile beneath her feet. Yet, this time, the sensation was more heightened than she remembered. She picked up her shoes and socks, leaving through the door, letting her bare feet touch the stone path as she moved toward the front yard where she first met Sage and Gwynn.

She sat down at the table, letting her feet glide across the cool grass. The blades tickled between her toes as the high sun fell on her face. She relaxed into the chair and closed her eyes. Within minutes, Sage and Gwynn emerged from their house. Gwynn was holding a glass of water with a slice of lemon. It glimmered in the sunlight like something out of a commercial. Sage followed closely behind with their striped gray cat hooked to a red harness. Silas leapt out into the yard, munching on blades of grass. Gwynn set the glass down in front of her and sat down in his chair.

"How do you feel?" He asked. Sage was sitting tailor-style in the grass with Silas, bearing resemblance to innocent children playing in parks.

"I can't even explain how it feels," Anya said, taking a sip of the water—it was cool and clean.

She didn't taste the bitterness of chlorine on the tip of her tongue, but the water was sweet and rewarding. "It feels like my body is just in this continuous state of vibration," she said.

"We've raised your vibration, my dear," Gwynn said. "What you're feeling is your own energy."

"It feels amazing."

"I've tried many different methods of healing, but none have touched me or healed me like Awakenings have," he said. "I abandoned prosperous careers to help people heal through Awakenings."

"How don't more people know about this?"

"Well, like I said before, people fear what they don't know."

"Right," Anya took another sip of water. She looked around the yard, down at the cat pouncing on a butterfly. She felt the sun on her skin and the trees seemed a brighter green now. "I also experienced... something."

Gwynn and Sage waited for her to continue.

"This is going to sound strange, but I felt like something pulled me off the table. A bunch of images flashed through my mind, and I landed on a picture of a calm ocean. One minute I'm looking at it, the other minute I'm actually in the picture."

Gwynn and Sage looked at each other and smiled.

Anya looked between them. "What?"

"I think you just had an out-of-body experience," Gwynn said.

"How?" She said, astounded. "I've never even—"

"You asked for it before getting on the table," Sage replied. "You may not have intentionally done it, but you asked for it."

"Wow," Anya said. "I don't know what to say. It was... incredible. It was like I was actually hovering over the ocean."

Gwynn smiled. "In time, we'll teach you how to astral travel on demand."

"After what I just experienced, I would like that," Anya replied.

"So, Anya, when is your birthday?" Sage asked, still clinging to the leash tied to her cat. They were an oddly pleasant couple so far, one she felt a strange kin to.

"April 21st," Anya said.

At that, Sage nodded and disappeared down the stone path toward the Awakening room, leaving Silas on the grass to bathe in the sun. She returned a moment later with her fist tightened around something. When she arrived at the table and opened her hand, she held an imperfectly shaped clear stone with speckles of white and swirls of black at the center.

"This is salt and pepper diamond, otherwise known as a Galaxy Diamond. It provides protection, promotes creativity and spiritual energy, and awakens change and new beginnings. Plus, it is a good fit for you, considering your connection to the stars. Keep it close. By your bed is best," Sage said. Anya took the stone from her palm, feeling its smoothness in her fingertips.

"I would like to set up some more sessions for you. Maybe once a month," Gwynn said. "If you are feeling motivated to learn more about the Pleiadian part of yourself, we will work up to that in a few sessions," he said. Anya was not only ready but willing. At this point, she was convinced she wouldn't be able to get enough of this warm feeling reluctant to leave her.

"Let's set it up," she replied.

"Great. Now, when you go home tonight, take a salt bath, make sure to drink a lot of lemon water, and try not to drink any alcohol or smoke weed. Those two things can lower your vibration."

"Write your dreams down in a journal. We can talk about them at your next session," Sage said. "And if strange things happen or you get met with difficulty, give yourself a little bit of grace. It's all just a ripple from today."

"Okay. Sounds good," Anya said.

"You did great today, Anya. We usually meet a lot of resistance during a first visit," Gwynn said. "You, however, must have reached your breaking point. Otherwise, you would have been fighting yourself just like most of them," he finished.

"Some of our visitors are usually looking for a quick fix to a deep problem. They aren't willing to put in the work to solve their own riddles," Sage remarked. "Sometimes, great healing takes a lot of work, sometimes harrowing work, and it is never easy to look at the ugly within." It had taken Anya this long to look at her ugly, but she feared she might just be getting started. She tried to view it as an investment in her happiness rather than a project or a problem she needed to solve.

Anya sat with them for another half hour before scheduling her sessions, paying, and finding the road back to Cripple Creek. Before she left, Gwynn and Sage gave her deep, heart-to-heart embraces. They were the kind that eliminated anxiety and cured depression, which she welcomed wholly. They felt parental; soothing. As she walked out the front gate, she turned to ask a final question.

"Hey, what do you put in that coffee? It's heavenly."

Gwynn looked at her and smiled. "Love."

Anya smiled back at them, watching Sage nod in agreement. She closed the gate behind her and got into the car.

Anya felt a cosmic shift in herself.

The experience with Gwynn and Sage was the crack in the iceberg threatening to break her away from what now seemed like her old life. It was perhaps the only threat she was content with welcoming. Many questions were ringing between her ears, ones only they were meant to answer.

How did they get into this profession?

How do people trust that this works for them?

What exactly did they just do in there?

How did they know she held onto judgment and anger if she didn't even know it herself?

For once, Anya was starting to believe in the higher powers that ruled over her parents. But this was a different kind of higher power, more authentic, more loving, full of glorious and positive intent—less a tool for control, more a tool for connection. It had been a sliver of what she was searching for.

Anya didn't know what might be in store for her over the next few weeks. For the first time in years, she felt she was on the right path toward a true sense of the belonging she so craved.

TWENTY-TWO

When he asked to see her this weekend, she said she had plans without letting him in on what she might be doing. Although mysterious, he knew she was not obligated to tell him anything she didn't want to. Sam was desperate to see her again, to spend every free moment with her if he could. Each time they were together already, he was left only wanting more. Sam needed to be patient. But was she ready? He still wasn't quite sure.

Time would tell.

Her free spirit, curious nature, and complex existence were revealed ever so beautifully as he got to know her. But, like all free spirits, she needed to drift. Any attempt to cling to her and she could evaporate in his fingertips.

Possessive natures were dangerous. Sam had seen what possession does to the women he had roped in many times. Their eyes lit with the desire to possess something, someone they weren't able to have. It was cruel of Sam to play this game, to give the appearance that he was available for that kind of ownership. Having been the one who enticed them into his space, he had created these thirsty and proprietorial monsters. And when they had transformed into these monsters, he suddenly didn't like them anymore, even though he was their creator.

It was terrible what he did.

Somedays, Sam wallowed in his guilt, recalling how many hearts he had played with. Most of them faced months or years of emotional recovery after he led them on. They'd send him lengthy texts explaining how he'd hurt them, hoping he would be heartbroken, feel remorse, care, and suddenly change his mind to give them another chance.

He never cared.

He never handed out second chances.

As he grew and changed, the guilt piled on. He never let it go either. Feeling as if he deserved the shame as a punishment for ruining women and the way they might perceive other men after him. Sam hoped most of them had found a safe place in the arms of another. That they went to bed at night, feeling warm kisses on their foreheads and words of love whispered in their ears. In the worlds he made up for them, men thoughtfully and intentionally loved the women he had shattered—loved them until they were pieced back together. He imagined the men professing their love and devotion to them amongst flower-ridden alters, crying at the end of aisles at the sight of their women in white. He hoped wherever these women were, and many of them had left this Cripple Creek, they were happy and loved by someone who didn't use them to get what they wanted.

But the worlds Sam built for them, they weren't real. It was a selfish attempt to right his wrongs in his mind. Convince himself that things always work out, so he never had to face ownership for how he handled his relationships with women. One day he might forgive himself, even if they never did. Or so he hoped.

Sam meant every word he whispered to Anya in her kitchen and wondered if she knew just how serious he was about devouring every inch of her. Sam shuddered at the thought, replaying his own words in his head, watching her eyes flicker beneath those eyelids, seeing her body quiver as his body and breath surrounded her. Knowing his words helped her vanish from reality, he could barely wait to see how his touch would slingshot her into their sphere of bliss.

It would be the most incredible high he would ever experience in his life, one that he would never want to come down from. He imagined experiencing everything with her—each glorious occasion of their two intertwined vessels beneath bedsheets, long adventures to unknown territories, and talks so intimate, deep, and authentic they interrupted their maddening existence in the world.

He even imagined the most mundane of things. Christmas mornings with horrid matching pajamas. Playful spats over how to fold the kitchen towels. Him knowing exactly how many freckles dotted her skin. Her knowing just how he liked his coffee in the morning. Snuggling up to terrible movies. Sitting in dead silence. Watching her read her books. Her watching him play hockey.

Since Anya was gone this weekend, Sam tried to dream up the next few days without her. In reality, they hadn't spent many weekends together just yet. Summer in the Gold Camp District should be savored and as frequently as possible. Sam knew he should be out at crystal lakes, fishing until the sun fell hot at the end of the earth, pondering his existence in the depths of the mountains beside a fire. That should be the way he ended all of his summer days.

Sam moved into a small room just beyond his bathroom, where his camping gear was. He owned a small tent, a tightly compressed

The Lost Pleiad

sleeping bag, and a single sleeping pad. Carrying as little as possible on any trail was always the best, in his opinion. Taking all the items, Sam filled his pack with an extra pair of clothes and warm socks, just in case. He shoved an entire box of tinfoil into the free space in his bag, which he planned to use for cooking his fish over a fire, and packed a single fork, a few cans of beer, a jar of salmon eggs, and a few jars of Power Bait. Sam strapped the sleeping pad to the top of his pack, the tent to the bottom, and then latched a strap to the sleeping bag, which he planned to carry over his shoulder. Sam fed his fishing pole into a long tube that would fit right next to his box of tinfoil.

It was still Saturday morning. The only question now was where he was going. Most of the time, he didn't know. Making it up as he went was usually his style. Sam looked into his yard, flipping through possible locations in his mind, thinking of the locations for camping not too far from where he was now, desiring to go someplace he wouldn't be bothered. There was Bison Reservoir, but he liked visiting his favorite places in moderation, so he never grew tired of them.

"Eleven Mile," he said out loud. Eleven Mile was beautiful at night, with great fishing. A lot of people might be there, but if he found his own quiet space, he wouldn't be bothered too much.

Eleven Mile rested out in Lake George, Colorado.

It was a Colorado State Park known for its marvelous vistas, outstanding fishing, and scenic hiking and biking. On a day like this, Sam expected to see a lake ridden with colorful kayak-shaped specks cruising around the shore and speed boats drawing pictures in the water with their wakes.

He planned to fish most of the day, mainly catching rainbow, brown, and cutthroat trout. Then, he would find a place to camp before sundown, enjoy his beer and smokey fish filets as he admired this countryside at night.

Sam set out in his white truck, becoming a speeding blur against these boring cliffsides and towering boulders. It was an hour's drive to Eleven Mile. He would drive through the Cripple Creek Mountain Estates, trying not to think of Anya as he passed the roads that led to her house—embracing the curves that led him through a tunnel of pine trees until he emerged to meet a small cow farm to his left as he raced around that curve. This route led him through Florissant, where he would take HWY 24 to Lake George.

Sam usually did these trips alone these days, but in the past, his best friend was usually a fun companion to bring along. But Zeke was lost, in Sam's opinion. Where he had first lost himself, he couldn't pinpoint, but Sam saw him, drowning his sorrow and haunting depression with alcohol and drugs. Satanic music always filled his home, making it seem like this dark passenger was possessing him. Sam missed his friend, wishing more than anything Zeke would just tell him what was wrong. They used to tell each other everything. Sam wanted to know why Zeke looked to alcoholism as a cure. Sam wanted to help and thought of confronting him about it but knew people wouldn't change or heal unless they were ready.

Since he couldn't see and know his beloved friend in the present, he remembered their past and how beautiful it was.

Running around in the mountains, doing everything together—chasing girls, stealing beer and liquor from their parents, smoking cigarettes at school, hopping the fences at the donkey pens to make penises in the snow with their feet. Zeke and Sam used to be inseparable.

Now, Sam was lucky if he got a phone call or text from him. The town was small, and he was more likely to run into him at the store. Not having his best friend around to share his thoughts with weighed on him some days. Perhaps that's why he had started telling his more painful truths to Bruce. He was the only person he truly trusted anymore. It made Sam angry, how disconnected he and Zeke were from each other.

Sam plunged his foot into the gas pedal, hoping it would sever his anger at Zeke. The two of them drifting apart meant that Zeke was unlikely to meet Anya. If things continued to get serious, Sam would want to introduce her to the most important people in his life, and yet there were very few amongst his hordes of acquaintances. Sam was ashamed of his friend and how Anya might think of him. How Anya would view the person he deemed a best friend.

Perhaps, he wasn't giving Anya enough credit. Knowing what he did so far, there was a chance she would be compassionate and benevolent. Maybe she would understand. Sam had to erase these thoughts. Nothing about them would change until that time arrived. Entertaining them any longer would ruin the day he was intent on having.

Sam sped down the paved roads, observing how the once jet black asphalt faded to a light grey, worn away by the sun. The hour passed quickly. Within minutes of entering the park, he was approaching a parking lot closest to a riverbank. He expected to see more people, but to his surprise, there weren't many. As expected, there were spots of orange, yellow, green, and blue colors where kayaks marked their existence on the water—speed boats in the distance left behind wavy trails of white. Eleven Mile Reservoir pleasantly reflected the deep blue sky while trees lined the river banks. Sam found a parking spot, slipping from the driver's seat, taking his heavy pack with him. His car alarm chirped as he walked hurriedly toward the bank.

There was a lot of daylight left, allowing Sam plenty of time to catch a lot of fish for dinner that evening. Staring at the waters and trees in view, he pulled the long tube from his pack, unscrewing the top to get his fishing pole out. His fingertips knowingly felt their way around each part of the pole, assembling the long thin shaft. Taking some of his bait out, he plucked a few salmon eggs from a jar and fed them onto the hook-like neon beads. Trout tended to like those. Sam rested his pack up toward the tree line, safely away from the water.

Casting his line, he watched the invisible string disappear into the landscape; pleasant thoughts of Anya and troubling thoughts of Zeke all falling away.

Each cast brought him a wealth of fish, some smaller than the others. He fought to reel them in as they bent the pole to submission. Cutthroats were some of his favorites to catch. He loved the harsh red coloring at the throat and how the scales reflected like mirrors in the daylight. The fish puckered up at him, searching for a single breath of water. Finding a large rock nearest to him, Sam unhooked the fish and knocked its head against it with one single swing and strung it to a stick for easy carrying.

After three good hooks and keepers, it became a game of catch and release. Sam carried this on until the late evening, but just before dusk started to make an appearance. He packed up his fishing gear, shoving it back in his pack, and taking the stick threading catches. Walking along the riverbank, Sam's next mission was to find a reasonable place to camp without causing any riffs with Park Rangers. He should be

The Lost Pleiad

staying in the campground, but he wouldn't dare. Camping should be an off-the-beaten-path kind of experience. Even if there was a chance Sam got in trouble for straying from a campground, at least he would have several moments or hours of impeccable nights of solitude in a single flat amongst the trees. Sam wandered a while, keeping track of his trail before finding the perfect spot. It was a single ledge looking over the reservoir, but trees hadn't grown there. It gave him a perfect view of everything around him, including the night sky. Anya would love this.

Sam set up his tent, which took some effort. Having another person would've helped immensely. He dragged the rainfly over the top, letting the fumes from the tent release in the breeze after being confined to a bag all winter. He laid his sleeping pad and his bag in the center of the small tent and zipped it up. Using sticks and leaves from the surrounding area, he took a lighter from his pocket and made a small fire, careful to contain it responsibly. It roared to life beside him about the time dusk approached, and the sky was a rainbow of deep violet and orange.

Sam retrieved his tin foil from the pack and lined up the fish on a single sheet. Covering it with another sheet, he clamped the edges together and set them on the fire. The orange cleared from the sky, leading toward darkness. The fire crackled beside him, almost in unison with the appearing stars. As if they were a symphony for their arrival. Sam cooked them until the fire was the only light left on the lake. Sam used another stick to take the tinfoil-wrapped fish from the fire, feeding the flames with more logs before fixating on his dinner.

The fish was hot and delightful. Sam always loved how no salt and seasonings allowed him to savor the true taste of things. A mind trick that reminded him we didn't need to overly garnish things that were already great. Popping a can of beer open, he took a long sip letting the warm bubbles prick his tongue before burning down his throat.

The crispy and smokey fish was gone within minutes, and Sam was content. Digging his heels into the dirt just near the edge of the small cliff, Sam admired the static fireflies clinging to the sky, the things that Anya loved so much. Anya told him she was Pleiadian, and he thought about what it meant to her to be Pleiadian; what it would mean to her if he was accepting of it. Sam wanted to understand better and hoped time together would afford him that opportunity. He took another long swig, the light from the flames of the small fire dancing on his cheeks to illuminate his golden-brown eyes.

These were the moments in time he lived for. Sam wanted to tell Anya just how much he contemplated his existence. How, like her, he was also searching for his place in the world. Although, to him, his idea of a place in the world would be different than hers. It wasn't so much a location he was looking for, but a person—someone who felt like home. If he could find that person, he could take that home with him, wherever he went in the world. But maybe he wouldn't take that home. Perhaps he would follow that home wherever it went, abandoning all things.

If Anya became his home, he would follow her anywhere.

TWENTY-THREE

Karmyn and Bee sat across the table with their mouths gaping open in awe.

The restaurant around them was loud, unlike their silence. The drinks in front of them had been untouched since Anya started her story about Sam, their night cooking dinner together, and his words that set her on fire.

"I cannot *believe* he said those things to you," Karmyn shrieked. "My legs are clenched. How on earth did you not jump his bones right then?"

Anya laughed uncomfortably. "I honestly don't know. I've never dated someone who said things like that to me," Anya felt her cheeks burn. Sam wanting to devour her, put his mouth on her. She could relive his words day after day and never tire of them.

"I didn't think he was this interested in me after seeing him with that girl in the museum."

"Yeah, what the hell was that about?" Bee asked.

"I'm not sure," Anya replied. "I haven't gotten around to asking him about it. Our last two dates have been amazing, so I kind of forgot."

"Yeah, it sounds like it," Karmyn shrieked again, finally taking a sip of her drink. "Aren't you glad I told you to go on another date with him?" She boasted—Anya, nearly unwilling to agree.

"Yes. I am very grateful you pushed me to go on another date with him," she said. "I'm starting to… I don't know… like him," Anya admitted, she was actually starting to like him a lot. Bee smiled, finally taking her first sip. Anya did the same.

"Well, that's not bad," Bee said. "It seems like he is doing whatever he can to prove he is serious about you."

"Yeah, but guys will say and do whatever they have to just to get in your pants. Don't you think?" Anya asked. The wise Bee answered.

"Not always. A bachelor could go years bouncing from girl to girl, but when the right one comes along, and he knows it, he'll drop all his bullshit to pursue her until it works. That's what happened with my husband and me. We've had lengthy conversations about his past and how things changed when we met. How things just clicked," Bee said.

"Do you feel like things have just clicked?" Karmyn asked. Anya honestly didn't know what "clicking" even felt like.

"I'm not even sure," Anya answered honestly. "I've never been in the realm of anything remotely resembling love. I don't have anything to compare it to."

"You would know," Bee said, taking another sip and eyeing the waiters as they drifted from the kitchen with steaming plates of food.

"And if I don't know?" Anya asked. Karmyn and Bee both stayed silent, conjuring up an answer. Anya knew they wanted to say the right thing, to instill the hope in love that she had lost for many years. They were desperate to see her happy with someone.

"If you don't know," Bee said. "It's possible he may not be the one."

"But, if you don't know right away, just give it some time. Get to really know him and trust him. That may be your issue," Karmyn said.

"Yeah, I do have some trust issues," Anya said.

"And rightly so," Bee added. "The flaming trash piles who've come into your life have not represented the male species well."

"I know that when you're not trusting, you're not open to the idea of something long-term or different than what all these assholes have made you believe about love," Karmyn said, her drink nearly gone now. Anya had only taken a sip of her non-alcoholic beverage, twirling the glass on the table and watching the cold beads sweat down the side of the glass.

"You're very right," Anya said. "It's just a terrifying risk."

"Attempts at love are never not a risk," Bee said. Anya knew she was right.

"Let's talk about something else," Anya suggested.

"And not about the hunky man whispering naughties to you?" They all laughed. Karmyn was always the animated and funny one. She could provoke a laugh from Anya at any moment, even if they were nosy quips that irritated her.

"What else has been going on with you?" Bee asked Anya. How things managed to be focused on her life all the time baffled her. For once, Anya would like to sit and listen to their lives, which they claimed were too uninteresting and routine.

"You look different, by the way," said Karmyn. "Like you're glowing. Did you do something different with your hair?"

Anya debated whether or not she should tell them about her trip to see Sage and Gwynn and her first energy healing session in her life. How meeting Gwynn and Sage and learning something, however small, about Pleiadians have given her some kind of hope in understanding herself. Anya didn't feel too different from her visit. But maybe she was different. Karmyn may be noticing that. Her ability to be nosy and observant usually annoyed Anya. At the same time, Karmyn was always the first to sniff out when something was wrong. Anya couldn't count on her hands how many times Karmyn sensed when something was spot on or spot off. It would only be a matter of time before she probed Anya for answers about why she was glowing.

Maybe the awakenings changed her in some subtle way only Karmyn could see. It wasn't uncommon for someone not to notice the minor changes in themselves. People may not see the things about themselves that have changed, even if they look at themselves in a mirror every day. No one sees a person's transformations like friends and family who haven't seen them in a while.

But telling them about her newfound path toward spirituality, which she still didn't understand herself, was a risky confession she wasn't sure about. What if they judged her for those thoughts or her journey toward self-love and understanding? On the other hand, what if they didn't judge her?

Where on her journey did Anya feel like she couldn't talk to her friends about these things?

Was it something she was afraid to admit to them or afraid to admit to herself? Anya could recall many times she was overridden with guilt and shame after being wholly transparent with a stranger who betrayed her trust. But those were strangers. Karmyn and Bee were her trusted friends, her closest allies. Surely they would love her and understand her regardless of her beliefs.

Why wouldn't they?

The beads of water running down her glass formed a circular pool that suctioned the glass to the table. Bee and Karmyn looked at her intensely.

"You alright, bestie?" Bee asked. Anya realized she had been pondering these thoughts for far too long. Heavenly smells from the kitchen wafted in at the exact moment the server brought their food to the table.

"I'm fine," Anya said. "I was just thinking."

"You were deep in thought there, my dear friend," Karmyn said. "You want to tell us what's going on in that beautiful dome of yours?" Anya looked up from the steaming plate of food in front of her.

A beautifully seared steak sat next to a heap of mashed potatoes drenched in pools of butter and crispy green beans. The only thing keeping her from digging in was the answer she hadn't given her two closest friends. At some point, she would need to stop hiding this part of herself, to stop letting these things keep her from the true transparency that made her relationships stronger.

It was time to stop holding back from the truth. If they walked away from her because of it, then she didn't need them in her life, right? Anya was tired of losing people. Losing Bee and Karmyn to her beliefs could swallow her into a painful oblivion, but she had to try. Of all the people she was closest to in her life, her parents excluded, Karmyn and Bee had been there. Not telling them her deepest feelings gave them no chance of knowing her deeply and being compassionate about the journey she was on.

Did she really believe her two friends wouldn't be loving after knowing her truth?

Like Bee had said, any 'attempt at love is always a risk.'

Anya loved her friends, and with respect to them and herself, she would have to tell them the truth.

Anya looked up from her plate.

"There is actually something I've been meaning to tell you guys," Anya said. "I've just never been sure how to tell you because it's rather strange." Bee and Karmyn perked up, shoving a quick forkful of food into their mouths before she continued.

"You can tell us anything," Bee said. Anya took a deep breath, feeling her nerves tense up, threatening to choke her words.

"So, do you remember when I told you about my favorite constellation?" Anya asked. Bee and Karmyn looked at her, careful not to make any facial expressions.

"Yeah," Karmyn said.

"I absolutely remember," Bee said.

"Ugh. This is so difficult to say. It feels weird," Bee and Karmyn started to develop worrying looks, so much that their cutlery was now still on the table.

"How do I even say this?" Anya said. "So, that constellation, Pleiades, the Seven Sisters. It turns out there is a whole community of people out in the world who believe they are part of the constellation. They call themselves Pleiadians," Anya pooled her hands in her lap, her eyes dodging the two sets burning into her. Both of them were silent as they listened.

"When I went to learn about it, I found a YouTube video listing traits of these Pleiadians. It helped identify whether or not you might be one," Anya continued. Bee was now resting her elbow on the table and cradling her chin in her hand. Anya swore she saw a smirk briefly pass over her face. "The more I watched, the more I felt like this was…

me. And I know that sounds crazy, absolutely batshit crazy. But, I don't know, I've always felt like… I didn't belong. Maybe this is why I don't? Maybe I'm not from here at all." Anya looked at them, their faces not showing disappointment or sadness but empathy. With each word, Anya loosened, her confession becoming easier to say.

"I wasn't sure who to talk to about it, being that it was such an odd thing. So, I found a couple down in Coal Creek who do energy work, hoping I might get some sort of confirmation from them about this possible identity. I went down there yesterday, and they gave me this energy healing session called an Awakening. They *knew* about Pleiadians and promised to help me get some answers about this part of me," she stopped. Anya looked at her two friends who hadn't said a word. They were waiting to see if there was more to the story before offering their thoughts.

"So, that's how things have been," Anya stopped. She took another large swig of her drink, wishing there was alcohol in it. She wondered which one of them would add their opinion and advice first.

"What were the traits of a Pleiadian?" Karmyn asked. Anya was still waiting to see if they would be outraged or quick to deem her insane. Her nerves had not settled just yet. Anya removed her hands from her lap and rested her elbows on the table, trying hard not to close her arms over her heart. She told them all the traits in-depth as they sat in silence.

"I could see why you would identify with that," Karmyn said, straightening in her chair. Neither of them had moved to touch their food.

"I've actually heard of this," Bee said. This didn't shock Anya at all. Bee was into all things that helped people understand themselves better.

"You have?" Karmyn and Anya said in unison.

"Yeah. They're supposed to be very loving and compassionate, right? Some of what I've read says that they were sent here to teach people more about love," Bee said.

"You shock me," Karmyn said with a smile. Bee gave a quick smile and side glance.

"I've come across these kinds of ideas when learning about personality types and enneagrams. Something I'm really big into," Bee said.

"What are those?" Karmyn turned to Bee.

"It's just other ways of helping you understand yourself. The Myer's Brigg personality test can help you identify if you are introvert or extrovert, intuitive or sensing, feeling or thinking, and judgmental or prospecting. For me, it's a way of just understanding people better, so I know how to interact with them and build stronger relationships. My husband and I have been using it in our marriage for years to help understand each other better."

Anya's story was getting lost in the conversation. She didn't know if she was supposed to feel seen or ignored.

"Oh," Karmyn said. "So, what am I?"

"I have an idea, but you should just take the test," Bee said. "I'll send it to you guys."

Anya had remained quiet, just listening and wondering if everything she had just told them forced them into denial.

"I heard what you said, Anya," Bee said, looking directly at her. "Were you afraid to tell us that?" Karmyn looked back at Anya.

"Yes. I was sure you would think I'm crazy," Anya said.

"I definitely don't think you're crazy," Bee said.

"I don't think that either," Karmyn said.

"What I do wonder is why you felt like you couldn't tell us," Bee inquired. "And I don't mean that in an 'I'm hurt' kind of way."

"I guess I just didn't know how true or realistic it was," Anya said. "I didn't want this to be anything that might make me lose either of you." Bee's expression moved from concern to empathy again. Karmyn looked at Anya, taking her hand.

"Anya, we love you," Karmyn said. Tears stung Anya's eyes.

"Very much so," Bee agreed.

"If you feel like you can't tell us anything, then we're not very good friends, are we?" Karmyn said.

"I love you guys, too," Anya said on the brink of tears. Bee's blue eyes softened as she placed her hand on Anya's.

"I'm sorry for whatever we did to make us feel like you couldn't tell us that right away," said Bee.

"I'm sorry for this piece of shit world making you believe you couldn't be who you are," said Karmyn. Anya started crying, not realizing how much she needed to hear that love and support. She was desperate for their acceptance, any acceptance from the people she loved most and her vulnerability was helping her feel whole. Bee and Karmyn were all she had.

"Thank you. So, you guys believe me?" Anya asked.

"If you believe that about yourself, then so do I," said Bee.

"Me too," said Karmyn smiled.

Anya would have to take this slow. Not overload them with too much information too soon. She saw what her full transparency had done to her relationships. Sometimes it drove them away. Sharing this shred of herself and gaining that acceptance was a positive first step toward finding that community and accepting herself—a step toward finding her place when she felt like she hadn't belonged for so long. If anything, Karmyn and Bee were there to remind her she very much had a place on this earth. She very much had a loving home.

"We all learned a lot about each other today, it seems," said Karmyn.

"We did," Anya agree.

"Can we please make sure to tell each other everything, no matter how insane it makes us feel?" Bee insisted.

"Absolutely," Karmyn said.

"I'm totally on board," Anya agreed.

That night, Anya felt lively. Feeling closer to her friends gave her new energy and confidence. She was feeling like she had a place in this confusing world and people should rely on. And if she felt daring, she could have one more.

After dinner and before driving home, she texted Sam.

"Want to come over and watch a movie with me tonight?" She asked. She stared at her phone screen and within seconds he replied.

"Absolutely."

TWENTY-FOUR

She was looking at a black canvas through a pair of virtual reality goggles. The goggles surrounded her, giving her a panoramic view—the view in a fisheye lens. She noticed the heavy weight of the cord pulling on the back of her skull, reminding her of her connection to something. In this black space, she could choose any earthly reality she desired.

The first destination, a green hill deep in the mountains, wildflowers bursting up from the earth in white and purple buds that opened instantly. Desperate to breathe the mountain air and take in the sweet scent of the wildflowers, the breeze carrying their aroma wouldn't invade her nose. The stiff, jagged navy peaks shot up into the sky like monstrous arrowheads, showing their majestic lack of symmetry, dusted in a pristine white reflecting the bright sun. She stuck her hands out in front of her, wiggling each finger before her, turning her hand over to see how real this virtual reality was. She danced in a half-circle, range of motion limited by her corded connection seeing the tall grass brush her calves and stomp flat beneath her bare feet. The sensation of grass didn't tingle against her skin, nor did the cool drops of dew wetting her feet. She felt nothing.

With the touch of a button, a new scene appeared.

Her feet, once flat on the earth, were now finding balance on a rocking boat. The sun rays had worn down the world's intense brown color to a faded tan. As the boat drifted downstream, it merged into clouds of mist steaming off the surface of the river and the banks hiding behind the mist. Above, the sky was a swirl of light oranges and periwinkle, rippling like the scales of a fish, reflecting in the still waters just ahead. A flock of Canadian geese sounded, flying above in a triangular formation. As she drifted past the grassy banks, the boat came to a knoll with a white gazebo perched on top. A swinging bench hung from within, but it was empty. The cool dampness of the river air feeding the lush surroundings evaded her. She felt nothing.

Her next destination was a perfect sunset on an empty beach. Searching in either direction, she saw sand stretch for miles and rows of palm trees line the white sands before the ocean waves reached to smother the earth. The water rushed in and drifted out like a gentle dance, each wave carrying its unique rhythm. The deep-orange sun stretched the length of the horizon, sinking beneath the line where ocean and sky met. She sat down on the sand, scooping the earth in her hand, hoping she might feel its roughness against her palm and between her fingers. But nothing. The sun dipped with each blink, the horizon cutting it in half. The ocean waters rippled up to leave a salty white foam at her feet. On the horizon, that same water made brushstrokes of navy blue and deep orange. To either side of her, the palm trees waved in the breeze, disrupting the seagulls. Dolphins leapt from the depths of distant and vast sea. Complete bliss.

Next, an urban city and her standing in the middle of a busy main street with taxis honking as they passed by. Pigeons cooed on the rooftops—someone passed by on a bicycle pulling a hot dog cart behind them. Imagining the taste of the savory hot dogs steaming past her, she sensed nothing. Others were in business suits or flowing dresses. Some listened to music reverberate between their earbuds. Peeking between the buildings, the sky was a stunning, vibrant shade of blue, brushed with a few wisps of clouds drifting with the slow winds sweeping above the rooftops. She didn't feel that wind, but she could see it carry the clouds. She didn't smell the car exhaust, but she could imagine its harsh odor. With a snap of her fingers, she was somewhere else again.

The next location was the bank of a river. The water trickled over the river rocks, forming little fits of whitewater before running into stillness. In some corners where the rock met the banks, spirals of river formed whirlpools and fishing holes where trout would live. Looking down at her feet dipped in the calm waters, she knew the chill should be stinging her feet. Yet, she felt nothing. Beside her was Sam with his naturally dark beard perfectly combed and matching brown hair slicked back. Wearing dark blue jeans and a black hoodie, he looked far off downstream, and she could see him smiling. His forearm propped up on his knee. Looking down at her hand, seeing his fingers tangled in hers, she felt nothing. He smiled.

"This isn't reality," he said to her.

"What?" She asked.

The goggles went black, and the whirring electrical sounds disappeared, leaving her in profound silence. She felt the weight of the helmet and the cord heavy at the top of her head—feeling fear. All scenes had disappeared into the darkness.

"What is this?" She said to the dark silence.

Then, she heard Sam's voice.

"Take off the goggles," he commanded. When she removed them, she was standing in the middle of a white road, violet grasses on the side of her, green trees towering up along the sides of the road. Flowers popped up in shades of opal, emerald, amethyst, and sapphire, sparkling like precious jewels. In the distance, where space was an infinite black, she saw a moon and other planets,

taking up a majority of the sky she could see. They were so close to her she thought she could reach out and pluck them from space.

Stunning people with silver hair walked by, donning intricate silvery clothing and gems resting at their third eye. They stared her down from head to toe, whispering to each other in musical tones as if when they spoke they sang.

She twirled around, seeing exquisite homes with softened corners and circular windows. In the distance were towering silver buildings with the same rounded features. Ovular silver vehicles hovering past her, and more flowers popped up from the earth, holding a moon-like glow. If possible, the stars were even brighter here.

Breathtaking.

Lingering in this spot, she looked down at her feet, seeing them bare against the white stone path—the smooth rock massaging her toes, balls, arches, and heels. The wind was cool against her skin, provoking a ripple of goosebumps. The musical whispers continued around her as she looked up at the sky. With each twirl released from her limited connection, this place encompassed a sense of familiarity. She could feel it all.

This heavenly dimension seducing her for too long, she realized Sam was nowhere in sight. Searching the crowd, a single head of brown hair would be easy to spot in the sea of silver manes. A panic rose in her chest. He promised he wouldn't leave her, that he would protect her. Where had he gone? The panicked twirls on this white road in search of him sent her into dizziness.

Someone approached her from the left side, slowing her spins to stillness with a soft tap on her shoulder. The musical voices she once heard in whispers transformed into words she now understood.

"What are you looking for?" Searching again, she didn't see that brown beard and brown hair slicked back. His jet-black hoodie disappeared into a *sea of silver drapes. The gleaming world around her fell away as she searched desperately for something, anything familiar with what she knew or the earth she lived on. No one was with her now. This wasn't home.*

Eyes bursting open, the night was still dark, but she could make out Sam's form lying next to her. She forgot Sam had come over last night. They must've fallen asleep after an intense movie and snuggling session.

More importantly, he hadn't left her.

In the shadow crossing his silhouette, she observed the freckles on his face. One was small, right beneath his right eye. Another was trying to disappear beneath his hairline. Sam had perfect unblemished skin, muscles that gleamed in the rippled moonlight working through the blinds, and a single strand of his hair fell to his forehead. Careful not to stir him from his slumber, Anya took that piece of hair, brushing it from his face, admiring how handsome he was.

Behind him, on the bedside table, the galaxy diamond caught a glint of the same moonlight shining on Sam. A twinkle difficult to ignore. Her dreams tried convincing her that he wasn't there or that he would be gone eventually. That unsettled her. As she stared into him, taking snapshots, he murmured in his sleep. Her eyes caught the movement of his lips and she wished she could kiss him right then. Slowly opening his eyes, Sam saw Anya staring at him.

"You're awake," he murmured.

"Yeah," she whispered.

"You okay?" He reached his one free hand up to feel her silky skin.

"I'm okay. I just had a dream," Sam moved closer to her, curling her into his space, grazing her cheek with his thumb. She thought she saw his eyes dart to her lips, but it was too dark to tell.

"Yeah? What kind of dream?" He questioned.

"I had a dream I was wearing virtual reality goggles. I was flashing through so many beautiful scenes. Some on sandy beaches, mountains, and some on rivers," she paused. "You were there."

"Was I now?" He shifted his body to move closer, his smile glowing in the dark room. "What was I doing?"

"You were sitting on a riverbank with me, holding my hand. Then everything went black. When I took off the goggles, I was on this planet. It was completely different. Everything was glowing, silvery, green, blue, and purple. But you were gone," she said.

"Well, I guess I can't very well keep my promises in your dreams," he said. "I'm sorry about that. It sounds lovely, though," he finished.

"It really was. For a minute, it was so lovely I forgot I lost you. When I realized you weren't there anymore, I panicked," she said. "Then, I woke up to see you hadn't left me at all."

He smiled. "Of course not. I'm not going anywhere."

"Okay," she brushed the freckle beneath his eye. She recalled the conversation they had earlier that evening. "Can I tell you something? About the person that made me lose trust in everyone."

"Absolutely," he said. "I'm dying to know everything about you."

"Is that so?" She asked. "Even the bad stuff?"

"Especially the bad stuff."

"Why, though?"

"Because if I know the bad stuff, I know just exactly how to love you," he said.

Love. Her heart skipped.

A place she had never been with anyone. Although, many times she had tried convincing herself she had arrived there.

"Okay," she smirked. "A few years ago, I met a guy on a dating app. He was incredibly handsome, super buff, and honestly stunning. We went on a few dates, and he talked about being into things spiritually, told me he was all about meditating, loved hearing my travel stories. Things seemed to be going good."

Anya broke her gaze from Sam, feeling hot shame rise in her. Telling him this next part wouldn't be easy. Reliving the memory was even worse.

"One night, he came over. Things got kind of hot and heavy, lots of kissing. When he started putting his hand up my shirt, I asked him to stop. I told him I didn't want to go too fast. By then, he had his shirt off. He was sitting against the wall throwing a fit because I wouldn't have sex with him. Then, like an asshole, got up to leave."

"Well, it's good that he left," Sam said. Anya stayed silent.

"It didn't stop there," she continued.

"Oh?" He said.

"For whatever reason, I believed I had a connection with him. For whatever reason, I was desperate for him to stay. Desperate to not be… alone. I begged him to stay and for us to start the night over. We ended up having sex," she said. Sam stayed quiet.

"After two weeks of dating, he showed up at my house for a date. While I finished getting ready, he told me he didn't want to date me anymore. He said, and I quote, 'it's just not as fun if it's easy,' and I started crying right then. I told him, 'you know you made me feel like shit for not wanting to have sex with you, right?' His response was, 'yes, I've reflected on that.' The crushing blow was the claim that I was too easy. After *that*, he was out of my life. I was miserable for months questioning myself and my worth." Sam was still quiet. Anya couldn't tell if he was just listening or silently conjuring up ways to ditch her by moonlight.

"Ever since then, I've never trusted the integrity of men and what they'll do to have sex with me. I've never trusted myself and what I am willing to do to fill whatever my void is," she finished.

"Well," Sam cleared his throat. Anya was still looking down and away from him. "Look at me," he said.

Anya couldn't. How could he want such a desperate and foolish woman? When she wouldn't look, his thumb and pointer finger lifted her chin to his gaze.

"He's a fucking asshole. What he did was wrong," he said. Anya felt a brutal sting in her throat trying to hold back her tears.

Why do I always cry at everything?

"He should have never made you feel like that," Sam said. "He is absolutely everything wrong with men."

"Yeah, but I let him in," she admitted. "It's partly my fault."

"Maybe. We do strange things while on the search for connection and acceptance. I know I did."

"So, you don't think I'm a hideous person for giving it up so easy?" she asked.

"Certainly not," he kissed her bare shoulder. "If you ever want to see how hideous a person can be, I'm willing to share." Anya smiled.

"Someday," she said. Someday, she would like to hear more about him and learn how she can love him for his darkness too. Deep down, a weight lifted, and relief settled in her chest. This is what vulnerability was, she thought—feeling accepted and loved for her darkness.

As much as she wanted to believe in the possibility of love, she had gotten in trouble with that eagerness. Every time, it had left her with

The Lost Pleiad

nothing. Keeping some part of her wall up was something she would have to do until she was certain he wasn't leaving. He had been diligent about bringing her wall down, collecting those bricks, and with each fallen brick, she would put up another. His bricks were stacking frighteningly faster than hers.

Anya had rarely heard any of his confessions even though he was ready to tell them. Somehow, she believed that no matter what he told her, she would believe it to be a tall tale. It was a trained belief that every story from a man's lips was embellished to place them in a sparkling light.

Trust wavered, but a small part of her wanted to feel like Sam could go to war with her doubts. The time it would take to know for sure could easily drive him off. A risk she was willing to take if it meant protecting her own heart.

That kiss lingered on her shoulder. All of his kisses seemed to do that. "Thank you for telling me," he said.

"You're welcome," she said. She watched him, lying in her bed, his shirt partially riding up to show his abs. Without noticing, she bit her lip, thinking of his mouth on her body as she writhed underneath him, his tongue and lips exploring every inch of her.

She wanted more than sex from him, from anyone. She craved intimacy and connection. But she couldn't deny how much she wanted to feel him touch her and transform those innocent kisses to her bare skin into something more thrilling. His eyes locked onto the lip she was biting. He leaned over to kiss her shoulder again keeping is eyes fixated on that lip. Anya closed her eyes, letting the feeling sear into her. He kissed another spot on her shoulder, then another, slowly working his way upward. Reaching up, he gently took her by the back of her neck. Anya inhaled a sharp breath, closing her eyes to savor every touch. Those lips kissed her cheek, tracing their path to an intimate forehead kiss, making her vibrate beneath her skin. Anya inched closer to him, arching herself into his space. The kisses worked their way back down, planting them like flowers on her nose and cheeks, until he was staring into her eyes and letting his mouth hover near hers. Her mouth went dry. Her whole body tensing next to him.

Brushing the hair from her face, he kissed her. Breathless, Sam pulled her into his chest, gently taking her mouth and massaging her tongue with his. Anya stifled a groan, trying to control herself from turning this into something more. She wanted to, but she wasn't sure if she was ready, afraid she might lose him if they went any further.

"You taste... amazing," he moaned between kisses. Anya was on fire, lusting desperately for more. She was on the brink of unleashing herself and mounting him right then but before she could go further, the intensity of the kiss faded into something more gentle. He pressed into her one last time, held her in his arms and then moved away. Anya struggled to catch her breath, feeling dizzy as he grinned at her. Sam was thinking the same thing, holding back just as much as she was.

Sam kissed her like she mattered. Like he cared for her.

"Goddamn you're amazing," he said staring into her and she smiled. Sam let her curl into his chest as they laid back down on her bed. Within minutes, he was snoring softly beside her, reminding her that times like these were more precious than the stories she recalled from past mistakes. From her cozy spot where she'd tucked into his side, she looked tiredly up at him, feeling like she could actually be happy.

TWENTY-FIVE

The fears consuming Anya for years fell away each moment she spent with Sam. The summer continued, flashing by as fast as the sun crossing the sky. They did everything together. Sam took her to his favorite fishing spots, to adventures deep in the San Juan mountains, nearly every night the two of them cooked dinner together. Sam always found a reason to run into her when he was in town, and when he did, she would light up. Anya was doing precisely what she had promised herself she wouldn't.

Falling in love.

Sam had spent these weeks doing everything he could to gain her trust, to prove he was there to stay. Every day, Sam made efforts, leaving sweet notes around her house and in the pages of her books, reminding her she was beautiful, referring to her as his 'cosmic angel.'

In that time, he learned she hated flowers as gifts but preferred tacos instead. She mostly hated how they were plucked just to die later. So instead of flowers, he brought her potted plants and tacos. Many of the nights they spent together, they told each other the stories of their lives. Anya got to see glints of who he was. Sam told her how much regret filled him when he recalled how he had treated women. It was the last girl he dated that made him rethink everything. Each woman he marched through just led him closer to realizing he was only hurting people while he helped himself.

The night he told her this, he cried.

Lamented in her arms as he was tormented with guilt.

It was the first time Anya had seen a man cry so intensely.

Her stoic father had never shed a single tear over anything, nor had any man she had known on a personal level. Men weren't allowed to show emotions. They weren't allowed to be anything other than a protector and provider. In spaces of vulnerability, men would be seen as weak, leaving so many of them trapped within their minds. All Anya ever wanted from any man was his willingness to be seen, be loved, let himself go, and stop the tough guy act. It was tiring being with tough guys and seeing how that façade ate them up inside and kept them from living a truly free and genuine life.

Anya was grateful he was sharing so much with her. She took every bit of it in without judgment, understanding how difficult it was to share the worst things about yourself and still desperately hope to be loved. It was a kind of bravery akin to singing karaoke in a full bar of strangers and hoping they liked your voice enough to clap along. Everyone wanted that kind of love and acceptance. From what she could tell, Sam was trying to resolve the guilt and shame, and in some ways, he had no place to go with his feelings. It's not as if the Gold Camp District was full of progressive minds that accepted others for who they were. And his friends, who Anya was starting to slowly get to know, reeked of toxic masculinity. Getting around a co-ed table at any bar, all women ever did was cringe at the grumbles of misogyny running rampant between gulps of beer.

These few weeks, things were turning out to be a stark contrast between everything she had known about men and relationships. She was in uncharted territory the more she let herself go with Sam.

What she knew better than anyone was this—too much of anything was never good.

And just as promised, Anya and her friends set a date for a road trip to California for a week. The longest time she had been apart from Sam since they got together.

It was beyond difficult, imagining what he might do in her absence. Would he lose interest in her? Would he find other ways to occupy his time? Would he realize he just wasn't into her at all? How would Anya feel even?

She applied the same questions to herself, thinking them intensely. Overthinking everything was something she was known for. Casting out the thoughts and their related questions, Anya decided to focus on something else.

Before her trip to California with Bee and Karmyn, she had another session with Gwynn and Sage. They agreed to meet once a month to dive deeper into Anya's connection to Pleiades. Somehow, Anya didn't care about it at the moment. Her newest infatuation with Sam obviously taking up her time.

The Saturday before their road trip began, Anya followed the familiar roads to Coal Creek to see Gwynn and Sage. Most of the summer was smothered with the bright sun, but not this day. Anya watched the dark clouds hang above. They were so dark, Anya wondered how it hadn't rained yet. She felt the galaxy diamond stiff in her pants pocket. Carrying it around had become a habit when it wasn't resting on her bedside table, feeling that if it was with her all the time, she would never lose it.

When she pulled into their driveway, they weren't outside combing the grass with their feet. Anya got out of her car, feeling the chilly wind blow hair in her face. She hurried to the front door, knocking three times. In seconds, Sage answered the door barefoot once again.

"Anya! So nice to see you, honey," she said. "Come in."

Anya was glad to leave the wind tunnel outside. She entered a large living room. When she looked around the room, she had only one way of describing this home to herself. Mr. and Mrs. Weasley's home.

On the walls hung various photographs, all signed with Sage's name. The bookcases shelved hundreds of books and figurines found their homes on any available shelf space left. To the left was a large wood-burning stove, sitting dark and unused in the summer warmth. To the right were mismatched chairs and couches pointing at a large TV and a single ottoman where Silas was now sitting alert, observing the stranger. In the dining area off the living room, Anya could make out Egyptian pictures framed on an unevenly textured, cream-colored wall.

"How are you, Anya?" Sage said. Anya returned her gaze to Sage, who was quick to embrace her.

"I'm doing well. How about you guys?"

"We're happy," she said.

"The clouds are horrid outside," Anya exclaimed. Gwynn emerged from the kitchen, where a stainless steel island winked from behind him.

"It means a big release is coming," he looked at her slyly, moving forward to hug her as well.

"That must be good, right?" Anya questioned.

"It always is," he says, looking at her with this strange knowingness. As if he knew what was about to happen in their next session. Gwynn motioned them to sit on the couch just in front of the windows letting in the gloomy hue from outside. Anya loved days like this. Rain always made her want to curl up in her nook with the latest book.

On rainy days, she would drink tea all day and watch rain stream down the big windows in her house like a waterfall. Hard downpours were far and few between. She couldn't recall the last time she was able to sit in her nook while it rained all day. The thought saddened her. The world had changed so much since she was a kid. It had been a long while since she had sprinted through puddles wearing rubber boots, trying to evade each raindrop that fell from the sky, a game she never won.

Anya loved the water.

The one thing missing from her Colorado mountains was the ocean. She craved the gravitational pull of the waves and the rough and salty residue left on her skin. She looked forward to her trip with Bee and Karmyn the more she thought about it.

But rain.

Lack of rain.

It was a sign that things were changing on this planet. Many ignored the change—blatantly denying its existence. As if Sage had been listening to her thoughts, she asked her if she wanted a cup of tea. Anya accepted the offer, finding a snug space on the fabric couch across from the leather one. Silas was eyeing her until she found her seated position, perched like a gray Sphinx. Once she sat down, his head lowered to rest.

"So, how have things been going?" Gwynn asked, fixating his teal eyes on her. Anya needed a second to collect her thoughts, wondering just where she should begin. She could start with Sam, but somehow she felt ashamed with how lovesick she had become in the past few weeks. Deciding to hold off, she told him about work and her upcoming trip to California with Bee and Karmyn. Sage listened from the kitchen, busy fixing her a cup of tea. When she came into the living room with the cup, it was steaming hot to the touch. Anya set it down to let it cool, fidgeting with her fingers, a sign that she always had something else to say but hadn't worked up the courage to say it. She wondered if Gwynn and Sage noticed this habit in her yet.

"Any dreams lately?" Anya stopped fidgeting to look up at him.

"Yes, actually," she said, realizing she would have to explain who Sam was. Anya felt anytime she boasted about someone she was with, the universe would just take him away from her. Not talking about him at all saved her from a jinx.

"Well, let's hear it," Sage said.

Anya told them the story of the multiple destinations she saw through the goggles and how she could only see and hear where she was in each destination. She couldn't taste, smell, or feel anything. She detailed her interaction with Sam next to the river. Then she told them about the final destination and her presence on a planet. She explained the silver buildings, the glowing flowers, the beautiful people, and how she searched for Sam but couldn't find him anywhere. Sage and Gwynn listened while the words poured out of her. She had talked for so long, the steam once rising from her teacup disappeared. This would likely be a routine for all future visits, letting her tea reduce to a shiver while she rambled away.

When she had nothing left to say, Gwynn sat silent. Sage fiddled with the rings on her finger, a soft jingle coming from the orchestra of bangles on her wrist.

"That is quite the dream," he said with a hint of a smile. "Great meanings."

"What does it mean?" Anya asked.

"Well, some spiritual masters say that when we have dreams, and we visit different destinations that seem outrageous or otherworldly, it's just our spirit body going to other places. These same spiritual masters suggest that as physical beings, we are living a holographic existence. We have a higher self creating multiple kinds of realities. Sometimes, in our dreams, that higher self visits those other lives. It's suggested that we as humans are not living a single linear existence. Rather, multiple realities exist concurrently." Anya wondered—were her lucid dreams taking her to other types of existences created by her higher self?

"What's interesting is in all of these destinations, you could only see and hear. Very puzzling," he finished.

"Why is that puzzling?" Anya asked.

"Well, we are spirits, living a human existence. We're supposed to feel all the senses. That's why we're here. You, however, experienced the opposite. You didn't feel anything at all. It makes me wonder many things about you," he said.

There was so much she was starting to wonder about herself, yet she still held few answers. Gwynn didn't continue but sat in thought, closing his eyes for minutes as if in search of an answer.

"Sage, do you have thoughts," he asked.

"I have some," she began. "It seems you're looking for your masculine side. Your masculine energy is seen as your active side, the one that makes things happen in the physical. The feminine energy represents the intuitive side. The things you feel in your gut. In dreams, women are seen as the feminine side and men, the masculine. Typically, the feminine and masculine energy are in perfect harmony when together. In dreams, this is represented in hugging, kissing, and sex—sex being the ultimate physical connection. Since you're looking for Sam, otherwise known as your masculine energy, this could mean you're looking for the active part of yourself."

Anya thought on this. Not quite sure what point she was getting to, but still listening, willing, and open.

"Is there a part of you that may not be taking action on something specific somewhere in your life?" Sage asked. Anya thought for a moment.

At work, she stayed pretty active.

With Sam, she didn't take action at first, but that was changing.

Perhaps she could be taking more action to be close to her parents?

Or...

It could be the very truth she had been avoiding all along.

It was true. Anya was putting in the work to learn more about her strange connections to things she didn't understand, but she was still hesitant, unwilling to believe any of it. A part of her did. Otherwise, she wouldn't be here. But an even stronger part of her was still in denial, driven by fears of what she didn't know.

Of the two things she could think of, where she wasn't taking action, this was the one constantly taking up brain space. Anya wanted to believe, but in so many ways, she just couldn't. It was easier living with what she knew, avoiding anything so astronomically out there. It was easier living in the world she had already believed in, not something out of Star Trek.

Anya was not ashamed to admit that she didn't believe this. So she did.

"I'm just not sure how much of me wants to keep looking into why I feel connected to Pleiades," Anya said. Gwynn and Sage looked at her. Anya couldn't sense any judgment or anger, just patience.

"Why is that?" Sage asked.

"I just don't know how much of it I believe," Anya replied. They both nodded in understanding. "It seems like absolute nonsense that I would believe something I can't see or hold over the various tangible things that already exist in my life."

Anya, winded after her answer, desperately looked at Gwynn and Sage, awaiting what they had to say.

"So, why are you here?" Gwynn inquired.

Because on some insane level, she really did believe it.

As much as the rest of her didn't want to believe it, she did.

"There's a part of me that truly believes it," Anya said.

"Are you afraid?" Sage asked.

"I'm beyond terrified," Anya admitted.

"Fear is a powerful motivator," Sage said. "What exactly do you fear?"

"What I don't know," Anya said. It was a simple answer but a truthful one.

"It's okay that you feel this way," Gwynn said. "Your efforts to be here are just proof that your questioning of it all will lead you into more enlightenment," he said. "Yet, there is another way for us to prove this otherworldly existence to you."

Anya found that hard to believe.

How could these two, living in the middle of nowhere, hold answers to life on Pleiades? How could they possibly know what that looks like? Denial was now thick in her bones, her solid foundation. As absurd as his claims were, she decided to humor him.

"What way is that?" She asked

"Astral projection," he said. "Many people we work with have found success with it. But it will take some time to master."

"How will it help?" Anya asked.

"It allows your spirit body to go to other worlds and dimensions all while keeping you tethered to your physical vessel," he said. Anya remembered what Sam said on one of their first dates about Marvel movies just being cinematic adventures easing us into the truth of what's really living in space. Then she had a thought.

"Like Doctor Strange?" She added.

Gwynn chuckled.

"Yes, like Doctor Strange."

Maybe she didn't entirely believe the concept, but having a movie's visual to refer to fed her imagination.

"And you can teach me how to do this?" A level of snark rising in her throat.

"Yes, we can," he replied. "But it'll take practice and patience. We likely won't start today. Are you interested in that?"

Anya considered it. Denial and fear were much stronger than her desires to know herself. Right now, she didn't have to make a decision, but she needed to give one to Gwynn and Sage. As Anya battled her indoctrinations, she blurted the first non-committal answer that came to her.

"Yes," Gwynn smiled at this. Anya saw a twinkle of excitement in him. Either he knew she was full of shit, or he looked forward to teaching her about astral projection. Anya felt the piece of stone present in her pocket, trying to remind herself of what Sage had said over a month ago. The stone brings change, imagination, and creativity. Maybe Anya could stand to use her imagination more or be more open to change. Either way, she would have to make a choice, and there was certainly no going back now.

Anya, Gwynn, and Sage went through the same ritual process of a reading, hand and foot washing, and then the energy session. Unlike the first and very emotional visit, Anya spent much of her time talking about her relationship with Sam. Gwynn and Sage looked pleased with her confessions. When they mentioned things would change for her, or she would feel a shift, Anya knew this fit in the category of things that resulted in change. Anya spoke less about her parents and avoided talking about her fears of so many unknowns.

She didn't cry this time. Didn't break. And when she didn't, they crumpled her colored drawing and burned it in the cauldron outside, saying nothing else. When it was over, Anya paid for her session and left, realizing however little she confessed to them still made her feel better, lighter, and more relieved. The only weights she carried were her fears and the stone in her pocket.

Without removing it from the deep space it settled in, she tried to remember just how much of a galaxy she could see in it. Recalling the one time she had genuinely looked at it other than the time it twinkled from the bedside table before her first kiss with Sam.

Driving home, Anya listened to music, watching the clouds darken above. Gwynn and Sage predicted heavy rain and release, which only reminded her that she hadn't released anything at all. Before she reached the part of the road where she would lose cell service, a message came through. It was from Gwynn. Not bearing to look at it directly, Anya commanded her phone to read it for her.

"Tell your heart that the fear of suffering is worse than the suffering itself," said Siri. How Gwynn had known this was a favorite quote from one of her favorite books, *The Alchemist*, was a mystery. Anya couldn't recall if she had even mentioned this book during their last few encounters.

The simple sentence planted a seed of thought.

Observing the lack of cars on the same road, she found a safe and flat space to pull over. She retrieved the stone from her pocket, admiring the jagged and imperfect shape. Looking into the stone, she found the random speckles of black and white, the pattern that coined its name, the galaxy diamond. Looking hard to find the galaxy in it, she tried to memorize where all the flecks lived. If no one knew better, this rock looked a lot like smokey quartz. To anyone, this was a meaningless rock bought at a store for $20.

What she was now beginning to learn about herself was too big to handle. That was the truth. She simply couldn't handle being someone, *something*, so far out of this dimension. Of being special. She needed more than the word of two people she barely knew—anything that would sway her beliefs.

Anya continued to stare into the rock that laid flat in her palm. Staring until the flecks of black and white sparkled like stars, hypnotizing her. A surge of peculiar energy surged through her, burning hot at her palm where the stone rested. Unable to tear her eyes away, she kept staring into the rock until the energy burned so hot, she nearly dropped the stone.

"Son of a bitch," she exclaimed.

When she took the stone from her palm, the heat disappeared, and the stone returned to coolness.

"That was weird," she said out loud. It could've been a sign. She should have paid attention to this sign. Then the words sent by Gwynn shuffled through her thoughts.

"Fear of suffering," she muttered.

A car sped by her.

Then another.

She thought about the times she had let fear consume her so much that she never leapt into anything, even if she desired it. Like climbing a rock wall fearing that she'd fall, knowing many most certainly do before they reach the top. Anya fiddled with the stone again, careful not to let it rest in her palm.

"Why am I afraid?" She questioned out loud, trying to make sense of this fear, going deep into investigation.

Why is this something to be feared?

Because maybe there is some truth to it.

Because if it were true, it would mean everything that she came to know in her life would fall apart around her.

But would that be such a bad thing?

Would being a more loving and more supreme being be so bad?

No.

Recognizing she is not only empowered but powerful is what was terrifying.

Humans are muted to their genuine strength. In the world of marketing, people play off others' emotions. She knew that well. They play off their fear, sadness, anxiety, and grief. Using it against them and enticing them to fill those voids with things they don't need.

Alcohol.

Drugs.

Medication.

Food.

Sex.

Things.

As a result, people will live in fear, anxiety, grief, and sadness for most of their lives. Did Anya want that? If this was her truth, what would she do if it was stripped away from her?

What if it wasn't her truth?

What if she lived on the jewel-toned planet to feel the love and warmth she had felt in her dream. What if she could leave this place for another place like that?

If she did, she would be doing it alone. No one would understand enough, or play into this idea enough, to consider an alternative existence.

She didn't want to do this alone.

She didn't want this truth to strip her of her friends, her Sam, everything she knew and loved. Even with the normalcy and comfort of her pain and struggles, she would be rid of that too, exchanging it for a comfortable experience void of everything else she had already created in her life. To accept one fully, she sacrificed the other entirely.

That was her answer.

This was why she was afraid.

The stone in her fingertips dropped to the floor. The thought of leaving all those things and losing everything she loved because she was driven to follow her heart. That was what she feared. The words Gwynn had sent her were part of a much larger story and more important message.

Following your personal legend and what you're destined to be.

How very big and frightening that pursuit always is.

In that story, the main character goes on his journey, passing up everything, even love, just to find where he belonged.

He gave up *everything*.

If Anya wanted to truly find her place, find the meaning of her existence, she would have to do the same, which was an excruciating fear. Tears came. Anya buried her face in her hands, listening to more cars speed by her, unbeknownst to tumultuous confusion happening in her car. Anya tried to convince herself it was okay to admit this fear. Yet, it made her feel so much more alone. In the middle of her sobs, she heard the rhythmic pounding of rain on the roof of her car.

Progressing from a slow drizzle to a waterfall-like downpour, the rain came, falling around her for as far as she could see. The phone chimed again—another text message from Gwynn.

"Good girl," it said. As if he knew. She dialed the number, trying to calm her sobs. He answered. Anya worked to stifle her crying, trying to say something. Anything. Fortunately, she didn't have to. Gwynn did instead.

"Let it out, girl," he said. "Whatever you're feeling, let it out."

She wailed on the other end of the receiver.

"I don't..." she cried. "Want to... lose everything... in pursuit of... what I am."

"You won't," he said. "You'll gain so much more than you could ever imagine by accepting who you are. Anyone who tells you differently is lying," Anya cried harder.

Those tears led the conversation while Gwynn stayed on the phone waiting for the crying to subside. After several minutes she was able to catch her breath long enough to inhale deeply.

"That's good," he said. "That was a big release, Anya."

Anya stayed silent, watching the rain plummet down around her, words unable to escape her.

"You've created a big void," he continued. "When we cry like this, we empty that space where grief, fear, or sadness use to live. We have to fill that space with something loving so no other darkness can come in, okay?"

"Okay," she responded.

"Do you know how to do that?" He asked.

"No," she said.

"Then, let's do it together."

"Okay," she muttered, still sniffing.

"Close your eyes," she did as she was told. "Take a few deep breaths. Let your body settle into your seat," Gwynn prompted her to relinquish the control of her body through meditation until she was met with a pleasant numbness.

"Now, we're going to call in the light," he said.

Anya took another breath, finally feeling relaxed.

"Imagine a stream of pink and white light filling you from head to toe." Anya imagined a bright shining white light with lines of pink and yellow filling the top of her head and flowing her down to her feet.

A warmth filled her. Soothed her.

She let out another breath, feeling full and even more weightless than she had before.

"How do you feel?" Gwynn asked.

"Much better," she said. "Thank you."

"You're welcome, my dear. Now, go have tons of fun on your trip to California, okay?" he commanded. "If you can, take a salt bath before you go."

"I will," she agreed. "Thank you again."

Anya hung up the phone. Looking in the rearview, she wiped away the remaining wetness on her face. She retrieved the stone from the floor of her car, quickly returning it to its home in her pocket. By now, dozens of cars had passed her. The rain continued to fall on her roof like a million sticks on a drum.

Putting her car in drive, she sped off, cutting through the walls of rain.

TWENTY-SIX

The rain pounded on Sam's roof as he built a fire. The damp from the rain outside was seeping through the cracks in his walls. Sam hadn't seen a downpour like this in a while. Weather channels could barely explain the impromptu shift in the weather forecasts. The entire region was getting hammered with rain. He hoped the rabbit and the Stellar Jays had found a good hiding place.

Sam packed his woodstove with crumpled newspaper and the dry sticks he had kept in the corner since winter. He was able to grab a few logs before the downpour soaked everything. With the flick of a match, he lit the fire. The newspapers blazed and smoked, the flames spreading quickly in ripples across the branches.

The door shut quickly, but he left the bottom smaller door slightly open to let air in through the vent. Once the twigs caught fire, he tossed a large log in and the wood-burning stove roared to life. Some residual heat built up just inches from the stove window, flickering a bright orange to light up his eyes.

He found his nearest black hoodie and a pair of grey sweat pants, pulling them both on to feel warmth.

The Lost Pleiad

Burrowing into his sweats, Sam loved the feeling of a fire, rain, and the sensation of his comfy clothes hugging his body.

Sam hadn't heard from her all day. As if she could sense he was thinking of her, his phone rang. Picking it up, he saw a candid photo of her flash on his phone. One he took at a brewery in Colorado Springs. She was looking at him with her Disney princess eyes while taking a swig of beer.

He answered.

"Hey, love," he said. "What are you up to?"

"Not much," she said. "I'm driving back from Fremont County."

Puzzling.

She hadn't told him anything about a trip to Fremont County.

"Oh?" He lilted. "What's down in Fremont County?"

"I want to tell you about it, actually," she said. A sentence that instantly relaxed Sam. He lowered himself into the corner of the couch, feeling the stinging chill that lingered on the fabric. "I'll be home in a little bit, and I need to take a salt bath. Want to come over in like an hour?"

"I just started a fire here," he said, looking out at the insane rainfall, realizing they had only ever spent time at her place. He loved her house, how it made him feel at home, how it instantly relaxed him, how it seemed to always be full of love. It never occurred to him to invite her over since he loved her space so much. There was also the other half of the house he still hadn't finished yet, which embarrassed him.

"Why don't you come here?" He propositioned.

"Yeah?" She said with a hint of delight.

"Yeah, of course," he said. "It is kind of weird you haven't been here yet. You may need a boat to get here, though."

"Ha! You're right about that. You don't have a bathtub, though," she giggled. And for the first time, Sam wished he had a bathtub.

"You're not wrong," he laughed. "Well, take your bath, do whatever else you have to do, and then come over here."

"Okay, darling," she said. Sam melted every time she called him 'darling.' "See you soon."

"See you soon," he replied.

Sam looked around his horizontal, plank-paneled bachelor pad and the contained fire in his wood-burning stove. While he considered himself pretty clean and orderly, his little studio area was cluttered. His hockey skates hung haphazardly just underneath his loft bed, and pieces of wood scattered the floor. His bathroom and the rock-carved sink needed a good wipe down. He didn't even want to look at the other side of his unfinished house. It was lucky he had some time to clean up before she would be getting here. Sam instantly busied himself to put his space in order, wiping down the stone kitchen counter that hosted a single hot plate and a dual sink. He tidied the cups on the log shelves just above the kitchen space, wiping those shelves too.

Sam hadn't thought about what Anya might think of this place. A sort of poor man's cabin, in his mind. However odd it seemed on the inside, he loved his home and what he had built for himself, even if it had its ghosts. But it was undeniable his space didn't accommodate much more than himself. That might've been why he always liked going to Anya's. Her home appeared to be a space made for at least two people, and it was much bigger than his space.

He looked up at the loft bed, which was unmade, climbing the ladder up to straighten out the blanket. Then he came down and vacuumed the floor just below. The vacuum growled when he switched it on. It sucked up bits of gravel and wood, sounding off like a coffee grinder working too hard. When he finished, he looked around, feeling a lot better about his space. Looking outside, the rain still hadn't let up. The sun was starting to set behind a grey curtain, and from a distance, Sam could see the haul trucks still running. They never stopped for anything, even rain. Lucky for them, the downpour would weigh the dust from the roads down.

Sam put the vacuum away and then slumped back into his couch. The wood still burned orange, kicking out heat, finally settling the damp he had felt earlier. Cleaning his house took all of thirty minutes, so he occupied the rest of the hour watching videos on the internet. Unable to decide just where to start his spiraling journey down a YouTube rabbit hole, he settled on a topic his lady was fond of.

Pleiadians.

He typed the words on his computer, watching them pull up on the 40" TV before him, giving him a much larger view. Hitting enter, dozens of pages came up, revealing a whole other world on this topic.

"Good God," he said to himself. "It's a whole damn community."

He scrolled through all of them, briefly reading their titles. Some of them focused on channeling Pleiadians. Others were meditations for Pleiadians. Others were people singing hymns in a Pleiadian language.

He played a hymn sung by a beautiful blonde woman. When the music started playing, the woman sang soothing tones, all with her eyes closed. Although a tad weird in his opinion, it was still quite beautiful. He had so many questions.

Was this language even real?

How did she learn to sing it?

Was she making it up just for the likes?

As much as Sam wanted to believe these things, he was reluctant to; stubborn to. But it was important to Anya, and he wanted to understand it better.

He closed out the video, scrolling further down to find something else to watch on the topic, finding a video of a woman speaking incredibly fast in a strange tongue as she channeled a collective of Pleiadians. He moved to another video discussing the traits of the Pleiadians.

In such a short time, he learned a lot.

This community of people believed in this Pleiades as if it were a place. They seemed to *enjoy* it.

Sam could now understand why Anya resonated with it so much. Although a peculiar way to identify, he still found it an endearing quality and unlike anyone he had ever known. For that, he knew he had found a treasure. How many other women would tell him such crazy things? The sheer courage it took.

As he finished his searches, wheels tore into his wet driveway, coming to a halt behind his white truck. Sam shut down the video search. Anya ran towards the only door she could find. When she stumbled in, she was already sopping wet.

"Holy crap," she said. "It is insane out there!"

"I know!" He said. "God, you're drenched. Let's get you out of those clothes." Anya smiled, tilting her head at him in uncertainty.

Sam rolled his eyes and laughed. "That's not what I meant.

He smirked, and Anya laughed.

"Are you sure?" she asked.

Sam instantly pulled her in for a kiss, feeling a new and better warmth cover him. He no longer needed that fire with Anya nearby.

He walked toward his dresser to find a dry hoodie and a pair of sweat pants.

"How was your day?" He asked. But she didn't answer. When he turned around to see why she was silent, Anya was standing in the middle of the studio watching him, her eyes wandering to his backside.

"What?" He laughed, looking confused.

"What is it about gray sweat pants?" She asked, placing a hand on her hip. Her golden hair dripped wet, without makeup, as stunning as ever. Sam turned, trying to look down at his butt.

"What about them?" He asked.

"Your ass looks amazing in them. And just so you know. That is a thing among women," she said.

"Is it really?" He said, shocked.

"Oh yeah," she said, practically swooning. "Chicks dig a guy with a nice ass in gray sweatpants."

"Well, I guess you learn something new every day," he laughed again.

He climbed up his ladder, retrieving a hoodie from the plastic bins that sat on top of his fridge, watching Anya from the corner of his eye as she searched his place.

"I really love your place," she said. Sam was shocked and happy to hear this.

"Really? Looks like a worn-down cabin," he said.

"I love small and unique places," she said.

"It is definitely both of those things." He said. "Thanks for liking it."

He climbed back down, handing her the hoodie. She disappeared into the bathroom, emerging a few minutes later to kiss him. Each kiss with her was just as exciting as the first kiss. Pulling him in, she made him forget everything else in the world.

"Mmmm," she said. Sam just smiled back at her. "You are yummy."

"Look who's talking," he brushed the wet hair from her face, looking at the blue of her eyes which were much brighter than the storms happening outside. She turned around, making her way to the couch, where she curled her wet hair into a bun. Sam followed her closely, quick to sit down next to her.

"I just love the rain," she stared out into the gloom in a most longing way. Like she was searching for something or missing something. She stared for so long, Sam thought something might be bothering her.

"You okay?" Sam asked. It was common of him to ask that question now. After several weeks, he regarded her as two things: his 'cosmic angel' and his 'profound thinker.' Sam always caught her just sitting there, thinking her deep thoughts, letting them consume her and bother her. He wanted so desperately to know what kind of things she thought about and most of the time, she told him. More than anything, he wanted to know so he could soothe her, prevent her from overthinking.

On the other hand, he was beginning to accept that this was just who she was. Instead of worrying about it, he decided to be a space for her to talk if and when she wanted to. He shifted into questions about what she was doing in Fremont County.

"So, what's in Fremont County?' He questioned. Tearing her deep gaze from the wet world outside, she looked back at Sam, staring deep into him instead. She hesitated, searching for the words. Another common trait of hers. Saying things with more intent and thought.

While things had gone well for weeks, it was clear Anya was still careful when it came to sharing the essential parts of herself. But looking at her now, Sam felt like she was more relaxed than before. More... out there.

It calmed him, but he was also curious about this new trait of hers.

"It's kind of weird," she said.

"I like your weird," he smiled.

"Somedays, I don't know why," she giggled nervously.

"Don't act so surprised," he smiled. "Okay, tell me."

"Okay, so around the time we started dating, I started going to see energy healers in Fremont County," Just when he thought she couldn't surprise him more. "I've been going down to them to make sense of that... thing I told you about."

"Being Pleiadian, you mean?" He asked matter of fact. Anya tensed her shoulders and jaw, dropping her gaze. She fidgeted with her fingers and then laughed nervously.

"Yes. *That*."

Just saying this out loud made her nervous, and that was obvious, her posture being the clear indicator. He realized how much courage it took for her to even say it out loud and wanted to calm her.

"It's okay, Anya. You can tell me this stuff. I don't think you're crazy," And with those words, her shoulders relaxed. Sam got up to find the nearest blanket, wrapping it around them for comfort. He watched her eyes rise to meet his. The more electric blue he had come to love was now much lighter, closer to slate gray.

"These people, we've been doing healing sessions together, getting to the bottom of some of my fears. The first time I went, we talked about my anger," Sam listened. Having never seen her angry, he couldn't picture it at all. "After the first session, they gave me this beautiful stone called a galaxy diamond. They said it was supposed to be helpful for me. That it would protect me and stimulate creativity and imagination."

"I've never heard of a galaxy diamond," Sam said. Anya pulled up a picture on her phone and showed it to him. They were beautiful stones. Some of them were so dark with black and speckled less with white. It honestly did look like a galaxy.

"This session, we talked about fear. They asked me what I was afraid of. I just couldn't pinpoint where I was afraid of anything. Almost everything in my life is incredible. On my way home, I pulled over on the side of the road. I held that rock and realized that I'm afraid this thing about me will tear me from everything I already know and isolate me more. When I realized that, I cried the whole way home." The glowing smile she came in with was now reduced to a frown. Sam pulled her in, hugging her so tightly she melted into him.

"You want to know what I think?" He asked.

"Of course," she replied.

"I think it's impossible for someone like you to be completely isolated from anyone just because of who you are," he said.

"You say that because you like me, and you're biased," she laughed.

"I say that because it's true. You're just too damn amazing. And if people don't understand that this is a part of you, if people want to walk away because of who you are, you don't want those people in your life anyway," he said.

"Yeah. I guess you're right," she sighed.

Sam felt her rhythmic breaths slow to match his own. They stayed like that for a while. For a moment, he thought she had returned to her thoughts. He imagined they had been a place of comfort for her for so long. Getting her to open up about these thoughts may be just what she needed.

"I know my parents will not accept this about me," she added in the silence. Sam didn't know what to say to that. Having had confusing parental influences in his life, it was hard for him to fathom having two parents who might not accept you for who you are.

"I'm sure they're more proud of you than you think," he said.

"They're very religious, and this goes against everything they're taught to believe. They, without a doubt, will not accept this. I promise you," Sam wanted to argue, wanted to be optimistic, but he didn't know their relationship well enough to form an opinion that could help, thinking it would be arrogant to try.

"You'll find out someday," she said. At this, Sam perked up. Meeting parents was always a big deal. Maybe not to her though.

"Oh, yeah? I get to meet your parents someday?" He asked.

"Sure. If they don't disown me for being an alien," she said.

"I prefer the term 'cosmic angel,'" he said.

At this, she lifted her gaze to find his eyes. She kissed him hard, pressing her body into his. Sam let her, feeling her weight fall onto him.

Sam loved how close they had become and how it conceived a greater connection unlike anything he had before. When he wasn't busy with other things, Sam craved her, mentally, spiritually, physically, sexually, and emotionally. He wanted all parts of her, and that want hadn't slowed or mellowed since the time he first laid eyes on her.

That night, they laid in bed next to each other, talking for hours. Sam remembered this would be the final night he would see her before her trip to California. He knew she would be back in a week, but he still dreaded her absence. Missing her was something he anticipated. He wondered if she felt the same way. Rather than hold back that feeling, he came out with it, saying it as honestly as she had admitted her otherworldly truths.

"I will miss you terribly," he said.

"I will miss you too, darling," she said. "I will be back before you know it."

Sam heard many great things about Karmyn and Bee over the past few weeks. How Karmyn pushed Anya to date him and how annoyingly nosy and wonderful she was. She talked about Bee being the wisest and most supportive friend she knew. It was more than obvious that Anya cared for her friends and valued them beyond words. He looked forward to meeting them someday.

"I'll bring you back some of the beach," she said.

"The only thing I want back from the beach is you," he said, kissing her forehead. Snuggling into the loft, they fell asleep, the fire slowly burning out below them. The cold started to creep in, cooling the room and drawing them even closer together.

The rain was starting to subside. As Anya snored softly coiled in his arms, Sam counted everything about her that he was grateful for. Reminding himself how easily something so terrific could be stripped away from him.

He hoped that with enough gratitude, the universe would let him keep her. That it wouldn't make him pay for the ways he had wronged women. That karma wouldn't strip him of the one thing that mattered most to him.

TWENTY-SEVEN

That morning, Anya raced out of Sam's door, giving him a million kisses as she left, promising she would text him when she arrived in San Diego. The rain had deeply soaked the earth. Apparent as her feet sank in the mud on the way to her car. A flock of Stellar Jays danced in the trees, happy to see the sunlight, and she saw the biggest rabbit of her life duck into a pile of wood.

She was going to miss Sam.

She hadn't told him about the rain. How Gwynn predicted her release would be linked to the downpour and that the heavy rain was of her doing. Mentioning the stone was too bizarre to mention too. Anya decided too much crazy truth would be too much altogether.

Trying to shake the anxiety surrounding her short separation from Sam, she drove home. Luckily, she had packed several days before they would leave.

Anya drove down the curves of the mountain, carefully watching for big horned sheep and deer. It was a long shot to see them since it was summer and so hot, but on occasion, they would hop down from the mountain and onto the road. The asphalt was turning from a dark to light gray as the sun-dried last night's rain away. The aspens perked up, showing the world their new shade of quenched green.

Anya's second favorite place in the world was the ocean. She would drive straight through the night to get to it, even if Bee and Karmyn fell asleep. Once they arrived, Anya swore to herself she wouldn't go to sleep until waves yanked her in with their gravitational pull, even if her friends whined about what a long trip it had been. She knew they would sleep the whole way anyway.

Anya picked up Karmyn first. When she came out of her front door, a duffle bag slung over her shoulder. Her husband, Jake, followed her to the front step, kissing her goodbye, while her two children trailed closely behind, pining for their mother. She kissed them too. That perfectly thick and wavy jet black hair of hers sparkled subtle shades of blue in the sun, and a tan glow radiated from her skin. She wore a pair of aviators, a black shirt that hung off her thin form, white shorts, and matching black sandals. Karmyn had many different looks, but Anya's favorite look was her adventurous one.

When Karmyn got in the car, Anya saw her stare out the window at her family, swearing a tear was formed at the corner of her eye.

"You okay?" Anya asked, holding still before shifting into drive.

"Oh yeah," she said. "You just never get used to leaving them, no matter how short the separation is."

Anya missed Sam already.

Perhaps they would have something similar one day. Maybe she would shed the same tears each time she left her family to go on a journey. Karmyn's husband waved at her from the door, blowing kisses in her direction. Karmyn blew kisses back.

"Okay, I'm ready," she said. "Let's go get Bee."

Bee wasn't too far from Karmyn's house. But really, anywhere in Colorado Springs wasn't that far. When they arrived at her home, Anya observed a similar goodbye ritual. Bee kissing her husband, Stephen, and their two children goodbye, watching them wave as she strutted down the sidewalk to the car. Bee was dressed in adventurous gear similar to Karmyn's, toting a large backpack with her dirty blonde beach waves already calling to the California oceans. She wore a pair of jean shorts, tan sandals, and a forest green shirt.—her signature color. Like Karmyn, she was on the verge of tears leaving her family for a short time.

Anya wondered how many kids she and Sam would have.

"What's that smell? Is that…" Bee sniffs Anya's hair. "Man smell?"

Anya rolled her eyes. Karmyn's white smile became way more than apparent.

Here it comes.

"You stayed at Sam's house last night!" Karmyn exclaimed.

"Yes, I did," Anya smiled. And she *really* smiled.

"Oh my god. Did anything happen?" She asked. "Look at your face! You're totally falling for him," Bee said.

"Perhaps," Anya said slyly. "And no, nothing happened."

"Really? You're glowing," Bee continued.

Anya laughed. "No, we haven't had sex yet."

"Damn, he is different from the rest of them," Karmyn said

Sure it could have been Sam alone making her glow this way, but maybe it was the sessions with Gwynn and Sage too. Karmyn sat in the passenger's seat, shaking her head in a strange sort of agreement. Proud of herself for forcing Anya into dating Sam more. Anya looked at them both and sighed.

"I'm very grateful for you both pressuring me to keep dating him," Anya said. How many more times would she have to say it?

"As you should be!" Bee said.

They drove down Uintah street toward I-25, the road that would carry them up to E-470 until they hit I-70. From there, they'd go west until they hit Grand Junction. This was the shortest route to Mission Bay Beach in San Diego, California. It was also the most beautiful drive. They agreed on making brief stops in Las Vegas and Los Angeles before arriving at their destination. One place for the adult fun. The other for tacos. But they needed coffee first.

Bee and Karmyn were in the car, practically shouting as they talked. Clearly, both of them were excited about this trip. As mothers and wives, Anya could only imagine how nice it must be to have a little break at times. Anya heard over and over how much work it was, being a parent, but with those confessions always came an undeniable, powerful love for their families. Every one of their children was well behaved, and they had husbands that glowed with love for them. In some ways, Anya couldn't understand how they would want to be anywhere else other than with their families.

Someday, she might find out for herself.

They reached Pikes Perk within minutes to get their ritual coffees and take their group selfie. Anya ordered her favorite, a hot caramel breve. Bee, a simple iced coffee with cream and maple syrup. Karmyn, a heavily sweetened vanilla latte with a dash of 'help me wake the fuck up,' as she called it.

With each sip, Anya let the creamy and buttery taste of half and half take over her palette along with the sweetness of toasty caramel. It was the perfect drink. How could cream, and butter, and fat be so good?

The Lost Pleiad

In one quick turn, they were speeding down I-25.

Minutes of driving turned to hours.

They drove around Denver to get to I-70, passing by Vail and Avon, waving hello to Hanging Lake since they couldn't make the stop, letting their jaws drop at the rocky cliffs of Glenwood Canyon. Salivating at the world's largest hot springs pool off the interstate as they passed Glenwood Springs. Driving past Silt and the KOA, where Anya stayed in a Campervan during her last birthday. She vaguely remembered the bald eagle perched in a tree and the river rushing by while she cooked bacon and eggs from the back of her rented van.

The next big city was Grand Junction, where they could see Grand Mesa from the interstate. The world's largest flat-top mountain, a monster trek the three of them still intended to conquer one day.

Grand Junction wasn't far from Palisade, a place famous for peaches and lavender. The lavender farm there held rows of purple shades crawling up small hills, covered with busy bees as Grand Mesa towered over everything in the west and the Bookcliff mountains crinkled like paper in the north.

After leaving Grand Junction, I-70 turned into HWY 50, shooting them into the state of Utah. They drove through the desert terrain, debating at length on whether or not they should stop at the Arches National Park. Ultimately, they decided not to. Anya was driving and desperate to get to the ocean. So that decision ruled in her favor.

Two stops were already enough.

In some moments, the car filled with chatter. Other times, they bopped along to their favorite genres of music, alternating between the playlists they've had on repeat. Sometimes, the three of them sat in comfortable silence, letting their thoughts carry them to far-off places.

When Anya caught herself thinking, she realized Karmyn and Bee were doing the same. She wondered what they might be thinking about, too but never asked.

In her silence, Anya thought about Sam, energy healing, and the galaxy stone.

She felt panic strike her heart.

The galaxy stone.

Had she brought it with her?

She relaxed, feeling no bulge in the deepness of her pocket where it always was, realizing she had left it at home on her bedside table—one of her two safest places. The stone had become so precious, losing it would wreck her like a ship in a stormy sea.

Anya wondered what Sam was doing. Probably working. It was a Monday. He was probably talking up some older strangers, reciting the same historical facts. No matter how many times he repeated his knowledge, his optimism and passion for the area never faded. He was just as excited to tell the 1,000th person about Gold Camp District as he was the first person. She thought of his thick beard, slicked brown hair, and his amber eyes—a starburst of brownish-orange in the daylight.

She missed him, and it hadn't even been a full day yet.

Eventually, Sam would meet Bee and Karmyn.

And her parents.

God. Her parents.

She could see it, the judgments they would pass under their breath; those same judgments would carry into their private conversations after he left. Judging him for having no religion, or having a simple job, making that into a soft lecture during their conversations.

The thought made her sick.

They would judge his profession and lifestyle, saying it wasn't enough to support a family, not knowing he was more stable and responsible than most people her age. There would be no way to save Sam from meeting them. Anya knew they would not give him a fair chance. Yet, somehow, she felt obligated to introduce him to them.

She was growing tired of her obligations to them.

Anya, stuck in her thoughts for so long, hadn't noticed Karmyn and Bee were fast asleep. By now, it was afternoon, and the drive through Utah was stunning. It was no Colorado, but Anya tried to see the beauties in all scenes of nature, not just her favorite ones. It was a desert wasteland for hours before the landscapes would return to mountains and trees.

Anya remembered this drive.

She did it as a child.

Their trek on I-70 would end with a junction at I-15, just before reaching Mesquite, Nevada. She stopped for gas, the halted car still not disturbing her sleeping friends. Las Vegas was a stone's throw from there.

Anya was nearing the Nevada border and the girls must have sensed or heard the sound of slots ringing because around Mesquite, they woke up.

"How long were we out?" Karmyn asked.

"About seven years," Anya said, eyes still on the road. "We turned around and went back home because y'all couldn't hang."

"Oh, shut up, An," said Karmyn with an eye roll. Anya laughed, amused at her own jokes. Usually, Karmyn was the one spawning eye rolls in her friends.

"Where are we?" Bee chimed in.

"Just about to hit Mesquite," she said. "And you know what I was thinking?"

"What's that?" Karmyn said, rubbing her eyes and sweeping her black hair from her shoulder

"I think we should do the zip line down Fremont Street," Anya said, glancing at the both of them to see their reactions. Bee's eyes widened, and Karmyn sat up even straighter in her seat.

"YES," Bee said. "A perfect idea." Anya wondered why they all hadn't thought of it earlier.

"I'm so down!" Karmyn added.

Mesquite was just over an hour from Las Vegas. As the day darkened, the glow of Vegas city lights took up the edge of the dark sky. Cutting through it like a glowing row of obelisks. The orange hue humming above the city somehow made the backdrop of everything around it a deep purple.

It had been years since Anya had been to Vegas. In the two times she went in the past, the city had changed so much. And that was just four years in between. New hotels shot up in full lights within those years, and more signs displayed crawling messages glittering on marquees.

Las Vegas was always working on herself.

Anya could only stand Vegas for three days. The energy was high, always, and if she didn't have enough energy to keep up, it tired her out. After the third day, Anya usually crashed until her flight home. But this year, although tired from driving, she felt strangely energized and ready for whatever trouble the three of them could get into.

Before they made it into the city that never sleeps, the lights glared down, tempting them to stop everywhere to explore, starting with the

Neon Museum not far from the interstate. Anya truly wanted to stop, but they were on a schedule. They had to make it to the beach in a reasonable time frame. The trip was more than 17 hours from Colorado Springs, not counting any stops they made. If they lingered here too long, they would miss the whale watching tour, which Anya was thrilled to go on.

Fremont Street wasn't far from where they were, but with the traffic heavy beneath the sparkling lights of Vegas, it would be the better part of an hour before they got there. Anya rolled down the window, feeling the scorching heat rush into the car. She listened to the city noise, tuning into the music, ringing slots, and chattering people, trying to live more in this moment, practicing gratitude for where she was and who she was with.

From the corner of her eye, she saw Bee and Karmyn's faces light up as Vegas clung to their cheeks in rich luminescence, highlighting their delicate and beautiful features.

No matter how many times they came through Vegas, they were still always enthralled by it. Anyone was. Sure, people tired of the party scene, but some viewed it as a kid seeing a brightly lit Ferris wheel at a carnival for the first time or fireworks popping off into the dark sky on the Fourth of July.

From Vegas, the intensely lit buildings drowned out every sparkling star situated in its usual place, hiding all constellations and muting them for eternity. Or until this world ran out of energy. Anyone would have to drive through desert for miles just to find a place the noisy lights wouldn't take up the sky. Anya could never live in a place where she couldn't see the stars. Not seeing them now was killing her.

The traffic carried them to Fremont Street, and for another thirty minutes, they struggled to find parking. Bee had already looked up and ordered tickets to the zipline known as SlotZilla.

"There are two ways to fly," Bee said.

"Let me guess; one is a wuss one, and the other is not a wuss one," Karmyn said.

"Damn straight."

"Which one did you pick?" Anya asked.

"What do you think?" She laughed.

"Of course," Anya said. "Not a wuss one it is."

"It sends you headfirst, superhero style. How dare you think I would pick anything else," Bee said.

After finally finding a space in a parking garage, they found SlotZilla. The excitement tore into Anya. She had done zip lines before, even though it frightened her. The most terrifying one she had ever done was at the Royal Gorge Bridge. SlotZilla was an 11 story zipline inspired by a slot machine.

Go figure.

From the top, superhero flyers shot out from the giant slot machine, a 114-foot drop just beneath them and over 1,700 feet worth of zip line ahead as they descend beneath the world's largest video screen. After five blocks, the three little space cadets would end at the Golden Gate Casino. This was probably the closest Anya would ever come to feeling like a bird in flight, and she was ready to enjoy every terrifying moment of it.

Anya, Bee, and Karmyn climbed up the stairs to the 11th story of SlotZilla, giggling along the way. Deep anxiety and excitement settled in.

The Lost Pleiad

The young guy from SlotZilla strapped them in, helping them step into their harnesses and tighten them until they lost all circulation. The young man looked almost too young to work anywhere in Vegas, but that was happening to youth today. He helped shove their belongings, which weren't much, into the bags that would follow them on the way down. All three of them hung from the harness on their bellies, letting gravity pull them into the slicing tension of the harness. They were ready to plummet headfirst toward a sea of people stumbling drunk beneath them.

They waited behind a large door, anticipating the thrill of this coming ride. When it started opening like a garage door, it was time. Released in an instant, Karmyn and Bee shrieked, gaining incredible speed on the shallow decline toward the casino. Anya lagged gratefully, marveling at the mass of people herding beneath her. Some shouted up at her, some waved. Anya waved back. She stuck her arms out but kept her eyes open, feeling the wind beneath her make-believe wings. The anxious feeling and the fear were gone now with each passing foot and zip of the line. She savored every wisp of wind, every flash of light dancing above her, every person below who craned to look at her, the biting tension from the harness at her pelvis, the sight of her two friends copying her same birdlike figure.

The platform at the Golden Gate casino drew closer and closer. Anya held onto her euphoric feeling of flying, hoping it would last until she arrived at the platform. The fear of it all ending pressed against her, tight like the harness. But she held on, not letting her arms brace her for the stop. Instead, she held them open like she would swan dive into a pool of water.

Bee was first, then Karmyn, and trailing behind, Anya.

They swung to a halt at the platform as the people helped them out of their harness. Anya arrived last, letting the jerk of the stop rock her back to reality.

"Hot damn, that was amazing!" Bee shouted.

"That was dope as fuck," Karmyn said.

"I seriously could do that again and again," said Anya.

"Oh yeah, me too," said Bee. "Best $150 ever."

"What?! This was $150 for all three of us?" Karmyn exclaimed.

"Yup," Bee said, pleased.

"I love Vegas," Anya said.

"Drinks and snacks are on me," Karmyn said.

The three of them found their way downstairs to ground level, intent on walking the five blocks they had just traveled back to the car, making short stops at key places along the way. Anya was high on energy and adrenaline, thankful to finally match the liveliness of her fellow princesses.

They walked together, arm and arm, weaving in and out of the crowd, watching the people dressed in a variety of exotic attires—a woman with clothes painted on, a single thong covering her most private areas, and a pair of thigh-high Spice Girl platforms laced to perfection. Shirtless men with cut bodies were everywhere, whooping between slurps of swirled, colorful, icy alcoholic drinks as tall as them and too large for one hand. Someone dressed in a unicorn suit—the lights from the colored arches above waved at them, helping change their normal hue to shades of purple, blue, orange, pink, and red. It was well past 6:00 p.m., so they had missed the Viva Vision light show. Before going any further, they ducked into the nearest casino, putting some money in slots just to get a free drink.

Beers all around.

Once getting their drinks, they left the casino, finding a group just nearby dancing to the music blaring from the 550,000-watt stereo system bouncing underneath the rainbow video arch. The three of them joined in, swaying their hips to the music until their legs were shaking.

They stopped at the Hotel California Casino to rub Happy Buddha's belly for luck and tried the free slot machine outside of Binion's and the Four Queens, winning nothing. The drinks were hitting them harder than intended. Having chosen sleep over food, it was bound to happen. They ended the five-block strut back around the same location as SlotZilla, finding a White Castle where they bought and devoured several burgers.

They sat for a while, laughing about the person in the unicorn suit, remarking on the hotness of the guys hollering in all their drunk messy existence down Fremont Street, wondering how many women those men would be taking home that night. They sobered up from their one beer, empty burger wrappers littering the table before them.

Anya was still full of energy, blaming her current adrenaline rush on their evening roaming around Fremont Street. Soon the adrenaline Vegas afforded her would wear off, and she would feel tired again.

That was almost guaranteed.

They ordered more burgers for the road, getting energy drinks from the Walgreen's diagonal from the White Castle and walking back to the Crosstrek parked in the Fremont Street Parking Garage. The few hours they spent in Vegas were fun, and part of her wished they could stay. Part of her wished she could take much longer trips with her two friends.

After braving the city traffic again, they managed to merge their way back onto I-15, moving southbound past the hotel-casinos shining like disco lights in this desert. Past The Mirage, the creamy marble Caesar's Palace, the Aria's Hotel—which looked like an odd silvery shark fin—the black pyramid from the Luxor beaming a single light into the dark sky above, and a giant sphinx perched beside it.

With each mile left trailing behind them, the dazzling lights from the city disappeared, but a neon glow hung over the horizon for a long while before the sky was silent with dark again.

As they left that light behind, they entered into darkness and a new desert terrain surrounding them. Anya downed her second energy drink of the evening, watching her friends find a comfortable position to fall asleep in.

By now, she should have been sleepy, but she was still full of energy. The stars returned to their rightful spots in the vast. If they were any brighter, they might steal any Vegas show. She was pleased to see them again as they winked at her from the light-years away. While artificial light orchestrated by humans was undoubtedly something to swoon over, nothing could beat the twinkling stars she had fawned over for decades.

"I know you've never left me," she said to them quietly in the space of the car, music softly sounding throughout the tiny cabin like a sweet lullaby. From Vegas, Los Angeles was just over four hours away. Anya checked the clock buried deep in her dashboard.

It was after 3:00 a.m.

Where had the time gone?

Time hadn't mattered since they jumped in the car. Thinking now, Anya couldn't recall a single time she looked at the clock on the way to

Vegas. She was too busy forming an even deeper bond and closeness with Bee and Karmyn.

Too busy with her thoughts.

Too busy dreaming about her oceans in California.

Too focused on the road ahead.

When she traveled, time didn't matter. She stopped keeping track when she wasn't succumbing to the schedule and routines always before her. Time only mattered on her vacations when she had to catch planes, trains, boats, or busses. Going from a life of routine to something freer, that was the kind of life she wanted to live. She imagined everybody wanted that life. One free of responsibility, free of obligation to anyone and anything. One where the only times that mattered were when the sun rose and set. Wanting to live a simple, stress-free life and work a job that paid a lot was the biggest critique millennials like Anya faced. They were dubbed lazy and entitled because of it.

A group who wanted a big paycheck for very little work.

A group that valued play more than work.

A group different from the earlier generations.

That same group, and many others, were stuck in circumstances passed down by the generations before them. Coddled by 'everyone is a winner' trophies, never knowing the meaning of failure or the hard work required to find success. Most of them were in jobs they hated, or loveless relationships, taking care of children they weren't ready for. Some spent time arguing on social media, hiding behind computers instead of making insults to strangers faces, as if it gave them some sort of power. To Anya, people appeared to be surviving but never really living.

Driving down this road, it would be easy for her to escape everything back in Colorado and just drive away. It would be easy to leave her family and friends behind and take off to a place where no one could find her, where she would never have to resign to obligation or judgment. On days when stress dominated her life, she had thought about leaving everything behind once or twice. But now, it was something she just couldn't fathom.

Leaving her best friends.

Leaving her parents. She somewhat cared about that.

Leaving Sugar.

Leaving Sam.

She had too much she could lose if she dropped her life and went somewhere where no one could find her. If it were any of them, Anya would go through the same excruciating pain and depression.

In her shoes, she couldn't imagine losing any of them, even her parents. Thinking how any of her wrong actions could affect others in negative ways stung like it was something already happening. There was always room for disappointment in relationships. That was certain. But tearing a piece of someone's heart away with a single selfish action was what Anya would never be able to do. She tore her gaze from the headlights slicing through the dark and glanced at her two beloved friends slumbering.

Karmyn had the seat leaned back and her head cocked to the side. Bee was lying down to take up the entire back seat, her head resting on Karmyn's soft duffle bag.

Anya thought of just how lucky she was to have so much when others had so little. She had friends who loved her and accepted her, while some stayed in toxic and demeaning friendships. Hands stiff on the wheel, Anya smiled amidst the black that swarmed her vehicle, feeling grateful.

By 7:00 a.m., the three of them would be in Los Angeles, searching for the best taco place money could buy, eating as many as their stomachs could handle, and prancing back to the car with food babies so large, they got compliments on their pregnancies.

Bee and Karmyn slept like babies. Anya felt like that mother who wanted to wake them and be in their presence, loving them so powerfully that the time they spent sleeping was too much time away from her. But like that same mother, she loved them too much to wake them for her own sake.

Instead, she listened to their breaths, the snores that were barely there, and recalled the many years they spent being friends—the countless adventures they had gone on. The millions of hours of laughter and smiles that took up their evenings. The times they spent together picking up their tragedies spread out in shattered pieces across their lives.

She vowed to never leave them.

Not ever.

TWENTY-EIGHT

Bee and Karmyn were awake, helping Anya search for a good place to get coffee. They could've gone with Starbucks, which they did love, but what they loved more was supporting small local coffee shops. The coffee always seemed to taste better. They assumed it had been made with more loving intent than massive corporations raking in millions a year.

Los Angeles was an hour out of the way from their initial route, but nothing could keep them from their Los Angeles tacos. As soon as they found their coffee, they would make their next stop at Leo's Taco Truck.

Unable to find a café or coffee shop nearby, they resigned to the Starbucks not too far out of the way. They received their normal orders, all in the largest possible sizes; Anya ordering an extra shot, feeling the fatigue of the long trip finally start to creep in. They arrived at Leo's, but the truck still hadn't opened yet. They still had a few hours to kill before then.

They sat in their car near the taco truck, trying to figure out their next move—all of them with talking stomachs.

"What if we just went downtown to walk around for a little while," Karmyn asked.

"Yeah." Said Bee. "I could stand to stretch my legs for a little bit." Anya was too tired to get up and go for a walk. Perhaps now was a good time for a bit of shut-eye so she could make it to Mission Bay Beach safely.

"Sounds good," Anya. "I think I may get a little rest while you guys are walking around."

"That's probably a good idea," Bee said. "You've been a real champ this whole trip."

"Yeah. I can't believe you've stayed up this whole time," Karmyn added.

"I just had a lot of energy, I guess," Anya said.

She drove to downtown parking on the street near the Flower District.

Anya told them to be back by 9:45 a.m., so they could go to Leo's. She gave them the keys and shared her location with them on their phones to find their way back. As soon as they hit the pavement, she locked the door and was out.

Towering pillars of marble surrounded her, all of them traveling infinitely down halls, eventually ending in darkness. It reminded her of the Mines of Moria in the Lord of the Rings: Fellowship of the Ring.

Anya's shoes were light on this ground. With each step, she bounced to a soft drift and almost a delicate grace.

Something was up with gravity.

If she didn't know any better, this could be the world's largest courtroom lobby, museum, or... something else.

She walked along the pillars, all of them identically cut with perfect precision to reveal smooth and even ridges. She was sure she was lost. This maze of marble showed no signs of life, just an orange-gold light hanging from the ceilings.

As she walked, she listened for the sound of anything, barely hearing her footsteps.

Was this a dangerous place?

A safe place?

Then, from the corner of her eye, she saw something small dash behind a pillar. A trail of fabric peeking from the place the pillar met the floor.

"Hello?" Anya called.

No one responded.

"I know someone's here," she said louder, feeling the pace of her heart quicken and her skin tingle with fear.

She walked toward the pillar, stopping several feet away, trying to focus her attention on the last place she saw movement. A silver-haired girl peeked from behind the pillar, her sky blue eyes cutting through the dim orange glow.

"Hi there," Anya said.

The girl stared at her, still not revealing her entire self. Anya reduced her voice to something smaller and more soothing.

"It's okay. You can come out."

The girl's crystal blue eyes stared wild at her. Just when Anya's fear was about to rise to new levels, the girl emerged from her hiding place, walking into view. She was small and nimble. No immediate threat was apparent, but she still said nothing.

"Are you lost?" Anya asked.

The young girl shook her head slowly, still focusing on Anya. "Well, my name is Anya. What's your name?"

Anya crouched down to eye level, making herself even smaller. The girl parted her lips and prepared to speak when her eyes shifted to something standing behind Anya. Anya noticed her change in posture, the eyes that hadn't left the place they were fixated.

The hairs on her neck rose to attention. She stood back up, straightening her posture. Turning slowly, she came to face a grizzly man with similar hair as the child and a thinning beard to match. His face seemed kind, but his eyes were sunken and sad. He looked at her quizzically, moving to close the space between them. Anya took one step back. When he opened his mouth to speak, his words came out in a baritone of notes that Anya didn't understand.

Rather than say anything, she just stared at the man, not sure how to react.

Should she run?

Should she scream?

She just shook her head.

The universal signal for 'no.'

Or.

'I don't understand.'

The man's face never harshened but reflected the same confusion Anya knew occupied her face. He took one step closer.

Anya didn't move but straightened again to try and make herself look bigger next to this monster of a man. He looked down at the floor, searching his thoughts. Clearing his throat, he opened his mouth again.

Once.

Then twice.

But still nothing.

As if he didn't quite know what to say. His blue eyes worked into her, looking hard to identify her. Searching for answers as to who he was without bothering to ask. His eyes narrowed like someone trying to read a text too small and difficult to read. Like he was trying to figure out who she was. The third time he opened his mouth, he surprised her with a question in a language she understood—a hint of music behind his words.

"Who are you?" He boomed.

His voice was smooth and velvety like silk, a vibrato so soothing and warm like she had heard it somewhere before. Anya turned around to see if the girl was still lingering behind them.

When she returned her gaze, the man was standing nose to nose with her, his eyes now a thin blue border surrounding the dilated black terrors of his pupils and the whites of his eyes now red with fury. They pierced deep into her.

"Who are you?" He shouted.

Anya let out a shriek. Her screams vibrating between the infinite marble pillars.

"Whoa!" Karmyn screamed. "Where's the fire?"

Anya woke up to her two friends staring at her in alarm.

"What?" Anya asked, looking at them, wondering what happened.

She had been dreaming again.

She sat up in her seat, adjusted the chair to its regular attention.

"You were screaming," Bee said, still looking terrified.

"I was?" She croaked.

"Yeah," Karmyn said. "It was freaky."

"I was dreaming," Anya said simply.

"What happened in the dream?" Bee asked.

"Must've been scary as shit for you to scream like that," Karmyn said. Anya had remembered the dream. It was too shocking not to. It would be weeks before she could rip the crazy blue and black-eyed stare from her memory.

"I honestly can't remember," she said, but she remembered all of it. Her dreams were becoming increasingly stranger. "I'm okay, though."

Karmyn and Bee looked at her in disbelief. Irritated, Anya snapped back at them.

"Guys, I'm fine. I promise," she gave a sweet smile to reassure them.

Both of them softened at this with only a hint of apprehension. Anya saw the tension in their shoulders relax at her words. She looked at the clock, noticing it was now 9:50 a.m.

"Well, good!" Karmyn sat back in her chair, aggressively putting her seatbelt on. "Because it's taco time!"

"Hell yeah!" Bee said, a clicking seatbelt following closely behind Karmyn's. Anya found her seatbelt click, forcing a smile, although the memory of her last dream had shaken her greatly.

The tacos were divine. Juicy pieces of well-cooked carne asada topped with nothing but cilantro and finely chopped white onions.

They gorged on three perfect street tacos, tasting the smokiness of the grilled corn tortillas crumble with each savory bite. The tacos were so good. It helped Anya forget about the intense blues eyes that sucked her in like a black hole in space.

Tacos *almost* helped.

They climbed back into the car, this time heading toward east Los Angeles to catch I-5 down to San Diego. For the next two hours, they drove until the road practically merged with ocean. They traveled for miles, hugging the guard rails separating the road and hills from sea. Seeing the ocean extend for miles before meeting the edge of the sky.

During this stretch of the trip, all windows would be wide open, and summer hits blasting from their windows as they cruised down the San Diego Freeway. I-5 would run them straight into Mission Bay Beach. As they drove, they were the epitome of every top-down, hair waving in the wind, hot girl summer trip seen in movies.

When the music had silenced some, the three of them rehearsed their itinerary, starting with Anya's stubborn request to hit the sand in Mission Bay Beach before even arriving at the beach house.

"I don't know why you wouldn't just go to the ocean in L.A. or pull over on the side of the road and go stick your feet in the water *here*," Karmyn said.

"Yeah, what's the big deal?" Bee said. They were always giving her shit.

"It's my one stubborn request! Can we just not question it?" Anya laughed, having no real good reason for being this stubborn.

"...There's ocean. There's ocean. Oh, look! There's some more ocean..." Karmyn muttered, giving Anya a wicked side glance. Anya just rolled her eyes and laughed back at her.

"HEY! I will turn this car around," Anya threatened with a smile.

"Yeah, okay, MOM," Karmyn said.

"You won't do anything. You silly goose. You drunk goose!" Bee cackled from the back seat.

"So what exactly are we doing tonight after you dig your toes into the Pacific?" Bee asked.

"We're going to go check in..." Anya said.

"Okay," said Bee.

"Then we're going to go to the liquor store..."

"Uh-huh..." said Karmyn.

"Then we're going to get some beers…"

"Yes," said Bee.

"Then we're going to put them in the fridge…"

"Okay?" Karmyn's face twisted in confusion.

"Then we're going to go out and get some dinner…"

"Now, you're talking," Karmyn said.

"Somewhere nice…"

"Obviously," said Bee.

"Then we're going to come back and swim in that ocean for hours…"

"Yes, girl," Karmyn said

"Then, after we're tired from swimming…"

"Say it loud!" Said Bee.

"…we're going to drink those beers on the beach until the sun sets. Then go inside and pass out until tomorrow's adventure comes up with the sun." Anya finally finished. "How's that sound?"

"Can't threaten us with a good time!" Bee remarked. Anya continued with the plan more seriously.

"I think tomorrow we're doing the whale watching, right?" Anya said.

"Yeah, I booked it," Karmyn said. "We're going at 11:00 a.m."

"Then we're just doing whatever sounds good for the rest of the trip?" Asked Bee?

"That's the plan," said Anya.

"A lovely plan," said Bee.

"If we do say so ourselves," added Karmyn.

"I can't tell you how much I have needed this trip," Bee continued. "This year of homeschooling was intense."

"Tell me about it," Karmyn said, craning her neck to look at Bee. "My kids are no longer preschoolers, and the homework they give us is so much. I can't imagine what you're going through."

Although Anya couldn't relate to this part of their lives, she didn't mind listening to it. Anya could only glean the craziness that parenting was. If the chance to help either of them ever arose, she would take it.

On one occasion, Anya dropped a whole evening to play video games with the kids while Bee and Stephen went out for a date. Anya had even taken Karmyn's kids to school on days when she was sick and Jake was already off to work. It seemed fitting that they would look forward to this trip. Anya listened intently as the two of them talked through their daily routines, making note of the things that bothered them or made them happy. Taking mental notes in case she needed to help them down the road.

They arrived in San Diego fast, as if they traveled through a wormhole to get there. They drove on Mission Bay Drive toward the ocean, the waves crashing hard to create foamy silhouettes of white. Taking a right on Mission Bay Blvd, they drove down the road until they reached Liverpool Court, taking a right. In one block, they took their last turn onto Bayside Lane, pulling alongside the tan house with the brick-laid fence. They retrieved the key from the door handle so they could park the car in the garage.

"Last one to the beach buys a six-pack!" Anya yelled, taking off in a sprint toward the sound of waves and the smell of salty ocean air. Karmyn and Bee took off after her in their sandals, trailing closely behind. The three of them maneuvering between houses, sprinting down long, narrow sidewalks to see who could reach the water first. They ran until the hard earth turned soft beneath their feet.

But they didn't stop there.

The race wasn't over until they were waist-deep in the ocean with their clothes on.

Anya was first.

Dry sand.

Wet sand.

Wet sand and seashells

Skeletons of the last wave.

Then both feet.

Feeling the first touch of water, Anya hurdled over little waves until she no longer could, resigning to slowly wade into the gravitational pull of the ocean waves sweeping her back and forth. She immediately ducked beneath the water, smoothing her golden hair back, feeling the water in her nose, and stinging her lips. When she bobbed back up, Karmyn was the next one in, followed by Bee.

There they were, the three wet Disney princesses with glimmering white smiles and an impossibly bright summer sun casting rays on their shiny strands of soon-to-be sun-kissed hair. People already on the beach were looking at the three full-grown women splashing in the waves like children. They didn't care.

They huddled together, swinging their arms around each other, feeling the waves nudge them out and draw them back in. Mother Nature's way of telling them she was both fierce and tame. Anya kissed both of them on their cheeks, feeling them tilt into her. Their shorts and shirts were heavy with saltwater. God knows where their shoes even ended up.

So far, this was the best summer Anya could have ever asked for.

For this and many other delightful reasons.

TWENTY-NINE

Sam sat on his couch, wondering what he used to do before meeting Anya. The only things he did were go to work, go to the bar, go fishing in the summer, and play hockey in the winter. He lived and breathed all of those things very well in singlehood. However brief Anya was gone, he felt a piece of himself was missing.

It was morning, and he was an hour away from starting his shift at the museum. At least he had something to keep him busy while she was away. But it wouldn't keep him busy enough. While at work, he would have to find other ways to occupy his mind to keep from going crazy.

Since leaving yesterday, Sam hadn't heard from Anya.

"I'll be driving most of the day, so I probably won't answer any texts. But I'll call you when I get there," she had said before climbing down from his loft bed. Sam agreed.

He wanted her safe.

Focused on the road.

Alive, so she'd come back to him.

Sam waited patiently for her to call him but still heard nothing yet. It was already the second day. The more silent she was the, more he missed her terribly. He would have to endure five more days without her before he could see her again. Sinking into the couch, he heard his coffee machine sputter to a halt behind him. Not bothering to get up just yet, he took his phone out to scroll through some of his favorite images of him and Anya together.

One picture was of them soaking at Mount Princeton hot springs, her shining hair twisted into a silky bun, skin wet, and eyes bluer than blue jays. Another was of them kissing before walking into a movie theater, his arm catching a lot of that picture. Another was a picture of her sitting in her nook, reading a book. Another was her silhouette as she slumbered in her bed. And then, one of his favorites. The one of her sitting across from him, taking a swig of her beer while staring straight into him.

Sam had to convince himself the time together was still too short. But in many ways, he already knew how much he loved her. Society would tell him it was too soon and that he couldn't love someone this fast. Most of the time, they'd be right.

But not this time.

Her absence made him fall more in love with her. But, his deep need for her to be by his side always was just as real as his desire to let her be the free and adventurous spirit written into her bones.

People shouldn't cage birds.

He lingered on their pictures for a while. Moping. Sam put his phone down and got up to get his morning coffee.

Generous splash of sugary creamer.

Pour coffee.

Watch it swirl from a marbled brown and white to tan.

Perfect.

He sat back down on the couch, sipping his coffee slowly, admiring his collection of old colored bottles on the windowsills, looking out into the Aspens. Some blue, some brown, some green, some broken. But all old. He had found them on his property and just decided to keep them. Looking at them now, they made things look more cluttered. How hadn't he noticed this before? When he glanced around at the rest of his house, he started to pick out all the things he didn't like.

Suddenly, this space felt too *small*.

He looked at the small door leading from his studio to the bathroom, thinking of the unfinished part of his house on the other side. The part of the house he hadn't mentioned to Anya. If he listened more intently, he could hear the sound of the blue tarp flapping on top of his roof. A signal that he had stalled in some parts of his life.

Who wanted a man like that?

Anya was going to energy healing sessions, discovering strange parts of herself, putting painful work in. Sam just sat idle. Too comfortable and content and unmoved by what existed in his life already. His house was a clear indicator he had gotten much too comfortable.

What if I finished the other half of my house?

It wasn't like he didn't have time. On the contrary, he had more time saved up than most. Sam was sparked with a new drive to finish his unfinished project. After contemplating what his new hobby might be, he threw all other possibilities out, which weren't many. While Anya was gone, he would spend the hours he wasn't at work fixing up the other side of the house. He had the money to do it, but getting it completely finished in five days? That was surely impossible. But he would do what he could. He would do whatever he must to free himself from the pain of her absence.

Sam downed the coffee, now warm after he had nurtured his thoughts for too long. He drove to Bronco Billy's for breakfast, acknowledging the mountain of ore in tiers off the road, saying hello to the mountains situated in the opposite direction. Reminded of how small and large things could be if people made them that way. He barely talked to his favorite bartenders at breakfast but was still polite as thoughts of how to renovate were thick on his mind.

After breakfast, he drove back to Victor to open up the museum. In between customers, he searched the internet for ideas and layouts, choosing how he wanted to renovate the space. It was difficult not to include potential thoughts and opinions of what Anya might like. He intended to keep her in his life indefinitely, so he planned renovations to this house he suspected she would love. On the other hand, he worried he'd seem too hasty to include her in this part of his life.

He also wondered how much longer he would live in this weird limbo of: *"Can I just be fully, unapologetically, and openly in love with her and weave her tightly into my life already?"* and *"Don't rush this great thing you two have. She's not going anywhere."*

The bell to the front door of the museum happily clanged open. Sam switched on all the lights, bringing all rooms out of darkness into a cheery brightness. He did a quick sweep of the building, minding everything's place, his mind an accurate index of where all things belonged. He was anxious to start his research on what he wanted to do for the unfinished side of his house.

When he finished his sweep, he slid into the stool just in front of the ancient computer. He began clacking away at the keyboard, fiercely searching for interior looks, calculating the cost of materials, taking notes, and making lists of what he would end up needing. He could get most of the things he needed from Ace Hardware in Cripple Creek; lumber, paint, floor stain, plastic sheeting, nails. Some of the other things he would have to go down the mountain to get.

Sam thought about that space, walking through the empty side of his house in his mind, trying to map it out and remember every corner. The entire room was dark as hell and lifeless. The wood was coated in layers of the time it spent being unkempt. He planned to brighten it up, sand down the hardwood floors to a different shade, paint the walls a more welcoming color, maybe a faded green. Replace the light fixtures with something smoother and more elegant. He would give the windows a nice spit-shine.

The set of bay windows he had were a perfect place to build a nook or put a set of comfy chairs and a small table to enjoy morning coffee. If it were a nook, it would be the perfect place for Anya to cozy up and read. If he did either of those things, he would have to cut down the tree sitting directly in front of it. It would give them a grander view of the mountains seen for miles in the beyond. It was an old tree he had tried not to part with but would sacrifice it for the view. Plus, it was extra wood for his stove.

Sam settled on a shade of green after searching for a palette online. He picked a lighter caramel stain for the floor and half-moon light fixtures. He chose pairs of long fabric blinds in an off shade of white that would sashay on all sides of the windows. He took screenshots of these things and piled pictures of them on his phone.

The Lost Pleiad

Farthest from the front door that hadn't been opened in years, there was a room, no doubt it was haunted, by Halloween standards. That room would be done sooner than later. The space was even larger than his current studio. He could place the couch on the wall nearest to the bedroom, mount a projector above it, and install a screen that dropped from the ceiling. He and Anya could have intense cinematic adventures or watch hockey all from the coziness of their couch. He would have to Pinterest ideas to get it right.

Cleaning up, building, and designing all at once.

This ought to be fun.

Then there was the matter of the roof. The blue tarp waved at passersby, barely visible next to the tree he was going to cut down but easily seen from space. Fixing the roof would be the scariest part of this whole adventure. It was steep, and he would have to be careful fixing the considerable hole left in it, courtesy of a snowstorm from over a year ago. Luckily, it was the only place on the roof he had to worry about. The rest was intact. He could ask his friends to help but didn't want to bother them. He hated asking people for favors but loved doing favors for others. He concocted a plan—strap a rope and carabiner to a tree on the opposite side of the hole in his roof. Then he would strap himself in, using the strength of the tree to hold him steady in case he fell—It was a boyish and stupid plan, but a plan, nonetheless.

In the long term, this would be the living and gathering area. That would leave his studio space as the kitchen and dining area. He would add a real stove and more counter space. Somehow. He would have to move a lot of things around and knock down the half-wall that separated the couch from the rest of his living space. That would be the best place to put the dining area. He would convert his loft into storage space. He would find a new home for his hockey gear. It would be awkward going from the living space through the bathroom to the dining area, but nothing was perfect. Every home had its shortcomings.

Tonight's task was to clean the entire space, sweep everything, dust all the corners, clean the windows, take out the trash, and survey the room, placing all of his plans in their appropriate corners.

The roof would come first, then the floor, then the paint, then the nook or comfy chair area. Since he couldn't decide which one he should do, he decided to ask Anya which option she preferred.

Summer's tourists filtered in and out of the museum all day, briefly pausing his planning efforts in some moments. Each tick on the clock was a slow crawl, but the day would fly by if he didn't bother to look at it. He handled the people who came in out as quickly as possible to get back to his planning. Just a few more hours until he could escape the museum and start his home renovation projects. He wanted to finish as much as possible before Anya came home.

Sam was proud of himself for coming up with a plan to busy his mind. And with all this work, he would easily fall asleep each night. If he was more tired, he might drift to sleep before having a chance to feel the space in his bed where Anya was supposed to be.

When 5:00 p.m. came around, he raced, not far, to his home just down the road in Goldfield. He lived so close to the museum he could practically walk there. That was if he had afforded himself enough time to do so and took the initiative to make breakfast at home. When he pulled onto his property, he drove over the brush that had swarmed the path that used to lead to the front door. He backed his truck up closest to what was supposed to be the front door. Dropping the truck bed, he forced the door open hard. A thick layer of dust, leaves, and other gunk had accumulated over the years. When the door swung open, dragging a trail of sticks and leaves with it, the ample space brightened from sketchy and dingy attic-type to something he could consider living in. Cobwebs were everywhere. Thick layers of dust had gathered in all corners. He didn't even want to look at the haunted bedroom. It being a project was a severe understatement.

Sam had his work cut out for him.

The room was cold—a cold that had endured many years. There was another wood stove in the corner closest to the door. Unused for years, it probably needed a good chimney sweep. The space was much larger than he remembered. He walked through, hearing the floor creak with each heavy footfall. Snaking his way through the bathroom to his current living space, he found a pair of gloves mixed in with his hockey gear. He grabbed a stack of old cloth towels from under his sink and a broom from the corner beneath his loft. He took them to the other side of the house, setting everything on the floor. He went out back to his shed, trying to find an old bucket he could use for soapy water.

Finding one, he marched back inside and filled it halfway with hot water and soap, carrying it into the dank room. He set it down, taking a deep breath before he would unleash a fury of cleansing on this place. For the next several hours, Sam cleaned, scrubbing baseboards and windowsills, stripping the dead pieces of trim rotting at the edge of the floor, and throwing them in the truck bed. He scrubbed the windows to a cleaner view, reminding himself to call someone tomorrow about getting rid of the tree. Sam found other odds and ends stored here, things left behind from the last owner, which he never bothered to throw away.

Sam cleaned well into the evening until coated in sweat.

When he finally stopped to take a water break and get some dinner, he noticed a text message from Anya sent an hour ago.

"Hey, babe," it read. "We've made it, finally. We just came back from a dip in the ocean. The house is adorable, and I miss you."

Sam's heart. It was on the verge of bursting.

"Hey, my cosmic angel," he typed. "I'm glad you made it safely. Missing you terribly. Send pictures of the house. I hope you're all having a wonderful time."

Sam sent it. He looked around the big room that was once a dirty mess. Now, it looked somewhat livable. It was a definite upgrade from what it was before. With this new type of shine, he could see where everything fit better. A wave of excitement washed over him.

He changed into a clean shirt and a pair of jeans. If he left now, he might make it to The Side Door in time for a burger before the kitchen closed. He could tell Bruce about what he was working on this week, tell him about the woman he was most certainly falling in love with. It had been weeks since he had seen Bruce. He was so caught up with Anya and their time together that he seemed to forget everything else, including the only actual parental figure he had.

He drove to town, turning into the sloped parking space just outside the Victor Hotel and The Side Door. The bell to the door rang. Bruce was, again, busy behind the bar, and no one was in the restaurant. Sam wondered if it was always this empty. Bruce smiled at the sight of him.

"Hey, son," Bruce said.

He came around the bar, taking Sam in a hug. Sam hugged him back. "I've missed you."

"Hey, Bruce. I've missed you too," Sam took another look around the restaurant. "Is it too late for a burger?"

"Not for you," he said. "I'll get in an order with Leo in the back."

While he hobbled to the kitchen, Sam waited for his phone to vibrate in his pocket, but nothing. Bruce emerged from the kitchen, which was smoking, and returned to his place behind the bar.

"Something to drink?" He asked.

"Just water," Sam said. Bruce shot water into a glass for him and slid it into his hand. "How are things going?"

"Oh, can't complain," Bruce said, wiping down the bar top before moving on to cleaning other areas. "Staying busy. It doesn't look like people come in here, but they do. But I'm boring. How are you?"

"I'm doing good. I'm fixing the other half of my house up." Sam said. Bruce stopped what he was doing, looking up at Sam.

"Are you serious?" Bruce smiled. "You've been talking about doing that for a long time."

"Yeah, I know," Sam said. Bruce nodded, still not removing his gaze.

"What sparked the motivation?" Bruce questioned. Sam took a sip of his water, ending it with a smile.

"Anya," he said plainly.

"The woman we talked about?" He smiled.

"The very one," Sam responded. "I think... not think... know I'm falling in love with her. Is that crazy?"

"Absolutely not," Bruce said. Sam knew he was thinking of his wife. "This is wonderful, Sam."

"Thanks. Anya is out of town on a trip with her friends. I was thinking this morning that I've just become too content with where I was living, which is fine unless you have unfinished projects. I had no one forcing me to transform or move on to the next phase of my life," he said. "I've never really cared about someone else's well-being other than my own until now."

Bruce was looking at him proudly with the smiling eyes of a father. Sam thought he might leap over the bar just to hug him. Bruce looking at him like a son meant more to him than he would ever know.

"So, tell me what your plans are," Bruce focused on Sam, who had downed his water.

"I'm going to sand down the floor, paint the walls, install new light fixtures, and make the bay windows into either a nook, or a comfy chair seating area, depending on what Anya wants. I'll fix up the bedroom, repair the roof, and maybe paint the outside. Basically, finish the house," Sam said in one breath.

Bruce continued to smile proudly.

For the next hour, they talked about Anya as he gorged his way through a juicy burger while Bruce got to see Sam bask in a new kind of happiness.

Sam helped him close down the restaurant and put up the chairs, even though the day had been exhausting. Bruce shut off the lights, letting a dark wave cross over the empty tables and upside-down chairs. There was still brightness from the Victor Hotel lobby shining in as the two of them walked out to his old beater truck with dents in it.

"You should let me knock those dents out for you one day, Bruce," Sam said.

"Nah," Bruce replied, waving the offer away. "It gives it character."

Sam laughed, shoving his hands in his pockets.

"Sure it does."

Before hobbling to his truck, Bruce shifted toward Sam, taking him in a tight embrace. Sam melted into the hug, smelling the grease and smoke from a day's worth of work, noticing Bruce was holding on much longer and more tightly than he had before.

"I love you, son," he choked. "I'm so proud of who you are."

Sam tried not to cry.

He tried to live up to the reputation placed on all men to never shed a tear, not even for a close father figure. Sam tugged back on his throat, feeling the aching urge to weep. There would be no holding onto these emotions. Not anymore. Sam cried into his shoulder.

Sam loved Bruce, like a father, even though he had never said it out loud. Sam had been dormant, afraid, apathetic, serious, stuck, and content with the bare minimum. Living his life this way afforded him less of a risk of getting hurt or losing someone he loved again. He was breaking free of his shell, feeling emotions he had never bothered to acknowledge, taking risks with his love again.

His love for Bruce, a beloved guardian, and father, resulted from his most recent abilities to wake up, be seen, and change. And he indeed was changed by these last several weeks. Whether that had to do with meeting Anya or was just habitual changing of the seasons, he didn't know. Sam did know one thing for sure; one thing he had never admitted out loud but was about to.

"I love you too, Bruce," with those words, Bruce cried too, clinging tightly to his shirt.

How long had it been since he had heard someone tell him, "I love you?" How long had Bruce needed to hear those words? Sam promised himself to see Bruce more often. Not just at work, but at home too. He decided he would take the responsibility of a loving son.

He promised to keep this momentum of transformation going.

THIRTY

The small boat rocked back and forth at the surface of the relentless ocean waves. Anya fit snug into her life vest, viewing the shore from a distance, miles of ocean between her and solid land. The city landscape hung over the tan beach, a wavy line in the distance.

They had been on this boat for an hour already and seen no whales. Anya was frowning, although she hadn't known it until Karmyn said something.

"Jesus Christ, cheer the hell up!" She exclaimed, shocking Anya back into a smile. "You always seem so melancholy and reflective. What is that about?" Anya knew she tended to stare off without reason.

"I'm not!" She yelled back, returning her frown to a smile. "I just really wanted to see whales today."

"Yeah, us too," Bee said. "Don't worry. We still have like two hours on this boat." Anya tried to stay optimistic.

"Yeah, you're right," Anya agreed.

"Let's go get some lunch," Bee invited.

"I think I'll sit here for a little longer. You guys go, and I'll find you in a minute," Anya said. Karmyn and Bee nodded, lacing arms to go find their lunch.

As much as Anya loved the ocean, she feared its deepest parts. She was tickled with wonder for the life that existed there but also terrified with what you might find or what might swallow you whole. She felt the same way about space.

If there were a way people could breathe freely in either worlds, earthlings would've discovered mysteries and secrets of each strange universe by now, letting the world know that people weren't alone in this galaxy.

If she could transform into a whale, she could access their teachings, learn to survive underwater, and sing beautiful songs for all other animals and people to hear. If she could reincarnate as any animal after she died, it would be a whale.

Looking off into the sea that went on forever, she pleaded and prayed that she would see a whale, even if it was in the distance, even water shooting from a blowhole. Closing her eyes, she made that prayer silently to herself. *Please show yourself. We paid a lot of money for this shit.* She stared out into the sea for a long time, searching the waves for any sign of ocean life.

A breach.

Spy hopping.

A fountain of sea spray from a blowhole.

The distance splash of a mammal jumping through the surface.

Anything.

But she saw nothing.

Everyone had retreated inside, unamused by the lack of activity promised for a whale-watching expedition. Feeling the tightness of her life vest, she glanced around. No one was here to judge her if she took it off.

She unbuckled, letting her chest expand to take in the ocean air. She hadn't realized how little she was breathing. Each breath was therapeutic.

Heavenly.

She had missed these ocean breaths.

Now, it was just her alone clutching the boat railing and the silent man at the helm just above her focusing on the waters around him. There wasn't much to focus on, in her opinion. She looked down into the ocean, curious about how far she could see into its depths. All she saw was a terrifying deep blue.

An undiscovered world.

An unknown universe.

Nothing else.

She stared harder, looking for even the tiniest silvery fish to glitter by. Then a shadow appeared.

She leaned toward the water, focusing more intently on the place she saw the shadow, swearing she had seen... *something*. The light of the day must have been tricking her. As she moved away from the railing, the boat shifted from the other side hard enough to tilt the boat and throw her headfirst into the navy deep. Her eyes closed in reflex. Water filled her nose. All around her was silence.

No worries. She knew how to swim.

Opening her eyes, feeling the sting of saltwater, Anya idled under the surface, seeing infinite blue all around her and single beams of sunlight filtering through the water like glittering flashlight beams. Waves rocked above her, but the world around her was a smooth and comforting blue. Lingering there, she realized just how beautiful it was to be in silence, feel the water hug her in all places, and be surrounded by so much space and unknown. Her golden hair waved beside her, brushing her shoulders. Her soaked clothing let her sink further. She would only be able to stay there for a few more seconds until she needed to return to the surface to breathe.

Savoring the solace and fear she felt all at once, Anya felt a heavy presence, shifting the water behind her, yet, not the hovering boat she had sensed above her all along. The black eyes centered in rings of blue flashed into memory, sparking a familiar sensation of something looming behind her like the beastly man who shocked her in a dream.

But this wasn't a man.

It was something else.

Treading water, she turned.

What breath she still held in her chest left her as she came nose to nose with a gray whale. So close, she could touch its nose and feel the sharp white barnacles clumped together in random spots.

Above her, Anya could see a dozen heads peering down into the water from above, looking worried. They could stand to worry for a few more seconds. Anya continued to tread water, floating in this majestic blue, face to face with a gentle beast. Whales were a reminder that some things bigger than us can crush us but instead choose not to. The whale moved inches toward her, slowly and gently shoving its nose into her stomach.

Anya's let the nose softly nudge her, instinct leading her to one thing—embracing the animal. Hugging its nose and resting her body there, she felt the firm whale skin against her arms and the barnacles threatening to slice her skin.

This had to be a dream. She hugged harder, letting the barnacles dig into her skin, but not enough to break it.

The Lost Pleiad

It hurt which meant it was *real*.

Anya could've suffocated, let the saltwater fill her lungs. If she could have chosen any moment in time to die happy, it would be this moment.

The water shifted again, the giant nose thrusting her upwards toward the surface in one swift motion. She met the warm air feeling an instant coolness on her wet skin. The commotion from the boat was of both panic and amazement. A dozen hands were reaching for her, and a blue and white life raft tossed at her.

The giant creature broke its connection with her, disappearing into the deep.

While the whale had brought her to the surface, it was also the culprit for her plunge. As it left, Anya felt an emptiness in her. A hole in her heart she was unaware could even exist. Like she had severed a connection that was always meant to be there.

When she was a child, she had crazily dreamt of swimming with whales. She had considered being a trainer until she learned what captivity did to whales.

Before then, she found every single book in a library that talked about cetaceans, taking notes, dubbing blue whales as her favorite, taking in all shreds of knowledge about them, and carrying it around unable to use in any normal conversation.

She learned Killer Whales are classified into three types—resident, transient, and offshore. Orca pods come from different parts of the world and speak different dialects. Belugas are the only whales that could turn their head from left to right. And there are two types of whales—toothed and baleen whales—each type using its teeth and bony plates to eat fish differently. She was enchanted watching videos of Inuit people chew on gummy pieces of whale blubber, wondering what it tasted like. She did a presentation on Sperm Whales in fifth grade, kids laughing every time she said 'sperm.' She decorated her room with various whale items, and her walls were painted a shocking blue. Her favorite biblical story was even Jonah and the Whale.

Anya was nothing short of obsessed.

Her love for these giants was so great, she pleaded for a place to keep one as a child, telling her parents they could build a pool and keep it there. But her hopes and dreams for a watery pet were crushed when she discovered she couldn't have a whale as a pet.

She was nine years old then.

The nine-year-old in her was doing backflips while everyone screamed around her. They yanked her onto the hard surface of the boat, helping her hurdle over the railing. Karmyn and Bee were next to her instantly, fighting their way through the crowd swarming her.

"What in the actual fuck?" Bee screamed.

"Get out of the way, goddamn it! That's our best friend," Karmyn yelled while Bee trailed closely behind. Both of their motherly instincts were kicking in. "Give her some space for chrissake."

"Are you okay, bestie?" Bee shrieked, crouching down beside her. But Anya was smiling erratically.

"I'm fine!" She exclaimed.

"Are you mad?" Karmyn screamed louder. "You are not *fine*."

But Anya was fine.

"What happened?" A random person hollered from the back of the crowd. Silence fell over everyone as they waited for a response. She looked around at everyone intent on hearing her story. Anya let the sun warm her and then spoke.

"I don't know. It happened so fast," she started. "I leaned over the railing to look down, and something nudged the boat. I just fell in. Then, I felt this presence behind me." She looked up, noticing everyone was hanging on her words, leaning into her, taking in the whole story just as Anya experienced it.

"When I turned, there was a gray whale there. Right in front of me," she said.

A woman gasped.

Karmyn and Bee looked at her with bewilderment. "Then, it swam towards me."

"It did not," someone shouted.

"It did," Anya assured loudly. "It stuck its nose right in the center of my stomach. It was so large. It took up my torso and then lifted me to the surface. Almost like it was protecting or saving me."

From the outside of the horde, a man shoved his way through. The Captain—although he didn't look it without a beard and fancy captain outfit.

"That is incredible!" He said. "I just checked our radar, and there was definitely a whale here. You just had the experience of a lifetime, young lady."

Karmyn and Bee were still in partial shock and worry, but she would explain to them the other more magical details once everyone else disappeared from earshot.

"Everyone give her some space," the Captain ordered.

But as he said the words, sprays from whale blowholes rained in the distance. A raspy sound of water shooting into the air before evaporating into silence.

"Whales!" The man shouted from the helm.

The attention shifted from Anya to the pod of whales just off the bow. The horde disappeared from around her, leaving Karmyn and Bee.

"Holy shit, you guys," Anya exclaimed. Standing up, she noticed she was shaking, and her legs gave way beneath her. Karmyn and Bee swooped in to lift her.

"You are not fine," Karmyn insisted.

"I swear, I'm fine, Karm," Anya said again.

"You guys have no idea what I just experienced," she said, looking at both of them. "That whale, it… and this will sound weird. It was like it came in for a hug."

"Really?" Bee questioned.

"Yes," Anya said seriously. "I can't even explain it. It was the most amazing feeling ever."

"Those things are monsters," Karmyn said with fear on her tongue. She and Bee walked Anya over to a nearby bench far from the railing.

"Gray whales are so gentle," Bee said. "Most whales are. The only ones that could eat you are Killer Whales or maybe Pilots."

"Exactly," Anya said.

"Whatever, they can still run you over, An," she was right.

"But it didn't. It just nudged me to the surface, like it was saving me," she said.

"That's fucking amazing," Bee said, giving in to the experience much faster than Karmyn was allowing herself to. "How often can you say that kind of thing happened?"

"Almost never."

Anya couldn't even explain what she felt to herself. When she got back to the house, she would try to write it out. Permanently sear the memory of it into her journal using curvy lines of ink. Doing whatever she could to preserve that memory. She would reimagine that scene hundreds of times until it burned into her mind.

Strange things were continuing to happen with Anya. Things she couldn't explain—the strange dreams, the downpour before her departure, the hotness of the galaxy stone in her palm, and now this. How long would these unexplainable instances continue? If they were all going to be this wonderful and life-changing, she didn't want them to stop. Anya felt a new wave of motivation and dedication to explore this magic starting to consume her life. She was willing to go down this rabbit hole if it meant feeling a connection like she did with the whale.

Anya could've never fathomed an experience like that.

She couldn't wait to tell Gwynn and Sage.

She couldn't wait to tell Sam.

It was all part of her shift in beautiful consciousness. So far, nothing about that shift had been terrible. Gwynn and Sage warned her of these shifts and Anya was hungry for more.

The whales loitered in the water surrounding the boat for more than an hour. For many on the tour, that experience was money well spent. The boat tour came to an end as the watercraft sped over the stubbornly angled waves. By now, Anya was nearly dry, feeling the saltiness of the seawater sticking to her skin. Anya, Karmyn, and Bee were now back to normal conversation, having moved past Anya's inconceivable moment like it was nothing.

It was *something* to Anya.

She was sure it meant something. Desiring to share it with others who might appreciate it or understand it more than Bee and Karmyn could. Anya could see parts of them were in denial. Not that her friends didn't believe it happened, they just didn't seem to understand the feeling and intent behind the moment. It was the connection she felt with the creature that was difficult to explain in a way that didn't transcend their reality.

When they reached the dock, they hopped off, feeling the steadiness of the land. Anya felt the gravitational pull from the earth, sad to leave the unsteady waters that rocked her back and forth.

The three of them hitched a 20-minute rideshare back to their rental. It was still early in the day. Since salt already soaked her skin, it was convenient for her to head straight back into the water. They decided to make another trip to the place where sea and sand met, intent on rushing the waves until their muscles relaxed and the sun tired them out.

Anya would never be able to get enough of the ocean. And with her latest experience, it nearly clinched a space in her heart for favorite spot in the world.

It was now a close race with the mountains. Before they left for the beach, Anya called Sam. She closed her door and dialed his number. He answered instantly.

"Hey, darling," she said.

"Goddamn, it's good to hear that sexy angelic voice of yours," he said. "How's my beach babe?"

"I'm amazing. You won't believe what happened today, Sam," she said.

"Well, I'm on the edge of my seat already," he said. "Tell me."

"Okay, so… I'm on the whale watching expedition," she said. "And everyone had gone inside the cabin to eat lunch. We still hadn't seen any activity. So I was standing there on the boat, looking out and, this next part is weird…"

"I would expect nothing less from you," he chuckled. She laughed too.

"So, I leaned over the railing to see down into the ocean. Then, something nudged the boat so hard I fell into the water," she said.

"Oh my god!" Sam yelled into the phone. "Are you okay?"

"Oh, yeah! I'm fine," she assured him. "But that's not the best part."

"Sounds pretty terrifying to me, but go on," he said.

"So, I'm in the water, and I don't have my life vest on. And I feel this like, presence behind me. I turn around, and there I am nose to nose with a gray whale."

"No. Fucking. Way."

"Yes fucking way," she said back. "I was just there, treading water in the presence of this beast. And then, it swam towards me and put its nose in my center. I literally hugged the whale's nose. Then it lifted me to the surface."

"That is incredible," he said, thrilled, awe rising in his throat. "I can't believe that happened to you."

"Sam, it was beyond amazing. And there was this insane feeling like we were connected or something. Being in the ocean like that, unable to breathe, being surrounded by nothing but infinite blue and unknown was terrifying. But I wasn't scared at all. I felt *safe*."

"Wow. I'm speechless. How often do things like that happen in your life?" He asked.

"Almost never," she said. "Anyways, I had to call and tell you that. I felt like you would appreciate it."

"Oh, I certainly do," he said happily. "How is the rest of the trip?"

"It's awesome here. We're about to go swimming until we can't anymore," she said.

"Sounds excellent," he said.

"How about you? What are you up to?" She questioned.

"Just work. I do have a surprise for you when you get back," he said proudly.

"Oh, do you now?" She said with a voice of intrigue.

"Yes, I do."

"Well, I can't wait to see this surprise. But mostly, I can't wait to see you," she ached to see him again.

"Same here. I miss you," he said.

"Anya! Let's go!" Karmyn called from the other side of the door.

"I miss you too, darling," she said back. "I have to go. Got to swim."

"Have way too much fun," he pleaded.

"I will. See you in a few days," she ended the call.

"Princess Aurora! Get your cute ass out here!" Bee hollered. With that, she emerged from the room and ran out the front door.

THIRTY-ONE

Over the next few days, Sam worked hard at the museum and hard at home. By the time his week was over, he had finished sanding the floors, finished several even coats of floor stain, painted the walls, installed the light fixtures, and cut down the tree in front of the bay windows. The roof was complete, and he only almost fell off twice. The trim still needed to be nailed to where the wall meets the floor. He hoped the bedroom would be squared away before Anya came home but just didn't have enough time.

The walls were a muted shade of green. The bay windows were clean, nearly transparent, the trim around them painted white. The ceilings were white, making the room appear even brighter. And the light fixtures curved in a half-circle, shining a milky shade with LEDs encased in them. The wood-burning stove was polished to a new shine, although the chimney still hadn't been cleaned. The door was now clean and functioning, but it would be replaced soon. Sam even had laid a more clear path from his driveway to the front door.

What he had was a good start, but he still had a long way to go.

Anya would be home in a day. That was enough time to get at least one friend of his to come over and help him move some furniture to the other room, starting with the couch and TV. Those were the only things he could move. He didn't have extra furniture to add and didn't want to place anything in front of the bay windows until he learned what Anya liked. Depending on what she decided, he may even build it himself.

Who could help him move this couch?

He could ask anyone but genuinely hated asking for favors.

He could ask Zeke. The one person he wanted to call but hadn't called or seen in months.

Most days, when he missed him, he would just push the thought to the back of his mind—their separation and quickly deteriorating friendship too painful to process or give attention to. But after sharing that moment with Bruce, how closely he was connecting with Anya, Sam was on a vulnerability and connection rampage. Somewhere in the past few weeks, he had opened a gate, become more willing to acknowledge his emotions, and let people in. Perhaps now was the time to make amends. Zeke was his best friend, after all.

Sam picked up the phone and dialed Zeke's number. Surprisingly, he answered on the second ring.

"Hey, buddy," he said rather cheerily.

"Hey Zeke," he replied, shocked with his sunny demeanor. "How it's going, man?"

"Oh, it's going," he said. "How about you?"

"Can't complain," he replied, an uncomfortable silence hanging between receivers. Sam called him, so he should keep the conversation moving.

"What are you up to today?" Sam asked.

"Not much. I just got off work," he said.

"Yeah? Feel like coming to hang out a bit?" As if surprised by the question, Zeke answered.

"I would like that a lot," Zeke replied happily.

"Great! We can have a beer and can catch up," Sam offered.

"Actually, man. I've been sober for two months now," Zeke said proudly.

"No shit," Sam said, surprised. Zeke had succumbed to years of a drinking addiction. It was an addiction so powerful, Sam thought he would never make it out alive. As much as he tried not to think about it, he was sure it would only stop if it killed him.

"Yeah. I still smoke weed, though. It was time for a change, I guess. I kind of had to do something after the last time they pumped my stomach," Zeke said. "Doc said if I didn't get my shit together, I was on a one-way trip to the morgue."

"Christ, man. I didn't even know," Sam said.

"Yeah. I was ashamed. I kind of just woke up after that, you know? Checked myself into rehab and have been sober ever since," Sam could've cried right then, listening to his best friend confess this.

I'm crying at everything now? What is happening to me?

"I'm proud of you, buddy," Sam said. "Well, come over later. We'll celebrate your recovery with a Coke. I'll tell you about the amazing girl I'm seeing."

"An amazing girl? Here?" Zeke was surprised, and rightly so.

"Yup," Sam said.

"How amazing?"

"You have no idea."

THIRTY-TWO

Zeke arrived at Sam's house well before sunset. He had more surprises for him than he realized. But everything would be easier to explain once he got there. Zeke's old beater car pulled up behind his white truck. When he stepped out of the driver's side, he was thinner than Sam remembered. Healthier.

Before now, Sam had always remembered him as overweight, red in the face, miserably sick looking. Zeke was far from that now. Not only was he thinner and smiling, his shoulders were pulled back, and he stood up tall, not shrinking to the small person he thought he had to be.

Sam wasn't sure if he could expect a sober Zeke, but looking at him through the window, Zeke had not been lying. Sam felt guilty for not believing his best friend. There had been so many times he'd given Zeke that chance and had been left disappointed. Sam came through the door to meet Zeke outside. The feeling of missing him sending him at a near run to greet his friend.

They smiled when they saw each other. In their past, they had never shied away from hugs or affection between two grown men. Seeing Zeke now, he was desperate to hug him. Zeke appeared to be desperate for one too. Maybe it was the emotional evening he had with Bruce the night before. Maybe it was all the time that passed between seeing each other. Perhaps it was Anya stepping into his life. Whatever the reason, he felt more vulnerable than normal.

"Hey, buddy," they hugged, giving each other pats on the back.

"You look great!" Sam exclaimed. "You didn't tell me you lost weight too!"

"Yeah. Sort of a side effect of sober living," he responded. Sam looked at him and blinked. Zeke's posture curled inward at Sam's gaze.

"Stop looking at me like that. I'm not a piece of meat, Sam," he said jokingly. Sam laughed.

"Come on, let's go inside," Sam said, leading the way in. This time, he pointed him in the direction of the front door, through the path he had recently carved on his property.

"Why are we going through the front of the house?" Zeke asked.

"You'll see," Sam said. They walked on the path. Zeke was ahead of Sam. As the door opened, more light entered, lifting the muted green to an even happier shade.

Zeke stopped at the threshold, his eyes darting around at the sight of it all. Walking in the rest of the way, he looked down at the newly stained floors, the new light fixtures, the clean windows.

"You've been busy," he said, stunned. "It looks amazing in here!"

"Yeah. I needed a project," Sam said back.

"I can't believe you got it started after all this time," Zeke said. "You haven't wanted to do anything like this since…" Zeke turned to look at Sam, and he was already nodding.

"Yeah, I know," Sam replied.

"What got you going again?" Zeke asked.

"Anya, mostly," Sam said shyly. Zeke stopped wandering the room to look at him.

"The girl?" He smiled.

"The girl," Sam smiled back.

"You need some furniture in here," Zeke said.

"Yeah. I need to move the couch in here," said Sam. Still stubborn to ask for a favor.

"Well, let's do it. I'll help," Zeke said. The two of them shuffled out through the door that led to this current living room. They swung the back door open. It was a small space, and getting the couch out would be difficult. Several times they tried to find the right angle, taking turns squeezing around the half-wall, which shrunk the already small space. After a few tries and several accumulated beads of sweat, they managed to shove the couch through the back door, rounding the side of the house to the open front door and walking it effortlessly in. They pushed it up against the back wall closest to the unfinished bedroom.

"Damn. That couch is a stubborn bastard," Zeke said. Sam looked at the couch, which looked more deflated in such an open space.

"It looks hideous," Sam said, staring at it in disgust. "It might be time to get a new one."

"Or you can get those covers for them now," Zeke said. "They're fancy looking and stretchy, like women's yoga pants."

"Eh, well. That would have to do for now," Sam said, unsatisfied.

"Well, you want to make your lady comfortable," Zeke said, giving in a good slap on the arm. "So, tell me about her."

"Man, where to start," Sam began. "She's the most real woman I've ever come to know on this planet."

"Well, that's saying something since you've met everyone in the world just working at the museum," Zeke said. They both walked to the deflated couch and sat down. Sam breathed in a light fusion of mountain air, fresh paint, and floor stain.

"She loves the outdoors, loves beer, and is the sweetest and most thoughtful person when it comes to caring for others. But she's humble too. When I look at her and see how beautiful she is, I guarantee she doesn't see that same beauty in herself. But I notice. Not just in her looks, but in the way she moves, the way she talks, her shyness, and her bravery. Anya has let me really see her. She has never put on a face to please me or win me. She's been herself this whole time," Sam's gaze burned into the walls in front of him as he envisioned her.

Sam realized just how in love with her he was the more he talked about her. He hadn't told Zeke the more secretive parts of Anya or her connection to the stars, feeling he may not quite understand. He felt those conversations were sacred moments shared between them. Maybe it was something she would tell people on her terms.

"You love her," Zeke said. Sam felt Zeke's eyes on him. He tore his gaze from the wall, tears threatening to pool in his eyes.

"Yes," Sam said plainly. "I think I really do."

"Wow," Zeke smiled. "Does she know?"

"No, I haven't told her."

"Are you going to?" Zeke asked.

"I'm not sure," Sam said. "We haven't known each other for very long."

"What does that matter?" Zeke asked.

"I don't know," he mumbled. "Is there a certain kind of timeframe for falling in love with someone?"

Zeke thought for a second. "You want to know what I think?"

"Yeah, I really do," Sam said.

"I think if you love her, you should tell her," he said. "Who gives a shit about the proper timeframe or all the fucking books out there on how soon or late you should love someone."

"Yeah, you're probably right," Sam said. But the thought of telling her scared him. What if she didn't feel the same? What if it was too fast for her? What if she left him because he was too forward?

All negative outcomes of speaking those three words came before the best possible outcomes. What if he told her he loved her, and she didn't feel the same? He could picture it—the pain rendered by another and how it could break a person completely. The hurt so deeply ingrained in his bones, no other woman would be able to scrub them clean. Years after his death, people could still find that heartbreak etched in his ivory skeleton like a code they must decipher to truly know him.

Sam wanted to love Anya wholly and unapologetically and had dreamed of doing so for weeks now. More than his desire to love her, he wished that same love was reciprocated. But Sam knew her heartbreak, how a single month or two wouldn't suffice. How those two months were nowhere near enough to show her just how much he loved her. He wondered how long it would take for her to fully let him in. The fear of losing her, of not convincing her how much he loved her was a powerful motivator.

Zeke stayed for a long time after that. Sam told him everything he could about Anya, leaving out the most fascinating parts, selfishly keeping them for himself. From the time he arrived and the time he left, they moved what furniture they could from the studio, which wasn't much—a TV and a side table. They talked about Zeke's sober journey. How he almost died from drinking too much liquor at a casual party. His visits to AA meetings in Colorado Springs, how he was seeing a therapist and working through the deep-seated pain that drove him to a bottle. He begged for his job back a third time. Zeke wasn't embarrassed anymore but grateful for all those who forgave him after how destructive, mean, and miserable he had been.

It was hard for Sam not to cry with him.

Sam learned the slightest thing could drive someone to alcoholism. What was a minor issue to Sam might be significantly larger issue for someone else.

He always had to remind himself of that.

As Zeke spoke, he talked about the series of small moments that knocked him down. Girlfriends who broke up with him, living paycheck to paycheck, friendships that stopped working, dreams shot to hell, and his never-ending comparisons to others. After so many of these, he just stopped getting back up. Before he knew it, the bottle had replaced his best friend and anyone around him who was good. Sam knew what Zeke was going through would only be the beginning. That he had a long way to go to heal whatever had hurt him. Pain couldn't heal overnight, especially deeply rooted pain. But pain could heal over time when acknowledged and worked through. Sam knew this and considered himself on the upper end of overcoming pain.

In talking to Zeke, Sam saw hope for him for the first time in many years. Like he would really do it this time. Like he wouldn't relapse. From what it seemed, Zeke had a tribe of people helping him through this time. Sam felt guilty for not being a part of that tribe for as long as he was. For not being more optimistic about his most cherished friend.

What he did know is that Zeke was here now. That fact told him their friendship meant something, that it could last. He was telling Sam everything, catching him up on all the things he had missed in the past few months. For once, Sam saw his friend again, imagined him coming along on fishing and camping trips, imagined him meeting Anya, imagined being there when he received his five-year and ten-year chips for sobriety. Sam imagined the two of them living out their friendship over several decades until death took them.

That night, Sam went to bed, recalling the day with his best friend. Feeling refreshed, rejuvenated, and absolved of all worry. Everything surrounding him in life felt better than before. When had it happened? Where had there been a shift in his gratitude for the things he held close to him? He thought of the most obvious answer, considering how unrealistic it was for a person to not only change you but change your attitude and environment.

But Anya, she was like the sun a flower needed to grow and bloom. Before her, he was a seed, buried, shrouded by darkness, never tended to, never watered, and cared for. But as if the ground around were fertile again, he pushed past that darkness, emerging into the light, growing tall with each drink of the sun until he opened himself up to the world.

Sam believed nothing would ever save him again, and he would be stuck in his darkness and melancholy, covered in a face of happiness. It did fool everyone and for a long time. But there was absolutely no hiding it now.

Sam was a different person—changed only by one person in a matter of weeks.

Amazing what *love* could do.

Hearing his best friend confess what he was going through and doing it with such courage, Sam felt the need to do it himself.

Now was the time to tell her the thing he had been hiding from her. The one thing few knew and he rarely talked about with anyone but those closest to him. Anya had shown herself to him in her most authentic form.

It was time he did the same.

THIRTY-THREE

It's incredible how fast a road trip goes when returning home. On the way to a destination, each second creeps by while all passengers squirm in their seats. Everyone is anxious for a break from their ordinary lives. On the trip home, this road is so familiar and remembered, so people sink into boredom and sorrow, grieving for the slice of heaven that used to exist just hours ago. The way back home is foreseen now that it's retraced—each curve of road, that mountain in the distance, the river that crawls over rock, you remember it all until arriving in your driveway. At least, this is what most people felt when going back home after a long, much-needed vacation.

Not Anya. Not this time anyway.

On the way back to Colorado, time crawled by even slower than their trip to San Diego. Getting back to Sam, being in his arms, feeling his words whispered in her ear, the gooseflesh following the chill that ran up her spine at the sound of his voice—she couldn't get back to that fast enough. It was impossible not to plunge her foot deep into the accelerator so she would get home faster. How dare she have to obey the laws of the road when a perfectly handsome and incredible man waited for her back home.

The Lost Pleiad

Anya still wouldn't quite allow herself to identify what she felt for Sam. The doubt caused by a man's attention was something she clasped onto without a second thought. What she did feel for Sam was a deep fondness that increased with each day, even when she wasn't in his presence.

Without the stops, the trip home was much shorter. And like the trip to California, Anya had no intention of stopping to rest anywhere until she saw Pikes Peak or until she was collapsing in Sam's arms.

After grueling hours of driving, they arrived in Colorado Springs where Anya dropped off Karmyn and Bee at their homes. Hugging them goodbye, they shuffled to their front doors, looking refreshed, rejuvenated, and equally saddened by another grand trip coming to an end. As soon as their children charged them at the door, Anya saw their momentary sadness instantly transformed into joy.

How wonderful, the three of them enjoying their time together so much and having something so splendid that they were left with sorrowful 'until next times.'

Before putting her car in park, she shot Sam a text, letting him know that she was on her way back to Cripple Creek and coming straight to his house.

He fired back with a text within seconds, excited for her arrival.

"You hungry?" He asked.

"Famished," she replied.

Another hour crept by.

Green aspens blurred by as she hugged the road's edges, delivering her into the mountains at a steady, swerving incline. Anya settled on an Allen Stone playlist she had been binging, belting each song at the top of her lungs. When she arrived at the Gillette Flats surrendering to the mountains before it, her stomach fluttered like the beating of a hummingbird's wings.

From here, she could take the back roads and end up at his doorstep within a matter of fifteen minutes. Ten minutes if she pushed on the gas. Anya recalled the exact place she had stashed the sand dollar that she intended to give him, recalling his words, *'The only thing I want back from the beach is you.'*

At this rate, she would be rushing back to him for the rest of her life. A thought that terrified her and excited her all at once. Anya had barely spoken to Sam during the entirety of her trip. Just enough to know that when she drove back home, he would still be there. An uncommon trait in her past romantic endeavors.

Anya wondered what he had been doing this whole time.

She imagined him perched on a boulder above a lake, casting a translucent line into the water, or sitting still in the silence of nature and fixating on the wagging tails of brown trout scurrying into the murky brown water. Maybe he was stationed at his work computer with a quizzical brow focusing on whatever work task needed extra attention. Moments like the ones she could conjure up in her mind were ones Anya dreamt of without even knowing it. Sam was starting to be everything she didn't know she even wanted.

Anya tried to recount all the moments she had built up a person in her mind. The image of them took the place of the person they were in reality. How that part of her imagination always got her in trouble, one way or another. It was always a possibility that Sam wouldn't be the person she had romanticized. How the absence of a person, even for a week, could change the way you thought of them. How she had seen this happen so many times with men.

The Lost Pleiad

When it came to travel, Anya was permanently changed, even if it was the simplest or shortest of trips. No matter the sliver of time Anya spent traveling, she always came back a changed person. What made her think she hadn't changed this time? That answer was simple.

The fact that she brought back treasure for Sam.

She couldn't remember a time she brought a souvenir home to a lover or if she had ever done that. Was it a memory she blocked out after years of heartbreak? Or was Sam the first person she could fathom doing that for?

Perhaps this was the start of something real. As much as she hoped for that, Anya knew better than to sink into that trap. She was always the one limping away, bloodied, and years later, scarred.

Anya was in constant battles with herself. Fighting over whether she should surrender to whatever was building between her and Sam or if she should run and keep protecting her heart.

Anya rounded the corners, watching the guardrails snake between cliffs and trees like silver snakes as houses specked into view. Goldfield was nearing, and so was the familiar man-cave she would snuggle up in. She could practically feel Sam's beard brushing the nape of her neck. Her skin started to feel hot. The doubt and the hope that occupied her mind space whenever she was with Sam or anticipated their time together, it was now fading away. The long stretch of road brought her to a bend that forked off into a dirt one. To the left was Sam's house. The blue tarp on the roof no longer flapped in the wind. Sam could live in a cardboard box at this point, and she wouldn't care.

Anya sped into the driveway, screeching to a halt right behind his truck, so close she almost tapped his bumper. It was startling enough that he emerged from the house beaming with a smile. His beard was combed, and hair partially slicked back with a single strand hanging above his eyebrow like usual. Anya shuddered, unable to leave her car fast enough, realizing she hadn't showered for over almost a day. He rounded the front of her car, meeting her at the driver's side door.

"Give me your mouth," he said, taking her so quickly, feeling the heat of his body push her into her vehicle. The keys were still in the ignition, sounding an annoying ding that disappeared with each fiery kiss from Sam. His lips were sweet and minty; he had brushed his teeth. The whiskers from his beard tickled her cheeks, wisping their way to her neck. She let out an aching moan.

His mouth was better than San Diego, Christmas, Disneyland, and any other great thing in this world. Anya was sure he would take her right there in the back of her car. She would have let him.

Anya was dizzy, drunk on his kiss. He smiled, recognizing the struggle she was facing as she tried to find her focus as his eyes evolved to the shade of a fiery phoenix.

"I've missed you," he said.

"I've missed you too," she replied, not knowing just how much until this moment. He kissed her again, this time dotting her cheeks, nose, and forehead with smaller, tender pecks. How dare he stop after she had driven nearly a day just to be near him.

"I have something to show you," he said. The car persisted with dinging, stopping only after he reached into the car pulling the keys from the ignition.

"Oh, yes. The surprise," her heart was now fluttering in more ways than one. He laced his fingers into hers and led her through a newly cleared path, her brain firing into investigator mode; something changed. But before she could reach her conclusions, they were at a

The Lost Pleiad

door, opening up into the other side of his house, which she had never seen. Anya walked in, admiring the beautiful green shade on the walls, the frosted light fixtures, the bay windows letting in the summer light. She saw the couch they snuggled in, the TV sitting in front of it on a stand made of fresh cedar planks. She could smell the lasting fumes of paint and varnish, the welcoming aroma of the cedar. Sam walked her into the center of the room, his eyes following her as she made a round.

"Sam…" she started, stopping to stare at him. "It looks incredible in here. You did all of this while I was gone?" Sam looked hard at her, still beaming, proud of his work.

"Yeah," he said. There was a long pause. She tore her eyes from him, looking at all corners of the room, noticing its emptiness and how large the room looked without anything in it. Sam rushed over to the bay windows. "I thought this would be a nice place for either a small dining table and four chairs so we could entertain. Or maybe it would be a small side table with two comfy chairs where we could sit and have coffee in the mornings."

Anya watched him dart around the room. Frozen in silence.

"I thought we could install a big projector screen in the middle here," Sam pointed up at the ceiling and then at the wall above the couch. "…then we could watch hockey or football or have movie nights here." He rushed to the door next to the couch, opening up the door. "Maybe we can make this a bedroom."

When he opened the bedroom door, she didn't follow him. She was giving him a sand dollar, a dead sea creature, when it appeared he was giving her a place in his home.

Sam noticed her prolonged silence. Leaving the door ajar, he turned back to her, his once beaming smile now replaced with a worrisome frown. He shoved his hands deeper into his pockets and glanced at the floor. Anya felt tears gather at the corner of her eyes.

"You did this for me?" She inched closer to him. Sam buried his hands in his pockets so deep there were likely to be holes.

Sam hesitated before responding. "Yes."

Anya stared at him. His head dropped to his chest as if facing defeat. Anya could barely contain the tears, feeling astounded by the gesture and efforts to fit her into his life. He was giving her this incredible gift, considering her presence and possible existences in every corner. It was a feeling she hadn't experienced, one that stopped her dead.

She looked at the bay windows momentarily, walking over to them to feel the freshly dried paint on the windowsill trim. She looked out the window, noticing the pink fleshy color of the tree trunk in front. It had recently been cut down and laid sideways on the side of the house, waiting to be cut into smaller chunks.

Anya looked back at Sam, who was avoiding her gaze. No one had ever done anything like this for her. Anya searched the past few months of memories she shared with Sam. Recalling every time he proved to her that he was here to stay and how he had done so much with very few words and all action. She recalled the moment he promised he would prove it to her, and here he was, proving to her by making space for her in his home. No one had ever given her such a gift.

"I think," she sniffled, Sam's head jerked up, anxious for whatever words came next. "I think we should put the comfy chairs here instead of a small dining table. But we should plant more trees nearby, so there is a new place for the Stellar Jays. Sam smiled, and tears shimmered at the corners of his eyes.

Anya walked over to Sam, taking his cheek in her hand. He stared at her with his softened golden eyes, taking her by the waist and pulling her close. He kissed her again, this time more gently.

"I love you, Anya," he said. *There it was.*

Words she never thought she would hear again. Words she never thought she would hear and *believe.*

"I love you," she replied. The very words uttered freed her from a cage she had built herself into. No longer did she have to pretend to be strong. No longer would she have to protect her heart from shattering, not when Sam was around. A wave of relief washed over her like the fresh swells of ocean waves. To have a man who loved her and really saw her was all she ever wanted.

Anya's want for Sam built up like iron at the core of a blazing supernova. He was gravity pulling at her center until she exploded, sending light hurtling through the black. Sam, her beloved gravity, kneeling to the push of her own nuclear energy, desperate to emerge.

It was the death of her old self.

Akin to that of a dying star.

Anya was bursting into oblivion after several lonely years in the silence of her own space. And with this death, she was reborn, like the Helix Nebula swirling with new and exciting colors.

Sam kissed her, but it was different from the innocent ones she came to know and adore. He craved her like she craved him. Sam's lips traced a hungry path to her neck, lingering there briefly. Anya's skin seared with euphoria as his hands gripped her curves. Her fingertips grazed his thick arms, tickling his skin.

He hungered for every inch of her he promised to devour wholly, slowing the once powerful kiss to more delicate motions of intimacy.

Sam let his lips flutter at her ear, breathing softly to create shivers that would arch her back in tension. That a single breath could make her body shudder was unlike any sensation she had felt. It was as if Sam remembered what that breath did to her, how it inspired a new kind of life in her.

Tasting his sweet mouth in hers, she moved her hands to his neck, running her fingers through his hair. His hands found their way to the rounds of her ass, grabbing it tightly. His voice trembled again like he would lose it at any moment, but he was patient and so slow with his pleasure, wanting to savor each moment and each inch of her.

Saying nothing, Sam drew back to look into her, grazing her plump cheek with his thumb, lingering there as if taking a snapshot of her beauty. His free hand paused at her waistband, threatening to tear them off her. He could do it. He could take her in any way he wanted, but Anya sensed he had other plans. Those fingers moved to the underside of her shirt, tickling her torso, feeling the softness of her skin until he could feel her breast in his hand.

Anya's trigger.

She let out a moan, feeling his fingers glide around her perked nipples. Anya, losing all control of herself, took his mouth in hers, ravaging him desperately. He responded with the same fierce wanting, pulling her closer to his body.

Taking her hand, he led her to his loft bed, getting a condom from his bathroom on the way, watching her physique wave a figure eight in his wake.

Sam stripped each piece of her clothing while her fingers danced around his face. She smirked at this thick beard, knowing she would feel its soft tickles on her skin soon. Anya removed his clothes, finally seeing the tight muscles in his chest, stomach, and arms like he'd been chiseled by God's themselves.

Anya wanted to taste him. Pushing him down on the bed, she climbed on top of him, kissing him again, moving her lips to his neck, down to his chest. Licking. Biting. Using her breath to tickle his skin. He writhed beneath her until her lips and tongue traced a path to his erection, swallowing him entirely. Sam cried out, which made Anya wet and ready. She stroked his cock with her wet tongue, letting his hands run through her hair.

"Please," Sam cried, unable to contain himself. "Not yet."

Anya smiled up at him, seeing his devilish smirk that told her he had more in mind. He reached for her, drawing her to meet his gaze, and turned her over to her back. From his knees, he looked down on her, letting his hands explore her body, feeling her everywhere.

Using his breath and touch, Sam's lips met her skin, tracing his journey south, intent on evoking an out-of-body experience. Those heavenly lips sailed across her buttery skin, flicking the hardness of her nipples with his tongue, his hands cupping the swells of her breasts. Each delicate touch made her disappear from reality into a place of bliss. His path extended beyond the mountains of her curves, making maps of her most sensitive spots until his tongue found the space between her legs. The tickling sensation and hot breaths met her skin before his tongue trilled her clitoris, making perfect circles as if he held a book on pleasing her with only his tongue.

Letting herself feel it all, she moaned; relinquishing all control of her body for an orgasm that would unhinge her from years of fear and sadness—freeing her from the place where negative thoughts of herself were held hostage like prisoners. When she let go, she quivered beneath him, her legs tightening, breaths going from a racing rhythm to a slow tempo.

"Oh my God," she moaned, opening her eyes to see the room spin around her. When Sam returned to her lips, she could taste her sweetness. His firmness hovered over the void she hadn't filled in the ways she desired for years. He tore the condom from the package and slid it on while she watched. When he pressed into her, she moaned again, feeling him slide deep within her. Finding their slow rhythm, she lifted her hips to meet his, letting him press into her so she could feel every inch of him plunge inside her.

Sam's slow motions brought her to the verge of exploding, their bodies whispering more wordless pleas. His arms flexed beside her, the golden glow of his eyes growing more hungry and bright even in the darkness. Anya felt her body tremble. Sam felt it too. She tightened around him, pressing harder into his pelvis, feeling her clitoris tickled again. He dropped his lips to meet hers as they climaxed together, howling into the corners of his bedroom.

It was Andromeda and the Milky Way crashing together. A collision of stars, planets, and moons in their two galaxies, filling the dark voids in their lives with ripples of light and destroying all darkness in its path before settling into delightful stillness.

Anya ran her fingers across Sam's hairline, wiping the perspiration that had formed on his brow. He just stared at her, his fingertips finding those same plump cheeks and twirling locks of her hair. Anya wrapped herself around him, feeling closer to him than ever before.

"My cosmic angel," he said, admiring the rivers, lakes, and oceans in her eyes. "For weeks, I've tried to find a word that describes how beautiful you are, but all of the words fall short of any and every word,"

Sam said. Anya smiled, kissing him, tasting her sweetness and the salt of his skin. "You are remarkable, Anya."

"Thank you, my dear," Anya said, kissing him.

"I should be the one thanking you," he said. "Saying I've never met anyone like you, whatever I say, it's just…"

"Ineffable. Hard to explain," she said. His wolf eyes returned to those sweet pools of honey.

"Yes, ineffable," he grinned. "How could I ever describe just how much you've captured me?"

"I ask myself that same question," she said, moving the hair from his face.

The pressure of his body on hers could be her weighted blanket, absolving her of all fears and anxieties. Relaxed wouldn't begin to explain how her whole body felt at this moment. Sam rolled to the softness of the bed, drawing her body close to his to let the moonlight bathe them.

"For many years of my life, I've dubbed mundane moments as spectacular, never truly knowing what was out there. Then, you found me," Anya said. "But Sam…" Anya stopped.

"What?" Sam asked, looking to see her eyes, which had dipped away from his.

"I'm terrified of what happens now. Now that I've let you in," her tears glistened in the moonlight, dropping to his chest and rolling off into the valley of darkness that fell to the bed.

"Oh, Anya," he said, hugging her tightly. "I would never do anything to hurt you. Ever. I will protect you with every inch of myself," Anya cried harder, releasing her sadness in his arms for the second time.

"Please promise me you won't leave me," she cried.

"Anya, I will do whatever I have to in this world to prove to you I'm here to stay. I will not stop until you trust me, and even then, I'll keep going," he said, squeezing her tighter.

"Okay," she muttered. "I believe you."

He took the blanket from the edge of the bed, wrapping them both into a cocoon of warmth and comfort while they nodded off. Anya was amazed by how his words encompassed a gentle, poetic flow. How his sweet loving voice, was an orchestra of silky and pleasant sounds.

Anya listened to his heartbeat. Listening for skips like she had done with many others before. Losing him now that she had found him was a profound fear suffocating her. She wanted to secure his place by her side. Life was transient after all, and tomorrows were never guaranteed. And she couldn't bear living with another heartbreak that might destroy her.

"I'm going to miss the loft bed. It makes me feel like a kid in a treehouse."

"If you want a treehouse, I'll build you one in the backyard," he kissed her forehead. Anya felt his flaming kiss again, wondering if that flame would ever die out or if her heart would ever stop bursting.

"Only if we get to build it together," she said. Letting the silence rest between them, Anya thought of the moment she saw Sam with the blonde woman at the museum.

"Can I ask you a question?"

He snickered. "Always."

"The day that I saw you with that blonde woman, what happened?" Anya didn't *need* to know and was surprised she hadn't asked already. Whether or not the answer was helpful or hurtful, she wanted to know.

Sam sucked in a breath.

"Well, she came into the museum that day by herself. I didn't know her and decided to walk through the museum with her to show her some of the highlights. She stopped at a photo of a couple from a long time ago and started to cry."

"Why?" Anya asked, suddenly interested in the stranger's sadness. Anya didn't like hearing people hurt at all, no matter who it was.

"Her fiancé had been cheating on her. They had planned a trip to Cripple Creek together. Instead of nixing the trip, she came on her own. I offered her a hug because I felt like she needed it," Sam finished.

Anya gripped him tight. "You do like hugs."

"I do," he muttered. It was midday, and the daylight brought a pleasing warmth to the room.

"That was sweet of you," Anya said.

And she meant it.

"There've been times where I haven't been so sweet," he replied. Anya stayed silent. "There is so much I've wanted to tell you about myself. Some of which is very shameful, but things I'm dying to tell you."

Was Anya prepared to hear those things? She had to be if it meant loving him fully. Eventually, she would have to accept him for his darknesses.

"You remember when you told me about the guy who hurt you?"

Anya cringed at the mere mention of it. "I do."

"I want to tell you about the woman I hurt," he said. Anya propped her head on her arm, nervous to hear what he did but happy to hear him open up, unlike most men had done with her.

Sam walked Anya through the history of him and this woman. Her name was Lori. He met her at Ralf's one night during karaoke. It didn't take him long to charm her, a truth about him Anya didn't particularly like. She had to remind herself he was not that person anymore.

"I knew she was not the one," he said. "She was convinced there was something between us and even asked me if I had felt the same. She asked multiple times. Each time, I told her I didn't believe we were meant for each other. Even after my answer, she would ask the same question, 'why do you hang out with me then?' I told her it was because I liked her."

Anya listened the whole time. Not interrupting his story, not judging him for something he couldn't change now. It was something she could tell he felt guilty about. She felt sorry for this woman, feeling a kinship with her and the heartbreak she was likely still working to overcome.

"I suppose she stayed around for so long because I told her I liked her and thought she was a badass babe. The worst part is, I let her stay. I let her spend time with me. I let her think I liked her and that I would change my mind about her. But I knew the truth. I wasn't going to change my mind," he continued.

"Then, one day, I woke up and decided I just wasn't into her anymore. I told her I was bored and didn't want to see her or have sex with her anymore. I told her over text."

Sam was crying, tears falling down his cheeks and fading into the pillowcase. Anya gripped him tight, knowing what it felt like to grieve and feel remorse for your wrongdoings.

"She was a good person. She didn't deserve how I treated her. For weeks after, she went around to everyone in my friend's circle, told them what a horrible person I was. No one believed her because she wasn't from here. I never corrected them. Even to this day, I never do.

That woman eventually left the town and never talked to anyone here again."

Sam broke into a heavy cry, sucking in air as he wailed into her. She curled him into his chest like a baby, and he sobbed fiercely. Anya felt for him and felt for Lori all at once. The things people do when they are hurt. Lori trying to tarnish Sam's image to his friends was an obvious sign of hurt. Yet, Anya still couldn't figure out what made Sam hurt so much that he did this to women.

"I ruined her," Sam cried.

"She will recover," Anya said. He lifted his chin from her chest, and his eyes were now swollen and red.

"Did you?" He asked, hoping for an answer different than what he already knew. The truth was, she never recovered from any of them. She carried the pain men had caused her like badges of honor, flashing their silvery faces to blind any other possible suitors. As time went on, the sting of those heartbreaks lessened, but they would always be tender wounds.

"No," Anya replied. "I don't think we really let those memories go, especially if they meant something to us. But honestly, I probably could have been better at managing my bitterness."

Sam sniffed, clearing the tears from his eyes and inhaling a deep breath. Anya hugged him tighter, hoping he could feel her love without saying a word. Sam clung to her, his head rising and falling with her chest.

"Thank you for telling me," Anya said, kissing his forehead. Hearing that truth wasn't as bad as she imagined. She loved him more for showing this part of himself.

So few had that bravery to be so transparent.

"Thank you for not hating me," he muttered.

"I believe you are quite stuck with me now," she said.

This made Sam smile. "Something that most delights me."

They lingered in silence a little longer. Anya let her eyes drift close, content with having him there. Being the protector of his heart like he was for hers. Anya knew there would be a road of love, truth, disappointment, and trust ahead for them. She knew they would fight about things, get frustrated and angry that they would say things they didn't mean. Although she wasn't well-versed in relationships, she knew nobody was perfect and that they would make mistakes. Anya would forgive him whenever she could and go through this entire journey, even if this part he shared wasn't the worst of it.

Realizing she hadn't slept in nearly an entire day, Anya fell asleep. When she woke, the day had fallen to night. She reached for the space Sam was supposed to lay in, feeling it empty. When she looked down, the area below her was silent. She couldn't feel the hum of the TV that used to be there or feel the presence of Sam's love.

She wrapped herself in the sheet and climbed down from the loft. On the floor were her bags. Sam must have brought them in from her car. Even the smallest things Sam thought of. She remembered the rough sand dollar tucked in a pocket of her bag. She fished it out, feeling the coarse texture and remembering the same coarseness of the sand at her feet just a day ago. Snaking her way to the newly remodeled side of the house, she found Sam sitting shirtless on the couch staring at the TV, a flash of blue passing over his face and the six-pack abs crunched into a slouch. She glided in his direction, sitting down beside him. He let her curl into the crook of his arm and planted a single kiss on her forehead.

The Lost Pleiad

"Hello, my cosmic angel," he said sweetly.

"Hello, my love," she chirped back.

He sounded cheery, but his stare was more absent than normal. On TV, a rerun of Letterkenny was on, a show Anya thought was kind of dumb but at the same time amusing.

"I got you something," she said. She recalled the moment she brought back the ocean for Sam. On the way back to the car, before sand transformed to paved asphalt and steady earth, Anya picked up a single perfect sand dollar. She felt the roughness on her fingertips. This specimen was more beautiful in its skeleton than the furry underwater creature it was before drying to death on the beach. Sand dollars were the currency of the ocean and sand, littered everywhere and turned into treasure by whoever picked them up and took them home. Each one had a different measure of value depending on how someone viewed it. She turned the sand dollar in her hands, noticing the slits at the edges and the perfect five-point lazy star in the middle.

A piece of the beach for Sam. Just like she promised.

Sam swiveled his gaze from the TV to find her eyes.

"Oh yeah?" He said with a smile. "I told you I just wanted you."

Instead of saying anything, she smiled, handing him the sand dollar. He twirled it beneath his fingertips, running a single pointer finger over the star shape in the center.

"Thank you, sweetheart," he said.

"Did you know that, depending on the species, sand dollars can be blue, green, purple, brown, or black?" She asked playfully.

Sam stared at the TV and responded plainly. "I did not."

"You okay?" She asked. He heaved a long sigh. The kind of sigh that told her he had been thinking for a while.

"There's something else I want to tell you," he said. Anya waited for him to say more. "It's about my parents."

THIRTY-FOUR

Anya stared blankly at her office computer. It was silent in this half of city hall, but the whiteboard of tasks was loud from the corner of her eye. Looking at the list of things she had to do in organized and straight lines, categorized by color and priority, only intensified her desire to procrastinate. So she sat, comfortably staring at nothing in particular. What was on her mind more than the tasks she would eventually have to get to was her conversation with Sam about his parents.

The thought of what happened to him made her sick.

But she was more sickened at never having asked him about them. In all the time she had been with him, she hadn't asked about his parents. Not once.

And she felt immense guilt over it. Anya theorized she never had because of her own relationship with her parents. She didn't particularly enjoy hers; why should she take interest in his? Her evasion of the topic was never intentional, at least not consciously.

In all the time she had lived here, no one had talked about what happened to Sam as a young boy. There weren't even brief mentions of it. No one in this entire town even mentioned his devastating past. It was as if everyone had made a secret pact to never talk about it.

Anya recalled the conversation, watching Sam's eyes well with tears, his muscles tense and his jaw clench. When Anya felt his body stiffen next to hers, she raised her head from his shoulder to look at him.

When she moved, he didn't bother to turn and face her. He just stared at the wall of the new living room he had just finished and spoke, as if a single ghost was standing there and he was having a conversation with it.

"I was fourteen years old…" he choked, "…when it all happened."

Anya listened. Not eager to pry when she witnessed the pain he was working through, trying to form his feelings into words.

"I came home from hockey practice, and it was pretty late. I usually tried to come home late because I hated my own house. It was always a mess. It smelled, and fly paper hung from our ceilings. Our dining room table was always covered in dirty dishes, old newspapers, trash, and rotting food that had been left out for days. I always tried to keep my room clean, but it was no place any adult or child should live in. Mom always tried to keep the place clean, even though my father was a slob. But I think she started to give up too. I wondered when or if I would ever give up, just like the both of them did. I never looked forward to going home, except if dad wasn't there and I had time with mom. He used to hit her. A lot. Sometimes he would hit me too. I was fourteen and nowhere near strong enough to stand up for her yet. I would weight train at school, hoping someday I would be strong enough to beat the shit out of him."

Anya ached, wondering how a man as sweet as him could suffer a gruesome past and still be a good person.

"That night when I got home, they were already shouting so loud I could hear them from outside. I tried not to make noise when I came in, but as soon as I crossed the threshold, there was my father, in this room, with my mother, holding his hunting rifle."

Anya covered her mouth.

"I stopped right there, looking at him with his bloodshot eyes and then looking to my mother, whose hands were raised. She kept asking him to put the gun down, but he had it pointed right at her head. He was a good shot too, especially when he wasn't drinking. Every year he brought an elk home during hunting season. Mom kept asking him to put the gun down. All he said was 'shut up, bitch' and kept pointing it at her. When I tried to step closer, his aim shifted to me. Mom panicked, screaming 'no' multiple times, asking him to point the gun back on her. I could hear her crying as she tried to coax him to put the gun down. 'Just put it down, honey. You were right. I was wrong. I won't spend any more money on things we don't need. I can return the skates for Sam tomorrow. I promise.' I remember those words, clear as day. I remember how she called him 'honey,' even though he had a gun pointed at her. It made me cringe. Made me furious. Mom kept inching toward him, and he started shaking. When she got close enough to the gun to try and take it, he shot her in the shoulder. She told me to run."

Sam was in tears, his words indistinguishable between sobs.

"When she shouted a second time, I sprinted from the back door, down the dirt road until I hit the pavement. I heard another shot ring out and sprinted toward Victor, trying to hug the curves and disappear into town. Then I heard footsteps running just as fast as me from behind. When I looked, he was chasing me, his rifle still in his hands like he was ready to stop and fire. I was too far away for him to see me, and it was too dark. It was like something in a horror movie. I ran as fast as I could, crying the whole way, and as I reached the Victor city limits sign, I heard the third and final shot ring out. I ran to the Victor Hotel and grabbed the first adult I could find. Bruce. He was sitting in the lobby taking a coffee break when I ran in the front doors. I told him what happened, and he called the cops."

Anya was crying now. Envisioning the whole night Sam painted for her as if she were there. She imagined his father sprawled on the road. Dead.

"It was a murder-suicide, started in this very house," he said. And from there, he broke open, like a dam that was too full and spilling over. What she could see flooding out of him was guilt—that he had lived and hadn't done more to save his mother. "I've never forgiven myself for her death, but I hope my father is burning in a special kind of hell for what he did."

Anya was unsure of what to say or how to say anything that wouldn't be insensitive, rude, or dismissive. She just sat next to him, feeling the heat of his body. She wrapped herself around him, cradling him in her arms where he wept hard. She looked around at the newly painted room and freshly stained floor. What ghosts had lived in here with him all this time? How was he able to sleep at night?

"How were you able to live here after that?" Anya asked.

"I didn't," he said, "Bruce took me in, became my guardian, and raised me until I turned 18. The property went up for sale multiple times, but no one stayed in it very long. The person who ended up staying in it the longest ended up losing it. It wound up at an auction. Bruce told me about it one day, and I decided to buy it. It had the worst reputation, so it was easy for me to get the highest bid."

The Lost Pleiad

"Why would you buy it when it was a host for such awful memories," Anya asked delicately, aware of being too invasive but also curious about his reasoning.

"At the time, I was like 24, and it just felt like it was time to face my demons," he said. "I didn't want anyone living in a house full of my family's ghosts. It felt wrong."

"That's a pretty bold way to face your demons," Anya said. She looked at the floorboards, wondering how long it took for the blood to come out. If blood was still there dried into the cracks. "Didn't it bother you? Living here?"

"For a long time, it did. But I figured the only way out of those memories was through," he said.

"That's why it took you so long to renovate this part of the house," she said. "This is where it happened, wasn't it?" Sam nodded. He wiped some tears from his face.

"My room was in the part of the house I live in now. So it was easier to just be there," he said.

"I didn't know any of this, Sam," she said, "I'm so sorry this happened to you." The word 'sorry' rolled off her tongue, and it felt too weak and insincere for something that altered a person's life this greatly.

"Thank you," he muttered, slumping back into Anya's embrace, letting his head rise and fall with the rhythm of her chest.

"How is it possible that no one around here talks about this? Like no one even alludes to it," Anya said.

"I suppose people feel bad about it still, or they're afraid they might open an old wound. I don't know," he said, "this town took care of me after they died. It might be just as painful for them too."

Anya hadn't considered what it must be like for everyone else. They must've felt guilty knowing there was something wrong happening at his house and doing nothing. Knowing if they said something, Sam might have a mother today.

"Why did you decide to remodel this side of the house," she asked.

"You," he said, snuggling closer to her. Her heart did backflips, and he wondered if he could hear it beating faster. "You're the first person who has made me feel hopeful for my future and forgetful of my past. I wanted to create a whole new life, erase the ghosts, and keep living forward."

Anya, brimming with even more love than before. Her heart was unapologetically full and bursting.

"I love you," she said. His head lifted from her chest to beam at her.

"I love you," he replied, those words even more delightful the second time she heard them.

Anya replayed the conversation several times after she left his house, continued replaying several more times after sitting down in her office chair.

Sam lost both his parents, given one was far more than a troubled soul, but he still lost them both. Meanwhile, Anya had two parents. Flawed and judgmental ones, but parents nonetheless. She had two, and he had none. It made her feel guilty for lacking gratitude and staying away from them all this time.

Anya considered calling them several times before she did. But hearing Sam's story made her think about them a lot. They didn't agree on everything, they didn't agree on many things, but when she

The Lost Pleiad

imagined their deaths, if they had ever happened quickly, she knew she would be devastated. His story was enough to make her call her parents without him having to remind her just how short life is and how she should be grateful she still has parents.

Anya let her pride live within her for far too long. And although she was determined to be right and stubborn, eventually, one of the three of them would have to concede. It was on this occasion, Anya decided to be the bigger person and call them.

She arranged for an evening to have dinner with her parents, mentioning she would bring Sam with, so they could meet him. Anya was terrified of them meeting Sam, of him being judged harshly for who he was and the life he lived. Anya loved his life and the simplicity of it. But her parents? She knew they would look down on him for that simplicity. It didn't matter how close she and Sam had become, how intimate their connection was, or even if it was given to them by God personally. Her parents were sure to judge it anyway.

Sam and Anya would meet them Friday down in Woodland Park at their house to have dinner. Anya worried about it for the entire workweek. Shortly after calling her parents, she called Sage and Gwynn, telling them about her 'meet the parents' night and how she might need some support the following morning. She set up another appointment with them as Gwynn briefly mentioned they would be discussing astral projection this time around.

Astral projection.

Anya felt a frisson, looking forward to what that would entail. She knew very little about it, torn between actively learning about it before arriving at their house or just walking into it blindly. Part of her didn't want to be psyched out by what kind of truths she may discover from astral projection. Another part of her was thrilled for what she might be able to do.

The whiteboard tasks hadn't moved, and Sami hadn't stirred in her office. Anya decided to steal a few more minutes of procrastinating to do a quick search on astral projection to satiate her curiosity.

She learned that when experiencing astral projection, the spirit leaves the physical body. With the spirit body, she could travel to other places while her physical body rested in a different location.

Astral projection falls under a myriad of other practices that fit under the umbrella of esotericism, a type of secret knowledge of movements devised in the West, including yoga, alchemy, meditation, astrology, spirituality, mysticism, and occultism.

If Anya's bible-thumping parents could see her now, dabbling in practices closely related to occultism, they would be fucking proud. Anya made a note not to mention that to them and to tell Sam to do the same.

Anya searched online for longer than she expected she would. Sami startled her when she entered her office.

"Hey! You want to get some lunch?" She offered, frowning at the whiteboard.

"You wouldn't rather skip your lunch for all this?" Anya gestured toward the whiteboard donning a painful grin. Sami walked over the threshold and positioned herself in front of a target hanging on the wall next to the doorway that said, 'bang head here.' She knocked her head in the center of the target three times. Anya laughed, getting up from her chair to stretch, feeling relieved to get out of the office.

"Let's go," Anya said, pushing Sami out the door and into the darkened city hall. She stopped in at the clerk's office to announce their departure and left the building. Four blocks down Bennett, Anya could see the herd of donkeys stopping traffic. Outside, shop owners were hanging plants, shirts, and signs from their awnings, not exchanging friendly talk. Anya laughed at this, at their unwillingness to be friendly to one another. In the past, she had tried to initiate something that resembled a Chamber of Commerce meeting, but it had ended up in arguments and frustration. Anya decided it wasn't worth her time. If the local shop owners wanted to be divided, so be it. She had more important things to worry about.

That Friday, Sam arrived in his shiny white truck, her man on a white stallion. He dressed casually, as Anya instructed. She wanted him to be his authentic self instead of dressing up to be someone he wasn't just to please her parents. She wondered if he was anxious about meeting her parents now. Now that she knew his story.

"Remember, don't mention anything about me being an alien or that I'm going to see spiritual gurus in Fremont County. They will lose their shit," she yelled from the bathroom. He snickered as she poked an earring through her ear.

"I won't say a word," he shouted back. When she emerged, Sam looked up at her, grinning mischievously as he sat in her book nook with Sugar curled in his lap.

"Man, how on earth did I get so lucky?" Anya blushed.

"Are you kidding me?" She strutted over to him and kissed him. "I'm the lucky one."

"Better to be lucky than good," he said, getting up. Sugar pounced from his lap to a new location on the dining room table. Anya beamed at him. "I have something for you."

"Love, we don't have time for sex," she said, laughing.

Sam laughed. "That's not what I meant. I have an actual gift for you."

"Oh," she said, surprised. "What's the occasion?"

"No occasion," he said. Sam dipped his hand into the deepness of his pocket to fish out something small enough to disappear into his fist. He opened his hand, and a silver chain dangled from his fingers. It sparkled as it swung in the light, revealing a single silver disc at the bottom. On the front were black dots formed into the constellation Pleiades. Anya choked back tears, admiring the silvery necklace, her eyes darting back and forth between her thoughtful gift and the man of her dreams.

"It's beautiful, Sam," she turned around to let him fasten the delicate piece around her neck. Feeling its coolness on her chest, she looked down to see the black stars dotting the silver disc. When she turned around, he was smiling proudly, eyes heavy with love for her. Love so strong, Anya knew if she had nothing else in this world, she would be happy.

"For my cosmic angel," he planted a kiss on her lips.

"You're amazing," she said. "I have ways to thank you later."

"Oh, I'm sure you do," he said with a hint of sultry that made her skin sing and her body tense.

"Okay, we have to go, or we'll be late," Anya commanded. She brushed Sugar's soft black fur with her fingertips and made way for the door, Sam trailing behind her.

In less than thirty minutes, they were arriving at the edge of Woodland Park. Anya directed him around turns that curved back to a house nestled in a forest. Sam parked his white truck in the clean cement driveway.

The Lost Pleiad

No one came out to meet them.

When they arrived at the front door, Anya rang the bell, her heart thumping in her chest. She peeked through the frosted windows, seeing blurry figures come into a less blurry view as they neared the door. Anya grabbed for Sam's hand, hoping it would bring her comfort.

Months without seeing her parents, and then seeing them now, was a kind of nervousness she kept putting off. Before now, she hadn't thought about what would happen when she saw them again; hadn't thought about seeing them again at all, assuming they would just always be there and never leave.

The front door opened with a click, revealing Anya's father.

Anya had forgotten just how young he looked. Time had been kind to him, showing little greying in his hair. His eyes softened at the sight of her like he was relieved to see her after all this time. But those same eyes held a twinge of resentment, the eyes of a disappointed father.

"Hey, Dad," Anya said, looking directly into his eyes. They shifted quickly back and forth between her and Sam. "This is Sam."

"A pleasure to meet you, sir," Sam said in a type of politeness that made Anya sweat. Sam put his hand out.

"You can call me Cole," he said. Cole took Sam's hand, shaking it firmly. Anya relaxed, but not much. "Come in."

They came in the front door, Anya feeling a little less unwelcome. She stole a glance from Sam, who grinned slightly as if telling her it would all be okay. The entryway opened up to a living area with high ceilings. Two sliding doors let in extra light, and windows on either side of the doors stretched to the height of the ceiling. To the left was a balcony, the second floor of the house. This wasn't the house she grew up in, but with the nice furniture, muted artwork, and elegant interior design, it was a beautiful home. Her childhood connection to it didn't exist here. What connected her to this place and made her feel at home was the aroma of garlic and chicken from the kitchen. Her mother was making Anya's favorite casserole. Perhaps they weren't as mad at her after all.

As they entered the living room, Jada emerged from the kitchen off to the right, hands buried in a towel while she forced a smile.

"This is my mother, Jada," Anya said. "Mom, this is Sam."

Sam didn't put his hand forward but grinned. "It's nice to meet you."

"Nice to meet you too," Jada half grinned. "Dinner is about ready. You're welcome to have a seat. Can I get you something to drink? A glass of wine?"

"I'll take some wine," Anya said, moving to the couch to sit down. Sam followed took a seat next to her. Cole sat opposite of them in a single armchair.

"I'll take some wine as well," Sam said. Jada nodded.

"What would you like, Cole?" she said dryly.

"I'll take a glass of wine, too," Cole replied. A silence hung in the air. Anya didn't reach for Sam's hand, and he didn't reach for hers. Him sensing the tension of this moment. If anything, Anya was just glad to have him here for moral support. There was noise from the kitchen, Jada uncorking a bottle of wine. Anya could feel her heart rate increase again with each passing second of silence. Should she be waiting to be scolded and embarrassed in front of Sam? Would this be a pleasant encounter? It had been a long time since she brought someone home. Keegan, the man who ripped her apart, was the last one. She had brought him home to meet her parents. The whole situation felt so foreign to her, and she wasn't sure how to act until her father broke his silence.

"So, tell me about yourself, Sam," Cole said, burrowing into his chair. As he got comfortable, Jada came out with two glasses of wine, the first glass going to Cole, the second going to Sam. Jada didn't look at Anya, just returned to the kitchen.

"Well, I live in Victor, and I work for the Lowell Thomas Museum," Sam said.

"Lowell Thomas, the famous world explorer?" Cole asked.

"That's right," Sam said.

"I didn't know he had a whole museum," Cole said, appearing interested.

Anya was trying to listen, wanted to interject, but noticed her mother was gone so long, she thought maybe she had forgotten about her. She sat straight up on the couch while Sam seemed so relax with each sip of wine. Minutes later, Jada came out with a third glass, giving it to Anya but barely looking at her.

Her mother could hold a grudge.

While she sat in anxiety, Sam and Cole were deep in conversation, talking about Sam's love of hockey and sports in general. At least they seemed to be getting along. Anya loved sports just as much, but couldn't find a way to enter the conversation in comfort, so she sipped her wine silently. She eyed the kitchen, wondering when her mother would emerge again.

Sam placed his hand on hers, bringing her back to life in the present, startling her, so she nearly lost the grip on her wine glass. When she looked at Sam, he was smiling, and so was her father.

"Sounds like you found yourself an incredible man here," Cole said. Anya, surprised by the comment, smiled weakly. It was the truth, but she couldn't help feeling uneasy where she was sitting. "How did you guys meet?"

Sam looked at Anya. "Originally, she came into the museum to give a familiarity tour, but we formally met at Ralf's."

"What's Ralf's?" Cole asked, looking at Anya.

"It's a bar," Anya muttered.

Awesome

"Ah. I see," Cole stabbed with displeasure. He didn't ask for any more details, but Anya remembered that day she met Sam. When she came in, he was so cheery, cheerier than you would expect anyone working in a low-traffic museum. It was off-putting at first because who could ever be that positive? No one liked overly optimistic people. But then it became impossibly endearing, to the point where she fought her attraction to him, convincing herself she wasn't that interested. They hadn't talked about anything all that interesting at first. But what she liked about him most was his knowledge of the area when he gave the tour and how he told the stories with such enthusiasm.

Naturally, when she interacted with him at Ralf's, she pushed back from his advances, having felt these similar tactics from previous men. But, here Sam was, proving her right with each passing minute. After Ralf's, he invited her out for coffee, saying it was much less intimidating to go on a coffee date than a dinner date. Their first date was at the Gold Camp Bakery on a Saturday.

When he showed up, grinning, happy to see her, talkative, and invested in what she had to say, it bothered her. It bothered her that someone wanted to know her and be around her. In her mind, he wasn't the only man to behave like this during dates. She convinced herself that it couldn't be real. But oddly, she wanted to give him a chance. After their first date, they went on more dates, but she stayed distant and closed off in his attempts to become closer.

Now, he was sitting in her parent's living room, introducing them. And not a week ago, he had told her he loved her. At the thought, she became paralyzed with fear.

Sam loved her. *Really* loved her.

No one had ever loved her and meant it. But Sam did.

And the fear that she had when she first met him returned. A fear worse than the original. A fear of losing him. If things didn't go well with her parents. If they didn't get along, or Sam didn't like them, Anya could lose him.

She couldn't let that happen. And just when she thought all would be well.

"Are you religious at all, Sam?" Cole asked because, of course, he would.

"Not really, sir," Sam said. At this, Cole frowned, gripping his wine glass a little tighter.

"Really?" Cole said. "Do you mind my asking why?"

"Dad," Anya set her wine glass down, her palms sweating. "Please don't."

"Dinner's ready," Jada said, emerging from the kitchen. Anya was happy for someone to change the subject finally. That didn't stop Sam from explaining himself.

"Well, sir. I lost both my parents when I was 14," he said. Cole's eyes widened. "My father was an abusive drunk who killed my mother and then himself. It's not that I don't believe in God. I just don't believe in any Gods who are okay with giving a child two parents, only to rip them both away."

Anya looked from her mother to her father, who were both frozen in place, and stunned by the answers. It was the first time anyone had ever shut them up about religion. They usually parroted some answer about 'God's plan,' which would've been hard to do with this situation.

Her father's cheeks flushed, and her mother looked like she cared for the first time since they arrived. Anya stiffened, feeling a grumbling in her stomach, and not from hunger. Mortified. Terror swept over her like a consuming plague. Maybe her parents weren't judging him, but judging Anya for her choice in men, wondering why she would choose a man with such a horrid past. She started sweating again.

Anya couldn't believe Sam. For someone who had never told that story to anyone, he was sure comfortable doing it now. She waited for any of them to say something, looking anxiously between them. So little time had passed from the moment of his confession, but the silence made it feel like they had existed in this place forever.

"I'm sorry that happened to you," Cole said, Jada drawing closer. Both of them looking concerned and compassionate. Anya tried to imagine what bible verse they might spit to explain the will of God taking two parents from a teenager but was surprised when they said nothing. It was much harder saying it was God's will when the person you're saying it to is someone you now know.

"Thank you. Believe me. Everything could have been worse after that. But I had a very good guardian. He is like a father to me," Sam said.

The sick feeling of what life would be like without her parents returned for the first time in a week, reminding Anya why she had returned home with Sam in the first place. No matter how different Anya was from her parents, she still loved them.

"Plus, everything that happens to you leads you to where you are. And I like where I am," as Sam said this, he looked at Anya deeply, taking her hand for the first time since arriving. His love shined for Anya. Surely her parents saw it too. Their faces softened in observance of Sam's silent confession of love for Anya.

"Well, dinner's ready," Jada said. "I made your favorite, Anya. Chicken and rice casserole."

Maybe her mother wasn't as mad as she thought.

The four of them spent the evening talking and laughing, going through a bottle of wine and an entire pan of casserole. Anya couldn't remember the last time she laughed with her parents. By the time they left through the front door, it was late in the evening, and Jada and Cole were practically swarming Anya and Sam.

"Let's please do this again," Cole said.

"It was nice having you both," Jada said so plainly.

Cole hugged his daughter and shook Sam's hand. Both of them looking surprisingly more forgiving. It pleased Anya but also made her angry.

"We will," Sam said. Anya waited for them to say they loved her, but they didn't. Having watched her boyfriend be just as honest, she attempted to do the same.

"I love you," she said. Jada nearly hesitated.

"I love you, too," Jada said an obligatory way.

"I love you, An," Cole said. "Please drive safely and tell us when you've made it home."

"I promise she's in good hands," Sam said, taking her hand in his.

"We can see that," Jada said dryly. They waved goodbye and climbed back into the Tacoma. Snaking down through the trees and curves until finding their way back to HWY 24, Anya stared at Sam for the first half of their trip, as if searching him for answers to an unsolved mystery.

"What are you looking at?" He laughed.

"How did you do that?" Anya asked.

"Do what?" Sam said.

"Make them like you. I mean, my mom still seems mad at me. But you make everything suddenly… *okay*," Anya said. Sam took her hand, glancing from her to the road.

"I don't know. I was just myself like you told me to be," he said. Anya felt sick, realizing how much of herself she had held back with her parents. How much of herself they still hadn't seen. It was different, Sam showing himself to them. But Sam wasn't in danger of losing them for being who he is. Anya, however, could lose her parents if she showed her true self. Perhaps that's why she hadn't done it.

"Why did you tell them about your parents?" Anya asked, desperate for his answer. "It just seems like something you wouldn't tell someone you barely know."

"Yeah, you're right," he replied. "But I figured, if these were to be my in-laws someday, I would want them to know me as much as possible. Eventually, that part of my life would come out, so why wait?"

Anya continued to stare.

He was already thinking about marriage? After just a few months of being together? Anya didn't know whether to be scared of how fast this was going or feel joy for finding someone already dreaming of marrying her.

The Lost Pleiad

"Well, they like you. That's for certain," Anya said, letting go of his hand to cross her arms.

"Were you afraid they wouldn't?" He asked.

"Definitely," she said. "They can be very judgmental of everything, including anything I ever do."

Sam lifted an eyebrow and gave a sly grin. Anya smiled too.

"You know what I mean," she said, smacking his arm. Sam laughed at her. "God, why are guys so dirty?"

"In all seriousness, though, you might just need to give them a second chance," Sam said.

"What do you mean?" Anya asked.

"I mean, I would love to have two parents of my own, even if I fought with them sometimes. And they love you," said Sam.

"How do you know that?" Anya asked.

"I know love when I see it," Sam said, looking at her. She grinned at him, realizing just how hard he loved her on any given day.

"I'm afraid they won't like me for who I really am. We disagree on so much. I don't follow religion, so they see me as a disappointment," Anya said.

"They don't. Trust me," Sam said. "Your dad looks at you with such pride and love. Your mom, although she tries to hide it, can't help but look at you. But you barely look them in the face."

Anya felt shame and sadness for her lack of closeness to her parents. Something she felt wasn't there but wanted so wholeheartedly. There had been a disconnect between them for so long, assumptions made on both ends. But with Sam there, observing from the outside with better clarity, he could see three adults who loved each other just wanting to do so freely and afraid to for fear of rejection.

"You're right," she said, crying. Sam's face switched to worry, and he took her hand and held it to his heart.

"Whoa. Hey, it's alright," he said. He searched the road for a safe place to pull over—not many places to choose from going up the mountain. He was able to find a pull-off for trucks going less than 30 miles an hour. Putting the car in park, he reached over the center console, taking Anya in his arms. She felt his warmth, burrowing in his chest, letting herself cry.

"I missed them so much," she sobbed.

"I know you did, love," he said, tightening his hold.

Anya felt her hope expand, filling the corners of her heart. Perhaps this world that she felt so alone in was only lonely because she made it so. She had pushed people away, failed to trust their realness, failed to trust her own realness, while Sam inspired her by being honest and trustworthy, all in a fell swoop.

This man was not only healing her with his love. He was healing the world around her too.

THIRTY-FIVE

"Sage smells like weed," Anya said out loud. Sage was dancing around Anya barefoot with a burning smudge stick. The smell was pleasant, soothing, but if people didn't know any better, it really did smell like weed.

"What?" Sage chuckled. "No, I don't. I haven't smoked weed in years."

At this, Gwynn and Anya laughed. How refreshing it was to have someone older than her parents with such openness and humor.

Anya laughed. "I don't mean you. I mean the smudge stick."

"Yeah, it does kind of smell like weed, doesn't it?" Gwynn agreed. "Never tried the stuff myself."

"Why not?" Anya asked.

"Just was never appealed to me," Gwynn said, piercing her with his ice-blue eyes.

"I never liked how it made me not feel," Sage said. "Anything like drugs, alcohol, or food can keep us from really feeling our emotions as they arise."

Anya had never thought of it that way. She flashed through moments from her past where she had used alcohol and food to numb herself from pain, eating her weight in Oreo cookies every time a man broke her heart, or she felt deep stress.

"Working through your emotions is the best for your growth. We've always believed that. That's why the work we're doing is so important. People don't feel enough," Sage said.

"So, neither of you drink or smoke?" Anya asked.

Little clouds of smoke drifted around her before disappearing into thin air.

"Nope," Gwynn said. "Life is our high. Who needs hallucinogens when you can go deep into meditation and have visions of your own?"

"I don't think I've ever had a vision," Anya frowned.

"You probably have. You may not remember," Gwynn said. Anya tried to recall a moment in time where she might have but couldn't muster a memory. "But dreams are a variation of visions. And we know you've had those."

"What is it like? Having a vision," Anya asked.

Sage put the smudge stick down in its abalone shell, letting the burning leaves slow on their own. Silas hopped up onto her lap and started purring like a diesel generator. Anya stroked his soft fur while he nodded to sleep.

"It depends on what you're asking for," Gwynn said. "If you set out to get an answer from the Universe, you may not always like what you get. But if you're in stillness, you can see all kinds of incredible things people can't begin to imagine. But visions are wonderful. Sometimes, the visions are so surreal. It feels like it's what I'm actually living. Like something out of a movie. If I could live in vision and mediation all the time, I would."

"Why don't you?" Anya asked seriously.

"Because my spirit came here to experience life, to live in the physical body. And when you are in constant mediation, you miss out on things you can experience in the present," Gwynn finished.

"So, then why meditate at all?" Anya asked.

"It's important to be balanced in body, mind, and spirit. If one of those three is off-balance, then so are the other two. If you live too much in the world, you forget just how connected we are to everything around us. If we live too much in spirit, we lose our physical experience and those connected to us in the physical. If we live too much in our minds, we lack compassion and become selfish, greedy, or resign to ego. Balance is important," Gwynn said.

"So, if I disconnect from the church and my religion, does that mean I'm cutting myself off from my spiritual self?" Anya asked.

"Do you feel like you are?" Sage questioned.

"Sometimes, but not really. I don't feel like Christianity resonates with me," Anya said. "It feels kind of... ridiculous."

"If it doesn't, then it doesn't," Sage responded. "Your connection to religion or spirit is a very personal relationship. We value all religions and spiritualities. We're both Catholic, but a problem we see with churches is their attempt to control people, what they think, and what they believe without giving them much choice to decide for themselves. Less often does their vendetta include true connection to the spiritual self."

"If you did resonate with it, it's unlikely you would be here searching for answers," Gwynn voiced. Anya knew he was right and she was looking for answers. Within the past few months, her world had changed along with her perspective, and she was starting to see her connections to things change in drastic ways. The world was improving around her. Had it been because of her pursuit in understanding herself better? She thought so.

"So, how will this work today?" Anya asked.

"Astral projection takes focus and practice," Gwynn said. "If you don't find yourself traveling at all today, don't be discouraged. We will keep practicing until you have become comfortable with the process. Right now, we are just going to show you the way. Whatever journey you take from there will be your own."

Months ago, she would've never believed something like this was possible, and even now, she was still somewhat hesitant and resistant. But if something about this session could change her mind, perhaps other possibilities would be more fathomable.

"The first step is quieting your mind," Sage said. "We're going to start you off with a meditation."

"Okay," Anya complied. "Is there a place I'll be going?"

"We'll guide you to somewhere easy first," Sage said. "Go ahead and close your eyes."

Anya closed her eyes, feeling the cat on her lap and her arms limp on his furry coat. She couldn't see Gwynn and Sage, but she could feel them behind her. Could smell the hints of cedarwood and ylang-ylang from their soap. Could hear the jingle of Sage's bracelets as she moved.

"I want you to take five deep breaths," Sage said. Anya started with the first one, letting the air fill her lungs, holding it for a split second, and releasing it through her mouth. "Imagine a liquid white light entering the crown of your head… feel the top of your head relax, then your face, then your neck, then your shoulders, then your arms…"

Anya imagined the liquid white light filling her body, felt a tingling numbness crawl over her skin as she felt all parts of herself relax. Sage's voice sounded like a slow-running river, soothing and hypnotizing. Anya felt the prick of fingers above the bridge of her nose. Sage's fingertips. Soft circular motions were made on her forehead, and with each motion, she felt the tingling intensify.

"Now that you are fully relaxed, think of a single object you hold dear. Think of all its aspects. How it feels in your hand, what it looks like, what it smells like." Sage said.

Anya imagined the galaxy diamond instantly. How warm it felt in her palm, but not just warm, hot. The weight of it sinking into the middle of her hand. The smooth sides of its multiple surfaces in her fingertips. The firm edges. The stone was nearly clear, swirled with black on the inside and white specks. She felt the stone in her hand, letting the light twinkle on the surface each time she twirled it. As she focused on the stone, Anya felt all stress, fear, and worry fall away, along with the present reality. Thoughts, hesitations, and resistance didn't crowd with her mind. Instead, she held the weight of this small stone in her hand. Sage's soft voice came into her ear.

"Now, imagine where that object is," Sage instructed. Anya imagined the stone sitting on her white bedside table. She imagined the white table pushed up into the corner of the wall and the single scuff mark on the corner revealing the reddish-brown of the wood she'd painted over. She imagined the single small and vibrant green Gollum succulent forced to the edge and the small lamp with the navy blue shade. A matching white side table sat on the opposite side of the bed with a matching lamp. She saw the cloud surface of her white plush comforter draped over her bed, the navy stripes that ran across the foot of it. She noticed the walls, how they opened up tall and wide to create space to breathe. Taking in a deep breath, she imagined the scent of lemongrass wisping from the diffuser sitting on top of her dresser. A hardcover book sitting beside it.

"Hold onto those thoughts," Sage said. "Now, imagine lifting from your physical body and floating up like a balloon."

Anya imagined herself lifting from her physical and felt her skin hum intensely. As she did, her eyes opened, as if in a dream, but she was in control. From her own eyes, she watched herself lift from her body. She noticed her weightlessness, her density falling away as she lifted from the chair. She looked down through her silver etheric form, stunned by the glowing appearance, noticing her physical body beneath her. In an instant, she spirit snapped back to her physical.

"Concentrate, Anya. Don't pay attention to your physical. Focus on the moment," Sage said as if she could see her spirit body struggling to move upward. Anya shifted her focus, imagining again that her spirit was rising from her body. Willing herself to lift again, the sensation of falling back into her physical form arrived in her thoughts. When her ethereal body lifted from her physical, it hovered for a split second before dropping down again. Anya could feel the chair hard beneath her again. Frustration filled her, removing the peace she had willed herself into. She exhaled an irritated breath.

"Let it go, Anya," Sage said. "Let's try again."

Sage started from the beginning, inviting Anya to take five deep breaths, feeling the white liquid light relaxing into her body. Anya did as instructed, finding her sense of calm and peace again.

"Now, imagine you're that balloon, Anya," Sage said. "Don't let your fear and resistance get the best of you."

Anya imagined the silver cord again, noticing its hints of blue and slight streams of gold. Feeling its thickness pull at her center.

"Good, Anya," Sage said. How did she know? "Now, try and lift from your body."

Doing as instructed, Anya willed her spirit to lift from the physical. With more intense focus, Anya felt her resistance attempt to move in but took one deep breath to regain her focus. The hardness of the chair fell away beneath her, the heaviness of Silas on her lap disappeared, and all physical sensation was lost as she came to float above her own body. Silas, disturbed from his slumber, looked up at her silver form.

Gwynn was in mediation too, but she could see him sending streams of pink and gold light from his heart center to Anya's heart center. Sage was behind her, feeding the same colorful light from her palms on either side of Anya's temples.

"Now, see yourself going to that object, the one you pictured earlier," Sage instructed.

Anya remembered the weight of the stone in her fingers. Anya's weightless body shifted in an instant to her bedroom. Nearly everything was in place except for a few things. The lamps were on the floor, and the book was gone from the dresser.

Remembering the stone, she willed herself to be near it, and instantly she was there. She looked down at the galaxy diamond resting on her bedside table between her plant and her lamp. Reaching for it, she took the stone in her hands once again but didn't feel anything.

But everything still seemed was so *real*.

How could this be so real and so unlike a dream?

What once was a simple thought and visualization was now her present moment and space. With each second she spent in her ethereal being, she started to forget her physical reality. Being in a state of weightlessness, without the worries of the world drowning her, no worries about how she would eat, or sleep, or live, it was no wonder people escaped into meditation so often.

As she settled her feather-light self on the edge of her plush bed, feeling the stone as the only dense weight. The world around her sang at a vibrating frequency like a pleasant song. Anya heard Sage's voice echo into her mind for the first time since she arrived here.

"Anya, I want you to start finding your way back now. Think of your body, and will yourself to slowly let yourself come back. Don't rush," Sage instructed.

Anya nodded at her request returning the stone to its place on the table and telling herself to calmly return to her physical body. Within a blink, she had returned to the house, watching Gwynn and Sage flash past her until she had settled into her body. Until she felt the hard chair beneath her, felt Silas heavy on her lap, and smelled ylang-ylang.

"Very good, Anya," Sage said. "Now, take a few more deep breaths."

Anya breathed in deep, letting the real air fill her real lungs. Her body felt the familiar purrs of Silas, who was slumbering again in her lap. The soft fur was now apparent between her fingers.

"When I count to five, I want you to start feeling the sensation in your fingers, your hands, your arms, your feet," Sage said. "Slowly start letting sensation return to all parts of your body. When I reach the count of five, you can open your eyes. One…"

Anya let sensation return to her fingers, hands, and arms.

"Two…"

Next, her feet, legs, and torso felt a lively tingle.

"Three…"

Then, her neck, shoulders, face, and top of her head vibrated to life.

"Four…"

She took another deep breath, feeling her body return to a normal state, yet feeling lighter and more serene than before.

"Five."

Anya opened her eyes, seeing Gwynn there, his eyes opening at the same time. Both of them were grinning pridefully. Anya looked around at the room, feeling more aware of everything in it. She noticed the bird figurines that rested on the shelves, filled to the brim with books. The Daddy Long Legs curled up on the corners where the wall meets the ceiling. The forest green wood-burning stove still collecting ashy dust from winter. The black and white photographs decorating the walls around the room. The bright orange color of their couch and the matching armchair.

"Well?" Gwynn asked, anxious for an answer. Anya was speechless, remembering where she had just been, disappointed that it was now over, but feeling more aware of herself and all things around her as if just being in a state of silence enhanced that.

"I don't even know how to describe what I just did," she took her hands, wrapping them around her body like a hug, feeling her soft skin and the presence of her own body. "How was I able to do that?"

"The first part of the out-of-body experience is willingness, which you had," Gwynn said. "You did struggle with it for a moment, but you were able to let yourself live in the possibility and the realness of it."

"You were a natural," Sage grinned.

She considered all the places she would be able to go if she practiced enough but frowned inside when she realized she would only be able to see it all and not feel it.

"If I practice enough, I will have the ability to go anywhere?"

"Yes. Anywhere," Gwynn responded. Anya's first thought was visiting the moon or Jupiter or seeing the Milky Way from an outside perspective. Then it hit her.

She could go to Pleiades.

But there would be no planet there.

Just a cluster of stars.

She scoffed at the thought.

"Pleiades doesn't have a planet, though," Anya said, sounding defeated. "Just stars and space debris."

"How do you know there is no planet in Pleiades?" Gwynn asked.

"Astrologists say so," Anya replied. Gwynn looked at her with a raised eyebrow.

"We only see less than 1% of what's out in our universe. How could we possibly know that for certain?" Gwynn asked, smiling like he knew something she didn't.

"Anything is possible," Sage said. If Anya hadn't experienced what she just did, she might not believe that last sentence.

Now, she did.

THIRTY-SIX

For weeks after her first out-of-body experience, Anya spent hours trying to spark her astral travel. And for weeks, she was unsuccessful and frustrated.

She would try before work, after work, and even prayed to God that he would help her conjure an experience while she slept.

But nothing.

She was starting to doubt her ability.

Before long, she started believing it wasn't real at all but a magic trick of some kind. Maybe she needed Gwynn and Sage to be there each time, but how realistic was that? Was it their presence that calmed her and kept her rooted to earth?

She tried to provoke an experience, desperate to feel the same weightless and freeing experience but ultimately lost patience. Her hopes of seeing the moon and Jupiter for herself, that was out of the question now. Seeing if Pleiades was a real place? Even further out of the question. Perhaps she wasn't as much of a natural as Sage and Gwynn thought.

She searched the internet for ways to induce an experience, hoping someone had an easy how-to guide detailed somewhere. But most of the knowledge was in books people wanted her to buy. She settled on one, *Adventures Beyond the Body* by William Buhlman. He promised to teach people how to experience out-of-body travel.

A few days after buying the book online, it arrived at her front door. That day, she was planning to meet Bee and Karmyn for coffee in Woodland Park.

Anya was tempted to cancel plans and put the world on hold so she could disappear into the pages of the book. Amongst the first several paragraphs, the man detailed his apprehension toward the experience. Convinced the only reality that existed was the one where he could feel and touch anything within his grasp. Everything else, heaven, God, or other fairy tales, were stories to keep people trained.

Anya related to the way he questioned out-of-body experiences. She had doubted the universe's otherworldly possibilities just as much as him, even after what she had done just weeks ago.

And she was frightened.

She could barely imagine what existed beyond her in other dimensions. She knew there were far too many possibilities to be created and explored. She knew how limited the current world was with their imagination, so how would it be any easier for her to dream up other worlds?

After a few chapters, Anya was out the door and driving to Woodland Park, her mind loaded with thousands of questions she couldn't wait to have answered. Perhaps she could get those answers more quickly if she talked to Gwynn and Sage. With no service going down the mountain, a call to them would have to wait.

Pulling into Café Leo, she could see Karmyn and Bee just walking in, their hair sparkling in the Colorado sun. Getting out of the car, she ran to catch up with them, nearly tackling them with hugs. The three of them walked in together, ordered their coffee, and then found a cozy booth to snuggle up in.

At the table, Anya's mind drifted into an internal monologue. She went over all the questions that were taking her attention, zoning out as she remembered the weightlessness of her first astral projection experience in her bedroom. What about going to the moon? There was practically nothing there.

For years she thought it always resembled the Death Star from Star Wars and always found it strange that when she looked up, the surface was always the same pattern. How long would it take for her to master astral projection? Why was she having so much trouble? What would or could she see on her journeys? How could she envision Pleiades if she had no idea of what it looked like?

Her thoughts took her to a strange and unengaged silence, suddenly disrupted by the mention of her name.

"An!" Karmyn nearly shouted. Anya nearly fell out of the booth.

"Yeah?" She said.

"You disappeared for like five minutes," Karmyn said.

"You've been acting so weird these past few months," Bee said. "Are you okay?"

Anya answered immediately. "Yeah. I just have a lot on my mind," she said, shifting the mug on the table.

Karmyn and Bee looked at her as if waiting to hear more.

"What?" Anya said, annoyed.

"We're waiting for you to tell us, that's what," Karmyn asked.

"I don't know," she said. "It's weird."

"Is it any weirder than how you've been acting?" Karmyn asked.

"Probably," Anya muttered, thinking how crazy she'll sound if she tells them.

"Try us," Bee invited.

How should I tell them this time?

My spiritual body left my physical body through mediation. *No.*

I turned into a silver spirit, and astral projected to my room. *No.*

I believe in other dimensions, and these two crazy hippies are helping me visit them. *No.*

She can't say any of these things, but she had to say *something*.

Bee and Karmyn were staring, almost glaring at her, trying to provoke a confession. Anya cleared her throat.

"I've been trying this thing," she said, not looking at them. "I've been working with Gwynn and Sage, my energy healers, to master astral projection."

"Okay," Bee said. "Like out-of-body experiences?"

"Yeah. Like Dr. Strange," Anya said.

"The guy who travels through time in a blue elevator?" Karmyn asked innocently.

"That's Dr. Who," Anya said dryly.

"Same thing," Karmyn said, taking a sip from her coffee cup. Bee giggled.

"It's really not," Anya said. "One is time travel, the other is spiritual travel."

"So, which one have you done?" Karmyn asked.

"The spiritual travel one," Anya said, feeling tense.

"Uh-huh, and which one is that again?" Karmyn kept asking. Anya felt like she would burst with anger, feeling small and crazy. She wished she had kept her mouth shut.

"Okay, so you've been practicing astral travel?" Bee asked.

"I had my first experience with astral projection a couple of weeks ago," and as she said it, she was bracing for their potential expressions of shock, but nothing came. "Gwynn and Sage helped me relax into a state where I could come out of my body and travel somewhere."

Karmyn seemed less likely to speak now. But Bee had questions. "So, where did you go?"

Anya hesitated, trying to think of how best she could describe it.

"I sort of… flew to my bedroom," Anya said, feeling stupid.

"You flew?" Karmyn asked, eyebrows raised.

"Not physically," Anya said. "Like my spirit body did. Whatever, it's dumb. I shouldn't have told you."

Anya was feeling a hint of rejection, immediately jumping to the defense. Explaining this amazing thing couldn't be done rationally. She wondered who else would look at her like a crazy person—wondered if Sam would look at her the same way.

"Why are you getting frustrated?" Bee asked.

"Because the more I try to explain it, the more I feel like I'm being judged," Anya said, looking down into her almost empty cup.

"Who's judging you?" Bee asked. "Not us. Sounds like you're doing a fair bit of that on your own."

"We're just trying to understand what it is," Karmyn asked.

"It's just… the more I try to talk about it, the more bonkers I sound," Anya said. "And, I don't know, I experienced this amazing thing that I can't explain, even to myself. Even after going through it, I can barely convince myself it happened. It felt so much like a dream or something only portrayed in movies," Anya replied.

"Like Dr. Strange," Karmyn said.

Anya smiled a little. "Yeah."

"It sounds like you're really in your head about it and possibly afraid and judgmental of what you went through," Bee said.

"You guys must think I'm mad," she said.

"Not at all. I mean, it's weird, and I don't understand it," Karmyn said. "But we still love you. Remember, we talked about this weeks ago. You can tell us anything. And it seems like you're going through a major change and life shift."

Such an observation from Karmyn only calmed her slightly.

Anya had felt this way her whole life, had been friends with Karmyn and Bee for almost a third of that life. Somehow they were just now picking up on how much she questioned her existence. She was just now picking up on it herself.

"Have you guys ever questioned why you were here or what the whole point of being here is?" Anya asked. As the both of them searched for the answer, Anya hoped for anything she could grasp to relate to her dearest friends.

Anything.

"Not really," Karmyn thought.

"I mean, I have sometimes, but not at length," Bee said. "I'm pretty happy with my life."

Her heart fell, making her feel even more alone in this crowded cafe. She assumed asking more questions or telling them more details would make her feel better, but it didn't.

Anya worried no one would be able to get behind what she was starting to learn. Who else could possibly understand this other than Gwynn and Sage? They were her closest link to what she was questioning and what possibilities existed.

"Let's talk about something else," Anya said, feeling even more frustrated than she was this morning. Her face was plastered with a fake smile and a game of pretending to be lively in conversation. When it was time to leave, she hugged her two friends, letting them drive off in the opposite direction. Making the climb back up the mountain, her hope to feel understood faded away like a pleasing autumn into bitter winter.

This was a solo journey; one time and reality were slowly convincing her she would be doing alone. No one could understand this when the world learned to believe in things far more tangible. Even the magnitude of what she was learning herself was shocking. And if it was shocking to her, someone already on the search for answers, it was probably more shocking to others who weren't inclined to entertain other possibilities to begin with.

When Anya pulled into her driveway, it was approaching early evening. The front door rushed open, revealing to her an empty house with a single furry black phantom gliding at her feet. Anya swooped her up.

"I know at least you'll love and accept me no matter what," Anya said, kissing her nose. Sugar replied with a lick from her sandpaper tongue. She set her down gently on the dining room table, patting her on the head, and then picked up her phone to call Gwynn and Sage.

They answered on the second ring.

"Hello?" Gwynn said.

"Hey, Gwynn," she mumbled.

"What's wrong?" He questioned as if he could sense her already. There was dead air as Anya choked back tears and the overwhelming loneliness amongst her even more plaguing feelings of defeat.

"I'm feeling a little lost and frustrated," she said, the sour taste of sadness clinging to the back of her throat.

"Tell me what's going on," he said. Anya sat down at her dining room table and started tracing invisible figure eights on the wood. Sugar jumped up to be near her.

"I've been trying to astral project for weeks since I last saw you. I haven't gotten anywhere. What's wrong with me?" Anya questioned, noticing her quickly arriving sobs. Gwynn didn't say anything, just let her cry. "I tried to tell my friends about what happened. It felt like each word I said made me sound crazy. All they did was stare at me. They're my closest friends, and I thought they would understand me. Accept me."

"Oh, honey," Gwynn said. "Not everyone will understand your journey. Not everyone will want to. Not everyone, even your most beloved people, will accept you. But it doesn't have anything to do with you. They're stuck in their own fear and lack of acceptance. It's scary to watch someone you love search for a deeper meaning when they're stalled."

"But why?" Anya cried. "How could people who swore to love you create conditions around where that love will end?"

"I don't have an answer to that," Gwynn sighed. "But what they feel is not a reflection of you or their love for you. I'm sure they love you very much. Can I ask you a question?"

"Sure," she sniffed, going to the bathroom for the entire box of tissue to wipe her nose. She sat back down at the table. Sugar, sensing her sadness, laid down beside her arm and started licking her furiously in an attempt to soothe.

"Are you afraid?" He asked.

"What?" Anya asked.

"Are you *afraid*?" He asked again.

"Why would I be afraid?" Anya asked back.

"What you're doing and the answers you're looking for—they are very much outside of the norm and what everyone is taught to believe. Does it frighten you how much that sets you apart from everyone else?" Gwynn asked.

"Yes," Anya admitted. "This world is all I know. If I pursue this other world and all its knowledge, I risk losing everything here. My friends, my parents, Sam…"

"What makes you think you'll lose them?" Gwynn asked.

"The way my friends reacted to me saying I tried astral projection and liked it," Anya said. "They must think I'm nuts."

"Do you think you're nuts?" Gwynn asked.

"Sometimes," she replied.

"Do you think it's possible that what you feel about yourself shows on the outside? Imagine if you were confident in your decisions and the journey you were going on. Would you be caring so much about what your friends thought of you or how crazy you looked?" Gwynn asked.

"I imagine not," Anya said grudgingly.

The more right he was, the more she realized this journey for answers might steer her out of a life she already settled into. It was a good life, full of good things, but it lacked purpose in a vital area. "I've always felt like I didn't belong here. I thought if I went on this path, maybe I would finally find that purpose, that place where I belong. Now I feel like I'm even further away from finding belonging."

"You haven't really begun to consider all possibilities of where that might be, Anya. Be patient with yourself," he said. After knowing them for just a few months, it was hard to say where this would all actually go. Had she even given it an actual shot? What she had to work through and the beliefs she had to overcome were challenging her daily. It was difficult, exciting, and terrifying all at once.

She didn't want to give up.

She was just complaining.

Feeling sorry for herself.

What she wanted was to feel accepted and loved for who she was, no matter how strange. To hear it from the key people she loved and admired most. Where would she find that kind of acceptance?

After a significant amount of silence where Anya was deep in thought, Gwynn spoke again. "Are you busy tomorrow?"

"No," Anya said, knowing she would probably have a nose in her book or that Sam might be asking to spend time with her.

"Come to the house tomorrow morning around 7:00 a.m.," he said. "We're going to go somewhere."

"Where?" She asked.

"Somewhere to get you out of your head," he responded. "Bring your fly rod."

"Okay," she said. "I'll be there."

"Do me a favor tonight," Gwynn said lastly. "Go outside, take your shoes off, and put your feet in the dirt for a while. Take a book outside and read or listen to music."

"Okay," Anya said sadly.

"We'll see you tomorrow," Gwynn said.

"See you tomorrow," Anya said back. The line went dead. She put down the phone and started crying again. Feeling sorry for her poor self and how she couldn't seem to find a sense of peace or a sense of self-understanding, she got up from her chair and took off her shoes. Barefoot, she walked over to her stack of books, passing over the *Adventures of the Body* to choose something a little less intimidating. When she selected her book, she strapped a harness to her beloved cat and walked outside in her bare feet.

Heeding Gwynn's instructions, Anya walked the paved driveway to a patch of dirt near the trees. She placed her bare feet on the earth, still warm from the heat of the day, the small pieces of jagged rock jabbing into all areas of her feet. Sugar strutted to the nearest tree and started clawing at it. Anya shifted her feet on the rocks until she was comfortable with the stabs in her arches. Sitting down on the paved part of the driveway, she opened the book to the first page. Sugar collapsed at the base of her outdoor scratching post and watched Anya with her golden blue eyes.

Anya read until night fell, her feet still rooted firmly in the dirt. Anya reeled in her furry companion, letting her fall into a deep sleep and purr on her lap. Anya looked over the tree line at the fading daylight. Tonight's canvas was a gradient of bright teal and a thin line of yellow just at the horizon. Up above, the stars were glittering into view. She searched the sky, saying all the constellations she knew by heart in whispers.

There was her Pleiades. Faintly shining four hundred light-years in the past. Within eyeshot and burning light at an unachievable distance. A world she was desperate to know but afraid to get to.

She felt impossibly small and insignificant in this big universe. Tied down by limitations and beliefs. Beliefs that were never really hers. If she could just sail out into the dark with the snap of her fingers, everything in her world would be better.

Who she wanted to be threatened the loss of everyone and everything she loved most. She realized just how fickle the world could be if she didn't fit into their box.

And that was frightening.

Anya found a comfortable spot in the back of Gwynn and Sage's Honda CR-V. They hadn't said where they were going yet, and Anya didn't want to ask.

Anya watched from behind the front seat where Sage curled her locks around her finger as they swerved on HWY 50 toward Salida. One of her favorite drives of all. Halfway through the valley, they pulled off to a dirt parking lot and picnic area near the Arkansas River. Gwynn hooked a Colorado State Park permit to his rearview mirror, and the three of them got out of the car. Sage retrieved a cooler of food and drinks from the back, and Anya and Gwynn took their fishing gear out.

This morning, Anya's hair was pulled into a ponytail and looped through the back of a hat that said 'Taurus' on the front. She dressed like she was going to the gym, an outfit suitable for her waders. It was still hot in Colorado, even though autumn would be on its way shortly. Hot enough to warm her skin, while the water was cool enough against her rubber suit.

Walking down to the bank, Sage laid a blanket where the river met the earth. She took off her sandals and dipped her feet into the river swirling at the bank, watching nature pass by.

Gwynn and Anya slithered into their waders and put together their fly rods. From May to October, she could fish the Arkansas using mayflies, caddis, stoneflies, midges, or hoppers to bring home a lot of brown trout. Any drive along a rushing river would certainly afford the sight of anglers waist-deep in a river, their thin fishing lines catching the sun.

The two of them waded into the river, not so deep that the current could take them, but deep enough to feel coolness cut them off mid-thigh.

In silence, listening to the rushing river and the cars speeding by, Anya and Gwynn whipped their neon lines back and forth, letting the flies brush the ripples of the water for a split second before letting it rest at the surface to drift downstream.

Anya felt the smooth line loosely gripped in her hand as she pulled it back toward her, feeling for the slight jerks from fish tricked into dinner. When nothing bit, she reeled her line, starting the process over again.

Fly fishing was an art, a soothing practice, an intoxicating way to connect her with nature. When she was focusing on each delicate whip of her line, she was focusing on nothing else. Her doubts, thoughts, and frustrations all disappeared with the hypnotizing sight of her beloved Arkansas River. Together, she and Gwynn caught and released dozens of trout, doing so in silence, applauding each other when they managed to hook something.

Sage sat at the bank, her toes still deep in the water being massaged by the river stones. She watched the two of them as the flecks of glitter on her cheeks caught the sunshine from above. After a few hours of fishing, Sage waved them over to eat lunch. They sat down at a picnic table and pieced together items to make sandwiches; cold cuts, cheese, pickles, mustard, mayo, and potato chips with French Onion dip.

"How long did it take you to learn fly fishing," Gwynn asked.

"Not too long," Anya replied.

She was feeling lighter now, more relaxed. Thoughts of this day being over too soon were quickly denied any attention.

"Did you ever get frustrated at first when you were trying to learn?" Gwynn asked.

"Oh yeah. All the time," Anya replied.

"I had a hard time learning, too," Gwynn said. "But once I learned, I loved it so much I couldn't stop. Some days, I fished so hard, I would dream about it for days after."

"Me too," Anya said. "Even the learning process, as frustrating as it was, was still fun to me."

"Did you ever think you wouldn't get the method down?" Gwynn asked.

"No," Anya smiled. "I pretty much knew I was going to master this skill. There was no doubt in my mind."

"How'd you know?" He asked again.

"I just felt it," she said. Gwynn paused for a moment.

"You mentioned you struggled with astral projection last night," Gwynn said. Anya's smile faded slightly.

"Yeah," Anya replied sadly.

"Are you enjoying the learning process?" Gwynn questioned, taking a bite of his thick sandwich. Sage watched the two of them, crunching a few potato chips between her teeth. Anya's sandwich laid untouched.

"No," she responded.

"Why not?" Gwynn asked.

Anya searched her mind for an answer. "It feels like this thing I'm desperate to learn overnight. And when I don't learn it immediately, I just get frustrated."

"But great things take time and patience, right? Just like your fly fishing skills," Gwynn said.

"Yeah, you're right," she sighed.

"When we're desperate to hold onto something, it pulls away from us. Most things, even what's non-tangible, don't like being possessed. If they are, there's unhappiness there," Gwynn said earnestly. "There's nothing wrong with taking the time to learn."

"You don't need to be so hard on yourself," Sage said, grabbing Anya's hand. "A lot of people in this world are very lost. Instead of facing the unknown, they stay in the known. It's a comfortable life, sure, but you don't get to live very courageously. But by doing all of this, you're going to get so much more delights than anyone can even dream of. But only if you trust in yourself. You should be proud of how far you've come."

Sage's loving and encouraging words made Anya feel hope again. As she sat with them, the sun fell to the outsides of the valley, casting a cool shade on them. Across the river on the railroad tracks, a herd of Big Horn Sheep crept in.

How could these two always know the right things to say when she needed to hear them most? She thought of her parents, how hard they were on her, how much discipline and judgment she faced daily before she was off on her own. If only her parents were like Gwynn and Sage, maybe then her life would be different, less confusing.

She felt guilty for wishing it.

Anya arrived home early that evening. The days were shortening, a sign of the coming autumn. The distance from her car to the front door let the cool evening air brush her skin. She felt her phone vibrate in her hands and announce three chimes in a row.

A text message, missed call, and voicemail.

All from Sam.

Without looking, she put her phone away.

She needed to concentrate.

Talking to Gwynn and Sage gave her new ambition and reminded her of just how powerful she was when she had patience with herself. That perhaps she was putting too much pressure on the desire to travel. Talking to Bee and Karmyn made her think—the fear of what the universe could show her was just as big of a factor in blocking her progress.

Anya changed out of her river clothes into a new shirt and pair of leggings. She found *Adventures Beyond the Body* and continued reading through the chapters with profound speed, lapping up each word and story the author shared. Reading about the vibrations and the tingling sensations he felt in his body, she tried to recall that same feeling but couldn't.

As she read, she noticed a similar trend to all of his stories and journal entries detailed in the first few chapters—as he honed the skill of astral projection, he recited the same phrase just before he induced his out-of-body-experience.

Now, I'm out of my body.

Anya wondered if it would be that easy for her. If she could jump from her body just by saying a few words. But it took him ten years to master. She was told she was a powerful creator before. Why wouldn't she be able to create astral travel? Anya was determined to make it happen and prove to herself she could do this.

When she grew tired of reading, she shuffled off to bed, Sugar following like a shadow in her wake. She crawled beneath the sheets, noticing the moonshine striking her galaxy stone on the bedside table. Over time, the stone had shifted places, being pushed toward the wall and out of sight by books, glasses of water, and charging cell phones. She had nearly forgotten about it. Anya took several deep breaths letting her eyes weigh heavily. While the soft vibrations for her purring cat rippled at her feet, she felt her body relax, her body tingle, her mind drift.

"Now, I'm out of my body," she whispered, slipping between sleep and awake, she felt a shift in herself and the familiar weightlessness from weeks ago.

THIRTY-SEVEN

Anya's puzzling absences were becoming worrisome to Sam. When he did spend time with her, she wasn't present, staring off into walls or forgetting to finish sentences—things people with Alzheimer's did. He tried to convince himself it was her work, that she was tired or busy. Even with his texts and calls to her, some of which went unanswered, he tried not to worry. Yet, something wasn't quite right.

He knew what happened when people started pulling away and could think of all the possible nerving reasons someone might lose interest. He also knew what happened if he tried to pull someone back in.

Holding onto someone he loved but felt was slipping was like flying a kite. He had to keep the kite string with loose hands, gentle hands, letting the kite fly at will. If he yanked too hard on the string, it could catch the wind just right, just hard enough to snap and float away. Then he would lose it forever. Sam has to reel his kite back in slowly, let it fall with the wind, only then will it reach his hands.

Sam thought of the most diplomatic ways to remind her that he was still here, that he still loved her. His biggest fear was losing her love or losing her entirely.

Sam had finished the unused half of his house, restoring the old bedroom with new coats of paint and bright lights. He had hung sheer curtains to help let the light in, making it into a dreamy white heaven, perfect for slowing mornings, breakfast in bed, and love-making. Just thinking about Anya in bed with him made him shudder, reminding him just how crazy he was for her

Sam had moved most of his furniture into the other side of the house, rearranging kitchen appliances and dining room furniture into a more cozy setting. Now, he needed to knock down the half wall to open up the space more. His loft bed was now a storage place, His hockey skates were still hanging death traps from the underside. In the corner where the couch used to be, he put his fridge. Where the fridge was, he put a small table and two chairs far enough away from the woodstove but close enough to keep warm. He imagined mornings having breakfast at that table with Anya. This place was starting to feel like *home*.

But a house isn't home without a woman, or so he heard.

It was true. But even truer was how Anya felt like home.

If Sam wasn't with Anya, he was with Zeke, rebuilding time lost in their long-term friendship. On weekends they would go on hikes to lakes deep in the mountains, camp near the shore of a lake, drink beer beneath the stars, go drunk night fishing, and then fish in the early mornings.

As much as he loved spending time with Zeke, he missed Anya's presence. Missed seeing her smile when he made terrible jokes. Missed the way her hair fell on her shoulders. He missed what she felt like in bed next to him and the adventures they took together.

It was painful without her.

Trying to conjure up ways to see her, Sam recalled their previous dates and the things she loved. Smiling at the very thought of the things they did together.

Sci-fi movie marathons.

Nights in front of a campfire looking at the stars.

Hikes to the tops of mountains.

Breakfast and coffee in small cafes.

Long drives to the state borders and back.

Rafting and fishing in rivers.

He had fallen so in love with her, the idea of losing her would break him completely. If he lost her, nothing would ever be the same for him.

Sam glanced at his phone, anxiously waiting for a reply from the last message he sent, or the last phone call he made, something he was often doing. Feeling uneasy, he remembered something Bruce had said when he and Anya were first getting to know each other.

Talk to her instead of assuming the worst.

Sam looked at the clock. It was nearly 9:00 p.m. and dark. Looking out the window, Sam could barely make out headframes under the nightshade. He picked up his phone, swiped to his favorites, and tapped her name. The screen showed an icon of her picture, her golden hair, and ocean eyes.

The phone rang and rang until it went to voicemail.

THIRTY-EIGHT

Her body was vibrating, skin rippling like water activated by someone dropping a pebble into it.

Now, I'm out of my body.

Everything felt dark, and her skin tingled. Her body felt stuck as if it existed between sleep and awake. Where was she?

Now, I'm out of my body.

She would repeat it until she believed it. Anya kept willing her mind into silence and clarity, trying not to cloud it with her thoughts. Nothing happened. Everything continued to stay dark; her body still vibrating. She said again with stronger intent.

Now, I'm out of my body.

As she said it, the weightless feeling returned, the lightness of a feather or cloud on air. She sat up. Lifting her arms, she looked at her silver form.

At the foot of the bed, Sugar perked up, staring at her in the darkness of her bedroom with her golden eyes, Anya noticing her silver form didn't shimmer back at her from their reflection. Anya closed her eyes, saying it once more for good measure.

Now, I'm out of my body.

With her words, the rest of her form rose from her physical self. Drifting there, Sugar's eyes followed her as if following a ghost. Anya considered where she might go. Somewhere easier first. Anya felt the tug of the silver line at her belly button and fiercely willed herself to think less of her own body.

The silver line was her safety line. Feeling confident that her body wouldn't be lost, Anya envisioned where she wanted to go. So many places came to mind.

Sam's house.

Greece.

The moon.

The Sun.

Jupiter.

Anya chose one, reminding herself she had nothing but time. That she should be patient, just as Gwynn and Sage said.

She settled on the moon, imagining its silky greyish-white surface in her mind, collecting pictures she had seen on the internet, videos of people bouncing on the milky grey surface, and combining them with the versions of the moon she conjured in her mind. She pictured each white craters and crevices, the black sky speckled with white glimmers surrounding her.

Just thinking it, the silver form drifted up into the sky, going toward the black abyss. She imagined venturing closer to the bright white moon that reflected the nearby sun. She shot into the atmosphere with a delicate grace, the world disappearing beneath her, states turning into continents floating on a canvas of blue. She passed through the arched dome that created the Earth's sphere until she was hurtling through space like a rocket.

Stopping, she twirled away from the vastness in front of her to see her very earth below. It looked so quiet, unmoving. No waves and currents of the ocean mapped out in foamy swirls. No chattering people or honking car horns, no music or movies playing in the background. No barking dogs. No motorcycles whizzing by.

Just a calming silence.

Alarmingly quiet.

Twirling back around, she stared into space, a world as far and wide and unknown as the Earth's ocean. The white stars were even more spectacular in this view but still far away at a glance. To her right was the moon, becoming larger as she closed the distance between them. She steadied her feelings of awe and surprise, maintaining a calm that would keep her from snapping back into her physical body. Thinking to herself, she willed her silver form forward toward the moon. The earth continued to disappear behind her, now resembling a blue, green, and white marble. As all characteristics and details of her world fell away, she started to notice the moon's imperfections. The craters, the crevices, the lack of life, bits of dust, and rocks knocked loose from lack of gravity.

Within minutes, she was entering its atmosphere, shooting herself toward the surface of the grey dirt. When she approached the land, it was barren.

Empty.

Lifeless.

Silent.

Stunning.

This greyish white against a black sky filled her with tears and joy. She placed her silver feet on the ground, feeling nothing at all, not even the bumpy terrain beneath her feet. She spun in circles, letting herself see space in a panoramic view. When she let the moon around her stop spinning, she sat on the earth, wishing she could feel the moondust, the jagged rocks, and the rough dirt beneath her.

But she felt nothing.

Hours passed as she sat on the moon.

Constellations and other stars similar to the sun became more apparent in her view. She spent hours counting the stars, picking out the ones she knew and the ones she didn't. She thought about all the planets. How far away they were. Beautiful glints and winks in a black sky. Knowing that if she neared them, they would start to take the shape of perfectly spherical orbs with painted swirls of color. Drawing even nearer, she'd noticed its imperfections, its craters, its mountains, its lakes. What once was a perfect sphere from a distance looked flawed up close, but it was still beautiful. Anya wondered how differently people would see each other if they all recognized these same admirable glints within each other. They were just as beautiful up close as they were from far away. How many saw each other just for their glimmers in the distance and could still adore their stunning rocky terrains and tall mountain tops?

She searched the sky for Pleiades. Unsure of where to look from this place. She remembered no planet was there like astronomers kept saying, and the thought saddened her.

Her body started vibrating with intensity, reminding her of her physical roots to something in her human reality.

Anya felt her focus waver, her silver form fading.

The tug on her belly button pulled her from the sky and precious time out of her body. In minutes, she was being tugged backward at an

The Lost Pleiad

alarming rate, hurled from the moon's atmosphere and back into her own.

She was hurtling toward the earth, turning her body to see the land below her speed into view. Farmlands cut into perfect brown and green squares, dark grey roads cutting making paths in thin lines, cars driving on them at the pace of ants beneath feet.

The weight of her body pulled her in long before she could feel the spirit and physical connect. The vibration grew, shaking her bones and silver vessel. The details of her earth becoming more carved, lights from homes and street lamps shining brighter than the stars she was just counting. She fell through the trees, into her home amongst the forest, through her ceiling, and back into her body.

When she woke, she could feel the strong vibration of her cellphone on her bedside table. The blue hue shot up toward her ceiling, lighting the room. Next to it, the galaxy stone had shifted places again, but Anya swore she saw a white glow fading from the black and white speckled stone.

As she regained her composure and her body's tingling sensation vanished, she looked at her phone. Time had barely passed.

It was Sam.

The single force reminding her why she loved Earth.

A fond connection she was letting herself lose.

The bond intent on grounding her to this planet.

Her body still quivering, Anya reached over and grabbed her phone. Without listening to the voicemail, she called him back.

"Hey," she said in her sweetest voice.

"Hey, love. What are you doing?" he responded.

"Just lying in bed," she said back. "What are you doing?"

"Missing you," he said. "It feels like I haven't heard from you in a while, so I thought I'd call."

Anya felt guilt snake through her body and coil at the center of her stomach. "I'm sorry I haven't responded," she said.

"Are we okay?" He asked, a nervous tremble ringing in his voice.

"Of course we are," she responded gently. "I've just had a lot going on."

There was a brief silence. That was the standard sentence someone said if they didn't want to tell the whole story.

"Can we talk about it?" He pleaded. "Please."

"Of course," Anya replied. She glanced at the clock, shifting her body to sit upward.

It was past 9:00 p.m.

Anya feared the more she went on this path, the more she risked losing Sam and anyone she loved. The more she loved Sam, the more this spirit world fell behind. It made her realize balancing the spiritual and physical was more challenging than she thought.

"Do you want to come over?"

"God, yes," he said. "I will be there in 15 minutes."

"Okay, love. See you then."

Hanging up the phone, Anya curled up beneath her covers, recalling her time on the moon, recalling the pleasant vibration and weightlessness brought on by her out-of-body experience. If only everyone else could experience this too and see how incredible this feeling was, maybe they would know about their access to universal knowledge and spiritual travel. She desired to tell Sam and explain the sensation to him. She thought of ways to convince him or encourage him to try it himself.

Sam was knocking on her door in less than 15 minutes. When he came in, he swooped her into his arms, hugging her like they had been apart for months. He took off his shoes at the door, leaning over to pet Sugar. Anya took him by the hand and led him to her bedroom, where they twisted together under the covers.

"You want to tell me what's been going on?" He asked. "You've always been a mysterious one, but you have me stumped these days. I feel like there is something you're not telling me."

Anya ached to tell him without fear of judgment. But she knew that's not how the world was. There was always someone who would judge who you were or what you do with your life. Sometimes it was even the people closest to you. She yearned for the ability to tell her secrets, whether good or bad and still be accepted and loved. What she kept forgetting was how Sam had been the most receptive of everything odd about her. He had listened, encouraged her, never judged, never made her feel small for what she believed. He took her on long drives to the darkest places to marvel at stars and meteor showers. Invested time watching documentaries and reading books, just because he knew what this world meant to her. He called her his cosmic angel. He genuinely loved her, and yet she had doubted him still.

What was holding her back?

She judged herself; questioned herself. Anya still wasn't sure of this path she was going down or if she planned to continue walking it. She knew what happened to people who discussed things like this. People who welcomed otherworldly possibilities with open arms were institutionalized, confined to white walls in psychiatric wards, and left behind by the people they loved most—all in the pursuit of finding themselves and universal truth.

Anya thought of how her two dearest friends reacted to her and how Gwynn and Sage did, too, considering the reactions of the two very different types of people, using their reactions to help her determine which way Sam might lean. She wasn't sure if she would risk losing Sam entirely by telling him the truth. Yet, she knew by not telling him, she was likely to lose him even faster. There was always the possibility he would accept her for what she was coming to believe and experience. But it was more than saying, 'I'm spiritual' or 'I'm an alien.'

One is an accepted truth.

The other could easily pass as a joke.

Despite her fears and uncertainties, Anya convinced herself it was right to tell him where she was going, even if it meant she could lose him.

"I'll tell you," she said. "But I have to preface by saying that I'm scared to tell you this. Scared to lose you."

"You could never lose me," he said, holding her close. "I love you."

Oh my heart.

"I love you," she said kissing him. "I've been experimenting with something a little different these days. Gwynn and Sage have been helping me."

"Okay. What is it?" He asked.

"Astral projection," she said, gulping down the lump in her throat.

"Like out-of-body experience?" He asked again. "Like Dr. Strange?"

Anya smiled, thinking of Karmyn. "Yes. Like Dr. Strange. Have you tried it?"

"Never. But I believe it's possible," he said.

Anya perked up at this.

"Really?" Anya smiled. "You believe in it?"

"Of course," he said. "Anything is possible. Have you successfully done it?"

"I have," she replied. At this, he smiled.

"What's it like?" He asked, appearing genuinely interested.

"It's like nothing I've ever experienced," she said. "It's amazing. Sage helped induce a sort of meditation, then asked me to picture an object. I pictured the galaxy stone."

"That's an interesting first thing to picture," he said. "Why did you pick that?

"They said it would be easier focusing on an object before focusing on a place," she said. "I thought of the stone, what it looked like, where it was in my room, what the room looked like, what else was in my room."

Anya started to feel a tightness in her chest. Anyone could imagine their favorite place from thought. This next part was less believable.

"Then, as if thinking were my only vehicle, I was out of my body, in my room, holding the stone. It worked," she said. "I felt weightless, tingly, and… free."

"Wow," Sam said. "That sounds incredible."

"Yeah, but after that first time, I struggled to do it again," she said. "I was getting frustrated and was feeling hopeless."

"Why, though?" He asked.

"I was desperate to feel that way again," she said. "And nothing was happening. But then I talked to Gwynn and Sage, and they helped me through what was blocking me."

"And what was blocking you?" He questioned.

"Desperation, fear, impatience," she replied. "I was desperate to master the skill but afraid of what I might be able to do with it."

"That makes sense," he said.

"Does it?" She inquired. "Because I feel like when I talk about it or express what I'm going through, it doesn't make sense at all. Or that people will think I'm crazy."

"Why do you care what people think so much?" Sam asked. It was something she could never really answer.

"I don't know," she said. "I've always cared, ever since I was young."

"So, your parents are the root of the issue," he stated matter of fact.

"I mean, I wouldn't argue with it," she said honestly. "They're the most judgmental parents on the planet, but what child still wouldn't strive for their parents' approval?"

"I wouldn't know," he said sadly.

Anya was amazed at how often she was consciously ungrateful for having parents at all. She hugged him tightly as if they could get any closer without morphing into one being. "Were you able to astral project again after talking to Gwynn and Sage?"

"I was," she said.

"And where did you go?" He asked. And even though she couldn't feel the shine of Earth's light permeating on her skin or the moondust at her fingers, she recalled her brief time visiting the moon.

"The moon," she responded. Sam smiled at her.

"And what is the moon like?" He asked.

"Just as you would expect. Completely and spectacularly out of this world fantastic and every positive thing you could imagine. It was Christmas, Thanksgiving, Disney World, and Dollywood all rolled into one," she said. Sam snickered, touch his lips to her forehead.

"Dollywood, huh?" He chuckled.

"Damn right," she said.

"You, my cosmic angel, are stunning and out of this world perfect, and I am so lucky to have you," he said. Anya felt the strength of his arms and love fold around her.

"Better to be lucky than good," Anya said. Sam grinned and kissed her lips. "Are you sure all of this stuff I'm telling you doesn't bother you?"

"It doesn't bother me even the slightest," he said.

"Why not?" She asked.

"Because I love you. And if I am to love you, I have to love you for everything that makes you who you are. Including things you think make you crazy," he said.

"And you don't think I'm crazy?" She asked.

"Well, that's an entirely different question," he laughed.

"Well, what's your answer, mister?" She questioned.

"I mean, every girl has to be a little crazy," he teased.

"Oh, whatever," she laughed. "I want to be able to tell you anything and everything."

"And you can. Always. Not only are you my girlfriend, you're my best friend. Best friends should be able to tell each other everything," he replied.

"You're right," she responded.

Sam was her home. Her safe place. The place she could go to in confidence. Her bright white moon in a sea of black silence. That had never wavered or changed, so why had she doubted him? Anya was ashamed for every time she ever doubted his love for her.

Most anything she ever felt afraid of, stressed about, anxious about, or insecure about wasn't because of how other people thought of her, but how she thought of herself.

If she could start to internalize better and identify her insecurities were of her own making, maybe she could change for the better. Perhaps she wouldn't go into her life with fear, sadness, anxiety, and lack of belonging.

Perhaps this place, right here in Sam's arms, was the place she belonged. The final destination in her adventures toward finding home. Or maybe this was the beginning of creating that home within herself.

THIRTY-NINE

Navagio Beach. She'd never been there before, but she could imagine it, thanks to Google. Standing atop this cliff, she imagined what it might be like to feel the jagged rock beneath her feet, but she couldn't feel it. She knew she wouldn't feel the stomach tugging sensation that came with the steep fall down such a deep cliff. Nor would she feel the water heated by the Greek sun touching her skin or the gritty sand between her toes.

Beneath her was a cerulean body of ocean so bright, it looked like blue raspberry Jell-O chilled far past its time. A few white boats the size of her pinky fingernail from this distance sat idly on top like something from a miniature model kit.

To the left of that body of blue was a perfect tan beach nestled in the curve of a rolling cliff topped with trees. Laying on it like a beached whale was a rusting shipwreck half-buried in sand with white waves lapping at it.

There were two ways to visit this cove, by boat or by air.

This wasn't the first time Anya considered jumping and free-falling. This time she wasn't afraid. As her calves tightened, ready to lunge forward and leap into the vast blue ocean below, a wave of people rushed past her tossing their bodies from the cliff and screaming with delight.

Everyone had a parachute attached to their back, but not Anya.

She smiled, watching them drop rapidly until their bodies became smaller in view. Anya inched closer to the edge of the cliff and lunged forward, giving herself space between the cliff and the wide-open air she wished she could feel rush past her.

Her vessel sailed downward, following the troupe of others whose parachutes opened up into a rainbow of colors, all fluttering like butterflies until settling on the beach below. She followed them as if she could still feel the draft of air they left behind, riding their path like an exhilarating roller coaster until the cliff behind her became smaller, and the ocean beneath her threatened to swallow her whole.

Wide and welcoming, she drifted toward the shipwreck, letting her body fall with grace like that of a feather. When her feet touched the ground, she saw the sand glittering like millions of rhinestones underneath the bright sun. Tanned bodies darted off into the oceans, which looked more forceful from here. She watched them from the beach, wishing she could feel those same waves tug at her ankles. Hoping this was her existence right here and now, and she could live all of these lives simultaneously like the spiritual guides suggested she could.

Anya moved to the rusting ship, which now towered above her, its dark brown exterior graffitied with things like "I love Greece," the names and dates of past visitors named 'Lena' and 'Carl,' or pictures of anchors carved into the thin layer of rust. Years of rust created holes showing the old ship's dark interiors and maybe even flashes of some ghosts. She walked to the front, finding the first large opening. The few doors she could see were covered with a sandy floor as she maneuvered through the hull of the ship to explore all the places she might play hide and go seek. Door after door, she journeyed through, ignoring the layers of graffiti, instead trying to imagine what it was like for people who lived or worked on this ship when it was alive and kicking. Imagining the ship stocked full of smuggled things like cigarettes and alcohol, and on some occasions, humans. She walked through, slightly crouching in a space barely tall enough for her.

After navigating through halls, she came back the way she entered, finding the familiar tan beach and insanely blue sea just before her, looking for the perfect place to sit and enjoy the view undisturbed.

Astral travel was becoming a treasured hobby and preferred outlet for seeing places in the world she couldn't reach by foot or car. Imagine how much of the world she could see if she could just keep—.

Wait.

Sam's coming.

FORTY

Autumn came fast, but winter came even quicker. Time flew through shades of warm leaves falling from branches like nature's confetti. Now it was bare trees and bushes resembling white skeletons frosted with snow from freezing nights. Anya juggled her relationship with Sam, her stressful job with the city, her friendships, time with Gwynn and Sage, her newfound spirituality, her somewhat improved relationship with her parents, and her newly loved skill of astral travel.

For one single person to manage so much and still feel singular peace was becoming a challenge.

Anya followed the teachings from *Adventures of the Body*, realizing that the skill of astral travel would take work and possibly several years to master. There were days when it wasn't easy—days where she felt defeated and hopeless in her abilities. At times, her mental space was too clouded with obligations and thoughts or what reality expected of her. The stress took over far more than it should've. Many days, she sacrificed time in her spiritual body by doing more "earthly" things.

Since learning how to astral project, she had seen and done many great things and journaled about every single instance out-of-body. Once, she was suspended above the ocean, seeing nothing but water and sky on all sides of her. Another time, she was swimming alongside a mighty blue whale and her calf. Other times, she was exploring the center of nebulas or watching dying suns burst into stars. Once, she hovered aside her blazing sun, watching it swirl with waves of heat and lava. Anya mostly went places she could envision or places she had seen in movies. Imagining other worlds was a different story.

She wasn't able to venture to the center of her galaxy, not without knowing what it looked like. Her imagination was sadly limited. Visiting other galaxies was just as difficult. The daunting task of using her imagination to build a world as it is and not as she interpreted it sent her into moments of depression.

If she couldn't imagine places she hadn't been to, how could she imagine a place like Pleiades? There was always the added fact that planets still hadn't been discovered there. It was still just a cluster of blue stars burning four hundred light-years in the past.

Anya and Sam had taken up space in his home during the winter months, hiding away from snowstorms covering the towns. Tourism was slow and monotonous, and they lacked energy on weekdays, even when the sun was out. They reserved weekends for binge-watching television, diving deep into documentaries, TV series, and movies, watching all of them one after the other. Anya stuck her nose in dozens of books and did as much research as she could on Pleiades and astral projection. She hoped she could find something, anything that might signal life far beyond this planet.

After telling Sam about it, he never really asked about it. Not that he needed to. Anya believed him to be content and accepting with whatever her spiritual practices were. After her visits with Gwynn and Sage, he asked about what they did. Anya would tell him about her healing sessions, breakthroughs she was making with fear, anxiety, and insecurity. Sometimes she would cry about the pain she was facing or celebrate her healing achievements. Sam would listen intently each time, locking eyes on her as she spoke about each session. Going down to see them in winter was more difficult with the weather in Cripple Creek.

One thing Anya and Sam always did and looked forward to doing in secluded mountain winters was stargaze. Colorado had some of the best stargazing in the nation around wintertime. It's during the winter months that the moon shined bright in the shivering dark skies—the meteor showers glittering even more brilliant as they shot hot across the sky. On nights when they went stargazing, they loaded up the truck bed with all the blankets, sleeping bags, and pillows they could find between both houses. They took thermoses of hot chocolate or warm cider with them and bundled up in their thickest coats, gloves, and hats. Then they'd pile in Sam's truck and make a journey to a place where the skies were furthest from cities and blackest.

By the end of December, winter was the coldest it had been in years. Snow drifts were as high as the front door, and some days Victor and Cripple Creek were entirely shut down.

Anya learned January was the best time to view Pleiades. At that time, it would reach the highest point in the sky.

For New Year's Eve, Sam and Anya decided to spend the weekend together stargazing at a cabin in the mountains. Anya wanted to see just how high Pleiades was in the sky, having never noticed such a small detail before.

"Are you ready to go?" Sam asked, slipping into a thermal jumpsuit underneath a pair of sweatpants. Shoving his feet into a pair of thick merino wool socks before slipping into his warmest boots, he wore a thick beanie, a scarf tight around his neck, and snowboarding gloves.

"Jesus, where the hell are you going?" Anya laughed. "The truck has heat, you know."

"You know I don't like to be cold," he said. "We're kindred spirits in that regard."

"You're right about that," she said, and as she did, she slipped into her thermal jumpsuit.

By the time they left the house, it was only noon. Daylight was fading fast, and with the night came even icier temperatures. Leaving earlier meant they could avoid icy roads and arrive safely. Even with Sam's truck in four-wheel drive, Anya always felt much safer going anywhere earlier in the day.

Getting in the truck, they drove down the familiar winding roads until the town was left behind them, taking Teller County Road 1 to Florissant. The cabin they were going to was in Basalt, Colorado on the Frying Pan River. They were staying in the A-Frame Cabin at the Dallenbach Ranch just five minutes from downtown. Sam had planned the trip for months, making sure it was the perfect weekend for them both. He surprised Anya with their trip for Christmas.

When they arrived, the river ran so low and clear, rainbow trout were too easy to see. The Frying Pan River is known for its award-winning fishing. Anya and Sam planned on using their private river access to take full advantage of winter river fishing. After self-checking into their cabin, the two of them hauled their single backpacks inside the cabin to settle in.

The cabin was just as described; an A-Frame home that sat right on the river and steps that led right to it, and a red roof sliding steeply downward until it touched the ground. Fresh powder surrounded the cabin and clung to the red rock cliffs across the river.

There was a wooden deck complete with a table and chairs and large windows that looked out onto the river. Inside was a small living room, a small kitchen, a bathroom, and a bedroom cozy enough for two. A string of golden lights hung over the bed, giving the small room a magical touch.

The living room had a small TV, but the windows gave a clear view of the rushing river. Anya believed they would be spending time either on the river or naked in bed. Anya could imagine her and Sam wrapped up in blankets, sitting on the front deck drinking their coffee, or snuggling beside the firepit while the river carried the glittering moon downstream. So much magic would be made here this weekend and all without seeing a single spark from a firework.

Anya and Sam put up their things and made a trip to Basalt to get bacon, eggs, bread, fresh vegetables, butter, and rice from Whole Foods. They planned to eat whatever fish they caught for dinner, adding pan-fried vegetables on the side and cooked rice, both drenched with butter.

When they got back, they pieced their fishing rods together, securing spinning reels in place and using Power Bait to catch half a dozen brown and rainbow trout in shallow waters. With each cast, they hooked one, reeling it onto the snowy riverbank where it flopped and sucked in the dry mountain air. They filleted the fish right at the bank, scooping the guts out, feeling the cold sting of the air on their fingertips as they tossed the innards back into the river.

By the time the scent of fried fish and buttery vegetables filled the room, the world outside the cabin was black. They had started a fire in the stove to heat the cabin, eating their dinner at the table, playing footsie underneath, and making coy glances of what would come after finishing dinner.

A trail of clothes led from empty plates and wine glasses to the freshly made bed and warm glowing lights hanging above them. They made love, worshipping each other's bodies well into the evening.

Sometime after the fireworks quieted and Sam was snug under the thick comforter, Anya was up. Wide awake, for no apparent reason at all. Glancing at her snoring love, she saw his brown hair shine against the golden glow of the room, and his tanned skin and dark brown freckles on his cheeks, the long dark eyelashes perfectly resting on his skin. Watching each of his breaths, she realized just how much she loved him.

Grinning, Anya lifted her naked form from the fluffy bed, bundling up into thicker clothes and her pair of winter boots. Finding an extra fleece blanket in a closet, she wrapped herself up and snuck out the door to sit on the deck.

The boards made a creaking sound with each step. She settled into a metal chair and stared out at the rushing river, watching it glide over the river rock. The trees remained unmoved against the red rock cliffs, and the moon passed over the sky to disappear behind the other side of the world. The only light left was the residual one from their room bouncing between walls until reaching the glass double doors.

Anya was aware of the wildlife that could potentially wander into her space. Aware of how often she felt anxiety around a mountain lion stalking her in the background at night. But she usually told herself she was foolish for thinking it. She looked up at the sky, past the tree branches stretching over the cabin. Right above her was Pleiades.

Admiring the small constellation that resembled the Little Dipper, she memorized the pattern of the stars, how a big one shined brighter than the rest but appeared separate from the others. Most nights, the pattern was faint, but she knew it well. It was impossible for her not to see it. She looked for the slightest imperfection, a small darkness, or a shadow, anything that might indicate a planet—as if she could see one.

Perhaps it would be hundreds or thousands of years before people discovered a planet there if they ever did. If it even existed. Anya wished there was a way she could find out faster or know for sure in her lifetime.

But maybe she could ask. After all, she had been learning to hone her out-of-body practices. So, why couldn't she just try? But she remembered what William said in *Adventures Beyond the Body*—it was easier to go places she had been because it was easier to imagine.

There was a part in the book when he asked to see his past. His request took him back to a previous life he had lived. Anya wondered if she would see her past life or if a request to see her past would take her to Pleiades. Only then would she be able to see if that was a part of her existence, if that was a place she came from, or if she was just full of shit. Anya wrapped the blanket tighter around herself, starting to feel the cold metal plunge through the thick blanket and her clothes. Closing her eyes, she took a few deep breaths, listening to the peaceful world around her and the softly rushing river.

After her deep breaths, she said out loud, to no one in particular, "Now, I'm out of body."

She repeated the phrase a few more times until she lifted into black space. The cold metal nagging at her blankets disappeared; her warm body under her clothes did too, along with the Basalt outdoors.

"Clarity now," she said. In an instant, just as William had done in his book, she felt all things around her sharpen like a photoshopped image.

"Show me my past life," she said with even stronger intent. As she finished her sentence, her vision became blurred and cloudy. She blinked multiple times, hoping it would bring focus or clarity, but nothing. Behind the blur was movement. Forms up close, moving and gesturing slowly, mumbled words that didn't quite make sense.

She tried to make out the blurry forms, tried to see their colors. But then remembered her teachings.

"Clarity now!" She told herself. Instantaneously, the blurred forms sharpened and she saw a woman. She had glowing silver hair and the fiercest blue eyes she had ever seen, eyes nearly similar to her own. The woman was smiling down at her, saying words that didn't make any sense and sounded like songs. The woman's clothes were pastel, touched by the light to create a stunning sheen, but unlike clothing she had ever seen.

"What form is this?" Anya asked again. Instantly, she knew her form, that of a baby's. Still, she wasn't sure which baby and who might be holding her.

"Who is this?" Anya asked, and nothing answered.

Anya cried, wailing like a baby. The woman's smile turned to a frown as she tried to soothe her with her musical voice.

A baritone voice boomed from beyond her form.

Anya knew this was her past. She knew this was a part of her but wasn't sure when this was or where this was, so she asked.

"When and where is this?" She asked. Immediately, she was shot through a wormhole glittering in greens, blues, purples, and whites.

She traveled through the glowing tunnel for minutes before landing firmly on a white stone street. Around her were white homes with curved windows and roofs, silver buildings towering into the sky, luminous plants and flowers popping up from the aquamarine grass. Above her were spinning silver oval vehicles hovering in mid-air, passing each other in layers as if they would crash into each other, but strangely and intuitively maneuvering in a sort of harmony. People with silver hair and almond eyes passed around her, smiling and waving at her like her presence was normal. Anya had dreamt this.

Anya stopped one of them, opening her mouth to speak in the only language she knew. A silver-haired woman with sky blue eyes looked at Anya and smiled. The woman was clutching a young boy's hand loosely. He looked up at Anya, his eyes like his mother's, and she smiled down at him.

"Where am I?" Anya asked again.

The woman looked at her, confused. Anya repeated herself once more. If she wasn't on earth, this place probably didn't use English.

"Where. Am. I?" She said slower. The woman was still confused. Anya thought for a moment. She could ask for anything.

"Remove the language barrier," she commanded.

Anya repeated herself, confident they would understand this time. When she spoke, the words were still in English, but somehow the woman knew what they meant.

"Where am I?" Anya asked again, the words feeling foreign in her throat. The woman smiled.

"Pleiades," she responded. Anya grinned, feeling tears sting her eyes.

"Are you sure?" Anya asked.

"Of course" her voice sang.

And Anya understood.

"What language is this?" Anya asked.

"Saren Light Language" she said, Anya had heard of it in her research. Maybe those Pleiadian channelers weren't actually full of shit after all.

"It's beautiful here," Anya said, observing the world around her. The woman nodded. "Thank you."

"You're welcome" she replied with a grin. "Be healthy."

Anya watched the woman walk away and then turned in circles to view the world around her. She couldn't believe it. She had made it here just by asking about her past. But it seemed vaguely familiar. Like she had seen it in a dream.

Anya moved over to the grass, sitting down to let herself cry. She was so happy she could scream. All around, people stared at her, but she didn't care. For what seemed liked hours, she sat in the grass, viewing every detail of the world around her. But that feeling started fading, and the bright world around her disappeared. Suddenly, she was aware of her physical body and the earth it was still very alive on.

Within an instant, Anya was back on the deck surrounded by the night, the trees, and the river. The door creaked open behind her, and she heard Sam's heavy footsteps on the wooden deck.

"Hey, my love," Sam said in his tired voice. It was so sultry and smooth she nearly forgot where she just was. She ached to be back there but ached even more for Sam's touch.

"Hey, darling," she said back.

"What are you doing out here? It's freezing, and you hate the cold," he said.

"You're not wrong," she laughed.

Sam came behind her, kissing her on the top of her head. He was silent, looking out at the river with her.

Sam came around to face Anya.

"I think you shine brighter in the moonlight than you do daylight," Sam said.

"The moon's not even out, babe," she laughed.

"You know what I mean," he laughed too.

"I'm not sure I do," she joked.

"I don't think I've ever met someone who loved the night sky as much as you," he said sweetly. "Sometimes, I wonder if you love that sky more than me."

Anya didn't know if he was being serious or making a joke. The darkness around her made it hard to tell. Sam came around, lowering himself to eye level. She stared into his eyes, lightly lit by the golden glow from inside.

"I have had a lot of good things happen to me. A lot of bad things too," he said. "But mostly, I've been really lucky. Unbelievably lucky in the context of you."

"Better to be lucky than good," Anya said, glimmering at him.

"That's right," he replied with a smile.

Sam saying romantic things was an often occurrence that filled her heart. On a night like this, a weekend like this, and with months of a good relationship behind them, her heart was spilling over.

"Now, I may not be this big beautiful night sky, the moon, or the stars, but I love you more than anything else in this world," he said, dropping to a knee. "I will spend the rest of my life making sure you know that my love for you is as big and as wide as this universe."

Sam revealed a small dark box decorated with silver stars. He lifted the lid to reveal the most perfect circle, solitary stone on a silver band. It was as black as her perfect night sky but speckled with white.

A galaxy diamond. An engagement ring.

FORTY-ONE

Sam snapped the ring box shut at the sound of Anya's footsteps drawing nearer. He quickly shoved the box into the deepness of his pack, knowing Anya wouldn't venture there. For months Sam planned for the moment he would ask Anya to marry him.

He had loved her ever since he met her, if he were honest. Sam let himself love her in a way he hadn't let himself love another woman.

It wasn't a matter of if he would marry Anya. It was more a matter of when. If he could have, he would have asked her to marry him months ago. He hated how much he had honored society's rules of waiting, even though he knew this is where his heart would forever be kept.

There were millions of ways he could have proposed to her. Millions of ways to show her how much he cared, how devoted he was to her. For months, he had upheld his promises to her. Although some days she seemed a little lost in herself, that mysterious part of her would always be intriguing and exciting for Sam. But above all else, he knew this; she loved him.

For weeks, Sam's anxiety raged, and he did everything to make himself appear normal. As if he wasn't harboring the biggest secret in his world. He and Anya didn't have secrets anymore. They told each other everything ever since talking about astral projection, but Sam suspected she might be onto him.

The ring was kept at Bruce's house. Anya wasn't the nosy type, but if she stumbled on it by accident, his plans for the epic romantic gesture would be ruined. But with the ring not around, it felt like a piece of him was missing. This eternal link to her appearing invisible until the time was right.

Sam remembered the night he told Bruce about proposing to her, describing the moment he knew it was time to ask. It was something insignificant, which he didn't expect. But Sam figured that's how people usually fell in love. Slowly, but then all at once. Sam didn't think about all the big moments like meeting her parents, their first date under the stars, exchanging house keys. They were amazing moments, to be sure. But they're not the moments that made him fall in love with her.

It was a series of small moments strung together over time. Ones mapped together like stars in a constellation, each shining one a stepping stone to a larger story that could live throughout history, told over and over for generations to come.

"When was the exact moment you knew?" Bruce asked, grinning like a proud father. The moment came to Sam's mind instantly. They were in Colorado Springs, walking toward Acacia Park. Sam had her hand in his, and she was holding onto it so tightly as if Sam would drift away. They were coming around the corner to Josh & John's to get ice cream when a young girl came out of the ice cream parlor. She licked at a bright pink scoop resting in a perfect waffle cone. Already, pink streaks stuck to the corners of her lips, and the little girl was smiling.

As she walked out from the enclosed patio area, a guy sped by on his bike, startling the girl. She dropped her freshly scooped ice cream cone onto the ground, where it shattered.

The ice cream instantly started melting amongst the bits of cone. She looked down, defeated, and started weeping. Anya noticed her sadness and walked over to her.

"Are you okay?" Anya asked. The girl looked up, her eyes shining with grief.

"I saved up my allowance for this ice cream," she cried. Anya frowned, looking around to see who this child might belong to.

"I'm so sorry," she dropped to eye level. "Where are your parents?"

"My dad went across the street to get coffee," she said. "He told me to get my ice cream and wait right here for him."

Anya looked across the street at Coffee Story, a tiny home with a coffee shop inside and a line down the street. She looked back at the young girl.

"Well, how about we get you a new ice cream?" Anya asked. "Do you think your dad would be okay with that?"

The young girl nodded, her tears and sniffles subsiding. Anya, Sam, and the young girl walked back inside. Anya ordered a new ice cream, offering to load it up with anything else she wanted. The girl was lit up as she chose topping after topping to create a perfect ice cream an allowance couldn't buy.

The three of them emerged from Josh & John's with their ice creams.

"Are you okay to stay here and wait for your dad?" Anya asked, looking hopefully up at the line in the coffee place, which had drastically shortened. The young girl nodded, licking at her ice cream.

"Thank you!" She said.

"Oh, you're super welcome," Anya replied.

Sam took her hand, squeezing it tightly. She looked at him. Sam's perfect earthshine, blinding him with her bright love, that kind that could consume the world if she let it. Sam felt it radiating from her. They sat down in the grass across the street in the park, making sure the girl was safe until her dad arrived to get her. It was a fleeting moment. One of the rare times Sam could really see her without having to pass through her protective veils and walls. She was just perfectly being who she was.

Kind. Thoughtful. Sweet. *Loving.*

Sam knew how much he loved her.

He knew then he would marry her.

"That's a beautiful story," Bruce said. "Sounds like your Anya."

Now, they were hitting the road to Basalt. He only had to endure several more hours before he would ask her to stay beside him for the rest of his life and all other lives beyond this one. Sam hadn't thought of exactly how he would do it—just intended to feel that moment and go with it. He just hoped she would say yes.

They drove over four hours and cautiously through the Colorado mountains, mindful of the snowfall left behind, still cold and solid underneath cliffs and trees where the sun couldn't touch it. Hours on the road and no real breakfast for the day, Sam knew Anya would be hungry soon. Sam was so anxious the thought of him eating anything made him want to vomit but he decided he would force something down anyway.

"I'm so hungry. We have to get something immediately when we get into town," she said.

"Okay, sounds good," Sam said as if deep in thought. His face glistened with sweat, and his palms were moist.

"Are you hot?" Anya asked. Sam glanced over at her, trying to appear light and carefree.

"No, why?" He questioned.

"You're sweating, and it's not even hot in here," she said, looking forward. Sam worried she might suspect something.

"Oh," he said, trying to create a plausible excuse. "I think I just have too many clothes on."

"I think you're the only other person who hates cold weather more than me," she laughed.

By the time they got to the cabin and settled in, Sam was looking for a new hiding place for the ring so there was no chance she would find it. There were so many places he wouldn't be able to think of. The space was small, and there wouldn't be many opportunities to be away from each other. Before Sam unpacked his things, he wandered around the cabin, looking for any potential places to hide it. But found nothing. Thinking she wouldn't look there, he left the box at the very bottom of his bag and shoved it in a corner of the room.

That night, he had fallen asleep after their love-making. For most weeks, he hadn't been sleeping well. And although he tried to stay awake, he just couldn't. Sometime after 1:00 a.m., he woke up, feeling the empty space where she was supposed to be. It was a common habit for Anya to be up in the middle of the night. Almost always, he knew where to find her.

Out with the stars.

Sam shoved his feet into a pair of sweat pants, socks, and boots, tugged a shirt over his head, and slipped the comforter around him to

The Lost Pleiad

quietly move through the living room. He opened the door to the deck, intentionally stirring, so she knew he was there.

Every word he mouthed from then on was a blur. Heart racing, he could see his foggy breath on the winter air barely lit up by lights from the cabin. Before he knew it, he was down on one knee in front of her, putting his heart out there.

She adored him. Sam was ninety-nine percent sure she would say yes. That other one percent was the mysterious part that always found a way to shock him. As he asked the question, he could see the blank stare and eyes darkened in shadows darting between Sam's hopeful face and the ring barely glimmering in nightshade.

Her expressionless stare worried him. Was it too soon? Was it the dark that made it so hard to read her? Was this the nightmare proposal and rejection he saw in movies? It was difficult to tell. Sam was suddenly aware of how cold it was outside. With the way her silence was headed, he was starting to wish he had done this inside. Or maybe this was the entirely wrong moment. Nervous, Sam spoke again, trying to find his way through cloudy thoughts and wild uncertainties. Trying to be cognizant of what he was saying, adrenaline coursing through him.

"Babe? Are you okay?" He asked, prepared to get up. She looked at the ring and then back at him. A single tear fell down her cheek.

"Yes," she said.

"Oh, good," he said. "I was worried I just said the completely wrong thing or asked too soon."

"No," she laughed, leaning forward. "I mean, *yes*, yes."

"Yes?" He exclaimed. "You're saying yes?"

Anya nodded fiercely, leaping into his arms. He curled around her, feeling her warm body melt into his.

Sam lifted her into his arms to cradle her and took her inside. Kneeling on the floor to face each other, Sam pulled the ring from the box and tossed it on the ground. She lifted her hand to meet his, and he placed the starry ring on her left ring finger. Anya leaned in to kiss him fiercely, the heat of their bodies exchanged between parted lips.

"Are you ready to spend the rest of our lives together?" Sam asked.

"Hmmm," Anya said, looking up at the ceiling. Sam's heart dropped. "Absolutely," she said, kissing him again. And Sam's heart had never been fuller.

FORTY-TWO

"It's a galaxy diamond. One of your daughter's favorites."

"It's stunning," Cole said, giving Sam a gentle handshake. "Nice job."

"Thank you, sir," Sam said with a beam of pride while Anya twinkled under the living room lights. The look on her mother's face dimmed the brilliance of the ring.

Jada looked at Anya and Sam with a sort of jealously, observing the radiating love that told the world they were in a happy relationship. It was a love anyone would be jealous of. And Jada appeared jealous.

Anya wondered how often Jada wished for such a passionate and understanding love that knew no limits. She knew she and her father weren't as happy as Sam and Anya were.

Everyone in the room chattered enthusiastically except for Jada, who sat silently in the corner of the couch, away from her husband, seething with envy and a fake smile forcefully plastered on her face. It was when Cole lifted himself from the couch that she seemed to snap into the present moment.

"Well, this calls for celebration," Cole said, smiling so widely she thought his face might stick there.

"Dad," Anya laughed nervously. "It's the middle of the day."

"Who cares," he said, looking down at Jada. "Our baby girl is getting married. We couldn't be happier."

Jada looked like she was trying to appear joyful, but looking at her, Anya could see disapproval. Her father disappeared to find the bottle of champagne they had saved for special occasions, which didn't happen often in this house. His absence left an uneasy hole in the room. Anya shifted uncomfortably in her seat, trying to move closer to Sam for comfort. It was no shock when Sam cut the silence.

"I'm so grateful to have met your daughter, Mrs. Allen," he said. "She's been quite an amazing and irreplaceable addition to my life."

As he said it, he drew Anya near him, kissing her on the forehead. Anya closed her eyes, feeling his love. He did nothing but gleam at Anya, a gesture that seemed to further irritate Jada.

"Well," Jada started. "It's nice for Anya to have found… *someone*."

The emphasis on that last word was meant just as harshly as she intended, and Anya's joyful glow quickly replaced with a frown.

"What is that supposed to mean?" Anya said bitterly.

"What?" Jada said defensively. "It's nice you found someone."

"But why did you have to say it like you did?" Anya asked again, letting her gaze sear into her as her mother avoided eye contact.

"Come on, Anya," Jada relaxed into the couch, knowing she had struck a nerve. "You are reading into it too much."

"I know you," Anya said. "You think I don't know when you're being fake with your words or when you disapprove? I see it on your face right now."

Anya was now standing, towering above Jada to show just how grand she could be. Sam was still seated and silent, radiating his calmness and support. Anya started to tear up just as her father returned with a chilled bottle of champagne already sweating condensation and four upside flutes dangling between his fingers.

"Why can't you ever just be happy for me, Mom?" She shouted. "Every single thing I ever do receives automatic criticism from you. Every. Single. Time. I see how you look at Dad, and it's fine if you don't have a love like mine. But whatever unhappiness or lack of love you receive in your own marriage doesn't warrant you to criticize mine. And another thing, just because Sam doesn't fit your standards, which are ridiculous by the way, doesn't mean he is not a good man. Just because he is content with his life, lives simply, and isn't religious doesn't mean he's not worthy. Sam is a great man and I love him. Your behavior and beliefs are not going to change that."

Cole stood before them, wordless.

"What's going on here?" He asked.

"Mom is happy that I found *someone*," she repeated Jada's words verbatim, noticing Jada cringe at her tone. "And for your information, Mom, Sam isn't just *anyone*. He loves me for everything that I am, which is more than I can say for you. Come on, Sam. We're leaving."

In less than a few steps, Anya kissed her father on the cheek and passed Jada without so much as a glance. She took Sam's hand in hers and stormed out of the door, letting the slam vibrate the entire house behind her.

FORTY-THREE

Anya stared at her ring, admiring its perfect round cut and glimmer. For years she convinced herself that she would never find anyone and that it was hopeless. She believed there were no good men left in the world.

But now she was getting married to Sam.

He proposed to her beneath the stars, with a galaxy diamond, nonetheless. Nothing in the world was more romantic or perfect to her.

One thing she was starting to notice was Sam's impeccable timing when she was on one of her astral adventures. Each time she was close to figuring out something about Pleiades, he always seemed to interrupt. After what Anya saw on their trip in Basalt, she couldn't stop thinking about the new place she discovered. Finding it at the same moment of her engagement was also bizarre and strangely timely.

Pleiades was nothing like what she could dream up in her mind. It was something so beautiful, she couldn't stop thinking about it—the silver buildings and cars that reflected from the shine of many suns, the plants radiating in neon jewel tones, and the magnificent beauty of

The Lost Pleiad

every single being that strolled past her on the white stone paths. The air was filled with love, or so it seemed.

Anya wanted to go back there.

But she needed quiet—a place where she would be undisturbed.

This time she would find a different place other than her house. She'd shut off her phone and go somewhere no one could bother her, not telling anyone.

Anya thought of the perfect place. Somewhere she could have quiet without being disturbed. The first place that came to mind was a hotel. But there weren't many in Cripple Creek that didn't have constant noisy chimes from slot machines ringing away all day. She needed a different place and just for a few hours.

By the end of the day, Anya was checking into a hotel in Woodland Park just off the highway. Anya told Sam she would be enjoying a spa day with Karmyn and Bee for the evening. Although a lie, he knew she wouldn't be disturbed if Sam thought she was off with her friends.

The key unlocked her hotel room door with a light beep, and she was in a quiet space. She unzipped her small duffle, extracting a pair of black leggings, a loose-fitting gray shirt, and the galaxy diamond, which she suspected was helping her with astral travel at times given the way it glowed each time she went somewhere.

She peeled off her clothes to slide on the comfortable ones and then found a comfortable place on the bed, holding the heavy galaxy stone in her hand.

It took some time to quiet her mind and drown out residual noises; beeping car horns outside, the hum of the mini-fridge, and other occupied rooms running water. After multiple deep breaths, she felt the weight of her body, the clothes clinging to her skin, the weight of the galaxy diamond ring on her finger, and the weight of the galaxy diamond stone in her right hand.

Now, I'm out of my body.

Now, I'm out of my body.

Anya repeated the phrase over a dozen times before she felt weightless. Her spirit body lifted from her physical form, shooting her into space in an instant. She took in the black void that surrounded her. Not seeing a single planet or moon in sight as the shimmering stars cut through space. Anya closed her eyes again, imagining the place she had once been. The magically loving place she thought would never exist.

Take me to Pleiades.

With that thought, her transparent feet were touching the white stone ground. But this time, she was somewhere different. Around her, she sensed the same warmness as last time. As if these types of visits were a common occurrence. As a young girl, Anya dreamt of Pleiades as a city floating on clouds and waterfalls disappearing into the space below it. But it was much more than her childish imagination. Pristine buildings rounded at the edges to appear softer and less edged, unlike structures on Earth. Anya walked down the stone path, passing by the other people, the Pleiadian people. She admired the buildings around her, noticing the more minor details, like the exotic foods that she couldn't describe, meats and vegetables in inverted colors of the ones she was used to. If only she could smell their aromas too.

People waved at her, flashing friendly smiles. Anya walked for what seemed liked miles, trying to familiarize herself with this strange city. Flat streets would sometimes turn into uphill inclines and winding staircases that lead to even more beautiful parks and crowded streets. In the sky, Anya saw planets hanging impossibly close on the horizon. As she looked, she noticed a palace in the distance. Parts of it reaching about as high as the heavens and disappearing into the clouds.

Anya stopped a passerby in the streets, her long silver hair carried by the wind.

Remove the language barrier.

Instantly, Anya could understand the conversations happening around her. Then she looked to the woman and pointed up at the palace.

"What is that place?" Anya asked.

"It's the White Stone Palace," she responded. Anya looked up at the palace, which looked Disney beautiful.

"Who lives there?" Anya asked again.

"The King and Queen and six princesses," the lady answered.

"Six princesses?" Anya asked. "Wow."

"There used to be seven," the woman said once more.

"Seven? What happened to the seventh princess?" She inquired further.

"No one knows," the woman said. "It happened hundreds of years ago. That story was long lost."

"Hundreds of years ago?" Anya was shocked. "How long do people live on this planet?"

"We're immortal mostly, so we live for as long as we wish," she said again. "But time doesn't really exist here."

"That's amazing," she said.

"What planet do you come from?" The woman asked.

"I come from Earth," she said. "Do you get a lot of people from Earth?"

"Yes," she said. "But we have a lot of people from all parts of the universe and quite often."

"So, that's why people are so friendly to me. They see spirit bodies all the time?" She said.

"Yes," she said. "We are much more in touch with our spirit selves here. We are pure spirit."

"Is that why I feel so much love when I come here?" Anya asked. "It feels like the atmosphere is charged with loved."

"Pleiades is known for being very loving, but our past and history still has terrible things in it," she said.

"I think that is true for all histories," Anya responded.

"You seem to have many questions," the women stated. "You must be very new to visiting us."

"That's true," Anya said. "This is my second time coming here. Maybe my third, I'm not sure."

"Well, blessings to you," she said. "You're welcome to visit the palace. You will find that everyone here is very kind, especially to those looking for themselves."

"Thank you," Anya said. "What's the best way to get there?"

"Just tell yourself where you want to go, and there you will be," and with that, she nodded and walked away. Anya returned the nod and looked back up at the palace.

Take me to White Stone palace.

Anya was instantly standing in the courtyard, watching people go on leisurely strolls. Some of them dressed in silvery-blue gowns, with stiff collars, or tight pantsuits with an elegant sheen. Everyone looked so royal, perfect, clean, and content. Anya walked through the maze of turquoise hedges and periwinkle and white flowers with a dim glow

The Lost Pleiad

Anya imagined would be brighter at night. Trees with white leaves rustled in the breeze Anya couldn't feel. As she walked, she came around a tall hedge to see a couple sitting on a bench. Their robes were thicker than everyone else's and stitched with gold. The woman's silver hair seemed even thicker, laced into a perfect braid that pulled her hair from her face. Her eyes sparkled with a dazzling blue shade. The stoic man beside her, built much larger than her, had equally long silver hair and a long silvery beard. He seemed strangely familiar.

Anya felt drawn to them, desired to ask them the million questions she needed answered, wondering if they might know a little bit more about her connection to this place. As Anya neared, she saw the woman's head turn to look at her with a quizzical expression. People crossed through her gaze, and she worked to fixate on Anya.

Many people were walking in her path, so many that Anya lost view of the pair on the bench. Anya quickened her pace, following her path to the bench in a bizarre desperation. As she neared, the couple disappeared from their seat. Anya whipped around, searching the crowd for them, but didn't see them. Disappointed, Anya lifted her head and continued her stroll through the courtyard. Perhaps what she was seeing was a trick. Maybe they were spirit bodies from other parts of the universe, like her.

Anya tried to take in the world around her as much as she could. Watching the clouds above her sparkle in the daylight, imagining what they might look like on a cool evening. She imagined the feel of fallen leaves from trees between her fingertips or what it might be like to lay on the grass in a park and stare up at the sky, picking shapes from passing clouds.

As she continued to walk, she came to a canopy of trees with the same white leaves that glittered around her in the breeze. Walking through the tunnel of trees on a stone path, Anya came to a stone wall that looked out at an ocean, observing the aqua waters that existed only in her dreams or books.

Maybe the dreams she was having weren't so fake after all. Down below, she saw children playing in the rushing waves and heard their playful laughter rise into the sky to meet her ears.

Anya had never felt such peace and solace. She could stare out at this ocean for hours and never get bored. She searched the horizon for any sign of marine life, wondering if whales, sharks, and fish like those on Earth lived on this planet too. She wondered what they looked like.

Anya dreaded the thought of leaving this place.

As she looked out into an ocean view that stretched to infinity, Anya felt a chill on her neck and the hairs rise on her arms. She knew she was safe but also knew someone was behind her. When she turned around, the pair that occupied the bench was standing just in front of her. The man stood much taller in her presence, at least 6'8". A giant, manly figure such as his that could appear intimidating in any other place was instead a comfort. The woman stood about Anya's height, a tad shorter, but able to view her at eye level. Anya felt the desire to hug her but frowned inside, knowing she wouldn't feel it.

Admiring their silver robes, she could see the gold stitching more clearly. She noticed how they both held their chest higher, likening it to the way royalty carried themselves.

Both of them had eyes bluer than the ocean and bluer than any sky she could paint on a canvas. Anya assumed the language barrier was still not a problem but asked to remove it once more to be certain.

Remove the language barrier.

"It's beautiful, isn't it?" Said the woman. Her voice sounded like one Anya had heard before, one that could soothe a babe into a calming slumber. Anya turned back to the ocean.

"It really is," Anya said. "I feel like I belong here. I wish I could explain that feeling. But I feel it in my soul."

"That is a common sensation to many who visit us here," the woman said.

"I'm sure it is," Anya replied. "Why would anyone want to leave a place this beautiful?"

The woman laughed. The couple inched closer to the brick wall to gaze out at the ocean with Anya. The three of them chatted for a while. Anya asked many questions about Pleiades, learning it had been around for thousands of years. That millions populated the city. She learned thousands of spirits visited daily and that many of them usually ascended to live their eternal lives out on this planet. Anya believed it to be a lovely notion, considered a life like that, but instantly thought of Sam back home. It was the first time she had thought of Sam during this entire experience. Wanting to live here made her feel guilty. But she considered the possibility of him traveling with her; a lofty consideration.

The man and woman spoke of their daughters, how they all lived in the palace—boasting their intelligence, grace, and beauty.

There was a long silence as they sat together, looking out at the ocean.

"I know you," the woman said. Anya was confused. No one on this planet could possibly know her. The tall man looked down at the woman.

"I'm sorry," Anya said, looking questionably at them both and frowning. "This is only my second time visiting Pleiades. I don't know anyone. I was hoping someone could tell me more about my connection to this place."

"You don't understand," the woman said again. She looked like she might cry. "We have known you for a long time, although you may not know it."

Anya searched her thoughts. Maybe she was crazy. Perhaps she had been here more times than she could remember, or maybe she had been here in her dreams and just hadn't known it? Anya had done plenty of research on dreams and how spirit bodies could go to many different dimensions. It was possible.

"How?" Anya asked. The woman looked up at the towering man. "Wait, who are you?"

The man and woman smiled at her. "My name is Pleione."

"And my name is Atlas," his baritone voice boomed. "We're the King and Queen of Pleiades."

Anya remembered the lore of the Seven Sisters constellation. Two of the stars were named Pleione and Atlas—parents of the Seven Sisters. They mentioned their daughters earlier, but Anya hadn't pieced it together.

She could barely believe it.

Anya stood frozen in front of two physical forms of the brighter stars in the cluster, looking at people regarded as a pure myth and fantasy on Earth.

"You won't remember, but this is your home," Pleione said.

"I know I'm from here," Anya said brightly. "I know I'm Pleiadian."

The two of them smiled gleefully.

"You're not just any Pleiadian," Atlas said.

"I don't understand," Anya said, looking confused.

"We could sense your true soul," Atlas said. "Almost instantly."

"How could you sense my soul?" Anya asked. "Is that a normal thing on this planet? Sensing souls?"

"No. That doesn't happen with just anyone," Atlas said. "We could sense your soul because…"

Pleione looked at Atlas as he crumbled beneath his own words and then looked back at Anya.

"Because you're our daughter."

FORTY-FOUR

"That's impossible," Anya voiced in disbelief. This once extraordinary world falling away around her after hearing the last four words. "How could I be your daughter? Don't you have to be born in an actual place to be someone's daughter?"

"You were originally born here," Atlas said softly. "Hundreds of years ago, just before our last war."

Anya wanted to feel relief, wanting those words to make her feel like she finally had found where she belonged. But the daughter of legends and myths?

"If I was originally born here, how did I get to Earth?" The two of them looked nervously, love still radiating from them while Anya stood overwhelmed with confusion.

"During the war, you were so small, we had no way to protect you," Pleione said in a voice filled with a plea. Her way of enticing a sort of understanding. "We sent you down to Earth by our own will."

Anya let her form collapse to sit on the wall, wishing she could feel its rough texture and ground to it, but glad something was there to steady her, Pleione and Atlas rushed to her side, unable to embrace her.

"So, my whole life, not knowing who I am, feeling different, feeling out of place, that was all true?" Anya asked. "This is where I've belonged all along?"

The two of them nodded.

"We've been trying to find you for centuries," Pleione said.

"We've been accessing thousands of people's dreams," Atlas said, placing stories there, hoping each attempt would lead you back to us somehow."

"I can't believe this," Anya said. "How would I even get there from here?"

"We did a ritual, an ancient one that would send you down to into the first vessel being born on Earth at the time of your arrival," Atlas said, his voice breaking as he spoke recalling the memory. Anya was too shocked to feel sorry for him.

"We understand this is much to take in," Pleione said calmly. "We're prepared to tell you everything you want to know."

Anya searched her mind for any other questions about her past but couldn't seem to think far past this new truth to form a single question. All she felt was overwhelmed, confused, sad, and somehow even more alone than before. Shocked. In denial. Feeling betrayed and abandoned. Everything she ever wondered about herself, was true, and for years she felt insane for it. Just as she was feeling at home on Earth, she was learning *this* about herself. But she remembered how little she looked like her parents, how that alone was an indicator and a clear one.

"My parents have dark hair, and my hair is blonde. So blonde. Their eyes even, they're brown while mine are so blue. It never made sense to me how I could look so different from them. I always joked to my friends that I was adopted. I joked so much, my parents had to show me pictures of them holding me at the hospital when I was born. But this… this is too much," Anya said. "I need to go."

"Please stay," Pleione pleaded. "We've just found you."

"I'm sorry," Anya said, barely looking at them. She took one last look at the ocean and thought of her body in the hotel room. Within a flash, she felt her spirit slingshot back into the softness of the bed beneath her, and her body pulled down by gravity. The galaxy stone fell from her palm, radiance fading from it.

Feeling the softness of the mattress, she curled up into her pillows and wept. Whether it was relief or grief, she wasn't sure, but the tears were as real as the newfound discovery of herself. What a weight to carry.

How could she tell Sam this?

How could she tell anyone?

It's one thing to relate a sliver of herself to a concept or community of people, somewhat like the blindness seen in believing a religion. It's another to be an actual complete alien that didn't belong to this planet. How many others could say that was their truth?

The weight of this knowledge was tearing her from the inside out. So much of her life had been confusing, a lie, a never-ending search for understanding herself and where she belonged. All along, her intuition was telling her what she already knew. She didn't belong here. And yet, in a way, she had found her place here, found her place and her home in Sam. Found her sisters in Karmyn and Bee. Oh God. Sisters. She had six sisters. Even with what she knew, how could she exist in two places at once?

This all came as a crushing blow, threatening to cripple her very being and all that she ever knew about herself. Anya had an entire life she built over thirty years. Who she was, the things she learned, the places she grew up, the countries she traveled to, the friends she made, the foods she liked, the things she believed. All of those things formed during her entire existence on Earth. Everything she had ever built for herself could have been completely different if she had grown up on Pleiades.

Anya Allen. The daughter of Pleione the sea-nymph and Atlas, the titan who carried the world on his back.

Anya Allen. The daughter of Cole and Jada Allen of Earth.

It was impossible. Unfathomable. Insane.

She had asked for the truth, received it, and denied it.

Anya curled up into the world that she knew, lifted the bedsheets and comforters, sliding underneath to find more comfort. All her life, she had looked for that sense of belonging, the place where not only her body fit but her soul. She thought she had found that in her friends, in her Cripple Creek home, in Sam. But she couldn't be more wrong. All that she had learned about herself and the person she ached to know was what she wanted until it was finally given to her.

Belonging in two drastically different worlds made Anya feel more alone than ever before. And she could talk to no one on Earth about it.

Under the warmth of the sheets, she cried until she couldn't anymore. Until her cheeks dried and pillow drenched. Her tired eyes carried her to the edge of a deep sleep, into dreams that she wouldn't remember tomorrow.

Her temporary slumbers would be a calming break from her denial and resistance. The initial shock, or whatever heaviness laid on her chest, would be gone, at least until tomorrow. But that was enough for now.

The sky was a fusion of yellow, oranges, pink, and periwinkle floating above pastel seas with a fuchsia sun disappearing beneath the horizon. It was the perfect sunset, one she couldn't capture with a camera or paint on a canvas. Some things are meant to be enjoyed in the moment.

Anya was back at the stone wall on Pleiades, looking out at the ocean, watching planets and moons hang too close. Below her, the waves rushing to the beach sparkled with pink and gold glowing algae. At the stone wall, she sat on the edge letting her feet dangle above the steep drop. Her galaxy diamond was heavy on her left ring finger, perhaps the most solid object rooting her to her life on Earth.

"This is real, you know," said a familiar and soothing voice. "This is just another form of out-of-body experience."

Anya turned to see Sam. His dark hair combed back and dark beard trimmed to perfection. The colorful sunset brought a softer glow to his caramel eyes.

"What if I don't want to do out-of-body experiences anymore?" Anya asked. Sam swung his body over the wall, letting his feet dangle beside hers. "What if I just want to be normal now?"

"After all you've been discovering?" He asked, taking her hand. "Why would you want to give this up now?"

"Because it's terrifying," she said. "Because it could take me from you."

"Don't be silly," he said. "You could never lose me."

"You don't know that," she said, looking out at the ocean. "You could always lose anybody. I know I did."

"What do you mean?" Sam asked.

"I have, or had, a whole life here on this planet, and I lost that," she said. "If I never went searching for it, I would've never known what I had lost. I wouldn't feel like this."

"Maybe," Sam said. "You're lucky to have one family. But two? That's pretty extraordinary."

"And it's better to be lucky than good," she said.

"Got that right, baby," Sam smiled, looking out at the same ocean. The fuchsia sun was now a blazing red-orange, and the pastel sky was fading into darkness. The foamy golden pink algae below changed to match the night, transforming to a pleasing cerulean. Anya felt the warmth of Sam's fingers laced in between hers, recognizing how perfect and comforting it was. If only she could have both worlds. This one she was just learning about and the Earthly one where she was finally starting to feel happy.

"How would I be able to live in both worlds?" Anya asked after a long silence.

"We will figure it out. Together," he responded.

"I don't see how," she said. "How am I even supposed to tell you what I am? That I'm... royalty, but not just any royalty, alien royalty."

Sam chuckled. "Alien royalty. I would expect nothing less from my positively perfect cosmic angel."

"And I have so many questions," she stated. "Like, am I just magically a princess now? How often would I have to astral project to be there? Would you be able to come too?"

Sam didn't say anything, just squeezed her hand tighter as if he knew something she didn't. As the fuchsia sun disappeared beneath the horizon, the stars poked out alongside the monstrous planets still glowing from earthshine.

"Do you plan to go back and visit? After what you've learned?" Sam asked.

"I don't know," Anya responded. "I feel like the more I visit this magical place, the more my reality could fall away from me. The more I risk losing everything I've built in the only world I've ever known. I don't know anything about this planet, this life, or what it means."

"Well, it's your choice," he responded. "You have to do what's best for you."

"How do I know what's best?" She asked.

"You'll just know," he said. "You'll feel it in your bones, in your belly, your chest. It will ring through every cell in your body, that knowingness. I know because I felt that same knowingness the moment I met you."

"No matter what, I'll have to give up something I love," she said. The thought alone flooding her with dread and a sick feeling in her stomach.

"Perhaps you would," he said. The night was pitch black now, their fingertips still laced together. Anya laid her head on Sam's shoulder. His head turned toward her, and his lips met her forehead. "I love you so much, Anya."

"I love you," she said back.

"You know what we should do now?" Sam said.

"What's that?" She asked, looking at him.

"Jump."

"Jump?" She replied. "Why?"

"Why not?" He said, grinning.

"It's a long way down," Anya said, looking at the glowing algae beachlines below.

"Don't worry, my love," he said. "You're going to fly."

Anya knew she could trust him and knew this was just another out-of-body experience. Anya knew she could fly.

"Let's do it together," he said, grasping her hand. They stood up from the stone wall to stand on top of it. "On the count of three."

Anya nodded. "One… two," Anya felt the muscles in her legs tense in preparation to spring forward into the night sky. "… Three."

As she jumped forward, she felt Sam's grip loosen and release her. He stood still on the top of the stone wall while she dove into the world. When Anya felt the absence of his hand, realizing he was not coming with her, a wave of panic coursed through her, sending her spirit self back into her body.

Anya sat upright in her bed, feeling the heat of the stone through the layers of sheets and comforters. During each out-of-body experience or dream, the stone was activated, but she hadn't figured out why. She was crying in her sleep. In the darkness of the room, she felt a deep void, as if she had just lost Sam. The dream felt so unbelievably real. Losing Sam felt so real.

It took minutes to convince herself it was just a dream, but in truth, she wasn't sure what was a dream anymore. Was it this reality she was living in, or the one her spirit body had been traveling to? Everything was blurry and confusing. When her breathing slowed, she took up her phone and called Sam immediately, desiring to hear his voice. The phone rang several times before going to voicemail. She hung up before he voicemail sounded. When she glanced at the clock, it was 2:00 a.m.

Anya thought of her dream, Sam's plea for her to jump, wondering if it was a genuine request. If it was a sign of which direction she should go in. But the thought of being without Sam, of him not embarking on every journey with her, tormented her thoughts, and she hadn't even lost him. But nothing scared her more than losing him because she was losing herself to this truth.

The conversation felt so real, so rational, so full of optimism and hope. Even in her dreams, he was understanding and supportive of whatever path she decided to take, which is why she couldn't tell him or share the real truth of who she was, knowing he may not accept it.

Telling him this would threaten everything they were building together. And nothing would be the same.

She got up from her place in the bed and moved to the window, the curtains still drawn to let the city lights in. She searched the sky for Pleiades again, trying to find it amongst the stars drowned out by headlights, streetlights, and building lights.

But she couldn't see it, not in the noise of light. Instead, she turned her back to the window, to the stars, to the moon, to the place she now knew she belonged, considering turning her back on it for a while. At least for now.

FORTY-FIVE

Anya studied her computer screen, searching for wedding ideas. She decided on mint as a primary color while satisfying Sam's request that the men wear all black. She was calling it a "Very Minty Marriage."

"I want to keep this wedding simple, babe," she said. "Nothing too fancy or expensive."

"I'm on board with that," he said. Sam loved how Anya valued the simple things and enjoyed minimalism. She told him she wanted to buy more experiences than she did things. Memories lasted forever. Things could fade away, break, or disappear.

"What kind of cake do you like?" She asked, scrolling through a variety of tiered wedding cakes.

"Ooo, anything with almond flavor," he said. "I love almond."

"Good God," the scrolling stopped so she could look at him. "We really are made for each other."

Feeling her lips on his, Sam's heart lifted.

Sam always looked at the idea of weddings as daunting, terrifying. But back then, he could never see himself settling down with anyone. He never thought it would be a possibility for him. As a result, he never looked forward to it. But with Anya, he could imagine everything they would do in their future.

Moving in together.

Cooking a Thanksgiving turkey.

Putting up a Christmas tree.

Weekends watching movies.

Waking up to each other every morning.

Brushing their teeth together at dual sinks.

Enjoying morning coffee together.

Having their first child together.

Sam could think of the endless ways they would spend the rest of their future. Each thought caused excitement to surge through him.

While Anya made to-do lists, guest lists, and shopping lists, Sam allowed himself to worry about how Anya and her parents would repair their relationship. For weeks, she wouldn't talk about it, busying herself with work, planning their wedding, introducing her friends, reading her books, or spending time with him. Sam noticed she was actively staying more occupied than usual, more attentive as if she was distracting herself from something she didn't want to face.

Sam considered asking her, but he knew she would come to him with whatever bothered her, and if she didn't, Sam was there to remind her that he was a listening ear.

This hadn't been the first time Anya disappeared into something or from something. But this time was different. It nagged at him more than expected, and he couldn't exactly pinpoint why, but he decided to trust her.

"Hey, babe?" He inquired.

"Yeah?"

"Have you talked to your parents recently?" Anya sighed, closing her laptop to give him her full attention.

"Why?" She asked.

Anya was silent, processing the question, maybe her emotions. Sam was unsure of what was happening in that magnificent brain of hers. She was looking down at her hands, focusing on the shimmering diamond fit to her ring finger. Sam lifted her chin to meet his gaze.

"Hey," he said softly. "You can talk to me. We are in a safe space, and I will not judge you for how you feel."

"I know," she mumbled.

"Are you still planning on inviting them to the wedding?" Sam looked at her, waiting for an answer while she sat painfully silent. "If you say no, that's okay."

"I don't know, Sam," she said. Anya thought back to the moment she announced her engagement to Sam, the words from her mother—talking about Sam as if he was just another warm body in her bed and not someone she loved so deeply. Her father didn't even stand up for her. "I'm so angry with my mother for how she talked about you, and we don't have a shining history of bonding well. So it's like, what's the point? I don't think she is going to change. I don't think she wants to, and my father isn't helping."

"You don't know that for sure," Sam said.

"You don't know my parents," Anya said grimly

"Well," he shifted his posture to face her. "Tell me about them then."

Anya's eyes darted around the room. She frowned as she thought, recalling every negative memory from her childhood. It was amazing how the mind always went to the worst things first.

"They believe in everything the exact opposite of me and who I am. They choose to judge people who don't abide by the Bible, they reject anything open-minded or different, constantly look down on others who aren't like them, and judge people far too harshly."

Sam listened to her observation, holding a place of love for her while she spoke.

"I don't think my parents love each other. Not like you and I do, anyway," she said. "You can see it in how they interact. They're like Allie's stuck-up parents in the Notebook, always telling me what I can and can't do. By the time I was out of high school, I was so relieved because I felt like I could finally be myself. I didn't have to go to church every Sunday. I could take on hobbies they told me were a waste of time. I could be friends with whoever I wanted," she said. "I felt... free."

"It sounds like it was really tough," Sam said, pushing a strand of hair behind her ear. He thought of his parents, still wishing she could love her parents, appreciate their presence in her life when he had lost his. But a request like that isn't simple. What's toxic is toxic. That was one thing he learned from his parents. But no matter what, people will always love a parent. Just as Anya was about to continue, her eyes seemed to glimmer with a bit of hope and love.

Anya continued, a deep sadness appearing on her face. "My Dad used to tell me that I was one of their most treasured gifts, and he had prayed for me for his entire life. He used to tell me this every single night when he tucked me into bed. He told me I was a gift, and when I was born, a blinding light came in through the windows. He called it a sign from God." Anya shook her head, sniffing to keep from crying.

Sam saw her flash through the memories, showing a fondness for them before returning to sadness. "The older I got, the less he told me that. After a while, I convinced myself he just didn't love me the same. But then, I got older. He taught me how to camp, how to fish, how to kick a soccer ball. When we would go on camping trips, we would recite the names of the mountains together."

"I have a daddy's girl on my hands," Sam said.

Anya laughed. "That you do. Although, no one has ever really said it out loud. Dad and I will always fight, but we usually make up."

"What about your Mom?" He asked.

"My Mom..." she started, "I don't really know where mom and I went wrong in our relationship. I don't feel like we're close. With my Dad, I feel like I can tell him most things. But my mom, not so much. Of the two of them, she is the most critical. I felt like she was always judging me for the choices I made and the things I believed. Over time, I just grew to resent her. We haven't been close for the past several years."

Sam wished their bonds could mend, desiring to see them happy and well. But Sam knew better than anyone that forgiving anyone and letting go of resentment could take a long time. He still struggled with it himself. Instead, he decided to just see it happening for her.

"Do you have any good memories of you and your mom?" Sam questioned. Anya propped her elbow up to let her chin rest in her palm and dove deep into her thoughts.

"There was one day when I was eight years old. I woke up feeling really sick, terribly sick, like vomit sick," Anya said, "I wasn't the type of kid to get sick. That day, she had to work, but when she took my temperature, she didn't bother going in. Instead, she let me stay home. I remember she dragged her mattress out to the living room to put it in front of the TV.

She turned down all the lights, and she let me watch any movie I wanted," she said. Sam looked longingly at her, noticing just how stunning she was when she loved. "But the best part about it was, she laid with me the entire day, stroking my hair and whispering how much she loved me in my ear."

"That sounds lovely, An," Sam smiled.

"It really was," she said. "But nothing like that ever happened again. Nothing that could compare anyway."

Sam decided to let her sit in that thought, stew in it, remember it fiercely, hoping that it would sway her into calling her mother. There were so many times he regretted never telling his mother what she meant to him. Sam hoped Anya would never be tormented with the regret she would feel for not voicing the magnitude of which a person mattered to her.

"I really think you should call her," Sam said. "Tell her how you feel, at least. If you never do that, there will never be hope for a healthy relationship."

"And what if she never changes?" Anya asked.

"Then you move on, but at least you can move on without feeling regret for things left unsaid," he said. "You move on knowing you did everything you could to revive that bond."

Anya nodded in agreement and huffed. "You're right. And, man, do I hate that."

As they laughed together, he took her in his arms to hold her, feeling her melt into him. "I love you to every moon and back."

"You are too perfect for this universe, Sam," she said.

"Thank you, love," he said. "Now, let's get back to this super fun wedding planning."

"Okay," she agreed. "Where do you want to get married? I don't think I've ever asked you that."

"Isn't it supposed to be the bride's choosing? Don't brides make all the choices," he asked.

"I mean, we could, but how lame that would be, not planning together," she said. "It's not just my wedding."

"Dang, I was hoping to get off the hook," he joked.

Letting her jaw drop, she laughed. "How dare you!"

"Okay, how about this," he started. "What if we had a night wedding. Got married under the stars somewhere really dark."

"My God," she said. "I love it. But where? Where could we go that's dark but still beautiful."

"I have a place in mind," he said, half smiling.

"What place? Spill," she said.

"How about Dunton Hot Springs? You said you wanted to go there someday right?" He asked, already picturing the majesty of the area nestled in the San Juan Mountains. A town of renovated ghost-infested cabins and private hot springs. "We can rent it out for the entire weekend, invite just the important people. They arrange the whole thing. Meals and drinks are provided for the whole weekend, and we can go fishing or paddle boarding or horseback riding after. We can stay in the cabin with the private hot spring. It'll be perfect."

Anya stared at him in awe. "How long have you been planning to marry me?"

"Gosh," he massaged his chin. "Several months now."

"Okay, that's it," she threw her hands up. "I'm relinquishing full wedding planning control to you. That is the perfect wedding, and I barely lifted a finger."

"So, how much is it going to cost?" She asked. "How worried should I be for that cost?"

"Well, I called in a favor. I'm friends with a friend of the owner. So we're getting it for about a third less than the normal price," he said.

"Uh-huh, which is how much?" she asked.

"So, insanely high. Perfect wedding high. Rocky Mountain high," he joked again.

"That sounds pretty high, but I'm about it," she laughed. "How many people do we get to invite?"

"Forty-four people," he said instantly. Anya was already looking at their website to get the numbers. "Two nights minimum stay."

"Holy crap, that's expensive!" She said, ignoring his answer.

"Worth it," he said. "We can save a lot more if we get married in the Summer."

"Well, that's not far away at all," she said, her eyes a blue electric shade of excitement.

"Just a few months," he elbowed her. "You scared?"

"Hell no, I'm not," she said, leaning into him. "I'm excited to spend eternity with you."

"So, is June 15th a good day to start eternity?" He asked.

"Perfect," she said. "I only have like six people to invite."

"I have like two," he said.

"Well, I'd say we're on target," she said. "Do you think you could coax your friend into an extra discount on account of our super lack of a guest list?"

"For you, my love, I'll do practically anything," he said.

By the time evening arrived, Anya and Sam had wrapped up an entire plan for their wedding, the woodland arch decorated in white tulips, a small gathering at the reception, unlimited access to campfires and hot springs soaks. All they had to do was call to make reservations, formally ask their wedding party to join them, and then relax because there was nothing else to do. They decided they would take their honeymoon trip to the Maldives, a place Anya wanted to visit before the ocean swallowed the islands. Sam, amazed by how easy it was to plan, felt his whole body relax. The idea of having a wedding be an entire weekend party rather than a few hours of celebration was more appealing.

As they snuggled in bed that night, closing laptops, turning off phones, and putting away guest lists, Sam counted every great thing he was given when this world had given him so much pain. He thought of the parents he wouldn't have at his wedding and how he wished they could be there. Then, he thought of Bruce, the only father he had left in this world.

It hadn't hit him until now, but he felt genuine hope for a future filled with life and adventure after years of convincing himself he would never have it, nor deserve it.

Sam would have to wait months to say his vows to Anya. On a night like this, when she slept in his arms, her hair radiant in the moonshine spilling in through the windows and sinking into the sheets, Sam vowed to protect everything the world had given him in a massive wake of sadness and destruction—first, by being grateful.

FORTY-SIX

Her cell phone rang for a third time while she squeezed her slim form into her 5th wedding dress of the day. It was Gwynn and Sage calling. The woman behind her lacing up the bodice remained wordless until hearing the vibrations of the third and last phone call.

"Aren't you going to get that?" The woman asked. Anya twisted around to look at the woman, whose hair was tied in a tight bun, the hairspray sheen reflecting the fluorescent lights above, the black pencil skirt flattered her equally slim form, and a grey blouse buttoned up to her neck.

"It's not important," Anya said. But really, it was. The truth was, answering their call scared her. If she was tempted to tell them about her last spurt with astral travel several weeks ago. If she talked to them, she would have to face the very real truth she just learned. More so, they'd compel her to talk about the moment with her parents, even if they didn't know about it. They were like magic. They knew everything.

Anya wasn't ready for that. Not yet.

If she couldn't admit it all to herself, how could she possibly admit it out loud to anyone else? The vibration rang out for the last time, a lasting glow remaining on the screen before falling to black silence. Anya felt relief roam through her. She would deal with it later.

"Alright. You're all laced up," said the lady. "This one is lovely."

Anya stared back at herself in the mirror.

The dress was a cream shade, a poofy ball gown that made her feel like Cinderella, and she hated it. It wasn't her first choice, nor were the last four options she had just slid in and out of. Outside the dressing room was the pleasant chatter of Bee and Karmyn. They were already on their third glass of champagne as they tore through a third of a complimentary cake.

"I'm coming out!" Anya hollered. The chatter ceased, and Anya stepped from the dressing room where her two friends sat at attention. The couches they sat on were large and white, and although two bodies took up most of the space, one other body was missing.

Just another issue she didn't want to deal with.

When she stepped to the small stage to turn herself about in front of her friends, they gasped with approval.

"My God," Bee said. "You look divine."

"You think so?" Anya studied the dress, hugging her body so tightly she almost couldn't breathe.

"We know so," Karmyn replied.

"I kind of hate it," Anya said, looking at the cheesy beaded bodice and her chest plunging. Not classy or simple at all.

"Hey! I picked that one!" Karmyn exclaimed.

Anya turned to face her frowning friend. "I'm sorry. It just doesn't feel like me."

"Sure it does," Karmyn retorted.

Anya frowned. "Then you don't know me at all."

Karmyn crossed her arms and fell back into the stiff couch. "Well, fine. What else ya got? How many more do you have left to try on."

"Two or three, I think," Anya replied.

"Well, if this isn't the one, let's move on to the next," Bee said. "We'll find it. We've already gone through my options and now Karmyn's, so it's up to you, bestie."

Anya returned to the room, listening to her friends resume their conversation. She admired a simple cream-colored lace mermaid cut: no poof, no cheesy ball-gown beading, no oddly stitched patterns. The sleeves fell just below her shoulders, the bodice was easy, breathable, and the corset was absent. The last thing she needed was her chest being the center focus, and she wanted to be comfortable. The second option was a simple, plain, satin dress with a lovely sheen. She could see this dress on her in a mountain wedding. Although she loved it, she feared it would show every imperfection on her body. Satin usually did that. The third and final option was a long-sleeve white lace dress with a low-cut back. Like the first option, the sleeves stopped just at the top of her shoulders, and it would cover her chest. It was elegant, classy, perfect for an outdoor wedding in the San Juan Mountains.

Any of these wedding dresses would be great. If she hadn't valued her friends' selections so much, she would've tried them first.

As she peeled off the frosted cupcake dress, she heard her two friends speaking in barely a whisper.

"It's weird, right? Her not being here?" Karmyn asked.

"Yeah, it feels awkward," Bee said. "But she doesn't want to talk to her. Can you blame her?"

"No. But it's her mom, and this is her wedding," Karmyn said. "It doesn't seem right."

The Lost Pleiad

"It's not like her mom tried to apologize," Bee said. "Her mom should be the first to call."

"Well, you know how prideful and stubborn her mother is," Karmyn said.

Anya couldn't hear a response from Bee after that, nor could she see nods of approval or shoulder shrugs. She wondered what sad expressions lived on their faces right then. She wondered if they knew just how fed up she was with her mother. Anya focused on the three dress options in front of her, trying to drown out their words. The simplest choice she could make at this moment. The only choice that didn't seem to overwhelm her.

"That one," Anya pointed to one of her three options. The woman busied herself, letting the material fall off the hanger and into her hands. Anya was half-naked in from of this woman, wearing nothing but underwear and a strapless bra. The woman held the dress at her feet so Anya could step in, pulling it up past her butt, her hips, her torso. Anya slid her arms through a material that felt silky like butter. A dress feeling like a home for her body. Comforting and comfortable. Anya dared not look in the mirror just yet. All she did was feel. Feel that perfect dress rest on her skin like a soothing gravity blanket. Feel herself walking down a meadow of cut grass toward a woodland altar, and her beloved Sam standing there at the end to receive her, birdsong ringing between trees like something out of Sleeping Beauty and leaves acting as nature's soothing tambourines. A melody fit for the split souls that managed to find each other in a sea of souls searching for their other half. Anya felt it all.

Wordless, Anya gripped the door handle, turning it, delicately shoving it open to reveal the masterpiece upon her body. In an instant, her friends gulped sips of champagne, hid speechlessness with their hands, let tears fall to their cheeks. Anya knew then that this was it.

She stepped in front of the mirror, ready to see the beauty she already felt humming from within.

In the sparkling lights, Anya looked at her reflection, the lacy long-sleeves rippled at her wrists, the short train of lace trailing behind her, how it complimented her skin, and it felt like everything she had been looking for and then some.

"That is so the one," Bee said.

"You're damn right it is," Karmyn said, reaching for a tissue. "I stand so apologetically corrected."

"This is the one," Anya said, recalling the previous moments where she lived in the future of her perfect wedding with her ideal man. The spiral patterns of lace swept along her body in all directions like they were going somewhere but hadn't arrived just yet. The dress was gorgeous, and the thought that her mother wasn't here to see it brought her to tears before she could stop herself. The lady who stood in cheery admiration of Anya's selection now held a worried look on her face. Anya noticed how much older she was, how she was provoked to comfort her but held back from consoling a client, a stranger. Surely she had seen moments like this before. Bee and Karmyn rushed to her side, prepared to pick up the pieces of Anya.

"She should be here," Anya said. "Why couldn't she just put it all aside?"

Bee and Karmyn remained speechless, but for reasons other than the ones from just minutes ago. They held her as she cried in her wedding dress, as she mourned the loss of this moment, the one every little girl dreamt of, and how it could be forever tarnished by the absence of a mother who couldn't accept Anya and the person she chose.

But it wasn't just her mother, and she couldn't lie to herself about that. It was who she was becoming, the secret she clung to, the one that made her feel confused, helpless, and lonely. The parts of her that gaped open, giving new life to the void, the vacuum of endless sadness she always felt but couldn't verbalize.

The reality of her existence would never stop being true, no matter how much she worked to will it away. This wasn't her home. These people weren't her family. This moment, it wasn't just the grief of an absent mother, the suffering brought on by an absent life, akin to what adopted children would feel. Anya was blood and bone to Cole and Jada Allen, and yet, she wasn't theirs. Not really.

"It'll be okay, An," Karmyn said. "Everything will work out. You'll see."

She wanted to believe it. Desired to. "How?"

Karmyn and Bee exchanged looks, wondering how to tackle such questions when they didn't have a solution.

"I don't know," Bee said. "You just have to believe it."

"It's not just Mom," she wept.

"What do you mean?" Bee asked, following up with the standard question any bridesmaid asked a bride. "Are you having second thoughts?"

"No," Anya said.

"Then, what is it?" Karmyn asked.

The words were there, teetering on the edge of her lips, desperate to escape, be heard, understood, and accepted. Anya wouldn't say them.

She would wipe her tears, pay for her dress, put on a happy face, and go home.

When she got home later that evening, she hung the wedding dress hiding beneath a zipped veil in the darkest corner of the closet where Sam wouldn't bother to venture.

When she turned away from her wardrobe, the familiar sparkle of the large hunk of galaxy diamond winked at her. A stark reminder of who she now knew she was. She considered tossing it into an even darker corner within her side table, hoping she might forget about it, forget about what she knew.

Coming around the foot of the bed, she closed the space between her and the stone, debating on picking it up to feel its energy, afraid it might spark another meltdown.

She had looked at it so many times, but somehow it looked larger than she remembered. Too large, like the bombshell dropped on her just weeks ago. Was it really so bad, this being a possibility for her? All she would think about was what it would cost her or if accepting this in totality would strip her of the life she wasn't supposed to live.

Her bottom met the edge of the bed. Fidgeting, she couldn't tear her gaze from the stone and how she now possessed two of them. Each one connected her to places she was meant to be—each connection was big and terrifying. One held conviction while the other held the opposite.

If Gwynn and Sage were here, they'd make her feel better. They'd tell her how it was part of the Universe's plan. She would praise her for finding the home and belonging people all seem to be searching for. Anya would sit with them, tell them what she saw, what she heard, how it all made her feel, how magnificent it was and how that terrified her.

She would cry in front of them; the only two people in the world she was certain would understand this.

But she still couldn't muster the courage to answer a phone call or make a phone call herself. Perhaps if she said it out loud, and gave birth to this reality, let it breathe life, let it float on the air, or echo between the walls of her home. Would she find solace then? Would it make this secret any easier to grasp in her hands and her heart?

She reached for the stone, letting it rest in the softness of her palm, feeling the heat form between a once cold stone and her quivering palm—a little treasure reminding her that she had the answer to the bigger question now. What she would do with it was her choice.

Closing her fist, she tightened her grip around the stone, feeling its jagged edges dig into her hand, feeling the realness of where she was. This was real. This stone is real. This bed, it's real too. So were the plants and the diffuser spitting lavender oil from the dresser. Anything she could touch with her bare hands, that was real. And yet, what she discovered on Pleiades felt just as real even though she couldn't touch or feel anything.

Even receiving the answer to her biggest question, Anya was met with even more unanswered ones. She knew just how to get them. Astral projection was getting even easier even in the weeks she hadn't practiced. She could always return and get her answers. Somehow she knew they were waiting.

Holding the stone to her chest, she cozied herself on the bed, finding an airy place for her head to rest on the pillow, preparing her body for another astral experience. Closing her eyes, she recited the familiar words, the ones her tongue missed.

Now, I'm out of my body.

This time she said it once. In the black depths of the universe, she felt her power humming around her, how it rippled through outer space, disrupting galaxies, planets, stars, and suns.

Pleiades. She thought it, and she was there, surrounded by familiar views of jewel tones and smooth silver and white buildings that rolled like waves across the earth—separately and all together at the same time.

This made sense. This feeling. This place. There was no denying such a truth or a feeling. Even though she couldn't touch this world, feel it, breathe it in, it felt as real to her as the plants, the diffuser on her dresser, and the galaxy diamond clenched in her hand.

With a simple desire and thought to be at the palace, she was there, staring up doors that seemed to reach the sky. They were made of a white stone that looked smooth to the touch. To either side of her were guards looking much too less like guards and more like hostesses.

Remove the language barrier. She commanded herself.

"I would like to see the King and Queen," Anya said. The men, with their cascading silver hair, looked at her.

"Who might you be?" They inquired calmly in voices that hummed like singing bowls.

"I'm Anya," she said, hesitating. "Daughter of Atlas and Pleione."

The two men exchanged baffled expressions. Unable to believe it themselves. Anya held the seriousness on her face, confident they understood that she wasn't kidding. The two of them dropped their heads back, and the center where their third eye was began to glow in a white-silver light.

The doors shifted open with a loud bang, revealing a short bridge that would lead to an arched opening. She walked through the slivered opening in the doors, which were much larger when up close. They closed behind her as she made her way toward the arch. Beneath it was another set of doors already opened to reveal a grand hall.

Passing over the threshold were some of the biggest pillars she had seen, ones doubling in size and comparison to anything she could imagine on her own. They went on into infinity, seemingly able to host an entire planet of residents if desired. The pillars were the same soothing white stone, perfectly grooved. Anya ran her hand across one, hoping she would feel its smooth texture, but nothing.

The hall was empty except for a spot of light drilling into the stone floors. She pressed on, curiosity moving her toward the light, curiosity moving her to learn what it might be. As she approached, the light grew in size, like walking toward the Eiffel Tower and realizing it was still growing in size with each step.

That light came down from a skylight spilling a giant circle of glow onto the floor, twenty feet wide in diameter, at least. Anya stood in the middle of it, letting the light fall onto her, hoping she could feel its warmth. She closed her eyes, letting the light try to flood past her eyelids. As she relaxed, she heard the voices she didn't know she loved so much until then.

"That's the exact place we let you go," said Pleione.

Looking over, she saw Atlas and Pleione standing just feet from her, radiating a desperate kind of hope.

"We weren't sure if we would ever see you again," Atlas said.

"I wasn't sure if I would come back," Anya said. "It was… a lot. To learn what I learned."

"We know," said Pleione. Her calmness was magnetic. Anya glanced between both of them, looking for a shred of resemblance in them. A lofty attempt to feel as if she truly belonged to them. If they shared anything, it would be their blue eyes. But even then, they were shades of blue Anya didn't know existed.

"I have so many questions still," Anya said.

"We're happy to answer them," Atlas said. "Just... please don't leave."

Atlas, the mighty Titan, and the softness sounding in his desperate plea made her heart ache. Embracing him was out of the question.

"What questions do you have?" Atlas asked.

Now that she tried to think of them, she couldn't seem to pluck even one from the long list she'd been keeping.

"There's so many. I don't even know where to start," Anya said. She looked around the hall. "Is there a place we can sit and talk about this?

"Of course," Pleione said. "Follow us."

They both moved between the pillars, away from the skylight, and through the doors. Atlas and Pleione led her through more stone passageways that led past massive courtyards filled with alien flowers, trees, and fountains. The palace was a maze. She tried to document where she was, where they were going, but she lost track. After passing several doors, they came to a pair of smaller stone ones. Pushing them open, Atlas and Pleione passed through. Anya followed, emerging into a hall with impossibly high ceilings carved in stone and perfect arches. Along the walls were lights hovering like little stars, as if someone had captured them with their bare hands and placed them there. Silver floors were beneath her feet while she followed in the footsteps of Atlas and Pleione.

Inside the widened hall, there were two doors forked off to either side of the room. Atlas led Pleione to the left one, opening the door to reveal a much smaller room decorated with plush white furniture, blue and purple curtains that dripped around the window frames. The walls housed hundreds of books—a language Anya spoke. Admiring their collection, she examined the symbols, lines, and dots connected like constellations, but all forming separate letters that would fuse to make words. Their words printed and scribbled on paper. From the window was a stunning view of the city and the shimmering buildings clustered together and glittering beneath the sunlight. In the distance was the same ocean she loved so much, no matter what planet she was on.

Pleione motioned Anya to sit down in a chair. When she did, the form was unmoved. Anya tried to imagine what it might feel like beneath her, sitting on a cloud, resting in a waterbed, floating in water, she would never know.

Atlas and Pleione sat together on a couch across from her. It dawned on Anya that she could've been choosing a question to ask them this whole time.

"What would you like to know?" Pleione asked. Anya searched her thoughts, trying to think of the simplest one, which she hoped would create a domino effect for asking all the others.

"Well..." she started. She looked around the room, at the drapes, the books, the floors, and the walls. Remembering the skylight, she thought of her first question. "You said you lost me under that skylight. What did you mean?"

Pleione was the first to speak. "There was a war happening when you were a baby. We thought we were being defeated. Each time we looked outside, those fighting against us were moving closer to the stone doors. If they made it through, there would be nothing we could do to protect you. You were the youngest and most recent born. Your sisters were much older and able to take care of themselves." Anya looked at Atlas.

"But you're Atlas, the Titan who carried the world on his back," Anya said. "How could you not protect us?"

Atlas seemed to shrink, and Anya noticed the harshness in her voice when she said it. "I did fight, but only when I knew you were safe somewhere else."

"When was this war?" Anya asked.

"Over two thousand years ago," Atlas said. Anya was stunned.

"You're both over two thousand years old?" Anya asked, baffled.

"Yes," Pleione answered. "Time is not what you think it is here."

"Why did you give me years then?" Anya asked.

"To make it easier for you to understand," Pleione said. "We live in the remote past."

Anya frowned, remembering that looking at Pleiades from a telescope, she was looking at the star cluster as it existed four hundred light-years ago.

"So, if you're four hundred light-years in the past, does that mean you don't exist now in my time, and I'm just talking to ghosts?" Anya asked.

"Not necessarily. As I said, time and our existence are complex to outsiders. In this reality of ours, time is somewhat non-existent. You will understand with time," Pleione said.

Anya tried to understand now. "Time is an illusion?"

"In a way," Pleione replied. "We exist as our higher beings. Other parts of ourselves live separate but concurrent lives in other dimensions. Where we are now is the root of all those realities, all of which can experience the illusions of time."

"What happens when those realities in other dimensions die?"

"Their essence returns to their true vessel," Pleione said. "They ascend to a higher consciousness, accepting that the experience is over and they may start a new, different one."

"Do they choose their experiences?" Anya asked

"Yes," Atlas said. "They all do."

"If that's true, and you can choose experiences in other dimensions, why would they choose difficult or sad experiences?"

"Understanding all types of experiences, whether good or bad, can breed intense empathy and love for all, which raises the vibration of our universe," Pleione said.

"How come they don't remember their higher selves, though?" Anya inquired.

"When beings are born, they are born a blank canvas," Atlas said. "They forget everything. They will learn what is taught to them and spend their whole lives experiencing the world as they've been trained to know it. They'll spend their whole lives trying to find their true self. Some won't be able to reach such spiritual clarity in one lifetime. If they don't, then they create a new experience. Some would say, another lifetime. But the higher self usually chooses a destined life for this physical reality."

"So, having many lifetimes is real?" Anya asked. Pleione nodded.

"Why would someone from a place so incredible want to spend time being human? Being a human isn't all that fun sometimes," Anya said.

"We disagree. We're grateful for all human experiences, even if they are challenging. They help us understand the entire universe better," Pleione said.

As Anya chewed on this information while another looming question arose. One that seemed silly to ask and impossible.

"So, I'm visiting you in the past," Pleione nodded. "Let's say I physically traveled to Pleiades. Does this mean I would be traveling to the past?" The question seemed ridiculous, but Pleione's expression held no judgment.

"In a way, but, ultimately, yes." Anya made an effort to rationalize the situation, make sense of how they existed two thousand years ago in this present time, but four hundred light-years ago in her physical presence. It made her head spin.

"And you would remember me and these conversations we've had even though I'm basically traveling back to the future?" Anya asked again.

Pleione smiled. "We would remember."

Anya sat, feeling the emptiness of her non-corporeal form, yet still aware of her physical body existing on Earth four hundred light-years ahead.

"So, if your higher beings live here in this dimension and realities you've created to experience life are born in other dimensions, does that mean my higher being is walking around on Pleiades somewhere?"

Pleione and Atlas stared at her as if they knew something Anya didn't.

"If we hadn't let you descend, your spirit being would be here now," Pleione said. "But we sent your entire essence to Earth when we did the ritual. You're a Goddess walking amongst humans without even knowing it. Your true self exists wholly on Earth."

Anya said nothing. Just stared into the ceiling, her ghostly form paved in daylight, wondering if she had superpowers.

"But this body I'm in. It's not really mine, is it?" She asked.

"No," Pleione replied.

"Then, where is my body?" Anya asked. For the first time in their conversation, the two of them looked at each other.

"We set the blue fire to it, as we do with all of our deceased when their time comes," Atlas said.

Anya slumped in her chair. If she had no body here, she suspected there would be no way for her to exist here. A possibility she didn't know she wanted to exist until that moment. How would she ascend like others?

The silence lasted a long time. Anya searched for another question.

"Are all your other daughters still alive?" Anya asked.

Pleione smiled. "Yes. They are quite well. We would love for you to meet them."

Being an only child, Anya could barely fathom the idea of six other sisters and all of them at once. But the thought delighted her. She wondered what they looked like.

"Someday, I would like to," Atlas and Pleione grinned so brightly, the light from outside was outshone. Anya discovered she was pleased, feeling calmer than she had in past visits. She looked back at the shelves full of books.

"Do you like to read?" Atlas inquired.

"I love reading," Anya said. "It's a favorite pastime. When I'm in a story, I'm in a different life, a different one, possibly better than my own."

"Spoken like a true Pleiadian," Atlas replied. "Reading is my favorite pastime too." He lifted his large form from the chair, moving to a bookcase to extract a book. It had a smooth navy cover and silver embossed symbols. He opened the book, motioning to read the words aloud.

"Wait," she told him. "I want to hear what it sounds like in your language."

Atlas looked pleased and nodded in approval.

Return the language barrier. Anya willed.

Atlas started reading in the language of song she was beginning to grow accustomed to. It was a beautiful song, notes fitting together in a way that created words—his baritone voice bellowing melodies that made Pleione sway in the background.

Anya remembered mentioning to Gwynn that she had watched *Close Encounters of the Fourth Kind*. In response to this, he told her that theorists truly believed alien contact would be made with song and color. Listening to Atlas speak now, Anya wondered how those theorists could have possibly guessed that one. By the time he finished a passage, Pleione's eyes were shut, and she was grinning contently. Atlas closed the book and returned it to its home on the shelf.

Remove the language barrier. Anya commanded.

"That was beautiful," Anya said. "I wish I understood it."

"Well, maybe we can teach you someday," Atlas said hopefully.

"I would like that," Anya said. "And to be honest. This place is so lovely and so are both of you. Why I've been fighting to accept this, I don't know."

"We understand this is a big truth," Pleione said. "We are patient, and we are here should you want to be here too."

Anya felt lighter as if asking all of her questions emptied her uncertainties from her vessel. Knowing herself, knowing her thirst for knowledge, Anya would have more questions and soon. Her eyes shifted between the two of them, memorizing all parts of their faces so she could remember them even after she left.

Anya was beginning to feel an almost instantaneous love for them like she did with Gwynn and Sage. As she sat in the chair, she couldn't feel beneath her, she felt their energy, their essence, their love for her which always existed, giving her life even in death. A love like that was capable of anything, even transcending all dimensions. What Anya knew is she had found the bridge home, and she planned to cross this bridge often, especially after knowing everything she did. Especially knowing there would be more to learn.

"I have one more question," Anya asked. "If that's okay."

"Of course," Atlas replied. "Ask anything you please."

Anya smiled, nervously excited to voice her next question.

"What did you name me?" Anya asked. Pleione took Atlas' hand in hers. Their eyes shimmering with pools of tears as if the question asked was an honor to voice. Perhaps it had been several hundred years since they'd even uttered it. Perhaps they uttered it all the time in prayers and whispers. But this would be the first time Anya heard it for herself and the first time in thousands of years all three of them heard it together. As Pleione's lips shifted to part, Anya felt a tingle, a quiver, a shiver of excitement. And then came a single word that seemed to give her even more life than anything else had ever given her before.

"Merope."

Anya let the sound of her given name chime through her ears like a song with perfect pitch.

"Merope," she delightfully repeated in barely a whisper.

"Welcome home," Atlas said. "We've missed you."

FORTY-SEVEN

Her mood shifted almost instantly, and there was no way he hadn't noticed. So much time spent together afforded him the ability to know her, her actions, the way she moved.

"Have your parents called you?" He asked, thinking that was the reason for her chipper attitude. Anya was in the middle of cleaning up dishes after dinner. She stopped to look at him, the suds dripping from her wrists while the water continued to run. And with one question, Anya was reduced to her melancholy self.

"Nope," she said, returning to furiously scrubbing the nearly clean plate.

"You've been in such a great mood lately. I thought things might be okay with you guys now," Sam said, wishing he hadn't brought it up. Each word he vomited just lessened the happiness radiating from her.

"I don't know what else to do, babe," she said. "The way she talked about you and how she did it with you sitting there. It's not exactly my place to make amends here."

"Anya, I'm fine," he said, moving to wrap his arms around her.

He kissed her cheek, feeling the steam from the hot water rise from the sink. He turned off the running faucet and turned her to face him. "Listen to me. You have two parents, and although they are difficult, you can tell they love you. Especially your Dad. He adores you."

She looked at him with a softness that said empathy. "I'm just so mad at her."

"I know you are. And that's okay," he said. "But with the wedding coming up, the last thing you want is to regret them not coming."

He tried not to imagine the worst-case scenario. Or how a decision like not inviting parents to their daughter's wedding could consume a person with guilt and regret. Sam regretted every day not telling his mother just how much he loved her. He didn't want Anya to feel that way, even if her parents continued to live and breathe. Dozens of unsent invitations covered the kitchen table, all sealed shut, stamped and addressed except for one.

"I'm having a hard time forgiving," she said.

A sentence he understood. "It's understandable. But I think you should give it a try. You'll hate yourself in the aftermath, and I wouldn't be able to bear it. Neither would you. That big loving heart would beat yourself up forever."

Her wet arms were hanging around his neck as she peered into him with her most loving glare. She huffed in defeat. "Alright. I'll do it for you."

He smiled. "Do it for you. Not me."

"Yes, sir," she said.

With that, he kissed her, letting those perfect lips melt into his. Letting their bodies fuse together. Those smooth limbs of hers wrapping around him like a warm blanket.

Running his hands up her curves, he softly pushed her against the counter, pressing his groin into her, finding the place where shirt and pants parted to feel her skin. Letting his fingers tease at her waistband, his lips met the crook of her neck, taking in her scent. Slowly, his fingertips made their way to unbutton, unzip. When she sucked in her breath, he felt that fire within. The one he always felt with her. In one motion, his hand reached down to her most sensitive spot, leaving her breathless again, her body crumbling beneath his touch. She relaxed into the motion of his fingertips on her clitoris.

"You are heaven," he whispered. Anya let out a moan, gripping the edge of the counter to find stability. That beautiful chest rising and falling while he tickled her until she couldn't control herself. Within minutes, she was coming hard, her body quivering against his.

Sam kissed her intensely, letting her moans echo into his mouth and throughout his entire being. Devouring every sweet sound of her release, he gave her smaller, more tender kisses from neck to nose to forehead to lips. The rise and fall of her breast slowed.

"You can keep washing the dishes now," he said. She opened her eyes, looking around as if she was unsure of where she was, having transcended to another realm for the past few minutes. When she found herself again, she grinned at him with a sort of amazement that made him feel more than pleased. "What was that for?"

Sam always wanted to please her, first and foremost. "That was for you." He said, walking toward the table. He licked the open envelope and sealed it shut, placing it in the pile with all the others.

"You're very convincing," she stated.

"Oh, I realize," he admitted. "Call them tomorrow."

She half-smiled, nodding to the request.

Surrendering her ego for the good of all.

"Thank you, babe," he said, stopping by for one last kiss.

"No. Thank you," she said.

He wasn't sure what act she was thanking him for, so he decided it was both.

FORTY-EIGHT

There was a flutter in her stomach as she clutched the phone in her hand. A picture of her mother smiling on her phone. For a minute, she debated on whether or not she should call her.

"Anya?" Jada said on the other end.

"Hey," Anya replied.

The dead air was unbearable and seemingly infinite.

"How are you?" Jada stuttered.

"I'm alright," Anya said. "I thought I'd call so we could talk."

"Yeah," Jada said. "I think that's... good." The flutters in Anya's stomach grew from the flapping of bird wings to spinning tornadoes.

"I'm really mad at you, Mom," Anya said. "So mad."

Jada said nothing. Anya breathed on the other end of the phone. She was usually a frustrated crier, but this time it was steady, beyond frustrated, and angry. She was fed up.

"I know," Jada said. It was an opportunity for her mother to say sorry, and she still hadn't taken it yet, which angered her.

"Sam is going to be my husband," she announced. "My husband. Do you understand that?"

"Yes, I do," Anya's voice pierced through the phone. Her mother passed up another opportunity to say sorry.

"I will not have you treating him that way ever again," Anya said. "And if you do… I will never speak to you again."

"I'm so sorry, honey," she said, caving at that statement. "It will never happen again."

Anya felt relief, and surprise, believing from the beginning her mother wouldn't apologize for her behavior. Even now, her apology was barely believable. She wondered if her father talked to her about it after they left the house that night.

"Good," Anya said, not asking for an explanation, not questioning her behavior.

Anya, wanting to let this go as quickly as possible, didn't bother asking her to explain herself. "We're having our wedding in June this year. At night. Under the stars. At Dunton Hot Springs."

"Sounds wonderful," Jada said. "When are you going to find a dress?"

The silence that fell between them again, minutes passing in the awkward silence until it clicked that she had found a dress without her mother.

"I already found one," Anya muttered, feeling little remorse.

"I see," Jada choked. "I'm sorry I wasn't there for you. It's my fault."

"Do you really mean that?" Anya said in a tone of disbelief that bit and snared.

"Yes," she cried. "Yes, my darling girl. I mean every word."

Jada wailed into the phone, into her Anya's silence on the other end.

"Oh my God, Mom," Anya asked. "Are you crying?"

"It seems I am," Jada admitted. "The thought of losing you forever because of my stubbornness. It was enough."

"I don't think I've ever heard you cry," Anya said. "Ever"

"Sure you have," Jada was still crying, and Anya suddenly felt bad for her, softening at her sobs. "You just haven't heard it in a long while."

"When? When was the last time you cried in front of me?" Anya questioned.

"The day you were born," Jada said. "The moment I held you in my arms, the tears came, and there was no force in the world, not even God himself who could stop me from weeping with gratitude," Jada said. "You were and always have been an incredible gift… I'm just not always good at showing it."

"Mom," Anya muttered. "I wish I could hug you right now."

"Me too, sweetheart," Jada said.

"You know it's okay to talk about things. To let go," Anya said. "You don't always have to be strong, composed, and put together. And strength can also mean being vulnerable, which is the best kind of strength."

"Well, maybe you can teach me," she said.

"I can teach you," she said in a cheery tone. "If you're willing. It takes willingness to let go of things like this. Can you be willing?"

"I have to be," Jada replied. "I have to be for you."

"No, mom," Anya said. "You have to be for *you*."

Anya felt lighter, like maybe her parents could be at her wedding without judgment or jealously. But she'd believe it when she saw it.

"I love you, Anya," Jada said.

"I love you too, Mom."

"And Mom?" Anya said one last time.

"Yeah, honey?"

"I forgive you," she said, trying to mean it.

"Oh, Anya," Jada whimpered. "Thank you."

"You're welcome," Anya said. "I have to go now, but can we have brunch soon or something?"

"We can do whatever you want," Jada said.

"How about this Sunday?"

"Sunday is perfect."

"Bye, Mom," she said. "I love you."

"I love you," Jada replied. The other end of the phone went silent, and Anya clung to those three precious words, letting them ripple through her. In one big release, she cried until her eyes were swollen and red.

FORTY-NINE

Sage's smile was more sparkly than the flecks of glitter shimmering on her skin. "Wow." Gwynn had a similar expression of amazement. The three of them cozied up near one of their windows, where trees were sprouting new leaves to signal spring was already here.

"That's all you have to say?" Anya asked, finding she was smiling too.

"I'm pretty good at being open-minded and accepting with anything people throw at me," Gwynn said. "But this… it's so surreal I can hardly believe it. It's not often you hear a truth this big."

"Except when I told you I was Mary Magdalene incarnate," Sage smiled.

"Yeah, but that would really put people over the edge," all three of them laughed. "Tell them you're Jesus' virgin mother, and people will lose their shit."

"I know," Anya said, knowing full well that was the truth. Months ago, she struggled to believe in things that once felt impossible. But here she was living such impossibles. "When I think about it, I still feel like it's not real at all. Like some fantasy I've conjured up."

She had just spent an hour telling them everything. About her journeys with astral projection, how radiantly colorful that world was, how she could communicate with them, how her parents were royalty on a different planet in a different dimension, how she was special. A princess. It made her feel so girly and undeserving, but also proud and confident.

"You're The Lost Pleiad," Sage nearly shouted.

"The what?" Anya said, looking confused.

"The Lost Pleiad," she repeated. "There's a myth that the youngest daughter of Atlas and Pleione was lost from her sisters. There are many different variations of the myth. But that's you."

"Really? What else does the myth say?" Anya said, eager to know more. She had read over that information but ignored that being a possibility for her.

"Well, the youngest daughter, unlike the other daughters, married a mortal, while the other daughters married Gods." Anya thought of her recent engagement to Sam.

"Seems fitting for me!" She couldn't remember the last time she felt this excited. "Wow. The Lost Pleiad. How do I tell anyone about this."

"Well, ya don't," Gwynn said. "Not unless you want to go to the crazy house."

Anya chuckled. "I guess you're right."

"So what now?" Sage asked. "I mean, how often will you see them?"

"As often as I can," Anya said.

"Just through astral travel, though, right?" Gwynn asked.

"I mean, would there be another way?" Anya questioned.

"I don't know," Gwynn replied. "Did you ask?"

Anya looked at them in shock, surprised that she hadn't asked the question.

"I didn't," Anya said. "But it would have to be impossible for me to travel to space. Scientists are barely proving wormholes and time travel. Plus, I'm not an astronaut, and even if I was. It's four hundred light-years in the past, and I'll die of old age a million times over before I arrive."

"This all coming from the woman who found out she is a long-lost princess from a constellation buried in Greek myth," Gwynn laughed. "You can't believe or experience all that and then not believe in outer space's other possibilities. They may know something you don't."

Gwynn had a point. So much of what she learned was impossible, clinically insane, unfathomable by a simple human mind that always made things too muddied and complex. But the possibility of real-life space travel to Pleiades, she loved imagining it. It filled her up. It was a crazy fantasy, but one that pleased her, so she let herself feed into it, imagining the touch of those bright flowers, the smooth buildings gliding across her fingertips, the otherworldly smell of grass she decided would smell sweet, the wind on her skin, a warm embrace.

She could imagine it all perfectly.

There was nothing she couldn't imagine now.

Anya stayed for a few more hours, chatting with Gwynn and Sage about all the universe's possibilities. The two of them spoke of their outlandish past lives, how they discovered this wasn't their first time on Earth either. And Anya felt grateful. Happy to have such people to confide in when the rest of the world would think she was insane.

What a comforting feeling, finding the place you belonged.

She had a lot of those places now.

One was Gwynn and Sage's home, which smelled like melted myrrh and Nag Champa incense and always made her feel welcome.

Another in Sam, who made her feel safe, wanted and loved beyond measure, the single person she trusted more than anyone.

Then Atlas and Pleione, the home and love she hadn't known but found she cherished so much.

Anya was excited to get home, rest her head on her pillow, cradle the stone in her hand, recite those familiar verses that would sling her from her body, and return her to the starry dimension filled with wonder. Everything was perfect, the kind of perfect she had always desired.

Speeding back home from Coal Creek, she tried to follow the speed limit, driving a few miles faster to cut her time down. Every minute driving, she anticipated her arrival, feeling the excitement pulsing through her. It wouldn't stop. Not until her non-corporeal form was transiently snug in a chair beside Atlas and Pleione.

After seeing the world was full of possibilities the human mind wasn't ready to comprehend, she knew that anything was possible, even human space travel, like Thor hurtling through time and space in a glowing stream of pink and green light. Going so fast, she felt like she wasn't moving at all.

Home was just around the corner, in the trees, sitting silently and alone. For weeks, she had been spending almost all of her time at Sam's house. She usually came home when she needed to disappear for astral travel and be undisturbed.

She and Sam talked about where they would live after they got married but hadn't decided. Anya loved both places, loved the way Sam poured his love into a once shattered home. He was determined to create happier memories there. Although Anya couldn't experience that pain or those memories, she still felt them peek in from the dark corners of rooms. She'd told Gwynn and Sage about his family in complete confidence. Their recommendation was to smudge the whole house from back to front, letting the smoke carry the demons and shadows out through the front door as she went. Anya just hadn't gotten around to it.

Anya didn't want to give up her home, not really. She considered renting it out to tourists who would visit the area. It was close enough that she could do housekeeping easily and drop by to make sure all was well. It would be the perfect side gig, and lord knows Cripple Creek needed more hotel rooms. If she moved out of there and into Sam's home, she would miss the quiet seclusion. Sam's home was so close to the road and surrounded by other houses, plus there was constant noise from the mines. She wasn't sure if she would love it. But she loved Sam, knew his connection to this place, not for the horrible things, but the sweet things, like his mother. Sam had done so much to prove his love and proved it he had. And it was for that reason she leaned more toward living in his home.

When Anya arrived, the house was dark, with an even darker cat silhouette there to welcome her. Anya rushed inside, swooping up her fur dragon to bury her nose in the silky coat. Planting kisses all over her cute face.

"Hello, my Sugar baby," Anya said, putting her down to change into something more comfortable. Sugar was at her heels, desperate for even more attention. Anya was home less and less these days, and that made her feel guilty. She needed to decide where she would live soon so Sugar wouldn't be so alone.

On the side table next to her bed was galaxy diamond which managed to sparkle even in a dark room. Beside it was the recent book she was reading. Anya based the healthiness of her relationship on how often she was reading. If she was reading too much, she was escaping. If she wasn't reading at all, she was chasing. Anywhere else in between meant she held a healthy space for her time and time spent with Sam.

Sitting down on the bed, she grabbed the stone, feeling the excitement for her next visit writhe within her.

She started her routine, reciting her words, meeting the black space, and then shooting to the one place that was becoming all too familiar—the one a small girl used to just admire when her feet were planted firmly on the ground. A dream she had but never thought could exist.

Within minutes, she was at the stone doors between guards with glowing third eyes that let her walk through without asking, allowing her through because she belonged.

Hurriedly, Anya willed herself to the hall with the familiar silver floor and glowing sconces.

Waiting for her with impossibly wide grins were Atlas and Pleione. They seemed so much taller, more radiant, more brilliant now when she looked at them. Was it because they had found their lost daughter after thousands of years.

Was it because this place was pure love?

She imagined running to them, collapsing into their arms, letting her heavy body fall into them and feel their touch, feeling their laughter rumbled from their chests to meet her ears. Maybe she didn't see them as parents, not yet, but could an embrace, just a single one, finally bring her home?

"We're so glad to see you again," Pleione said. "We weren't sure when you were coming back next."

"I would come back every day if I could," Anya said. "But some days, I'm too busy."

"You have an entire human life to live," Atlas said. "You have to take care of your body there to visit us here."

He was right. "How have you been?"

"We've been happy," Pleione said. "The happiest we've been in ages."

"Me too," Anya smiled.

"You seem very excited," Atlas said in observation of her jittering posture.

"I am," Anya replied. "I have a question for you."

Anya couldn't wait to sit in a chair and have them approve her request to ask so she could blurt it out.

"Would it be possible for me to travel here?" Anya asked. Atlas and Pleione, expressionless, looked to each other as if they were having a telepathic conversation. The looks on their face didn't provide much hope, but Anya tried to keep her hope and heart lifted.

When they tore from each other's stares, Anya awaited their next words.

"It's possible," Atlas said. "Technology on your planet is not ready. But there may be another way."

"Really?" Anya gushed. "How? How can I do it?"

Pleione hesitated, carefully choosing her words.

"It may be possible through a stargate."

Anya hadn't heard of stargates but was determined to search for more information about them when she returned to her body.

"Great. How do I know which stargate?" Anya pushed. "How would you do it?"

"Thousands of years ago, there were thousands of stargates placed everywhere," Atlas began. "We haven't used them in many years, not since the last war. You would have to find one still active with energy, and you would need a sacred object. Like gold."

Gold was everywhere—especially where Anya lived.

Cripple Creek was still actively mining gold. Getting it would be the problem.

"But it's possible for a human to travel through one?" Anya begged.

Atlas and Pleione looked at the hope in Anya. "It's possible."

"I can't believe it!" She exclaimed. "I can actually come here?"

They nodded, smiling grimly at her, but she barely noticed. If she could dive into their embrace, she would. Anya spun in circles, looking up at the ceiling to see it twirl like a glittering kaleidoscope.

"I can't believe this is real. That this could have been my life," Anya said. She stopped spinning to look at them. "You have given my life a new meaning."

"We're happy you're happy," Pleione said.

"I'm going to do it," She said. "I'm going to travel here, smell the earth, feel the wind, taste the food, hug you both. Experience this world. Pretend for a day that this has always been my life."

This transparent vessel was an apparition but never felt fuller. She was so full, she could burst at the seams spilling light over everything it could touch. Happiness. That's what she made it out to be.

"I want to know everything about this place, about this palace, about this planet. I want to swim in the ocean and bathe in the light of all these moons."

"We can do all of those things," Pleione smiled, looking to Atlas. "When the time comes."

"Daughter?" Atlas said, and the smooth deepness in the way he said it only made her heart grow ten sizes. "We are so glad you have found us after so long. There is something we want to show you. Is that alright?"

"Of course," Anya replied. "I want to know everything."

"Follow us," Pleione moved to reach for Anya's hand but realized she wouldn't feel it.

Anya walked through more mazes of white corridors, watching her birth parents glide through with a sort of grace, robes trailing behind them. "We've wanted to show this to you since you came back into our lives, but wanted to wait for the right time."

The three of them stopped in front of a door. Atlas pushed it open to reveal a room with so much light it was glowing. The floors were the colors of sand, with smooth curved moldings in accents of blues and greens. There were tall windows letting the light pour in. To the right was an enormous bed, with tall white posts and cerulean drapes she could see through. On the walls were the balls of light hanging like sconces, as if she needed any more light. Shelves hovered from the walls holding dozens of books in the strange language she couldn't read but was desperate to learn. It looked so royal and yet unlike any royal room she saw in movies and magazines. To the left in the corner was a white egg-shaped crib that lay empty and dark. Anya turned to Atlas and Pleione, realizing where she was.

"Is this..." but they were already nodding. "This is my room?"

"It is," Pleione said. "We left it as it was and haven't changed one thing about it."

Anya walked over to the crib, wishing she could feel the edge of the empty vessel dig into her palms. "How lonely have these years been?"

"Very lonely," Atlas said. "We tried not to lose hope. But after a while, we couldn't handle the grief of losing you."

Anya felt sick, her heart aching for the parents who lost a child and the thousands of years they spent grieving that loss. Meanwhile, Anya felt guilt for how oblivious she was to her existence and the high she was on having just learned about it. But she could see the relief lifted when Anya returned to them. Anya thought of the single person she feared losing most, what it would be like to never see him again in an instant. For a moment, she was desperate to return to him.

"I'm so sorry," Anya said. And with those words, Pleione wept into her hands. Atlas took her in his large embrace, although Anya wished it could be her own. She desired to comfort her. Tell her things like, *It's okay. I'm here now. I've returned to you.* But the most significant part of her still hadn't returned home. Not yet. Anya knew better than anyone how crucial physical touch was for connection.

"It's not your fault, sweet girl," Atlas said. "We did what we thought was necessary to save you. We wouldn't change it for the world, especially with you standing in front of us now."

Atlas lifted Pleione into his arms, letting her bury herself into his chest, but now, he was crying too. Unusual for a man, but she was on a different planet now, one that dealt with emotions differently. She could feel that difference, that energy in the very air they were all breathing.

"Merope," Pleione said her given name, and it was just another beautiful lyric in a longer song she would never tire of hearing. "There is something else we need to tell you."

Anya moved closer to them, hoping to feel even a shred of the loving embrace she just observed between them.

"What is it?" Pleione looked at Atlas, wiping tears from her cheeks. Giving a nod of approval, Atlas turned to Anya.

"If you come here through a stargate," he started. Anya looked to them, their grins reduced to mere frowns. "It's possible you can't return to Earth."

Anya, who had built her own stunning Pleiades dreamscape, saw it vanish from her mind. Coming here meant leaving home and the entire life she knew. How naïve she was to see this as a simple vacation to another world.

"How do you know?" Anya asked, looking for a hopeful answer.

"No one from here has used a stargate in centuries," Atlas said.

"That doesn't mean it can't work, though, right?" Anya asked again.

"Anything not used or cared for after long periods usually becomes lost, broken, or forgotten," Pleione said. Anya thought of the Disney movie Atlantis.

"So I would have to choose a life?" Anya asked once more. Atlas and Pleione chose not to answer.

The cruel universe once working so much in her favor was now making her choose.

FIFTY

The torment of choice was ripping her to shreds. Her desire to visit the place she belonged was a one-way ticket rather than a round-trip.

Leaving it all behind here, after thirty years clawing her way to the places she'd dreamed of in her human life, it was something she couldn't consider doing.

But she was considering it.

Deep down, she was, and she hated herself for it. That night, Anya sent a loving text to her adoring fiancé, saying she would be going to bed. Instead, she searched the web for answers, looking for stargates, blog posts, theories from space dorks, videos, any evidence that she could still do this and return home.

She had convinced herself anything was possible, and she stubbornly held to that belief. Finding stargates was simple, but there was little to prove that human travel to places throughout the universe would be a possibility.

On her search, she found the docuseries, *Ancient Aliens*. She binge-watched professionals investigating strange points on the planet where energy was high, and giant-sized stones and boulders were too heavy to be placed together by mere humans. She watched hours of content and was starting to believe every single word of it.

Episode after episode, until dawn broke, she consumed all the information she could, searching for any Stargate that would resonate with her. By 5:00 a.m., it was too late to sleep, even for an hour. She shuffled to her kitchen to brew a fresh pot of coffee, the only thing she could stomach. *Ancient Aliens* continued in the background, telling her things she hoped would make her feel better.

While the coffee maker sputtered to life, she glanced over at the TV to see an expert talking about Lima, Peru. In the shot, they showed a slanted red rock with a large door carved out in it. Anya was reaching for a coffee mug when the image stopped her dead. She had seen this door; in a dream. Retreating from her cupboards, she hurried back to sit in front of her TV, turning up the volume.

She heard nothing else but the words, *Gate of the Gods*. The narrator took her through the area, which was five times larger than the average person. Seven meters wide and tall. Huge. The stone was cut like someone started carving space for a door with a laser but got interrupted. The center base of the larger door was an even smaller one that also led to nowhere, standing two meters high. In the center of that was a gouged hole in the stone. Protectors of the areas smudged the sacred area with burnt sage, donning colorful ponchos, standing in the doorway feeling its energy.

This was it. Her stargate home. She knew it.

She had the answer all this time without even knowing it.

This wasn't the only time her dreams had showed her things like this. She wondered how many of her dreams were messages just trying to point her in a direction. Recalling all of them over the past few months, it became clear someone was trying to show her something. Her parents sending dreams, just like they said.

All Anya could compel herself to focus on now was *Gate of the Gods*.

The person talking on screen spoke of the chunk of stone missing from the smaller door, how a large disc of gold was likely to fit there, like a key. Anya remembered Pleione telling her gold could act as the sacred object. The key to this gate home. The hole was huge, bigger than her heart. Anya knew exactly what would fit in that hole.

A Hershey's kiss.

Or that's what the gold miners called it.

It was a hunk of solid, high-grade gold extracted from the mines, very rare in a territory that mined most of it in the early 1900s. On occasion, they were lucky. Anya felt her heart rate quicken and then die. The last Hershey kiss they found was early last year. The CCPD had been guarding it until someone could retrieve it. It was gone.

Even if she could do that, which she wouldn't. Getting a piece of stolen gold to Peru was out of the question, and she was concerned with how much she even considered it. It would have to be something else. But the time the episode had ended, the coffee had been sitting untouched for thirty minutes. Anya looked down at herself, feeling both charged and tired like she just slammed a Vegas bomb at a bar. She needed to get ready for work. She needed to let her curiosity and looming obsession subside so she could focus.

Skipping coffee, she took a shower, cleaning the tiredness from her body. She slipped into some simple jeans and a shirt, willing herself to brush her hair and teeth, contemplating how she would make it through this day undisturbed by these thoughts.

In the mirror, she looked at the necklaces dangling on the wall. The only one sticking out was the silver disc with a black etched Pleiades on it.

She was the lost sister.

She made it on the front of this disc to become part of myth and history. It made her feel powerful, meaningful, and somehow even more isolated and lonely than before. She lifted it from the white hook and fastened it around her neck.

Looking at the clock, it was already 6:30 a.m. If she left now, she would have time to research *Gate of the Gods* a little more before Sami arrived. Sugar was asleep in the window but chirped at the unexpected hand grazing her neck. She resumed her slumber as Anya left through the front door.

She was to city hall in just fifteen minutes. Unlocking the green door, it swung open and into silence. Everything was dark and cold, even with the warmth of spring happening outside.

She walked to her office, switching on the golden light, taking the familiar path to her computer. She powered it on, watching the blue hue spark to life. When everything loaded, she opened a browser and kept searching on *Gate of the Gods*.

In Spanish, *Gate of the Gods* was Puerta de Hayu Marca.

It was discovered by Jose Luis Delgado Mamani in 1996. When he came across it trekking among the stone forest, he said he "almost passed out."

"Strange," Anya said. Page after page, she looked through the photos, marveling at her mind's ability to conjure this up in her dreams without consciously knowing what she was conjuring. If she had never seen it before, she couldn't place that memory within herself. Anya snapped into the present by the loud bang of the front door. Time had flown, and now Sami was passing through on the way to her office. Anya heard a large thump of her bags landing on the floor and then the soft boiling of a tea kettle.

Minutes later, she came through Anya's door.

"Good morning," she said, holding her cup of steaming tea, the opposite end of her teabag dangling on the outside of the mug.

"Morning, Sami," Anya replied, briefly looking at her. "How are you this morning?"

Sami walked to the whiteboard, which was overwhelmed with tasks in a rainbow of colors as usual. It seemed to never end, so Anya barely allowed herself to notice. When Sami came around to the farthest end of the board, she saw Anya's computer screen and the various images populating it.

"I'm good," she said. "That's the *Gate of the Gods*."

She took an innocent sip of her tea, and Anya spun in her chair to face her, stopping everything.

"You know it?" Anya questioned.

"Of course," she replied. "I'm a major archaeology buff. Did a whole dig near Assisi, Italy several years back. I'm fascinated by rocks and ancient things."

Anya glanced back at the screen. "What do you know about *Gate of the Gods*?"

"Probably about as much as you do," she responded. Anya felt her insides frown. "Some people have called it a gate to immortality. A portal to another dimension."

"You think it's true?" Anya asked hopefully.

"Not really," she said. "There's an explanation for everything."

"What's the explanation for this?" Anya asked.

"Well, It's a carved, unfinished building project from the Incan Empire. There haven't been many artifacts found in the area, which suggests that the Incans started the structure but abandoned it quickly into construction. It's considered a monolithic structure since it's carved stone created using bronze tools. The "door" measures seven meters by seven meters, with a small recess-like central feature at the center base," Anya knew this already but still listened. "It could be the beginning of an entrance, likely to an administration building or potentially a religious structure. The location of the *Gate of the Gods* is considered spiritually relevant area now, but we don't know if it was during Incan times. The proximity to Lake Titicaca and the submerged Tiwanaku temple, along with the significance of higher elevated plains to ancient peoples, suggests that it could have been the start of a temple or religious building."

Anya stared at her, stunned by her knowledge. "So, you *don't* think it's a portal to another dimension?"

"Likely not," she said, grabbing the tea bag and swirling it around in the cup. Anya observed her matter-of-fact stance, how Sami didn't notice Anya's hopes dying within her. "But, there are myths that say Gods traveled back and forth to check progress on humans and how they were advancing on Earth. Or something like that."

"They returned?" Anya asked.

"Apparently," she responded. "Very *Outlander* of them, don't you think?"

"Yeah," Anya muttered, thinking there may be hope after all. And if there was hope, that means she was considering, even if for a moment, to leave this world behind.

"So, what should we start with first? I think…" Sami's words trailed off while Anya sat in her chair, taking it all in. From what Sami said, there was a perfectly scientific and archaeological explanation for the massive unfinished door carved in stone. It was more tangible evidence than lofty dreams of escaping through portals and wormholes.

And here Anya was, feeling crazy again for considering other possibilities.

"Hey," Sami said, her face much closer to Anya now. "Are you okay? You're really pale."

Anya sat up straight, looking at Sami, who pushed her glasses from the edge of her nose to meet her face. "Yeah. I'm fine. I just didn't sleep well last night."

"Oh. I'm sorry," she said, stepping back from the desk. "I'll get working on some things I can handle without you and give you some time to wake up. Let me know if you need anything. Oh, and don't forget, we have the rodeo meeting tonight."

"Thanks, Sami," she left the office and returning her space to silence again. Before she could busy her mind with tasks other than her changing world, a text shook her entire desk.

"Good morning, my love," it said. "I hope you have a magnificent day filled with wonder. I love you to many moons and back."

Reading the text, she burst into silent tears, doing all possible to avoid alerting Sami. Torn between two worlds, Anya wished she lived in multiple places at once, especially after how much of the world she'd seen. But in those cases, she could jump on a plane and visit, inevitably able to return home.

This was different. Far from different.

If she went one place, she could lose one world forever.

If she stayed here, she would miss out on what her soul had spent decades yearning for. Anya knew very few people who answered their soul's calling and instead stayed behind to be in their place of comfort. People everywhere settled, sacrificing whatever piece of their soul dangled by a thread, fearing that they'll lose any and everything dear to them in the process of pursuing who they were. How many bought so much into the physical they had lost sight of themselves?

Anya had seen it countless times. People like zombies, shuffling through the world, unhappy, unfulfilled, and disconnected. Anya didn't want that to be her life. But she knew sacrificing what the world told her to be to live in a place she was destined to belong, she would lose it all.

What a hell of a decision to make.

It was no wonder the vast majority picked the safer option, which usually ended up being the most comfortable but also the hardest, rarely bringing true fulfillment.

Living the physical life and spiritual life equally and presently seemed impossible each time Anya thought about it. If people get lost in one, they lose the other. Entire courses and lifetime gurus were dedicating their lives to helping people balance the spiritual and physical self. But who had done it successfully? Cats maybe.

Sam, who had admitted meditating, believing in other worlds, being fiercely open-minded. He lived more in the physical than she did. Anya herself was spending more time in the spiritual than her physical, and if she wasn't in it, she was thinking about it. Maybe Gwynn and Sage were the only ones she knew who could do both.

As her knowledge and understanding of this universe expanded, she was more aware of the world she lived in and how people were brain-washed and prevented them from questioning and exploring other possibilities. They were shaped by what people told them to be shaped by. If someone else raised Anya, raised her in a different country, or had grown up learning a completely different language, her life would be different. She could be different even now if she willed it. She could strip away everything the world told her she should be or the things people told her to believe. Was it practical? Maybe. Would it be easy? Definitely not.

Anya had the choice to completely strip herself of doubt and all things she believed to be impossible and be free of resistance and judgment. But people loved their drama and melancholy. They loved the suffering and even enjoyed it. People worked too hard and never gave time to themselves. Convinced they had to work until they die, many waiting until the end of their lives to see anything other than an office setting.

The more Anya thought about it, the more she despised the same miserable routes all people herded through like cattle. Anya was starting to see this world with more clarity, more understanding. More than anything, she wanted to escape the suggested path she didn't want to take anyway. Anya felt like she was waking up, and it was grueling. Seeing so much of the world was more difficult than being ignorant of its presence around her. She wished people would wake up too so it would be easier, less lonely.

But she knew better.

People wouldn't change unless they were ready. And who was she to believe they had to anyway? Anya knew she didn't know it all, nor did she have the answers. She especially was in no place to judge people for their paths when she was unsure of her own path. Knowing each life is commanded by a higher self that chose these human experiences, Anya felt compassion for them.

Anya made it through her day, trying not to overthink or think at all. Focusing on work was a nice vacation from what she was forced to decide.

Today, she was doing planning for the annual rodeo. It was run by an association of business owners and well-known locals—all of them putting on the highest rodeo in the world, sitting at 9,494 feet. Anya sat at the table as one of the only women in the group, Sami and another shop owner being the other two. The men were arguing about which bands to bring and which food trucks to host. Each time one of the women tried to speak and give input, a man would talk over them. They always talked over each other.

One guy didn't want the hot dog vendor because they didn't like him as a person. The other thought their personality didn't matter if their food was still good. Thus, arguments ensued.

Anya hated it. The arguments. The conflict, the petty judgments that usually never circled around the overall crowd's enjoyment, but rather the association's personal preferences.

It was small-town politics that Anya never understood. It was the part of her job she hated the most. They didn't want her opinions, so she stopped giving them. It was an hour of her time she wasn't getting back.

After multiple attempts to provide input, Anya shut down and didn't try to speak or provide an idea. When the hour-long meeting was up, she left without a word—only saying goodbye to Sami as she left.

By the time she stepped out of the Brass Ass Casino to go home, the wind was blowing, and the leaves were rattling. She stood on

Bennett Avenue, the original face of the brick buildings preserved while the rest of the buildings were newer bricks stacked together to look authentic. Indicative of how she felt about this town and its people. Projecting realness when deep down, it was all fake. She looked up and down the roads, people coming in and out of the casinos. Jingles of slot machines sounded with each opening door, colorful awnings swayed in the door, the stiff and nauseating smell of cigarette smoke wafting up the street with the wind. Suddenly she felt annoyed with her world.

Watching the select cars pass by her, the sun was shining, and she let the mountain breeze blow through her hair. She crossed to the other side of Bennett, then walked toward the Double Eagle Casino and Hotel, past the empty pocket park, past the empty buildings people hadn't been able to keep open.

Anya thought often about how she ended up in Cripple Creek. Some days she couldn't believe she was even here and questioned how she had arrived. It wasn't really her place at all—just a stressful job, where she had to fight with locals to work together, and everyone had an opinion on how this town should be run, but no one wanted to compromise or work together. She had often run an event and gotten yelled at over the stupidest things like placement of tents or the date of events based on personal opinions.

Moreover, she was helping promote a town that thrived on gambling and alcohol addictions. A city that didn't care about whether or not they had a life-changing experience as long as they took people's money. Yet, on the other side, there was an effort to build up tourism and promote history and gold mining. But even that was greedy. A whole corporation kept sucking precious metals from the earth just so they could use less than a few grams to make cell phones or place golden bands on ring fingers to represent relationships that would ultimately end.

Anya didn't know how much longer she would enjoy this life in a small town, fighting to make it better but never getting anywhere.

Perhaps her frustrations were heightened. Perhaps she was too sensitive to it all. No matter, it felt like, in this moment, she had made the worst choice in being here, trying to make this life work. This wasn't really where she was supposed to be.

Anya was angry with how greedy and lost the world felt, how it had always been that way for her. Her new spiritual journeys were taking her away from it all like a glorious escape while at the same time heightening her irritations whenever she thought about how wrecked the world was. Maybe this was a reflection of herself. After all, the world revolves around choice. If the world is confusing, other people must be just as confused within.

She wanted to escape it all, start over. And it wasn't the first time she had ever thought that. On occasions, she dreamt of picking up her life, dropping everything, telling no one she was leaving, and then driving off to find a new place to live and be a different person. Just driving until she found a town that felt better than this one.

She could do it. She *might* do it.

But this time, she wouldn't be driving.

Anya reached her car and slid into the driver's seat, turning it over until it roared to life. She got back home, deciding to take a hot bath and let the entire day run down the drain. Anya dropped her items on the floor, slipped out of her shoes and clothes at the front door, not caring about putting them away. She went to the bathroom and turned the faucet on, letting the water shoot from the spout to fill her tub.

Anya's phone vibrated, but she ignored it, instead pouring a generous amount of Epsom salts into the hot water and an even more generous squeeze of bubble bath.

She stepped into the hot water before it was even half full, letting the water sting her skin. She slumped back, waiting for the water to reach the brim before turning it off. Sugar sat near the tub, a black apparition giving worrisome chirps, knowingly aware of Anya's distress.

After several minutes, the tub filled, and she was fully submerged. She dipped her head back into the water, letting her ears drown, so the world around her was silent. She closed her eyes, feeling that silence and the water still around her, trying to find peace and calm. Trying to let go of this day and how overwhelmed and defeated she felt.

Her eyes were closed until she heard a soft bang, prompting them to burst open. There was Sam, sitting on the toilet, looking down at her. She was startled to life, coming up to hear the world again.

"You scared the shit out of me," she said.

"I scared the shit out of you?" He said. For the first time in their relationship, Sam was frustrated, angry almost. "You didn't bother to answer my texts today, Anya."

Shit. She forgot to reply to him this morning.

"We're getting married in just a few months, you know?" His voice, hot with anger, his eyes a near blood orange. "I've gotten really good at being patient with you when you're aloof, Anya, but I don't know. Sometimes you feel so lost and gone, I don't know how to reel you back in."

Anya looked at him, his worried face, the tears threatening to spill on his cheeks, his eyes now colored a sad and faded orange. She was hurting him. She hated hurting anybody, and to his credit, she was lost and gone *a lot* these days. The fact that he noticed meant he knew her better than she realized.

"I'm sorry," she said. "I don't know what else to say. I had a bad day, I guess."

"Well, Anya, that's fine. It's fine if you have a bad day. Just talk to me about it instead of shutting me out. We're about to be married. I've given you every reason to trust me and confide in me, have I not?"

Anya felt sick.

Her tub filled with more than just water, but gallons of guilt, all of it spilling over onto the floor at his feet. She was screwing this up. When she didn't tell him what she was feeling or experiencing, she was hurting him. But her truths were too great to share, so powerful they might destroy her world and his with it.

"You have done everything one thousand percent right," she said. His hands met his face. A sentence like that should've eased him, but it didn't. He wanted answers for her behavior, for the secrets she was holding and unable to announce to the world and herself.

"But…" he said.

"But what?" She said. "There is no 'but' to anything. It's a fact."

"People usually accompany those statements with a 'but,'" he said.

"Well, I'm not," she said. "I honestly just had a bad day."

Partially true. "Are you sure that's all it is? You're not preparing to… leave me."

She sat up in the tub, quick to answer so he couldn't sense the hesitations and doubts she had been feeling all day.

"No, Sam," she said, reaching for him, her naked body dripping wet. "I'm not going to leave you."

He kissed her wet wrists and wept in front of her.

"I'm so sorry, baby," she said. "So incredibly sorry that I've made you doubt me, doubt us."

"Sometimes, I think of what it would be like to lose you," he said. "I imagine what that would even be like, what my life after you would be like if I ever lost you. And it feels so hopelessly empty and lifeless. Please understand. I've lost everything in my life. A lot of good things normal average people have. I can't lose you too. I just can't."

Anya was shocked, crying too.

He was roping her back into the world, rooting her to this ground, this Earth. She had promised to spend her life with him. And for that, she wouldn't be able to go where she should be. Anya had to live with what she had, live her time on Earth until she died. And in between, she would just visit Atlas and Pleione in her spirit body. It would have to do. She couldn't disappoint anyone in her earthly life. Not now.

Anya climbed out of the tub, wrapping herself in a towel and around Sam. They went off to bed, and she held him for hours, letting her love for him cover them both, hoping he could feel that energy rippling over the two of them.

Long after they held each other, they were sleeping. And after several weeks, Anya dreamt for the first time.

She was in the mountains, picking wildflowers springing up from the earth, a sign of life returning after it had just laid dead and dormant for months.

She picked periwinkle Columbines and other flowers dressed in white and yellow.

"We're going to make honey," someone said. When Anya looked around, no one was there. It was just a voice.

"The bees make the honey," Anya said to no one. "Not us."

"The bees are dying," the voice said. "Just like the Earth. It's our job to make the honey."

"They aren't dying," Anya tried to convince the voice. "There is much life to live here, and the bees aren't going anywhere."

Anya continued to pluck flowers, looking at the meadows of green grass that rose to the height of her hips.

"What will your choice be?" The voice asked

"What choice?" Anya responded, filling her basket with flowers in fuchsia.

"The only choice you have," the voice said. "You can't stay here."

"Why not?" Anya asked, feeling angry. "I like it here."

"But the Earth is dying," the voice said again. "It's not where you're supposed to be."

"Then why was I sent here?" Anya asked.

"That was a different choice you weren't a part of," the voice said.

"Well, I'm not leaving," she said even more stubbornly than before. "I have too many flowers I still need to pick."

When she looked down at her basket, the flowers she had picked were already wilting. Anya ignored them, picking more of the vibrant colors to cover the already wilting ones.

"Plus, I can't go," she said to the voice. "I don't have the key, and I need the key."

"You have the key," the voice said. "You've had it for a while."

Anya stopped picking flowers. "I think I would know if I had the key. I know a lot more than you think."

"You don't know because you've chosen to ignore," said the voice. "You have been ignorant your whole life, Merope."

"That's not my name," Anya said. "Don't call me that."

"Merope," the voice said again.

"Stop! My name is Anya Allen," Anya shouted.

"Merope," the voice repeated.

"SHUT UP!" Anya screamed louder, letting her voice echo into the mountains.

"MEROPE," the voice rose to a loud bellow, surrounding her, drowning out her echoes.

"NO!" Anya screamed once more, covering her ears. "I don't want to hear it."

"Suit yourself," the voice said. "You've made your choice."

The mountains, meadows, and flowers knew silence again as the voice disappeared. When she looked down at her basket, the flowers were dead, shriveled, and grey. She looked up to clouds winding above, a coming storm that turned the whole world grey.
A stream of lighting came down, striking her, letting her lie there in the tall meadow grass.

Anya sprang up, breathing hard. She looked down at Sam, who was unmoved. He was always such a heavy sleeper. Anya felt a ringing in her ears, the voice in her dream repeating itself, searing into her brain. She would never forget it, but she would try.

Lifting herself from the bed, she took a blanket from her closet and covered Sam with it. Now, she was restless, her body up and alert. She left through the front door, going out to stand under the stars. She looked up, searching the sky for Pleiades.

"I'm sorry," she whispered as if they could hear her from that far away. "If I left now, I'd give up so much. I hope you can understand."

Anya hoped they could.

She recalled the voice, the one that told her she already had the key. The sacred tool that would lead her to another world. She'd always had it or had it for some time. Anya thought hard, wondering what the key could be. Could it be her? She was royal, after all. Maybe it was something within her that was the key.

Anya closed her eyes, remembering Gwynn and Sage's teaching, letting their words echo through her mind.

"You have all the answers, Anya," they would say. "You just have to ask the question. Just get quiet and ask."

In her sessions with Gwynn and Sage, they had practiced this a lot. How to ask the universe for a sign or a vision and quiet herself enough to get an answer.

It was true. Anya had made her choice, but she still had to know. What was the key? She closed her eyes, listening to the crickets chirp, the leaves wave, the trees whisper to each other. Anya had practiced enough now that getting quiet was easy.

"What is the key?" She asked herself. Nothing showed. She took more deep breaths, trying not to be frustrated even though she was all day, and needed a break. Taking a few more, long, deep breaths, she asked again, with more focus and command.

"What is the key?" Anya asked.

Instantly, she was in the pit of Newmont Gold Mine, looking up at the still dark sky. All around were bulldozers, empty and lifeless. Not a single soul was in sight. She turned in circles looking for anyone. When she looked at the ground, she saw a mound of dirt the size of her fist.

Dig. Anya got down on her knees, scooping dirt with her bare hands, letting the rock jab into her shins and knees. Digging and digging, she kept feeling the cold earth beneath her fingers. The more she dug, the bigger the hole. A few more digs and she felt it, something hard, something jagged and uneven.

Gold. But it was too dark to see.

Give me light, she requested.

The moon opened up, shining like a massive spotlight on her and the mysterious treasure in her hand. She wiped it clean of the brown and red dirt, letting it shine brightly under the moon. After sweeping the dirt away, she looked down on it. It wasn't gold at all, although she assumed it was. Atlas and Pleione said it would be gold. Looking at it now, she remembered it. It was something given to her months ago. Something precious.

The galaxy diamond Gwynn and Sage gave her.

That was her key home. Anya had possessed it all along.

FIFTY-ONE

"Okay, so I'll see you Sunday night?" Anya asked.

She was loading her hiking backpack, getting ready for a trip to the mountains as per the summer Disney princess travel tradition. Anya took the galaxy diamond out of its dark corner in the back of her side table and shoved it into the bag.

"Yes, you will," Sam said, kissing her hard. "Have a great time."

"You know I will," and with that, Anya was out the door and hopping into her Crosstrek. She picked up her girls, made their coffee run, and then drove the winding roads to Clear Lake, the one place they chose to ring in the new summer.

"You think we should change up our mountain locations?" Karmyn asked. "I feel like Clear Lake is getting old."

"Don't you dare say things like that in this car," Anya said jokingly.

"What!" She exclaimed. "I'm just saying."

"You may have a point, Karmyn," Bee said.

Anya gasped. "Traitor. Fine. Where do you want our next destination to be? After this year, of course."

"Of course," Bee said.

"What about somewhere in the Sangre de Cristos?" Bee suggested. "Those mountains are so badass."

"Ooh, great idea," Karmyn said. "But it has to have a lake or a stream. Somewhere for us to swim. That is a must."

While Bee and Karmyn listed off ideas, Anya thought of the galaxy diamond, the key to her other world, the stone gifted to her by Gwynn and Sage. It was worth thousands in this world but priceless to those trying to discover other dimensions, and she decided to pitch it off a mountainside.

She wanted to rid herself of the temptation to leave this world behind. Tossing it into a mountainous abyss was a symbol of her decision to stay here. Before she did it, she would say goodbye to Atlas and Pleione, tell them her decision and make them understand why she chose this.

They didn't force her to come, but she saw the hope in their eyes when she asked about the possibility. Their chance to be united with a long-lost daughter was a hope served on a silver platter, a gift they long thought would never be given to them.

And Anya was about to rip their dreams to shreds.

Since learning about the Stargate, weeks had gone by. Building long-lasting bonds, learning about them and Pleiades, telling them about Sam and how much she loved him. She told them about her fierce friend and this job known as marketing, which they didn't quite understand. She told them about the parents who raised her and the challenging years she spent with them but didn't go into too much detail. Being the parents of a daughter raised by other parents had to be a touchy subject, but she liked to think they understood. Even so, the conversation would be awkward, at least for a while.

Anya told them she was looking for the key home, even though she already knowingly possessed the key.

For all they knew, she had decided to come home and leave everything behind because that was the right path to go on. She just hadn't had the heart to tell them she wouldn't be coming home. But she hoped the weeks she spent with them would soften the blow, help them to trust that she would be back, that she would visit often. She wanted them to feel like she would always be around.

Even though Anya had made her choice, she knew, deep down, she was destined to be on Pleiades. In her soul, she knew it. Everything over the last year was telling her this was her path. The doorway home, the key to that door, the family she discovered, all of those dreams fed to her in times of uncertainty, the fact that she had so diligently searched for these answers. Anya got everything she asked for. But people made choices every day that went against what they knew was right. Anya didn't plan to meet Sam and suddenly love her little world. Yet, life did that to people, interrupted them when they were already on one path, doing whatever possible to veer them into something different and test their loyalty and commitment to the journey.

She had committed to this life and this journey. It would be hard to leave behind, and she was afraid it would wreck her. If her spirit had nowhere to go after this, then so be it.

Anya still hadn't told Sam about what she had learned about herself or that her galaxy diamond was a key to a world she fantasized belonging to since she was a child. She thought it would be better that way. She didn't want him to find out this was a possibility. It would shake him, make him doubt their bond even more, and she wanted to comfort him.

Within hours, the three of them were at Clear Lake setting up camp. Anya planned to fall asleep in their big tent together and sneak out after her two best friends were softly snoring. She would astral project, probably for the last time in a while, at least until she had gotten married. The wedding was just weeks away. Anya would tell Atlas and Pleione about her life. Tell them she was getting married to Sam. She would tell them she couldn't come home, especially if she couldn't come back. They would cry or plead for her to change her mind. Anya wasn't sure what to expect.

When the night fell, and the only light at camp was the fire they built from twigs and leaves, they ate dinner together and drank beer until the night swelled with darkness. Tomorrow morning, they planned to climb the mountain on the other side of the lake, and then she would pitch the stone as far as she could into the rows of mountains, where it would shatter into a million pieces.

They crawled into their sleeping bags, letting the forest sounds rock them to sleep. Within several minutes, the alcohol running through their veins had wiped her two friends out. Anya snuck through a sliver of the open tent and zipped it shut. She moved to the fire where the coals were still hot, adding more wood until it came to life again. She laid down beside it to keep warm. And closed her eyes.

Now, I'm out of my body.

She felt her form shift from physical to spiritual, watching herself propel through the sky, traveling at unforeseen speeds. This time, she took it all in, watching stars, planets, suns, and galaxies pass her by as she hurled through the universe. She could be speeding through space for minutes, hours, days, or years and not realize it. It didn't matter. Time was nothing here.

Then, she had arrived at the white stone doors, walking between them. But this time, she went to her room, passing through the door like a ghost. She knew her parents would find her. They always knew when she was there. The guards always told them. Although she had seen a lot of the palace and a lot of Pleiades, she still hadn't mapped the place out in her mind. And when she visited, the three of them would only spend time in their studies or her nursery.

Anya drifted through gracefully, making her first stop at the corner where her egg-shaped crib was. Perhaps it was time they got rid of it, stop letting it remind them of the daughter they had now found. Anya smiled inside, happy that she had found her place, where she was from. This new life she was about to share with Sam was her home. It had always been her home. Her fate. As she looked into the empty crib, she felt the relief that haunted her for decades, the one she assumed adopted children felt when they went on a search for their biological parents. There was relief knowing where she came from, even if she never expected to come from anywhere at all. Soft footsteps interrupted those thoughts.

She could feel Atlas and Pleione behind her.

When she turned, she was met with the familiar sight of them and then an unfamiliar sight—six female strangers all stunning and all similar in appearance.

"Hi," Anya said. It felt like someone gut-punched her. She hadn't spent time with anyone else. "Who is everyone?"

She asked as if they couldn't hear her. The women started crying, holding each other inside embraces, grasping each other's hands.

"Is it really you?" One of them approached. Atlas and Pleione were emotional. As the woman drew near, she felt energy akin to what she imagined hers would feel like. She couldn't explain the similarity, but it felt like the energy and connection a pair of soul sisters shared. Then it hit her. She looked at the approaching woman and the other five women standing behind Atlas and Pleione.

"Oh my God," Anya said. "You're not…"

"Yes," the woman said back. "We're your sisters."

"We tried to have them wait," Pleione said. "We thought you might not be ready to meet them yet. We told them so much about you, and well… they were very insistent on meeting you as soon as they heard you arrived."

Anya stared at the six of them.

Complete goddesses with long silverish hair and touches of light. The one closest to her had emerald-green eyes with a hint of blue, more detailed features in her face, ones that appeared more mature. She pinned her as the eldest. The others had similar looks but different shaped noses and eyes colored like different precious gems. All different, but when placed together, Anya could tell they were sisters.

The oldest one opened her mouth to speak.

"I'm Maia. Your eldest sister. This is Elektra, Taygete, Alcyone, Celaeno, and Sterope. "

Anya knew all of their names by heart, but not once did she consider she would meet them.

How had that thought never crossed her mind? The more she looked at them, the more she could see Atlas and Pleione in them. Their small ears and pronounced noses, their almond eye shapes. Anya couldn't ignore the profound connection between them and how it seemed to intensify when everyone was in the room—like a massive force of gravity drawing her in.

"You are stunning," Alcyone announced. "I mean, even though this is not your body, you are still just as stunning as we could ever imagine."

Anya was speechless, unable to say anything, and consumed by shock.

"Are you okay?" Another one of them asked. Was it Taygete or Elektra? She had already forgotten who was who.

"I'm fine," Anya said. "I knew I had sisters. I just never thought about what it would be like to meet you. You're all insanely beautiful."

They smiled at such a pleasing compliment. "We've been dying to meet you. I'm Sterope. Don't you like how our names are so similar?"

Anya still wasn't used to hearing her given name. She laughed nervously and nodded.

"We know this is all overwhelming," Atlas said. "But we were hoping we could spend the day together, so you could get to know your sisters."

Anya hadn't planned on this or feeling the way she was feeling. She hadn't anticipated how deep her connection would be to this place and how that connection continued to grow. Anya hadn't realized how much she wanted siblings until now. She remembered begging for a little brother or sister when she was younger, but her parents told her she was a handful already.

Anya pointed to each one, trying to recall their names, starting with the obvious one.

"Maia, Elektra, Sterope, Taygete, Alcyone, Celaeno," as she pointed, they nodded in approval. "Sure, let's spend time together." All of them smiled, jumping in excitement. Anya found she was smiling too.

"We want to show you a day of what it would be like to live here in Pleiades," Alcyone said. "Goodness, I wish we could take your hand. But it looks like we'll be doing that soon enough!"

She spoke gleefully. Anya looked forward to time with them, feeling only slightly intimidated and overwhelmed by it all.

"Alright, where will we be going first?" Anya said, looking at them.

The women looked at each other with childlike innocence. "Well, we wanted to take you to get clothes, but we can't do that yet," said Celaeno.

"But we still want to take you to the market and show you the kind of food you can eat there!" Elektra added.

"We're going to have breakfast together first," said Taygete.

The six sisters beckoned her to join their group. As she walked toward the door, Atlas and Pleione remained unmoved.

"Are you coming with?" Anya asked, feeling nervous.

"We've spent a great deal of time with you already," Pleione said. "We thought we would let the seven of you venture out together on your own."

Anya smiled nervously. "Okay."

Atlas gave a fatherly grin, reaching his hand up to where her cheek was, although she was couldn't feel his touch on her skin. "Don't worry, darling. You'll have a great time."

With that, the seven sisters set off, walking out of the white stone doors to follow a path downhill and into the city. The women chattered all morning like hens in a henhouse.

"We can't believe you found us," Maia said. "Mother and Father were sad for centuries. They told us everything about you already, but we want to know more."

"How did you even find us, this place?" Asked Sterope in her innocent voice.

"Well, I guess I just always felt like I didn't belong on Earth," Anya said. "It always felt like a piece of me was missing. So I found a pair of spiritual masters who helped me tap into my higher consciousness. I read books about how to let my spirit body travel, and it led me here."

"You love to read?" Alcyone said. "That's lovely. Father loves to read."

Anya smiled, already aware of this and even more delighted to relate to him that way. "He's shown me his books. I don't understand them, though."

"Don't worry, darling sister, we'll teach you," said Alcyone. Each time they mentioned her being here soon enough, Anya felt a little piece of herself fall apart.

"What do you think of Pleiades so far?" Taygete asked.

"It's lovely," she said. "Like a heaven I always imagined as a child when I made up my own stories. There is so much love in the air, and kindness seems to exist everywhere."

"It's the nature of Pleiades," said Maia. "We are known to be very loving on this planet."

"Yes, I learned about it when I was young," said Anya. "I learned about Pleiades when I was ten years old. But I didn't know what that meant to me then."

"It's lucky you found this place," Elektra said. "Many people don't make it here in their first lifetime. Sometimes it takes multiple lives."

"Well, it's better to be lucky than good," she muttered. *Sam.*

The seven of them walked down winding paths, in between the rounded white buildings of quaint neighborhoods where children played on strange swing sets or kicked around colorful balls. It seemed just as normal as Earth life. Everyone looked at the seven women, walking together gasping in amazement, whispering about the returned sister.

Anya listened to her sisters introduce Anya as their lost sister, to which many applauded and even cried. They welcomed Anya back home. She let all the kindness bother her initially, but as they walked, Anya decided to let the day in, pretending she lived here. Like she wasn't about to tell them her decision to remain on Earth.

The rounded white buildings turned from cozy neighborhoods to a booming city bustling with people, silver hover cars, white bridges filled with people going on strolls.

Did people even work or have jobs on Pleiades? They had to. Otherwise, what else would they do? She would remember to ask at some point.

"Most of the people around here are very busy managing their spirit bodies on other plains. It's a life's mission. But like all things, we need breaks too. We must eat, we must play, we must experience our world just like our other beings in other dimensions," said Celaeno. They continued walking until they came to an alley with booths that stretched as far down as she could see. They were perfectly clean canopies with steam rising to meet the sky. The foods were various exotic colors, many of which were purple, blue, pink, and green. The same inverted colors she recalled from past visits.

"We want to tell you what the items are, but you might not understand, so we should just try a bit of everything," said Taygete.

"Sounds good," Anya said. But then she frowned. "Wait, I can't eat food. I can't grab or touch anything."

Sterope came to stand in front of her, carrying a worrisome look. "My goodness, that's right. We didn't even realize. I'm so sorry, sister. We must find something else to do."

"No," Anya said. "That's okay. You can tell me your favorites, and we can keep looking at everything. I haven't been to a market yet, and it's interesting."

"As you wish," Sterope said. They led the way, stopping from booth to booth, picking out their favorites, learning about her sisters. She learned Sterope loved sweet things. Maia loved a combination of salty and sweet. Taygete loved sour and tart things, and Anya found she loved watching her face pucker. Elektra and Alcyone both loved eating salty things. Celaeno, on the other hand, didn't like much flavor at all and preferred bland foods. She watched them purchase their favorite snack and devour it in front of her. She thought seeing people this happy and pleased all the time would be exhausting, but it was exhilarating.

"So tell me about all of you," Anya asked, watching them lick, bite, and swallow everything within their hands. "Are you married? Do you have children? What do princesses do on Pleiades?"

All of them giggled, but Taygete was the first of them to speak. "Well, myself, Maia, and Elektra, we are all wives of Zeus. Maia is the mother of Hermes, I am the mother of Lacedaemon, and Elektra is the mother of Dardanus and Iason."

"Wait," Anya said, stopping them. "Zeus, like *the* Zeus."

They all laughed. "Of course. Is that strange?"

"Not at all," Anya replied. "It's just not common for a man to have many wives where I am from. Less common is them being married to a Greek God."

"We love all on this planet," Elektra said. "It's very normal to love many people at once here."

"What about Alcyone, Celaeno, and Sterope?" Anya asked.

"Alcyone is the wife of Poseidon, the king of the sea, and has three children, Hyrieus, Hyperenor, and Aethusa," said Maia. "Celaeno is also the wife of Poseidon and has two children Lycus and Nycteus. And Sterope is the wife of Ares and the mother of Oenomaus."

Anya would have to brush up on her Greek mythology when she returned home.

"I hope I get to meet them all someday," Anya said, meaning it.

"You will," Maia said.

They walked down the long alley until booths thinned out and the steam disappeared. At the end, they came to a large plaza where people weaved in and out of paths on their way to different destinations.

"That was wonderful. I can't wait to try everything," Anya said, not stopping herself, letting her game of pretend continue. "Where are we going next?"

"We thought you would enjoy some music," Maia announced. "Do you like music?"

"I love music," Anya said. "It's a universal language!"

They tugged her along with a sort of invisible string, leading her to a large amphitheater. Inside were symphonies of soothing sounds coming from circular string instruments, long and curved white instruments Anya regarded as woodwinds but appeared to be very long with weird spaces between buttons. She was surprised at how different they were but how much they resembled instruments back home.

They sat in the best balcony seats, where they could see everything, and for the next few hours, Anya heard some of the best music she had ever heard in her life. It was soothing, like opera or classical music. It was something she would listen to if she were meditating at home, but better, even more relaxing, if that were possible. The instruments twinkled in the spotlights as sounds erupting from each delicate note plucked reverberated in the music hall.

Anya could listen to this music all day.

She wished she could take it home with her, listening so closely, she might be able to repeat the sound if she got home.

Home.

She would eventually have to return.

When the concert was over, the seven of them left the music hall. The night sky was arriving, letting the stars poke out and shine with the various moons rise at the end of the planet.

"We have one more place we want to take you," said Celaeno. They walked out of the plaza and into another neighborhood. From what Anya could see, no one seemed to live in poverty or struggle. Everyone helped each other. But she was sure there was much she wasn't able to see or had yet to learn. The homes disappeared around them, and thick rows of trees started taking their place. Between them, Anya saw the brilliant flowers she had grown fond of in all of her visits, bursts of pink light from what she assumed was their version of lighting bugs sparkled at eye level. The moons were so bright; outdoor lights weren't needed. The trees thinned, and stone paths turned to sand. In the distance, she heard waves softly lapping. When they came through the clearing of trees, there was the ocean, drinking in light from all the moons and stretching far beyond view.

The women rushed to the water to feel it on their feet, while Anya stood aching to feel it too.

"We're going to go swimming, sister!" Sterope shouted. "When you come here, you'll get to feel this divine water at your feet. It will soothe everything that ails you!"

As she finished her sentence, the other women were already stripping their clothes and their naked bodies galloping into the waves. The moment reminded her of a dream from months ago. Her sitting on a beach, watching her sisters dive in and bathe in the ocean and moonlight. Anya watched them all, crying at the beauty of it, realizing her dream was just a premonition into this wondrous world. She hugged herself as she watched them play, laugh, and splash in the sea, wishing she could join them. They held no other cares, just lived freely in the moment.

Anya wanted that. She didn't know how much until she saw it. But she wanted this family. Anya sat on the beach, wishing she could feel the sand on her palms and beneath her fingers. She remembered the dream now, the woman who sat beside her, encouraging her to be brave. Her mother.

"You must be brave. Give yourself a chance to see how brave you are." That's what she said to Anya, the girl afraid of the unknown but drawn to it. Even then, Anya didn't know that was her birth mother and couldn't remember her face in the dream. But now she knew what it meant, trusted what her dreams had been telling her all along.

Anya made it back to the palace with her sisters, and it was well into the night when they returned. Atlas and Pleione were delighted by the sight of them giggling together. A complete sisterhood mended and whole after thousands of years.

"Did you all have a nice time?" Pleione asked, kissing each of her daughters on the cheek. Atlas took each one of them in his strong embrace, hugging them tightly. Anya pined for the same, trying to imagine the warmth of his kisses and hugs.

"We had a lovely time, Mother," said Taygete. "She is stunning and everything we ever dreamed she would be."

Anya held back her tears. She had cried enough already today, but it was hard not to be moved by this whole day or changed by it. With the nine of them there, the energy in the room was a pleasant thrum like a circle of magnets drawn together. The only way to detach them was by force. The six daughters talked over each other, telling their parents about the day like excited children who had just been to the zoo. The innocence and happiness of it all, it was thrilling, captivating, addicting. Anya couldn't contain herself or her words. When she blurted it out, she was surprised by how good it felt. How normal and comfortable and easy it was.

"I love you all so much," she said. Their conversations ceased. Atlas and Pleione turned to her, looking impossible grateful. "This past day has been nothing short of incredible."

As she said it, the tears came. It was time for her to tell them the truth.

"There is something I need to say to all of you," they all listened intently. Hanging onto every word. "I…"

Anya began, her words sticking to the back of her throat.

"What is it, darling?" Atlas asked. Anya felt frozen, unable to say what she had scripted. Instead, she told them what she wasn't supposed to.

"I've found the stargate and the sacred treasure, the key to bring me home," the eight of them looked at her in shock, bright smiles taking up the length of their faces.

"Can you show us?" Pleione asked. "Just imagine it in your mind."

Anya closed her eyes.

She pictured the galaxy diamond with its rough edges and imperfections then showed the *Gate of the Gods*. They watched as the visions of the two things were projected from her third eye.

"How do you know?" Atlas said.

"They've been coming to me in dreams," Anya said. "I can feel that it's the right path.

"I can't believe it!" Pleione said. The women leapt into each other's arms, Atlas boomed a hearty chuckle, and Anya stood, wishing she could be a part of it all.

"I have had the best day," she said aloud. "But I have to be going. I wish so badly I could embrace you all."

"You will soon enough, darling," said Pleione. Anya blew them kisses, saying farewell, and with a single thought of her body, she shot back to the warmth of her campfire. When she felt its heat, she sighed, looking back up at the stars she just came from. Anya cried until she was too tired to keep her eyes open.

The following morning. Anya woke to her two best friends and the same swimming tradition. She bathed in the glacier lakes, drying off on the grassy banks and dressing in new clothes. Once dressed, they laced up their boots, slathered on sunscreen, and strapped on their backpacks. They trekked in a line up to the mountain peak on the other side of the lake, a strenuous hike for two hours. When they reached the top, they could see mountains for miles, uninterrupted by roads, undisturbed by people.

Out there was true quiet, true wilderness, a whole other world to be discovered. Maybe some already had. Maybe the world still had years to go. At the edges of the mountains, the three of them screamed nothing particular, letting the wind carry their voices on the wings of birds.

Anya felt the stone in her right pocket. The very one she promised to pitch into these jagged mountains to see it shatter on impact and disappear forever. She let it hum heavily in her pocket as she shouted over mountain peaks. On her left hand was the galaxy diamond engagement ring Sam gave her, weighing heavy and reflecting in the light.

Both stones were in reach. Both were possible paths to her future.

When Karmyn and Bee sat on a rock near the edge, Anya walked to a separate distant one, looking down at the mountains below. She retrieved the stone from her pocket, feeling it between her fingertips, staring into it, trying to memorize its shape before throwing it away forever—black with white speckles like stars. She looked out at the world around her, at the mountains reaching up to meet the sky, and at the two stunning women within arm's reach of her smiling brightly in the sunlight.

This was her home. It would always be her home.

But she needed to be where she belonged.

Stepping away from the cliff edge, she shoved the stone back into her pocket, clenching it tightly as she stared out into the mountains before her.

ACKNOWLEDGMENTS

This book lived in me for the better part of a decade before coming to life. The idea for it came to me years after I received a video from my father about whether or not I was Pleiadian. As detailed in the book, I cried through the whole thing. My mother Kathy, and my Father, Jim, have been incredible spiritual guides and supports throughout my journeys. Thank you both for your love. To my siblings, Kirk, Vili, Hillary, and Bea, thank you for always being proud of me. I love you all. Thank you for your support as I pursued my dreams.

For my best friends, Bee and Sami—I have some of the best friends in the whole world. Bee is yet another member of the spiritual family who helped me understand myself in ways I didn't know existed. I love you to pieces. And Sami, we've shared countless conversations about this book over tea and food. She gave me so many ideas for this book that were included instantly and gave me her most honest edits. Her knowledge of ancient things was a true asset. You are a spectacular friend and sister. I love you dearly.

I want to thank my dear friends, Randy and Nicole. Randy was the person who inspired me to do NaNoWriMo in 2017. I never finished a book back then, but it was always a goal. Thank you, Randy, for giving me a place to manage my projects and motivations. And Nicole, who created such beautiful cover art and other designs to help me promote this book. I am so grateful for your creativity and friendship.

And my former creative writing professor, and talented author, Iver, who helped me edit this book and always gave me such nurturing feedback during workshops while I attended CSU. It was awesome having you read this and thank you for supporting all my other writing since I've known you.

For the other English educators in my past who have inspired me to write since childhood—you have been remembered throughout this journey and made indefinite impacts on me. I am forever grateful for your teachings.

For Steve—much of my life opened up after meeting and working with you. Thank you for your love, patience, and friendship. Thank you for your knowledge and mentoring of Cripple Creek, Colorado. All of that information would never have been possible had you not been my boss and friend.

For my Nana, I will always be your little Starseed, and I miss you every day. And my Papa, for your endless hugs and love. And my entire family in Wisconsin and Colorado who believed in me and brought me up in such wonderful, loving, and creative environments.

For my Mama, Baba, Soe, Auntie, Jason, and Sam. All of you changed my life with your love and kindness. I love you so much. 给我妈妈，爸爸，姐姐，阿姨，陈果，和飞飞。你们六个用你们的爱和善良改变了我的生活。我非常高爱你们。

To Nick—who reminded me to keep living

And to the many authors I have read over the years. You have been inspirations and fairy godparents guiding me through. Thank you for creating your stories and sharing your light so I dared to share mine.

With Incredible Love & Gratitude,
Kelly

ABOUT THE AUTHOR

Kelly Branyik is an American writer who grew up in the Wet Mountains of Colorado, and comes from a family of writers. She attended Colorado State University–Pueblo, where she received her B.A. in English with an emphasis in Creative Writing. Nurtured by her family, who encouraged her to always pursue her writing, Kelly has composed dozens of pieces for publications around Colorado and a few other publications around the nation. However, her true passion for writing stemmed from her love of books, which have inspired her to become a novelist.

Kelly's first book, *It Depends: A Guide to Peace Corps*, is a guide for Peace Corps Volunteers looking to serve overseas. It was the #1 Best-Seller on Amazon in its first week for the Volunteer Work category. *The Lost Pleiad* is her first fiction novel.

She currently resides in the Pikes Peak Region of Colorado. She pilots a travel blog and still enjoys writing pieces for various publications. She enjoys cool mornings drinking tea, solo adventures around the globe, reading great books, and spending time with her family. You can learn more about Kelly at www.kellybranyik.com.

READ THE NEXT BOOK IN THE SERIES

Which home did Anya choose? Is she staying on Earth or traveling to her home in Pleiades? Join Anya Allen as she continues her journey to find where she belongs in the universe. Pearl of the Sky is full of more shocking twists and turns that you won't see coming.

Pearl of the Sky is the second book of The Lost Pleiad Series. Learn more about this book online at KellyBranyik.com or follow Kelly on Facebook, Instagram, and Twitter. #TheLostPleiad #PearlOfTheSky

CPSIA information can be obtained
at www.ICGtesting.com
Printed in the USA
LVHW041732221121
704140LV00012B/366/J